W9-CFK-264

A TENDER KISS

"Becca's got a chance for a future here and I won't let you ruin it and bring the shame of her illegitimacy out!" Elizabeth hissed. "I don't want to ever again hear my child called *a bastard*. Or have other mothers snatch their own children away when they get near her, like she has some terrible disease." Elizabeth impatiently dashed the tears from her wet cheeks.

Rand stood perfectly still. As if he'd sustained an unexpected blow. "People did that?"

"Damn you! A lot you cared!"

All the anger and fear and loneliness she'd suffered through the years surged within her. Flying into him, she pounded on his chest with her fists as hard as she could.

And he let her, taking the punishment as if it were his due.

Her anger left suddenly, taking her strength with it. Collapsing against his chest, she sobbed for all the pain she'd borne and all the loneliness.

"I'm sorry, Elizabeth. More than you can know." Rand caught her to him, stroking her shoulders and back, wishing to God he could go back and make everything different. "Not that it makes it better, but there hasn't been a day that I didn't think of you."

Her head came up. He could see need and disbelief at war in her eyes. She wanted to believe him. That was something, at least.

In her place, he doubted he would.

He was aware the exact instant the energy between them changed. Her lips were slightly parted, as if she were awaiting his kiss.

"I never stopped thinking of you."

With those final words, Rand lowered his mouth to hers . . .

Books by Victoria Dark

MARRYING MATTIE

LOVING ELIZABETH

Published by Zebra Books

LOVING ELIZABETH

Victoria Dark

Zebra Books
Kensington Publishing Corp.
http://www.zebrabooks.com

ZEBRA BOOKS are published by

Kensington Publishing Corp.
850 Third Avenue
New York, NY 10022

Copyright © 1999 by Vickie Hillman DuBois

All rights reserved. No part of this book may be reproduced in any form or by any means without the prior written consent of the Publisher, excepting brief quotes used in reviews.

If you purchased this book without a cover you should be aware that this book is stolen property. It was reported as "unsold and destroyed" to the Publisher and neither the Author nor the Publisher has received any payment for this "stripped book."

Zebra, the Z logo and Splendor Reg. U.S. Pat. & TM Off.

First Printing: September, 1999
10 9 8 7 6 5 4 3 2 1

Printed in the United States of America

To Paula Clyde Hillman, who has shown her support in many, many ways.

Also, my special thanks to Sherita, for helping my old brain understand my new computer; and to my critique bud, Margery, who gave constant support.

Prologue

Under a gray Kansas sky, a north wind whistled through the bare limbs of the old cottonwood tree and around the eaves of the square-built soddy. Nudging the back door open with her foot, Elizabeth McKay carried two tin buckets of snow and ice inside and put them on the stove to melt. The well had been iced over for more than two weeks. Luckily, the winter storm holding the land in its grip had dumped plenty of snow.

The nape of her neck prickled as she sensed someone at her back. A heavy metal click sounded behind the curtained-off sleeping alcove behind her.

"You can put your gun away," she said. Without turning around, she pulled off her muffler and knitted cap. "If I was with a lawman, you'd have been hog-tied and tossed across a saddle five minutes ago."

"No doubt you're right." The purely masculine voice was like dark silk.

Turning as she pulled off her mittens, Elizabeth found Dalton McClure, leaning negligently against the doorjamb, wearing only gray trousers. Tousled ebony hair touched his shoulders. Eyes of the same shade held a light of purely male interest as his gaze moved over her. An interest she tried to ignore, wondering all the while how a man could be so comfortable with his body that he could appear half-dressed without any nervousness at all.

He sure made her nervous. In all her nineteen years, she'd never met anyone like him. But growing up on the Kansas prairie, the nearest town tiny Salt Cedar Flats ten miles away, she hadn't met very many young men.

As if he understood and enjoyed the discomfort he aroused in her, he smiled, a flash of white teeth—as white as the bandage wound around his wide chest. With a long-barreled pistol in one hand, he finger-combed his long hair back with the other. But still he looked completely wild and dangerous.

She knew the effect he had on her was dangerous to her peace of mind.

"I have a lot to learn about this business of being an outlaw," he said ruefully.

Unwillingly, Elizabeth's lips curled into a smile at his audacity. And as his gaze moved over her face and touched her mouth, something warm fluttered to life in her abdomen. Suddenly, the heat of the kitchen seemed oppressive. She stuffed her mittens into the pocket of her coat, then pulled the coat off and hung it and the knit cap on pegs by the door.

From the moment she'd found Dalton wounded on the prairie—the same day the killer-cold weather hit—this man had stirred her senses in a most disturbing way. After loading him in the wagon, Elizabeth brought him home and dug the rifle slug out of his shoulder, grateful for what she knew of treating wounds from assisting the doctor in town. More grateful still that the bleeding had stopped and nothing vital seemed shattered or damaged.

Forced to deal with the wound alone, Elizabeth had wished a hundred times for her mother's help, but she'd been coming home from taking her mother, a midwife, to help with a birthing at a neighboring homestead when she'd found him. The weather, not unusual for a Kansas winter, had been too dangerously cold to go back and get her mother.

Trying to banish the sensations he roused so easily inside

her, Elizabeth busied herself checking the beans simmering in a cast-iron pot on the back of the stove.

"I stirred them a few minutes ago," he said.

"Oh." She put the spoon on the spoon rest and replaced the heavy lid. Knowing that he was still watching her made her completely aware of him. And aware of herself. "How's your shoulder?" she asked, turning. She resisted the urge to put a hand up and smooth her unruly honey-blond hair as his dark gaze moved over it.

"Well enough I should be on my way."

No. She didn't want him to go! "You're not strong enough yet."

"It's a good time. It will snow again tonight. Tomorrow at the latest. It will cover the horse's tracks."

"You can't take our horse," she said firmly. "We've only two. The gelding is so old, he won't make it a mile in this cold. We will need the mare."

"If they catch me, they'll hang me for a murder I didn't commit." He shrugged and winced slightly. "Might as well be for a horse I *did* steal." He grinned. "I'm sure they'll give it back afterward."

"Dalton!" Elizabeth snapped, exasperated. "I didn't dig that slug from your shoulder, or stay up with you fighting fever for you to head out on the prairie and die. You're not healed yet. I—"

"I'm healthier than you think," he said, cutting her off.

His tone held a note she didn't understand. "What's wrong?" She wanted to smooth the hair from his forehead, touch it and make certain the fever had gone. She didn't know how or when it had happened, but she had come to care a great deal for this man's well-being.

For this man.

"You're a beautiful young woman, Elizabeth McKay." His gaze moved over her breasts; then he looked back at the steaming pot on the stove.

Her body tingled in response to that brief glance. Looking down, Elizabeth noticed her nipples pebbled against the worn wool of her dress. Feeling warmth steal into her cheeks, she took her old shawl from the back of the kitchen chair and wrapped it around her shoulders.

What he made her feel! These wondrous feelings she'd read about in novels, but had doubted were real. Living isolated as she and her mother did, she'd never met a man like Dalton before. She knew instinctively she never would again.

And the feelings weren't only physical. As she'd taken care of him and they'd talked, she'd come to know him for the kind, caring man he was. Just seeing him or thinking of him brought a warmth inside her that felt too big to conceal.

He was such an exceptional man. Educated, a construction engineer by training—she could talk about anything with him, from the ancient ruins of the pyramids in Egypt to Miss Nightingale's work in the Crimea. That lady's writings about nursing and the techniques she'd developed had inspired Elizabeth to become a nurse.

Dr. Brown in Salt Cedar Flats was only too happy to offer her training over the last couple of years, in exchange for her free assistance with his work.

But Dr. Brown had never treated her as an equal. His training had been given with a superior air and criticism delivered in sarcastic tones. He seemed to think nurses were equivalent to servants.

Dalton was different. He acted as though she was his equal. Elizabeth knew she would miss him terribly when he left, and it was just her and her mother again—after her mother returned—with an occasional visit from her brother and his snooty wife to break the monotony of life on the prairie homestead.

When Dalton left.

Because he would leave. He had to, she knew.

Suddenly, she wished to God she had never met him. Then she could have gone on as she'd been living, vaguely dissatisfied, but not knowing what she was missing. Eventually, she might have married some wheat farmer and taken joy in her children, reading to them about faraway places and teaching them about the world beyond the seemingly endless prairie.

But then she would have never known she wasn't strange

for enjoying books and dreaming of the world beyond the narrow boundaries of her life.

Dalton turned back and laid the gun on the chest by the wall in the alcove, then came into the kitchen and lifted the lid off the beans. Picking up the spoon, he stirred the contents of the pot. "I added molasses and a bit of black pepper."

"That will give them flavor." Pulling her shawl more tightly around her shoulders, Elizabeth stared into the pot as he stirred.

As he did, he watched her in profile, trying to memorize the details of her face, like the way her bottom lip was just a little fuller than the top, and how her thick lashes shielded the expression in her wide hazel eyes. He wanted to remember how she looked.

"I should have been more alert and heard you when you came in. But I was finishing *Pride and Prejudice.*" He chuckled. "Probably why you never hear tell of erudite outlaws. Those who get caught up in reading novels are shot sooner in their careers. They don't survive long enough to achieve notoriety."

"Sort of like Mr. Darwin's theory of why animals evolved differently." She returned his smile. What a joy it was to talk of the things she'd read about, without being ridiculed for having odd notions, or looked at oddly. Her brother had so often belittled her for being "different," she felt like an oddity.

"Exactly like Darwin's theory. Survival of the fittest." Dalton smiled, his lips curving up at the corners. His gaze shifted back to the stove and the smile faded as he returned the spoon to the rest. "Maybe I'll take to the sea and visit the Galapagos. Since reading about them, I've wanted to visit the islands and see the differences in the tortoises from island to island for myself. Then, I could go on to the Sandwich Islands and climb to the lip of the volcano."

And while he was seeing these wondrous and strange places, she'd be looking out at the buffalo grass waving on the prairie, just as she'd done her whole life. The difference was she'd be remembering Dalton McClure and she'd feel the empty place he'd leave in her heart.

Elizabeth blinked rapidly. The thought of it was almost unbearable.

Though she lacked courage to tell him in words how she felt, Elizabeth found the courage to touch his face, trailing her fingers across the strong planes and angles of his cheek. His skin was rough with a day's growth of whiskers. Surprise, then warmth flickered to life in his dark eyes, and he caught her hand and kissed it.

She sucked in her breath at the sensations the action sent rioting in her chest. "Don't go. Appeal your conviction. Ask for a new trial. You said you were arrested and tried the next day, with no time to prepare a defense and prove you are innocent of shooting that man. That should be sufficient grounds to appeal the judgment."

"The lawyer who defended me was supposed to do that—after he sobered up." Dalton grinned sardonically. "Trouble was, they intended to hang me before he could get to Wichita to file the appeal."

He wound his strong fingers through hers. "I don't want them to find me here, Elizabeth." For once, his tone was serious, not teasing. "Or that I've been here. If people know we were here alone together for two weeks, your reputation will be ruined. You saved my life. I won't repay your kindness that way."

Something dark and needy lit his eyes as his gaze moved over her face. Although she'd never been with a man before, never even been kissed, her woman's heart recognized the look as purely male. Pure need.

And her woman's body responded. Very slowly, she moved against him, pressing her breasts against his chest, separated only by her wool dress and part of his bandage. Her nipples tightened at the contact, the feeling so delicious she wanted to gasp her appreciation. "You are noble," she whispered, her gaze on his lips, anticipating how it would feel if he kissed her.

"Elizabeth!" There was pain in his tone. "I'm not that noble. Don't—"

"You are the most wonderful man I've ever known," she confessed breathlessly. "I want . . . I want you to . . ."

Blushing, she left the rest unsaid, too shy to finish.

There was no need. He knew they'd both felt the need building between them since his wound began to heal. At every look, at every accidental touch.

"Don't," Dalton whispered hoarsely. But his hands slid up her back, gently pulling her closer even as the one word warned her away. "Don't. After I leave, you'll fall in love and get married to someone who can give you the life you deserve. Babies. A future—damn, I can't give you anything like that."

"You could come back after you've cleared your name." Elizabeth splayed her fingers on his warm chest. His male nipple hardened under her fingers. She looked at it, fascinated that his body reacted like hers. "Then we can be together."

"That might never happen." His face taut, he caught her wrist and pulled her hand away, but turned it up and kissed the hollow of her palm. Looking into her upturned face, Dalton saw her hazel eyes were luminous with desire.

The tip of her pink tongue wet her lips. "I know you'll come back. If you can. Right now, I want to be with you," she whispered.

"You don't know what you're saying." Even as he said the words, he was bending to kiss her. He could no more stop himself than he could halt his heart from beating. Though he'd tried to deny the desire that had been slowly, inexorably building between them, the truth was he wanted her more than he'd ever wanted a woman. Needed her, not just to satisfy his desire, which was growing undeniable, but needed her humor and warmth. Her innate kindness.

Needed her.

It was so damned unfair that he should find her now.

"I might not ever clear my name and come back for you. I might be shot down when I leave here. I wish I could make promises, but I can't and won't. It wouldn't be fair to ask you to wait."

"I understand that." Elizabeth wrapped her arms around him, pressing against him as tightly as she could. "I know you will if you can. But if you can't . . . if you—I want what we can have."

Dalton touched Elizabeth's face, smoothing his thumb over

her creamy cheek, then her moist lower lip. Her thick-lashed eyes darkened with desire and her lips parted. The look in them said she was certain.

Cupping her head, he kissed her gently, afraid to frighten her with the powerful need he felt. Her mouth was so incredibly soft and sweet, he had difficulty holding himself in check. He wanted to go slowly. Though she hadn't confessed as much, Dalton guessed she'd never been with a man before by her hesitancy as she returned his kiss.

The knowledge was potent, drawing a moan from deep within him.

Unable to resist, he thrust his tongue deep into her mouth, unwilling to leave any of the warm cavern unexplored. Her tongue met his—as if he was teaching her to dance, and she was following his lead. Slipping a hand between them, he found her breast and his need redoubled.

This time, Elizabeth moaned. He captured the sound in his mouth. Feeling his desire growing out of control, he tried to push away until he could contain his rampant need for her.

Holding onto him, Elizabeth whimpered and pressed closer, running her hands up and down his back and pulling him nearer, his arousal pressed against her abdomen.

"You don't know what you're doing." His voice was a rasp.

"Yes, I do. I'm a nurse."

The half-smile she had as she said it was his undoing. With a groan, he scooped her up. Though she protested that his shoulder might be reinjured, he barely heard as he carried her to the bed and laid her down. He sat down on the edge beside her. She looked up at him, trusting and waiting.

"Don't do this if you'll regret it," he told her. Although it took all the willpower he could muster, he'd managed to give her one more chance to call a halt to what was happening. But just how he was going to manage to leave her alone if she had second thoughts, he had no idea. "I can't promise you anything," he said seriously. "Lord, I want to. But I can't."

He wanted to promise her the sun and the moon and that they'd be together for always. She deserved so much more than he could give her.

He couldn't even promise her tomorrow.

Looking up at him, her hazel eyes more green than brown, Elizabeth wet her lips. "Do you care for me? Do you want to stay with me always?"

"Yes," he answered honestly. He cared for her more than he could express.

"Will you try to come back to me if you can?" She touched his face.

"If I can clear my name, all hell couldn't keep me away." Dalton turned his head and placed a kiss in her palm. "But I don't know how I can do that. I don't know how I could even start. The evidence, though circumstantial, was strong. I have to be honest with you."

Elizabeth smiled up at him. "I want to be one with you."

I want the memory, she added silently. If he didn't return, if he was killed before he could clear his name, she wanted the memory of his lovemaking. She knew she'd never meet anyone like him again.

Dalton was intent on storing up memories, too. One by one, he took the pins from her honey-blond hair and released the unruly waves she tried so hard to keep in an orderly bun. Combing her hair with his fingers, he fanned it over the pillow like a silken halo. The scent of lilacs wafted to him and he crushed it in his hand, inhaling the scent. Then he slowly unbuttoned her dress, kissing every inch of skin he exposed, memorizing every detail of her body.

For years afterward, whenever he smelled lilacs he thought of honey-blond waves of hair and thick-lashed hazel eyes.

Chapter One

"Stage is comin'." Wild Willie Bates thrust his head through the open door of the sheriff's office, his bushy red brows working up and down in excitement. "Only two days late this time!"

Rand Matthews nodded. "Thanks."

As Will disappeared, a breeze rustled the stack of wanted posters Rand had been looking through. Pulling open a drawer on the battered desk, which was the only furnishing in the office other than a potbellied stove and a rifle rack, Rand dropped the stack of posters into it. He went through each fresh batch as they arrived.

So far, the familiar name he was looking for hadn't been among them. And in truth, he didn't know whether to be disappointed or relieved. Anticipation had a way of wearing on a fellow.

Or maybe it was just that it seemed life was passing him by while he looked on, waiting for the worst to happen.

But he supposed life passing him by was a damn sight better than having it ended by a noose.

Shaking off the restless feeling that plagued him often lately, he scraped his chair back over uneven floorboards and stood, slipping on a leather vest with his sheriff's star pinned to it.

Maybe he should just move on. He suspected, like the sunshine spilling through the uncurtained window and the perfect spring weather outside, his luck couldn't last forever. He could sell his place—hell, he'd never done anything with it. And just head out wherever he took a notion to go.

Trouble was, he kind of liked it here in Willow. And he'd been footloose for so long, there was nowhere he wanted to go.

Except maybe Kansas.

Thinking about it, he knew he didn't want to go there either. Better to let the past stay buried.

Taking his hat down from the peg by the door, Rand glanced at his gun belt hanging on the same rack, and decided against strapping it on. Things were generally quiet in town.

Since Judge Blackwood had appointed him acting sheriff—serving out the rest of the term for his predecessor, who took off for the gold fields of Montana—Rand made certain things stayed quiet.

That was why he made a point of meeting whatever new people the stage brought into town and sizing them up, and making an appearance in the saloon on Saturday nights, when the lumberjacks and workers laying the railroad tracks came into town to spend their pay. He figured it was the least he could do in return for the judge giving him first peek at the wanted posters.

"Morning." As he approached the ferry landing, Rand nodded to Ezra "Squirrel" Perkins, to Squirrel's wife, Maivee, then to several others in the crowd of people gathered on the riverbank. Their interest was focused on the opposite riverbank, where the stage passengers were getting on a ferry built from boards salvaged from the bridge that once spanned the river.

Since the bridge had been washed out in last spring's floods, the ferry was the only way to cross the river from the main road. The railroad would have a rail line into town soon, so no one had been in a hurry to rebuild the bridge. It would be far easier once the railroad bridge was completed just to put an extension on the side, for buggies and wagons to cross.

''Quite a turnout,'' Rand commented.

''Well, Sheriff, Cincinat' has its opery house,'' Squirrel Perkins mused. ''Here in Willow, we watch the stage for our entertainment, too, and we don't have to pay two bits to do it.'' The former lumberjack chuckled at his own humor, then sent a stream of tobacco spit over the side of the rough dock and into the swirling McKenzie River.

''Ezra Allen Perkins, *must* you indulge in that disgusting habit in public?'' Maivee stabbed the point of her parasol against the planks of the landing and bent a reproving eye on the wiry little man. ''I will *not* have the new people coming into town thinking we're a bunch of mannerless backwoods bumpkins!''

''Well, then, Maivee, what kind a backwoods bumpkins do you want 'em to think we are?'' Squirrel drawled, and grinned as his wife puffed up like an angry setting hen. Laughter rippled through the small crowd.

Watching the exchange from a little higher on the bank of the McKenzie River, Rand pushed his hat back, privately admiring the man's courage. Maivee was a head taller than Squirrel and three times his weight. The joke down at the saloon was, when Squirrel was working timber, he liked to climb the big trees.

Maivee shook her parasol at her husband, and Rand wondered for a moment if he'd have to fish one of them out of the river. Then Squirrel dared to get close enough to whisper something to his wife. People near enough to hear laughed and stepped away from the pair, as though expecting blows.

But whatever Squirrel said did the trick. A blush rising over her broad face, Maivee snapped her parasol open and positioned it on her shoulder as Squirrel slipped an arm around her waist.

A woman at the back of the ferry snagged Rand's attention, and his heart kicked.

It couldn't be. . . .

She was dressed in shapeless dark clothes, and it was difficult to tell her size. A bonnet hid her face. He only caught a glimpse of it when she faced straight forward. There was no reason to think it was her. But something in her posture, in the way she held her head, struck a chord in his memory.

Then a little dark-haired girl claimed her attention, and he knew it couldn't be Elizabeth. This woman was probably the wife of one of the men on the ferry.

Rand tipped his hat back and expelled a harsh breath. It was because he'd been thinking of Kansas earlier, that was all. It was natural that would bring to mind the woman he'd left there.

Maivee and Squirrel stepped in front of him, Maivee's parasol blocking Rand's view of the woman.

It was just as well, Rand thought. He didn't want to think of Elizabeth right now. Knowing that she deserved better than a life on the run with a man convicted of murder was all that had kept him from turning his horse toward Kansas time after time. Leaving her safe in Kansas had been the hardest thing he'd ever done.

And the only way he could repay her for saving his life.

''Careful, Becca!''

Her heart thumping, Elizabeth McKay caught her four-year-old daughter as the child dashed toward the ferry's railing. Full and swift with spring runoff from snow melting in the mountains, the river swirled with currents and frothed white against boulders. Everything was so different from the flat and usually dry west Kansas prairie that Elizabeth tightened her hold on her daughter.

This had been a mistake. . . .

Everything about this country looked wild and dangerous—the giant trees reaching up into the sky, the imposing mountains and wild rivers. She felt tiny and insignificant. And vulnerable.

''Ouch! You're holding too hard!'' Irritation gathered in Becca's large dark eyes, drawing Elizabeth's thoughts away from possible disasters. Becca regarded their trip as a huge adventure, taking to the forest like a wood sprite. She never saw danger. Never dreaded the unknown.

Forcing a smile, Elizabeth picked the child up. "Sorry, pun'kin."

Feeling none too steady as the ferry's deck shifted beneath her feet, she sat down on her battered trunk and placed Becca on her knees. The ferryman hauled on a rope, moving the craft across the river a few feet at a time—entirely too slowly to suit her. The town of Willow was on the other bank, its dozen or so buildings overshadowed by the towering evergreens.

The male passengers from the stage crowded the square front of the craft, tilting it low in the water and making Elizabeth feel even more uneasy. Talking and gesturing, the men ignored the ferryman's warnings to get back. Didn't they know they could founder this contraption?

"I want to see my new papa!" Craning her neck in an effort to see past the men, Becca tried to slide from her mother's arms, but Elizabeth held her firmly.

"No! Anyway, we don't know what he looks like, now do we?"

Sighing, Becca stopped struggling. "How can we marry him if we don't know what he looks like?"

Ignoring the question, Elizabeth smoothed her daughter's ebony curls. Becca's sunbonnet, as usual, hung against her back. Although Elizabeth had tried to explain before, the concept of her mother being a mail-order bride seemed hard for the child to grasp.

Her too-big wedding band glinting in the Oregon sun, Elizabeth caught Becca's calico sunbonnet and placed it on the child's head, retying the strings.

Everything would be fine, Elizabeth almost added. Then she realized that Becca didn't need reassurance. The little girl wasn't the one who was worried.

Elizabeth wondered again if she was she doing the right thing, marrying a man she'd never met except through his letters.

The ferry dipped as it went through a small whirlpool of current, and her stomach lurched. Holding on all the more tightly to her daughter, she admitted to herself she was as apprehensive over her and Becca's future as she was over crossing the river in this crowded hatbox. She'd come so far, trusting a stranger's word, gambling that she could make a future for her and her daughter where no one knew her.

Had she been wrong?

What if he found out she'd deceived him? Would he throw her and Becca out with no place to go?

Elizabeth tried to breathe deeply to ease her nerves. But it was difficult with her corset drawn more tightly than she was used to. Back in Kansas she'd seldom worn one.

They had shared a room in Eugene last night with Lois, a fellow passenger, and this morning Lois had helped her dress, giving Elizabeth's corset strings an extra yank, saying that she should show off her tiny waist to her intended.

As she considered the enormity of what she was doing, Elizabeth felt as though she couldn't get enough air and her fingers were like ice. But she and Becca couldn't have stayed in Kansas, she reminded herself. Since she'd given birth to Becca out of wedlock, she'd become a social pariah.

Alone and shunned was no way for her to raise her daughter. And Becca had suffered, too, avoided by the other children whenever they'd gone into town. Not understanding people's cruel taunts. All because her mother had loved an outlaw.

Remembering Becca's father, she felt a familiar pain curl around her heart as she looked up at high evergreens lining the riverbanks and blinked.

He'd left without a word. On the run, convicted of a crime he didn't commit—she'd known he must go. But the way he'd left, taking their best horse and sneaking away in the night without even a note, it seemed as though he'd deserted her. As if she'd misplaced her belief in him.

When she heard he'd been killed by a bounty hunter, she thought her life was over. But her hurt and grief were only the beginning, soon overshadowed by the shame and degradation heaped on her when people discovered she was pregnant.

Men seemed to think she had become an easy woman and became free with their hands. Women crossed to the other side of the street to avoid her.

Even her own brother and his wife had snubbed her. And

after her mother's death two years ago, she'd been terribly alone.

Except for Becca.

From the moment Rebecca was born, holding her daughter in her arms made every slight and insult bearable. Becca was worth every sacrifice—even this one, traveling a thousand miles to marry a complete stranger, so Becca would have a normal life and a father.

Elizabeth's conscience smarted, but she firmly quelled it. Surely, pretending to be a widow so her daughter wouldn't bear the stigma of being a bastard wasn't so terrible. Why should Becca be punished because Dalton had been killed before he could come back?

Becca squirmed. Elizabeth pulled her tightly against her. "Be patient. We're almost to the other side, then you'll meet your new father and see everything there is to see."

Becca sighed dramatically, kicking her small high-button shoe against her mother's skirts "I'm patient. How long do I have to be patient this time?"

"Just a little while."

Twisting a look over her shoulder, Becca eyed her doubtfully from beneath the brim of her sunbonnet and thrust out her lower lip.

"That child is adorable!" Lois Mayflower sat down on the trunk beside Elizabeth and tickled Becca under the chin, eliciting giggles.

"And well she knows it." Elizabeth smiled, feeling a mother's pride.

Lois had boarded the coach in Salem, on her way to live with her brother and his wife in Willow and help out when their first baby came. Though Elizabeth had been drawn to Lois's openness and lively outlook, it felt odd to be treated as an equal by another woman.

But it warmed her, too. For the first time in years, Elizabeth felt she had a friend.

As the ferry dipped again, Elizabeth looked back at the receding bank where the ruined base of a bridge support thrust out into the water. The stagecoach driver said the bridge had been washed away in a flood last year. Which made her feel even less certain about trusting the ferry to get them safely across.

And when she got across, what if she found Hiram Smith wasn't the man she thought he was? He might drink. Or hit. Or hate Becca if he found out about her birth . . .

"Thinking about your intended?"

Whipping around, Elizabeth found a shrewd glint lighting Lois's round, deep-set eyes. "How'd you know?"

"You're looking back, like you're ready to get back on that bone-cracking contraption we just departed from and head back to Kansas," Lois said, referring to the Celerity Wagon drawn up before a way station that was little more than a shack nestled amid the tall evergreens.

"No. I . . . well, I guess second thoughts are natural." Elizabeth shrugged and shifted her hold on Becca, who was squirming again to get down.

"Sure they are." Lois grinned, showing a wide space between her front teeth. "And third thoughts, and fourth 'uns. Good Lord knows, I've never been able to bind up my heart long enough to give it to a man in marriage. Why, even though you've been wed before, I don't know how a man convinced you to come way out here to get hitched anyway."

"Hiram's letters were nice. He seems to be a kind man. Lonely, and needing a mother to help with his three boys. And there was no one for me in Kansas." Elizabeth pressed her lips together, wary of saying too much.

Warmth lighting her eyes, Lois patted her hand. "If that was true about Hiram Smith being a kind man when you left Kansas, seems to me like it still should be."

Nodding, Elizabeth was glad for the other woman's wisdom. "You are right, of course. It's just . . ." She sighed.

"Riskin' a lot?" Lois finished for her.

"Yes." Worrying the wedding band on her finger—her mother's wedding ring—Elizabeth wondered again if she'd made the right decision. Had she been wrong to agree to marry a man she'd never seen, letting him think that she was a decent woman? To claim to be a widow, to try and escape her past?

But what choice did she have but to deceive him? It was certain he would never have offered her marriage if he'd known the truth.

She'd had no choice, Elizabeth told herself firmly. She came to Oregon for Becca. So her daughter could grow up without being called a bastard. And pretending to be a widow was the only way to do that.

But she still felt guilty.

Making a silent promise to her child to see that she had that chance for a normal life, no matter what, Elizabeth kissed the top of her daughter's soft sunbonnet.

"Well, if it makes you feel any better, I'm sure this Hiram is just as nervous over the whole business as you are, don'tcha think?" Lois said.

Blinking in surprise, Elizabeth said, "I don't know why, but it does make me feel better." Grateful, she squeezed Lois's hand.

"Now, why don't you take a deep breath and relax," Lois advised her.

Elizabeth tried and felt the bite of whalebone stays. "I can't—get a deep breath, I mean. I'm not used to wearing this corset!" she confessed in a whisper, blushing at the admission. "I feel like there's a giant hand squeezing the breath out of me."

Lois laughed. "That's why I never wear one of the things." She winked. "After your intended sees how trim your figure is, he'll whisk you away to the preacher before anyone has a chance to try to steal you away. Then you can put the infernal contraption in a drawer and never look at again."

Elizabeth smiled. Lois was right. Just a little while longer, and she and Becca would be beginning new lives.

Looking up, she realized the ferry was nearing the other bank. A crude dock stuck out over the river, with a plank ladder on the side. She felt herself relaxing. Hiram Smith's letters *had* been warm and reassuring. He was a man she could count on. Hadn't he trusted her enough that he'd sent her almost two hundred dollars for the trip?

Marrying him was the right thing.

He wouldn't leave her without a word, like Dalton.

Caught unaware, Elizabeth sucked in her breath at the thought of Becca's father. Such thoughts always brought pain. Dalton was dead. It wasn't his fault he'd never come back for her, never known about their child, she reminded herself.

Lois nodded toward the people on the dock. "Think your intended is one of those waitin'?"

"I don't know." Glad for the diversion, Elizabeth looked them over. At her brother's insistence, she'd come out a month earlier than she and Hiram had planned for her to. Her brother had had a sale for their farm. Elizabeth only hoped Hiram Smith was among those waiting on the dock. "I wrote to him a week before I caught the stage, and I hope he got the—*oh!*"

As the ferry neared its destination, the men in the bow pressed farther forward. The square front dipped into the water.

"Back up, or I'll toss the lot of you overboard!" the ferryman growled. The men obeyed and the craft righted. Water painted ribbons across the rough planks, and Elizabeth caught her skirts and held them off the deck as the ferryman grabbed the rope and hauled it the length of the craft once again.

As the boat bumped against the pilings, a cheer went up. Becca pulled her corn-shuck doll out of her pocket and told "Miss Annie" all about what was going on.

The ferryman whirled a rope over his head, then sailed it. A stout man caught it and made the craft secure to the top of a post. Even before it was tied properly, several of the men were hefting trunks and carpetbags up. People on the dock caught the objects and handed them back to people behind them. Others called out to friends or greeted strangers.

Looking over the men on the landing, Elizabeth wondered which one she'd come to marry.

"Which one is my new papa?" Leaning forward against her mother's arms, Becca echoed her thoughts.

"I don't know, dear." Though she had sent her fiancé an old photograph of herself, he'd written that he didn't possess one of him to send and warned that she mustn't expect too much by way of looks. His last letter had expressed regret that he couldn't promise her love, stating his hope that friendship would be enough.

He was still grieving after burying his wife, and it was only because his three boys needed mothering that he was even thinking of wedding again.

Elizabeth respected his feelings and admired him for them. And she certainly didn't care what Hiram Smith looked like, as long as he accepted her daughter and gave her child a home.

A man moved from behind the crowd on the dock, and her thoughts whirled away like ashes scattered by the cool spring breeze. He was tall and wide-shouldered, his face shadowed beneath his flat-brimmed hat, and looking at him caused hot pain to spear through her.

It was a ghost. It had to be.

A matronly woman stepped in front of the apparition, the woman's parasol blocking him from view, and Elizabeth drew in a shaky breath.

It was the excitement of arriving at last, lighting a fire to her imagination. That was all.

Dalton McClure was dead.

Elizabeth and Lois rose so the trunk where they sat could be lifted up also.

"Well, I guess we'd better figger a way up yonder, without showing our everything!" Lois dubiously eyed the wooden ladder up the side of the dock.

Nodding, Elizabeth lifted her daughter onto her hip and watched the men clambering up the rungs. It wasn't long—only a few feet—but a challenge in skirts and petticoats. Becca leaned out so far that Elizabeth was hard-pressed to support her. "Don't squirm!"

"Miss Annie wants to see!" Becca held the corn-shuck doll up.

"Miss Annie will fall over the side!"

The man in front of them stepped back and bumped Becca. As her doll fell to the plank deck, the little girl gave her mother a wide-eyed look, as if to say, "How could you know?"

Then her small face crumpled and she struggled to get down and retrieve it. It was her only doll.

"Hurry before Miss Annie gets stepped on." Elizabeth set the child on her feet. But as Becca stooped to pluck the doll from the deck, someone else inadvertently kicked it. The corn-shuck body sailed across the rough deck and poised half over the side. Before Elizabeth could catch her, Becca dove for it. Shifting people made the ferry tilt, and the child plunged between the slats of the crude railing.

"*Becca!*"

Elizabeth dove to her knees, frantically reaching for her child. But Becca disappeared beneath the dark, swift water.

Chapter Two

A woman screamed. Elizabeth realized the sound had torn from her own throat. The sight of something under the water sent hope surging in her chest. Then the corn-shuck doll surfaced, already several feet downstream, carried by the fast current.

Suddenly, Becca surfaced, not as far away as the doll, but carried further with every heartbeat. *"Becca!"*

It might have been a mile. Elizabeth couldn't swim.

"Mom—!" The child splashed once, then went under, her scream changing into a gurgle.

"Becca!" Elizabeth's gaze was riveted to the water where her child had disappeared. *"Help her! Help her, someone! I can't swim!"*

Elizabeth hooked one leg over the railing. Lois caught her shoulders. *"Don't!"*

Elizabeth threw off Lois's hands. Everything seemed to slow, and she had all the time in the world to think about her actions. She had never been in water above her head. She would probably drown.

But if Becca died, it wouldn't matter. She wouldn't want to live.

Shouts and screams from the people on the dock came to her as if from far away. Before she got her other leg over the railing, there was a large splash. Someone had dived in further downstream from where Becca had last been seen.

"The sheriff will get her!" someone shouted from the dock.

A dark head broke the surface. His hair plastered across his face, the man shook his head once to clear his eyes and held his position, treading water.

What was he waiting for? The splintered railing bit into Elizabeth's fingers. Precious seconds hurried by, carried away with the swift water. *"Save her!"* she screamed.

Carried backwards by the current even as he swam, Rand was startled by the voice. He glanced up at the distraught woman hanging half over the ferry railing. And for an instant he forgot to swim.

Cold water stung his nostrils, snapping him back to where he was and what he was doing. He shook his head again, clearing the water and hair from his face.

Pulling hard against the swift water just to keep his head above the surface, he searched the gray-green depths of the river, watching for tiny bubbles to surface from the child's clothing—something to give him a clue as to where he should dive.

If it wasn't already too late. He prayed it wasn't.

And he prayed the child wouldn't be carried past him without his seeing her.

"Please save her!" There were tears in the voice now.

He didn't dare look up at the woman again. But he knew the voice all too well, although years had passed since he'd last heard it.

Elizabeth. Though his mind doubted, his heart was certain.

The child was Elizabeth's child.

One part of his mind registered the fact that Elizabeth had a child so she must be married. Well, what did that matter? She had been lost to him the instant he'd ridden away from her in Kansas.

He thrust the stray thoughts aside. Searching the water, he tried to peer into the depths for the little girl.

"*There!*" came a shout. He glanced up and saw Maivee Perkins pointing. She and the other people were moving along the high bank as the current carried him farther downriver. They could probably see deeper into the water than he could.

The child hadn't passed him. Good! He scanned the spot where everyone had pointed, trying to see under the water. *Where was she?*

His heart sounded like a gong in his ears, and an hour seemed to pass between each beat as Rand watched for bubbles, for anything, any clue to where the current was moving her. The river, high and fast, was frigid. Already, he couldn't feel his fingers and his legs were tiring. He was glad he'd taken a half-second to shed his boots before jumping in. If he hadn't, he never would have lasted this long.

Where? Where was she? How long could she stay under and live?

Something brushed his foot and he dove, snagging cloth. A tug showed it was something heavy—the child! Winding his fingers in the material, Rand kicked furiously, hauling the prize upward.

As he broke the surface with the girl, a cheer went up. It died just as quickly as he shifted her high on his shoulder, where she lay still and pale, her dark curls plastered to her little head. A trickle of water ran from the corner of her slack mouth.

Rand stopped fighting the current and just kicked to stay afloat, letting it carry him along as he thumped the child on the back, willing her to react.

There was no response.

His heart squeezing painfully, he spoke to her, urgent, nonsense words, as he thumped again. The wet lashes lay still against her too pale cheek. She was such a tiny thing. Her face and lips were tinged with blue. *Don't let it be too late!*

He thumped again, harder.

Nothing.

Trying to still his own shaking, he felt her cold skin beneath the point of her jaw and found a faint flutter of pulse.

"She's alive!" Rand shouted, hope surging, and he thumped. her back once more.

She came to life suddenly, flailing weakly and spurting water. As another cheer went up from the onlookers, Rand clasped her to his chest as she thrashed, fighting the water from her lungs.

His legs tiring as he kicked, Rand looked over his shoulder at the steep rock banks and the white water farther downstream. Now that he had the child, how was he going to get her out?

"*Yo! Here, Rand!* Pull to this side!" Squirrel Perkins waved his arms, catching Rand's attention. The wiry little man sat in the river up to his thighs, astride a fir that had fallen half into the water.

Kicking toward Squirrel, Rand felt the first knotting of a cramp in his thigh. Trying to ignore it, he swam on, angling toward the tree. Catching a branch, he pulled his way up along it until Squirrel could reach the crying child and plucked her from Rand's shoulder.

Squirrel got to his feet, scrambling up the wide trunk with the thrashing child. As he reached the bank, the crowd surrounded him and the group headed away.

Breathing raggedly, Rand hauled himself out of the water and lay on the rough trunk, his heart pounding from exertion. He heard the child's cries and coughs growing fainter as the crowd moved away with her. They'd be taking the girl to Doc Sedrick.

Elizabeth's little girl.

He closed his eyes.

Elizabeth. There hadn't been a day when he hadn't thought of her. Knowing that she was lost to him hadn't eased the pain. He remembered the concern darkening her hazel eyes as she tended his wounded shoulder, or warmed his nearly frostbitten fingers.

And he remembered the passion that lit their depths as he cupped her face, then drew her soft, eager body against his.

He shook his head. He'd been thinking of her just a short time before. And now she was here.

Now, she was a mother.

She must be married, committed to another man. When she would have been his, if life had treated them fairly.

Rage at all he'd been robbed of surged through Rand, warming his cold extremities. All because a Kansas sheriff had charged him with murder, refusing to listen to the truth or look for the real killer. Rand had been convenient. A construction engineer, he'd worked for the railroad, which a lot of folks hated and saw as robbing their land. He'd been tried and convicted the day after his arrest, his defense lawyer so drunk he fell asleep before the jury came back with their guilty verdict, although deliberations had only taken ten minutes.

If a man he worked with on the railroad hadn't blown the jailhouse wall, Rand knew he would have hanged. He owed Lucas Skinner his life.

Rand had almost made a clean getaway. The sheriff had gotten a shot off at him as he'd dove through the demolished wall, hitting him in the shoulder as he mounted the skittish horse Skinner had tied nearby.

Rand owed Elizabeth, too. She had saved his life. He rode as hard and as far as he could, but eventually blacked out from his wound and fell from his mount. Elizabeth found him half-frozen on the prairie and brought him into her home. She cared for his wound, sitting with him around the clock as she fought for him.

And her kindness and caring claimed his heart, even as her beauty fired need that had nothing to do with gratitude.

Leaving her had been the hardest thing he'd ever done. And Rand knew it was the only way he could repay her for saving his life.

Bright blue flashed as a jay flew between the trees. A squirrel chattered somewhere up in the boughs. Drawing in a deep breath of the tangy evergreen-scented air, he tried to let his anger go. Anger at what was past was a useless emotion.

Rand drew in another deep breath and released the last of the tension that gripped him. White clouds scudded across the strip of blue sky above the tops of the firs. Funny, yesterday there was nothing he wanted more than to see Elizabeth again.

Today, he wanted to ride out of town rather than face her. And her husband and child.

"Eh, Rand? You okay?" Squirrel Perkins called from up on the bank. "When I didn't see you nowhere abouts, I thought I best see iff'n you'd made it out o' the river."

"Just catching my breath." Rand sat up. "Is the little girl okay?"

"Yeah, I'd say so. Her and her ma's at Doc's right now." Squirrel hurried away.

Rand stood and carefully made his way up the sharply angled tree trunk, brushing past branches with half-dead needles. He would face her, of course. He owed her too much to do otherwise, though seeing her happily married would rip at his heart.

Hell, how could he blame her for getting on with her life? That was exactly what he'd meant for her to do when he'd left that winter night

"She'll be fine." Dr. Sedrick removed the stethoscope from his ears and dropped it into his brown leather bag.

"You're certain?" Elizabeth swaddled Becca in the towel the doctor had given her and briskly dried her arms and hair.

Becca was trembling from cold. Her clothes were a sodden heap on the floor. In Kansas as she was training as a nurse, Elizabeth had had only one experience with a drowning victim, a toddler who'd fallen into a horse trough. And that child hadn't been revived.

It seemed like a miracle that Becca was alive. Elizabeth couldn't stop shaking.

Doc said, "Yes, barring pneumonia, or—"

"Pneumonia!" Wrapping Becca tightly in her arms, Elizabeth hugged her and rocked back and forth. For once, Becca didn't protest that she was holding her too tightly.

"Now, I didn't say it's likely, and I didn't mean to alarm you." Dr. Sedrick bent a glance over the top of his half-lensed glasses. He was a small, round man, and his rather pointed ears and bald pate gave him the look of a kindly, aging elf. "In my experience, life puts enough on our plate to drive us to melancholia without our worrying over what will be served up next.'' He patted Elizabeth's hand. ''Now, I'll just go tell those people outside that everything's fine, then see if I can't help Mabel with that hot chocolate she's fixing for us.''

''Oh, she really shouldn't go to the trouble. You've both been more than kind already.''

''You two need something to brace you, after that experience. Doctor's orders. Besides, I'm rather fond of chocolate.'' He winked.

After he'd shuffled out, closing the door quietly behind him, Elizabeth held Becca closer still. Tears flowed freely down her cheeks as she rocked her daughter back and forth. Whether the movement was to comfort Becca or herself, she wasn't quite sure. Now that she was certain Becca would be all right, she was falling apart, and she was grateful that the doctor seemed to understand her need for time alone until she could compose herself.

The crowd that had followed them from the river talked in hushed tones on the porch. The sound of Dr. Sedrick's voice was muffled through the wall. After he spoke, a small cheer broke out; then Elizabeth heard their voices drifting away.

She sniffed and swiped at her cheeks. It was over now. Because of the sheriff's quick action, Becca was safe. The first thing she planned to do when she left the doctor's was find Sheriff Matthews and thank him!

Gaining some composure, Elizabeth sat Becca on her knees and started toweling her fine dark curls. Still unusually quiet, her child regarded her with solemn ebony eyes, holding onto her sleeves as if she was afraid to let go.

''I'm sorry I made you cry, Mama.''

Smiling, Elizabeth chucked her under the chin. ''That's all right, pun'kin. I'm crying because I'm happy you're safe.''

Touching her mother's wet cheek, Becca seemed to accept this with some reservations. Then some of her usual curiosity asserted itself and she peered up at the shelves filled with stoppered bottles and tins in the doctor's otherwise bare examining room. ''Is that all med'cines?''

''Yes, I suppose.'' Reluctantly setting Becca off her lap,

Elizabeth went in search of her luggage, and was grateful someone had placed her trunk and valise right outside the examining room door. She found dry clothes, and worried that there wasn't an extra pair of shoes. However, Becca decided walking around in her stockinged feet was a treat.

"How do you like it, dear?" Mabel Sedrick asked Becca later, seated in the Sedricks' parlor.

Becca promptly drained her blue enamelware cup in a most unladylike manner and smiled, a chocolate mustache outlining her lips. "Delicious!"

"Oh, my, that good!" The doctor's wife chuckled and took the child's cup. "In that case, I suspect you would like a bit more."

Becca nodded, hiding a yawn behind her hand.

"Oh, Mrs. Sedrick—"

"Mabel, please," she said, interrupting Elizabeth's protest. "And I realize you want to teach this darling girl good manners, but do let me coddle her this once. She's had such a bad time of it, falling in the river after your long journey." Shaking her head sympathetically, Mabel poured more chocolate in the child's metal cup. She had served the adults in fine porcelain, exclaiming how delighted she was for a chance to use her good dishes.

"Water was cold," Becca informed them.

"I'll bet it was! Here you go."

"Thank you, ma'am," Becca said, taking the proffered cup and promptly tilting it to her mouth.

"Drink it slowly, like a lady," Elizabeth whispered.

Blinking up at her, Becca stuck out her pinkies as she held her cup in both hands, and the doctor and his wife chuckled.

Lifting her own cup from its saucer, Elizabeth sipped the rich chocolate. Being seated in the Sedricks' small neat parlor with its sturdy dark furniture, just like any other guest, made her feel oddly uncomfortable. It had been so long since people treated her like an ordinary person, she would have to relearn how to be social, she decided.

After all, this was why she'd left Kansas, so she would be treated just like other people, and Becca would be, too.

"This *is* delicious. And Becca has never had chocolate before, so you'll have to forgive her enthusiasm." Smiling, Elizabeth set her cup in its saucer.

"Never had chocolate?" Doc Sedrick's gray brows rode high on his forehead. "I can't imagine life without chocolate, though the cost *is* exorbitant out here."

"Everything is exorbitant out here, having to be brought such a long ways by freight," Mabel said. "When it's finished, the railroad will help. But it's still only halfway here from Eugene."

"Where we lived in Kansas was rather isolated, and I never saw chocolate at the general store in Salt Cedar Grove—the town nearest to our homestead," Elizabeth said. "The only time I ever tasted chocolate was when I visited my Aunt May, in Lawrence." She added, "However, I don't remember my aunt's chocolate tasting so wonderfully rich and sweet."

"Oh, you have relatives in Lawrence?" Mabel clasped her hands, her eyes gleaming with excitement. "So do I! My sister is married to the dentist there. Fred Cook is his name. My sister's name is Jeanette. They've lived in Lawrence for many years."

Elizabeth placed her cup on the saucer, frowning as it rattled slightly. The chocolate on her tongue was suddenly bitter. Now she'd done it. She'd forgotten for a moment, relaxing her guard, just as if these people would have her and Becca in their parlor if they knew the truth.

Wife of the Lutheran minister, her Aunt May would no doubt know Mabel's sister. Very socially conscious, Aunt May made it her business to know everyone of any import, and a dentist's wife would certainly qualify. Elizabeth could imagine her aunt telling Jeanette Cook all about what a Jezebel her niece was. Then Jeanette would write Mabel.

"This was years ago. I was just a girl." Elizabeth smoothed her black skirt, smiling at her hostess though the skin of her face felt tight. "Now Becca and I have no one there."

Although she had stretched the truth a bit, it was essentially an honest answer. When Becca had been born, her aunt had written, calling Elizabeth a harlot and severing all further ties.

Though she'd lost her taste for it, Elizabeth took another sip of chocolate and cautioned herself to be more careful. The future depended on keeping her secret. Becca's future. Elizabeth would have borne the consequences of her actions, however foolish she had been not to realize she could conceive from being with Dalton McClure just that one time. But she wouldn't see her child looked down on any longer. Or called a bastard.

Lying didn't come easily to her, but she had to protect her little girl.

Becca yawned and leaned against her mother. Smiling, Elizabeth gathered her against her side. "You've both been most kind, but I should try to locate my fiancé now. Becca's exhausted."

"She's had a hard day, poor heart." Mabel smiled at the child, who yawned yet again, then closed her eyes. "She's already asleep. Oh, goodness, you can't wake her and take her all the way out to Hiram's place. And you, dear, are exhausted, too, and the roads are quite rough. Stay with us until Hiram can come fetch you."

"I wouldn't want to impose." Elizabeth's conscience pricked. Dr. Sedrick had already refused to let her pay him for his services.

"You wouldn't be, dear," Mabel assured her, rising. "Jonas could send the boy who does odd jobs for us out to the Smith place to fetch Hiram."

"Good idea. I'll find Johnny now." Dr. Sedrick rose and shuffled out of the room.

"You are more than kind," Elizabeth said sincerely. In one day, these people and the whole town of Willow had shown her and Becca more kindness than she'd seen in Kansas since Becca was born.

Used to being scorned, Elizabeth felt unworthy.

"Nonsense. If you'd like to pick her up and follow me, I'll go turn down the bed in our spare room."

Coming to Oregon had been the right decision, Elizabeth thought later as she pinned Becca's wet clothes to Mabel's clothesline. Mabel had reassured her about her choice of husbands, telling her Hiram was kind and gentle and as good a man as she could ever hope to find. His three boys were energetic and spirited, and while they were no longer babies, the oldest being thirteen, they did need a woman's hand.

A thrasher flitted in the lilac bushes in the corner of the yard. The blooms sweetened the air. Stabbing a carved wooden pin onto the rope line to secure the corner of Becca's pinafore, she promised the Smith boys silently that she'd bake and sew and clean. And love them, if they would let her.

If they didn't want to love her, that was okay, too. Either way, she wouldn't try to replace their mother.

As she pinned the last corner of the pinafore to the line, a man's shadow fell over the wet clothes.

"Mabel Sedrick said I could find you out here. I wanted to be certain the little girl was all right," said a deep voice behind her.

A voice that went straight through her. Prickles danced over her arms and her heart thudded in her ears.

"Elizabeth," the man added, soft and low.

Chapter Three

Finally finding her courage, she turned around and found the man she'd dreamed about for so long, the man she'd thought dead and lost to her forever.

Was he really standing within arm's reach?

It had to be just a hurtful illusion!

Still unable to believe it was he, she touched his chest. Beneath her shaking fingers was muscle and bone and heat. And a beating heart.

He was no apparition.

First Becca had nearly drowned; now Dalton was back from the dead. No, this couldn't be real. There had to be some other explanation. This man just looked like Dalton McClure.

He just looks like Dalton, that's all, she thought. *It has to be. If Dalton was alive, he would have come back for me.*

Staring at up him, she felt ill. Her vision narrowed as darkness closed all but his face, as if she was staring through a tunnel.

"You know my name," she managed to whisper, still unable to believe.

"Have I changed so much?" The lines bracketing his mouth deepened slightly. His ebony eyes were shadowed, sad and wary at the same time.

Shuddering, Elizabeth closed her eyes against the truth. *No!*

He touched her hand—a tentative, uncertain touch. And the slight contact sent a jolt skittering through her from the point where his callused fingers brushed her skin.

Trembling, she tried to catch her breath, but a giant hand squeezed her chest. First Becca. Now Dalton alive. Was this really happening?

"Elizabeth, I've missed you. I've missed you so much. I've thought about you— *Good God!*"

He caught her as she fell.

"Elizabeth? *Elizabeth!*"

As Dalton Randal McClure looked on helplessly, Mabel Sedrick called Elizabeth's name and chafed her pale wrist. Elizabeth lay on the settee in the Sedricks' parlor, where Rand had placed her after carrying her inside after she'd collapsed.

"Jonas!" Mabel called out as she set about loosening Elizabeth's tight, high collar. "Come quickly, and bring your spirits of ammonia!"

Elizabeth's gold wedding ring caught Rand's eye. "Why isn't she coming around? Is she . . . ill?"

"Did she say anything about feeling unwell before she fainted?" Mabel glanced up.

"No." Rand remembered the shock on her face just before she fell. Well, that he understood. Seeing her on the ferry earlier, he'd felt as if a mule had kicked him in the chest.

He'd also felt as though his heart was beating for the first time in almost five years. It had stopped again when he saw the little girl and realized she must be married.

"It's just all the excitement, I expect, and the heat. After the day she's had, I should have hung up those wet things for her."

"Excitement?" Rand frowned, turning his wide-brimmed hat in his hands as though measuring it. He'd been barely alive when Elizabeth had hauled him into her wagon, wounded and bleeding. As she dug a slug from his shoulder, she'd been sprayed with his blood, and had joked that at least he still had enough left in him *to* bleed. Though he had hurt like hell, he'd been drawn to laugh.

Rand smiled at the memory. "No, she isn't the type to pass out from excitement."

Mabel Sedrick's curious gaze found him. "She just arrived from Kansas. How do you know that?"

Realizing his mistake, he shook his head. "I don't." Feeling the weight of the woman's gaze still on him, he jammed his hat on his head. "I mean, she was rock-steady when her little girl fell in the river. If she was the fainting kind, she would have collapsed then."

Clutching a brown bottle, Dr. Sedrick shuffled through the door. "Damned corset has her air cut off, I imagine."

"Jonas! It's not polite to mention a lady's undergarments." Mabel blushed, tucking a strand of iron-gray hair behind her ear. "Or to swear."

"I'm a doctor. I'm exempt from being polite. Especially when a woman's sense of modesty endangers her health. I'll never know why some fool woman decided you all should wear those stupid harnesses."

"They are stupid and uncomfortable, so I assumed a man had invented the things." Mabel rose from the straight chair she had drawn up beside the settee and moved aside, letting her husband occupy it.

As Doc sat down, he took Elizabeth's wrist, checking her pulse.

"How is the little girl?" Rand asked. He wanted to shout at the doctor to hurry and *do* something. Or shove the man out of the way and help Elizabeth himself.

But he didn't have that right. He wasn't her husband.

"The child is sleeping peacefully." Mabel beamed at him. "You were very brave, Rand, to jump into that torrent after her. You're a good man."

"In spite of what people say about me." He winked, feeling uncomfortable with the praise.

"That *is* what people say about you," Mabel countered, with a wink of her own.

Doc Sedrick pulled the stopper from the bottle, and the

scent of ammonia permeated the room as he waved it beneath Elizabeth's nose.

Coughing and fighting to free herself from the odor, she came to life.

"Are you all right, young lady?" Doc Sedrick tilted his head back and studied his patient through the half lenses of his glasses.

Turning her face toward the back of the settee, Elizabeth nodded. Rand noticed her breathing was fast and shallow, but some pink was returning to her cheeks. Some of the tightness in his chest eased.

She was going to be okay.

Then his gaze was snagged by her breasts, full and round. They filled the bodice of her traveling suit, straining the fabric with the rapid rise and fall of her breathing.

Her breasts were much fuller than he remembered. And he had remembered. Small neat handfuls topped with delicious strawberry nipples that tempted him to taste and touch. And he remembered her mouth, soft and sweet. His kisses on her sweet mouth had made her tremble, but when he'd kissed those strawberry-tipped breasts, she'd caught flame. . . .

Shoving his hands into his pockets, he studied Elizabeth's wedding band again. "Where's her husband?"

He'd noticed that Elizabeth hadn't looked at him since she'd come out of her faint. Now, she closed her eyes.

The doctor didn't answer his question either. "Rand, if you'll excuse yourself, Mabel and I had better get that contraption off her."

Rand didn't want to leave. But as he was casting about for some logical reason to stay, Doc Sedrick frowned over his glasses. "Sheriff?"

"Sure, Doc."

As he closed the door behind him, Rand shook his head at his own behavior. It was the shock of seeing her, he told himself. After holding the memory of their loving close for so long, he would naturally see the differences in her appearance.

Damn, but she was a beautiful woman. Even more beautiful than the girl he had known.

Feeling the need for fresh air, Rand stepped out onto the Sedricks' porch, and he was almost bowled over by a tall female in a poke bonnet.

"Sorry." As he caught her arm to steady her, he recognized the woman who'd been standing by Elizabeth on the ferry.

"No harm done, I'm sure." She smiled, showing a wide space between her front teeth. Then her eyes rounded and she stepped back and looked him over from head to toe.

Slightly taken aback, Rand didn't think he'd ever been inspected quite so thoroughly before.

"Say, are you the feller Elizabeth's come out here to marry?"

As Mabel worked on the strings of Elizabeth's corset, loosening them, Elizabeth sat sideways on the settee, bending forward to give her access. His back to the women, Doc Sedrick busied himself pouring a spot of brandy from one of the bottles on the sideboard into a glass, then moved to look out through the lace-curtained window.

Elizabeth drew in a blessedly deep breath.

Alive. Dalton was alive.

"There we go," Mabel said, after retying the corset strings so the garment was much looser.

"Thank you. I'm so embarrassed. . . . I've never fainted before." Elizabeth concentrated on breathing slowly and deeply, trying to regain her composure.

"Think nothing of it, dear. I expect it was the stress catching up with you."

"And that damned tight corset," Doc said over his shoulder.

"Jonas!" Exasperation colored Mabel's tone as she helped Elizabeth pull her blouse back up over her shoulders. After it was buttoned, Elizabeth slipped the jacket to her traveling suit back on.

As she focused on the row of buttons closing the front, Elizabeth said, "I didn't even thank . . . the sheriff."

"Rand? I'm sure he understands." Mabel glanced at her husband. "We could use that brandy now."

"Rand." Elizabeth remembered "Randal" was Dalton's middle name.

And Dalton *was* alive. It hadn't been some trick her mind was playing.

"Rand Matthews. Drink this, young lady." Doc Sedrick handed her a heavy glass with an inch of amber liquid in the bottom.

Elizabeth took a wary sniff, and it nearly took her breath away.

"Go ahead. It's good for what ails you." A fuzzy gray brow dipped and rose as he winked.

Obeying, Elizabeth took a tiny sip and felt a pleasant burn all the way to her stomach. Looking at the liquor left in the glass, she said, "I've never had spirits before, and when my fiancé arrives, I shan't want him to think I'm fond of drink."

Doc frowned. "I'd almost forgotten. When Mabel called me, I was speaking with Johnny. He said Hiram's sister is taking care of the Smith boys right now, because their father has gone to float some logs down the river to the sawmill in Eugene. Johnny couldn't say just when Hiram is due back. You can ask the boys, when you're feeling better.

"However, right now," he added, "I want you to lie back and be still. I see my next patient coming up the street, but Mabel will be around if you need anything."

As Doc Sedrick shuffled out of the room, Elizabeth lay back on the settee, closing her eyes. She did need time to compose herself, to get used to the fact that Dalton was really here.

He was alive.

Warmth bloomed in her chest and tears threatened to squeeze past her closed lids. Until a new thought struck her—why hadn't he ever contacted her? She had heard nothing from him after the night he'd left, taking the best horse in their barn.

Then her brother had told her Dalton was dead, showing her the newspaper article, which declared the outlaw had been brought to justice. There'd been a picture of a bloated corpse in a coffin, tilted up for display.

Looking at it, she'd felt as though her heart was being torn from her chest.

But Dalton had been alive all along.

And he hadn't tried to contact her in all this time.

What that meant sank in quickly. He could have come back. If he had wanted to.

"I know you're disappointed that Hiram wasn't here to meet you. I don't know what he could have been thinking, taking logs down the river when his bride was arriving." Mabel shook her head.

Elizabeth opened her eyes and saw the older woman seated in the straight chair beside her. "I arrived earlier than we originally agreed on," she explained. "He must not have gotten my letter."

"Oh, I see. I had to wonder. Hiram Smith is usually one of the most thoughtful, honorable, dependable men in these parts."

"He is? I mean, I'm certain he is." Elizabeth twisted the gold band on her finger.

Mabel nodded wisely. "Of course, you're wondering what manner of man he is." She smiled. "After all, you've never met him, have you? Let me assure you, dear, you've chosen wisely. Hiram will make you a wonderful husband."

A wonderful, dependable husband . . . That was what Elizabeth believed from Hiram's letters. It was good to hear Mabel confirm it.

Elizabeth closed her eyes again. She'd come out here to marry Hiram Smith and give Becca a stable home.

And found Dalton McClure alive . . .

She drew a deep breath, her heart thudding heavily.

And what did finding Dalton was alive change?

Nothing.

Nothing at all. She had come to marry Hiram, a good, dependable man.

And marry him she would.

Chapter Four

Elizabeth pulled a blanket up to Becca's chin. Her daughter's small, dark head was nestled on the pillow, her eyes closed in sleep, her lips parted. Smiling, Elizabeth touched the child's velvet cheek. Thank God, she was going to be fine.

When her daughter had slept the afternoon away, Elizabeth had become frantic. After coming so near to losing her daughter, it was hard to believe she was really all right. But Doc Sedrick had assured her there was nothing to worry about. He'd said that it was natural, considering what Becca had been through.

After undressing, Elizabeth hung her clothes over a ladder-back chair in the corner of the small room, then slipped on her nightgown. Unpinning her hair, she finger-combed the tangles out of the tight waves as she remembered how Dalton had jumped into the river without hesitation and rescued Becca.

Though she didn't like the idea of being beholden to him now that she knew the truth, she owed him her life for that. However he'd failed her in the past, letting her think he was dead and going on his merry way, she would forgive him.

She would, she promised herself. Though she suspected it might take a while.

Her heart ached anew each time she thought of what he'd

done, letting her believe he cared for her, that he would return for her. When he must never have intended to at all. Taking up her brush, she angrily worked at a tangle as she remembered how she'd grieved after hearing he was dead. She wondered who'd really died.

The room seemed warm and airless. Parting the yellow chintz curtains, Elizabeth raised the window, wincing as the wooden frame groaned. The sound seemed to echo through the sleeping house. After propping a stick in the corner of the window to hold it up, she leaned on the sill, breathing deeply of the moist lilac-scented air.

Listening as crickets and cicadas sang their high-pitched trills and frogs croaked down by the river, she felt peace gradually settle over her. It was going to be okay. Becca's falling into the river and finding Dalton alive made for a rough start to their new lives. But it was going to work out.

Everyone told her what a good man Hiram Smith was. That had relieved her main concern in coming so far to marry a man she'd never met. From the way everyone described him, Elizabeth was certain he would accept her daughter and be a good father. He might even come to love Becca as his own, since his children were all boys.

Elizabeth fervently hoped he would.

Her conscience pricked her briefly over not telling Dalton that he'd rescued his own daughter from the river. But she pushed the feeling away. It probably wouldn't matter to him anyway. Even if it did, she had Becca to think of first.

Above the circle of tall trees, an almost-full moon shown down, surrounded by a sprinkling of stars. Heavy dew glittered like diamonds on the grass in the Sedricks' backyard.

And footprints in the dew angled across the grass to the house.

A man's footprints—too large and the stride too long for a woman or child.

Trepidation tightened around her heart as she leaned farther out of the window, trying to see where the footprints led. A dark shape detached itself from the house. Before she could draw back through the window, a hand closed over her mouth.

"Sssh! Don't yell." A voice hissed near her ear. "Be still."

She had no choice in the matter. Another hand around her shoulders held her immobile, despite her struggles to break free. Angry, she bit the hand covering her mouth.

"*Ouch! Stop it!* Elizabeth, it's me!"

Rand moved to where she could see him. But uncertain what her reaction would be, he kept his hand loosely over her mouth.

She slapped it away. "Dalton, you scared the life out of me!"

"Sorry." He stepped back slightly. Seeing her like this, he wanted to touch her, to assure himself that she was real. She was like a vision. Moonlight shimmered over her shoulders, turning her white nightgown luminescent and lighting the waves of her hair. The rapid rise and fall of her breasts showed how upset she was. But her eyes glowed in the half-light, as though she was happy to see him.

The last was just a trick of light, he knew. Though he'd never forgotten her, Elizabeth had gotten over him pretty quickly and gotten on with the business of life—her little girl proved that.

As he glanced through the window at the sleeping child, it hurt to know how easy forgetting him must have been. Judging by the age of her daughter, Elizabeth must have met someone and married right after he'd disappeared.

"Dalton, why are you here?"

Shrugging the disappointed feeling away, he looked up at the haloed moon. "Call me Randal, or Rand, if you don't mind. Dalton McClure is dead, and I'd just as soon he stayed that way. I've no urge for him to die twice, this time for real."

With his face upturned in the moonlight, he looked just the same, as if no time had passed. His straight dark hair just brushed his shoulders. The silver light etched the planes of his face, making her long to reach out and touch his cheek, explore the angle of his jaw. She could almost remember how it felt.

Clenching her hands, she was angry with herself for allowing such feelings.

"Believe me, I haven't forgotten you're an outlaw." She wished she could catch the angry words back. Her tone was harsher than she'd intended. It was no way to thank the man who'd saved Becca's life.

Sighing, Rand turned away, and his face became shadowed by the wide brim of his hat. Moonlight spilled over the broad width of his shoulders, making Elizabeth remember how sheltered she'd felt in his arms—a lie. A terrible lie she'd told to herself.

Older and wiser now in the ways of the world and of men, she knew he hadn't really cared.

If he had cared, he would have come back for her.

"You're angry." He said it as if it was a revelation. As if he hadn't expected her to be angry.

"I am not." To admit she was angry would make him think she cared. "I'm . . . surprised. Why are you here?"

"We need to talk in private. I thought this would be best. I was waiting here for everyone to get to sleep. Then I saw you raise the window." Pitched soft and low, his soft, deep voice slid over her like dark silk.

She crossed her arms over her breasts, willfully tamping down the feelings he stirred inside her. "If you're afraid I'll give you away, don't be. I'd rather no one knew we've ever known each other."

There, she'd done it again—let too much emotion escape with her words. The last thing she wanted to do was let him think she still felt *anything* for him. Not even anger.

Except for gratitude for her daughter's life.

Rand paused. Though that was exactly the request he'd come there to ask of her, the tone of her words was like a slap.

"Why?" he asked softly.

Could that be pain she heard in his voice? Elizabeth studied Rand's face, but his infernal hat hid his expression in a moon shadow.

"You haven't already told someone that you know me, have you?" she asked.

"No."

Leaning out of the wide window, she snatched the hat from his head.

''Why did you do that?'' Rand reached for the hat, but she ducked back into the bedroom.

''I want to see your eyes when you talk. It's unnerving to talk to a shadow.'' When she was certain he wasn't going to snatch it from her grasp, Elizabeth placed it on the windowsill between them.

''Then let me get closer,'' he said.

There was that dark silk voice again, making warm shivers go through her. Rand stepped closer, stopping near enough that she could have laid her head on his shoulder through the window. For a long moment, she wanted to do just that. To feel the heat of his body beneath her cheek and the hardness of his muscles beneath her hands.

He smiled, a slight wry twisting of his lips, as his gaze moved over her face in a way that made her pulse race. Her breath caught in her throat as she sensed he was thinking of her, too. Of being with her. And a heat only he had ever inspired bloomed low in her belly.

Then he looked past her at the child asleep on the bed, and his expression changed, becoming unreadable. ''I'm happy your daughter will be okay. Elizabeth . . .'' As his gaze focused on the child, he paused.

Her breath catching, Elizabeth looked from the little dark-haired girl to the dark-haired man. Could he guess? He had to guess—it was so obvious!

Impulsively, Elizabeth caught his hand, redirecting his attention to herself. ''Thank you for saving her. She is my life. I couldn't have borne it. . . .'' She was unable to say more.

Looking uncomfortable, Rand glanced at her pale fingers clasping his darker ones. ''I'm glad I was there to help.''

''I'm happy you were, too,'' she admitted, warmth surging through her. Happy he'd saved Becca. But more than that, happy that he was still alive. Even if he'd never really cared for her, some corner of her heart had been torn since she'd heard he was dead. At least, now it was mended.

Though a new tear had taken its place—discovering that he'd never really loved her. But this time the pain would vanish quickly. Now that she knew the truth, she would put the past behind her.

Rand said, "Look, I'm sorry I let you think I was dead. The man everyone thought was me was a bounty hunter. He shot my horse from under me, and would have shot me next if I'd let him." He paused, as if remembering something painful. After a moment, he said simply, "I didn't."

Rand turned back to her. "He looked like me in size and coloring, so I left my gun. It had my name on it. I took his gun and his horse and rode west. The next week I heard Dalton McClure was dead, his body brought in by another bounty hunter."

She snapped, "You never wrote to let me know you were alive."

Aware of the note of censure in her voice, again, Elizabeth could have bitten off her tongue. Now that she knew the truth, the last thing she wanted to do was let him know how badly he'd hurt her.

Surprise flickered in his eyes. He reached out and touched her cheek, but she took a step backward into the room, breaking the contact.

Rand paused, his hand held out for an instant; then he dropped it to his side. "I figured being dead was the kindest thing I could do for you, Elizabeth."

Her name on his lips was like a caress. Looking into his eyes in the half-light, she could swear she saw regret. Tall and strong and near as he'd been in so many of her dreams, she wanted to forget her anger and hurt and just feel his arms close around her.

And that would be madness.

How could she allow herself to be so affected by his nearness? She was an engaged woman, here to start a new life.

"Go away. As far as I'm concerned Dalton McClure is still dead," she hissed. Snatching his hat from the windowsill, she smacked him in the chest with it.

Reflexively, he caught it. "Elizabeth—"

"People tell me I couldn't find a better man than Hiram Smith."

He was perfectly still for the space of a heartbeat. "You couldn't."

"I came out here to marry him."

"I know. I talked with your friend, Lois. She told me all about how you lost your husband and came to Oregon as a mail-order bride. What I wonder is why. A widow as pretty as you should have had no trouble finding a husband, even though you have a child."

She wanted to shout that he'd left her pregnant. No man wanted a fallen woman, at least not as his bride.

But it had been her choice to make love to him. She wouldn't lie to herself and say he'd seduced her.

Now, she willed herself to remain strong. For Becca. This man had given her back her daughter's life. For that, she could forgive him for abandoning her, for letting her believe he would be coming back for her. Even for letting her think he was dead.

And her silly heart was all too aware he'd called her "pretty."

Sighing, Elizabeth shook her head. "Since the war, you should realize there's a great many more women in Kansas than available men. It was like that when you were there. Out here, just the opposite is true. So, I answered an advertisement for a wife."

"I never meant to hurt you." The words were so soft, she had trouble doubting their honesty.

"You did," she admitted reluctantly. "I cried when I heard you were dead."

"But it wasn't long before you were married." The words held a hint of anger.

So the thought bothered him, did it? Elizabeth didn't allow herself to examine why that thought pleased her.

She shrugged. "Life goes on, doesn't it? I got married in the early spring. Then Becca came along. We were planning a big family, but then my husband—"

"*Elizabeth!*" The harsh whisper engulfed her at the same instant Rand leaned through the window, grasping her around the waist. She found herself plucked from the bedroom as though she weighed no more than his hat. The cool night air caressed her skin; then she was pulled against a hard-muscled chest.

Unable to help himself, Rand covered her mouth with his. He wanted to shout in triumph as he felt her respond. The heat was still there between them.

The scent of lilacs filled his nostrils as he splayed his fingers into her hair, cupping her head and angling it so he could deepen his kiss. When he thrust his tongue into the sweet moist depths of her mouth, a surge of need shot through him. God, she was warmth and woman, just as he remembered. He thrust again and her breathing went ragged, as did his own.

Grasping Rand's wide shoulders, Elizabeth pressed against his hard length. Closer. She wanted to be closer. She felt she would never be close enough. When his hands slid down her back, pulling her to him, she sighed her pleasure. Then he cupped her backside through the fabric of her gown, and she felt the hardness of his arousal.

Her body caught flame. It had been so long since she'd been in his arms. So long since he'd taught her about a woman's needs, showing her the passion she'd never suspected she possessed. The way she needed him was frightening.

Elizabeth tried to pull back. Rand took advantage of the space between them to cup her breast, squeezing it gently.

He captured her gasp of pleasure in his mouth as his fingers found her nipple, already a tight hard nub. As he touched it, white-hot need jolted through him. God, how had things gone so far so fast? He'd just meant to talk to her. Now he was an inch away from laying her down in the dew-wet grass.

This was so right. They were meant to be together, he realized.

He should have never left her in Kansas—would have never left her, if he'd had a choice.

And she wanted him as much as he did her. She whimpered when his lips left hers, then trembled as he turned his attention to her neck, kissing the tender skin. When he moved to her cheek, he tasted salty moisture.

Tears?

The thought cooled his ardor as effectively as a bath in the cold river.

Cupping her face, Rand tilted it to the moonlight. "What's wrong?"

"That you could do this to me." Pulling back, tucking her chin, she added, "It shames me that it's so easy for me to forget that I'm betrothed."

"You're set on marrying Hiram Smith?"

"I am." Her head was still bent. The words were the softest whisper.

Rand was utterly still for the space of a heartbeat, sifting through the night sounds, trying to pretend he hadn't heard right.

"Not just for me. For Becca."

Releasing her, he nodded. Hell, he couldn't blame her. He'd never given her any reason to trust him.

But suddenly he wanted her to. More than anything. Still, what could he offer her? He had a decent-sized spread he'd never done anything much with. Because the old uncertainty had always held him back.

Crossing her arms over her breasts, she met his gaze, determination in every line of her body. "You'd better go."

He sighed, and plucked his hat from the grass and jammed it onto his head. "I understand."

God help him, he didn't want to.

Elizabeth squeaked as he caught her around the middle again, but to her surprise he set her back inside the bedroom. Not immediately letting go, Rand leaned inside and stroked her back, his big hands leaving trails of heat, prickles of need everywhere he touched her.

Somewhat less threatened with the windowsill between them, Elizabeth savored the feeling. Surely, it couldn't be so wrong. This was the very last time they would be together alone—she promised herself that.

"You can't deny there are feelings between us, Elizabeth. I've been just existing for a long time," he murmured. "But when I hold you like this, it's like I've found home."

Until you leave again! The words echoed in her head, but

never found her lips. He would. She could never trust him. No matter what his touch did to her body.

She stepped out of his grasp. ''Rand, I owe you for saving my daughter. It's more debt than I can repay. But I don't want to see you again.''

He stiffened, as though her words were a blow. ''I can't promise that. It's a pretty small town.''

Turning abruptly, he went back the way he'd come.

After he was gone, she closed the window and hugged herself. There was still desire between them, she admitted. But desire was a hot fire that burned out quickly, leaving cold comfort. Dalton—*Rand* had taught her that.

When he'd made love to her in that Kansas soddy, a blizzard swirling outside, she'd thought there had never been anything more perfect.

When he'd left, he'd shown her how wrong she was.

The only perfect thing that had come of it was Becca.

Now, what was best for her daughter came first. It had to.

Chapter Five

Feeling little appetite, Elizabeth absently stirred her porridge. The sunlight streaming in between red checkered curtains did nothing to brighten her mood. After Rand had disappeared into the shadowy night, she'd gone to bed, certain she would never sleep. Surprisingly, a deep, dreamless sleep had claimed her so quickly she didn't even remember pulling up the covers.

But this morning when Becca shook her awake at first light, Elizabeth had felt as though she hadn't rested at all. Since awakening, she'd been able to think about little else but how it had felt to be in his arms again.

That would never do. Finding that Dalton—no, *Rand,* she must remember!—wasn't dead had been wonderful. But to learn he could have returned for her after all, and had simply chosen not to, replaced the sense of loss she'd carried for so long with a sharper ache.

Sitting beside her on the wooden bench, Becca spooned her porridge down like a lumberjack. After she'd come so near to losing her daughter, Elizabeth still couldn't quite accept that Becca was truly unharmed. But this morning Becca was her usual self—as curious as a kitten and just as energetic.

Thanks to her father, the child had survived her misadventure none the worse for wear.

And Elizabeth knew she could never repay that debt.

Rand had jumped into the swift water, putting his life at risk without hesitation. And he didn't know it was his own daughter he'd rescued.

Elizabeth's heart pinched. Since she owed him so much, how could she keep that knowledge from him? Didn't he have a right to know?

And how could she tell him?

Elizabeth shoved her bowl away. Rand had done a selfless, noble thing. But he was the same man who'd abandoned her and let her think he was dead. She doubted he'd care if the child was his. Even if he did care, he was still a wanted man. He would leave again. If someone recognized him and it became known that Dalton McClure wasn't dead, he would be forced to run again.

"It's a beautiful day!" said Mabel, bustling in the back door carrying a wooden pail covered with a square of gingham cloth.

"May I help you with something?" Elizabeth rose.

Mabel dismissed her offer with a wave of her hand. "No, child. Johnny is cleaning a hen for Sunday dinner. I just brought these feathers in to put them to cure, before I wash them."

The older woman took the cloth from the top of the bucket, which was filled with wet, brownish feathers plucked off after the chicken had been scalded. Stooping, Mabel slid a wooden box from beneath the huge stove in the corner of the kitchen, where they'd be kept warm until they dried.

Frowning, Mabel plucked Becca's shoes from amid the feathers already inside it. "Oh, my. I'd forgotten I put these in here to dry."

"My shoes!" Becca shoved her last spoonful of porridge into her mouth. "May I be excused?" she said around it, looking up imploringly at her mother.

Deciding they needed to work on manners after their lives settled down, Elizabeth nodded.

Becca was off the bench in a flash and took the shoes from

Mabel. ''They're hard.'' A frown drew her dark brows together as she examined them, plucking a few random feathers off.

''Indeed, they are. Perhaps some mink oil?'' The last Mabel directed at Elizabeth. ''I have a tin in the cupboard beside the window. There are some rags there, too, you can use to work it in,'' she added as she carefully placed the feathers into the box, then picked up the ones that had wafted to the scrubbed wooden floor around it.

''Thank you.'' Elizabeth slid out of the narrow space between the table and the bench. ''I'd better do it now, if she's going to wear them to church. It was kind of you to invite us to go with you and Dr. Sedrick.''

''You're more than welcome. I'll be happy for the company. But I doubt Jonas will be back from his doctoring in time for services.''

''Is someone sick?'' Elizabeth paused, her hand on the door of the cupboard.

''No more than the usual complaints. Jonas seldom makes it back from seeing his patients in time for Sunday services. Word came this morning that Tom Fredrick was kicked by a mule, and Jonas went out to the Fredricks' farm to bind up Tom's broken rib. Jonas said afterward he was going to stop in and check on the Jones children. They have fifth disease. Thank goodness it isn't measles, as their mother first thought. Both make rashes, but measles are so much more serious.''

Propping the empty bucket on her hip, Mabel shook her head. ''Someone always needs him. I fear Jonas often overtaxes himself. He never knows when to rest. When smallpox swept through here a couple of years back, he ended up in bed with exhaustion.''

''That must have been frightening for you,'' Elizabeth said. Aware of the special closeness between the Sedricks, she understood Mabel's concern. Lacing her fingers together, she studied them, wondering if she'd feel that sort of closeness with her husband. It would be nice, after feeling so alone for so long.

Realizing it was Rand Matthews's image that came to mind when she thought of ''husband,'' and not any thoughts of Hiram

Smith, whom she had yet to meet, she shook her head as though to dislodge the image.

But in the short time she'd known him in Kansas, she had felt a closeness to Rand she'd never felt with any other human being, as though he was the other half of her whole. Remembering how they'd read books together and talked of far-off places, she felt a pain of loss anew that that had been taken away from her.

But not by his death, as she'd thought. He just hadn't returned.

Shaking her head, Mabel said, "Jonas is the only doctor between Eugene and Rosebud, and he has a very protective attitude toward his patients. But he's not young anymore. Not young at all. More and more people are coming into the area, and I fear it's getting to be too much for him. Though he would never admit such a thing, mind you."

"Perhaps I could help," Elizabeth offered. "I mean, in some small way. Before Becca was born, the doctor in the town near where we lived trained me to assist him as his nurse. I've had experience in assisting in surgery, too."

"Truly?" Mabel asked in wonder. "I admire you then. I fear I've a squeamish tummy. Jonas gave up a long time ago on having me help out with his patients."

Elizabeth said, "When I was younger, I read about Miss Nightingale's work in the British battlefield hospitals in Crimea. She was so heroic, fighting to create standards of care for the wounded—standards that cut the mortality rate in half. I wanted more than anything to be a nurse and help people as she did.

"And my mother was a midwife, so I guess she inspired me, too. I dreamed of going back east to train at St. Mary's in New York—or even in Miss Nightingale's school in London." That dream seemed so far away now. Another lifetime. "So, if there's any way I can help Dr. Sedrick, I would be happy to do so."

"I'll tell Jonas that. Thank you." Her eyes alight, Mabel smiled. "It would be so nice if he could have some help."

Elizabeth was surprised as the older woman gave her a quick

hug, then bustled back outside, murmuring something about making sure Johnny singed off the pinfeathers properly.

Staring at the door, Elizabeth felt awkward and uncertain. First, Lois had stopped by yesterday afternoon and showed deep concern over the fainting episode, promising she would be back today to make certain Elizabeth was all right. Now, Mabel's warm attitude toward her made her feel strangely unsettled.

Unworthy.

Since her daughter had been born, she was more accustomed to being treated as though she had leprosy than with kindness and consideration.

She shook her head over how she'd allowed the people back home to color her attitude about herself and damage her self-esteem.

"What'cha thinking about, Mama?" Ebony eyes blinked up curiously, eyes so like Rand's.

"About how nice everyone is here and how I'm glad we came." Elizabeth tousled her daughter's curls.

"Me, too. I'm glad we came." Becca smiled.

As Elizabeth looked in the cupboard for the tin of mink oil, Becca put her shoes on her hands and walked them along the bench. "Why did my shoes get hard?"

"Because they got so wet. Do you remember falling into the river?" Elizabeth located the tin and a soft cloth.

Becca nodded. "Miss Annie fell into the water. Now, she's in heaven with Grandma." Looking thoughtful, she sighed and tapped the shoes together. "I was there, too, but I had to come back."

Elizabeth's heart stopped. Then raced painfully. Her mother had caught pneumonia and passed away before Becca was two. "Pun'kin, I thought you didn't remember Grandma."

"I told you," Becca said with all the exasperation of a four-year-old talking with an adult who seemed not to have been listening closely. "She was in heaven and she had Miss Annie. She said she'd keep her for me." Wide ebony eyes met Elizabeth's gaze. "Grandma was beautiful, all sparkly and gold, like light."

Placing the tin and cloth on the bench, Elizabeth picked up her child, needing to hold her near.

Becca added, "I wanted to stay, but she said I had to come back. She said I had to come back 'cause . . . 'Cause . . ."

Pushing back out of Elizabeth's tight embrace, the child frowned at her mother. "I don't remember why I had to come back." She looked close to tears. "I promised Grandma I wouldn't forget, and now I can't remember."

"That's okay, Becca." Elizabeth kissed the top of her head, then hugged her tightly again, rocking back and forth as she held her child. "The important thing is you're all right."

"Shall we gather at the ri-i-ver . . ."

"Ri-i-ver!" Becca sang out enthusiastically, half a beat behind the rest of the congregation. She was unable to read the hymnal she held upside down, but didn't let that deter her from joining in.

"Where bright angels' feet have tro-od . . ."

"Have tod!"

On the other side of Becca, Mabel hid a laugh behind her gloved hand, the red feathers atop her hat bobbing.

Elizabeth bit the inside of her lip and picked up her daughter.

"Why did you pick me up, Mama?"

"You can see better from up here." Turning the hymnal around, Elizabeth whispered the words of each line. Becca showed her appreciation by singing them at the top of her voice.

One thing was certain, Elizabeth mused. Her daughter was not shy. The more people turned and looked, the louder she sang. Thank goodness these weren't the censorious looks Elizabeth was accustomed to. These people were warm and good-natured, amused by the child. People here were already beginning to accept them.

Because they were new, they'd drawn quite a bit of attention when they'd entered the church just before services started. Everyone had crowded around introducing themselves and asking about Becca's health after her adventure. Many people had praised Sheriff Matthews's quick action and admired his courage.

Elizabeth readily admitted that he deserved all their praise and more. She'd walked down to the river this morning and looked at the roiling water, and ice had touched her heart at how near she'd come to losing Becca. It was a miracle Rand had been able to pull the child out.

The song ended and the congregation sat down. Exerting her independence, Becca slipped off her mother's lap, settled on the pew, and immediately started impatiently kicking her foot.

"Do we sing again?" she asked hopefully.

"I'm not certain." Elizabeth smoothed the skirt of her daughter's pinafore, then gave her attention to the minister, who was reading from a long list of announcements about people who were sick, special church activities, and social events. She was pleasantly surprised when she, Becca, and Lois Mayflower were welcomed as new arrivals in town.

Waving discreetly, Elizabeth smiled at Lois, regretting that they hadn't had much chance to talk the afternoon before. In truth, she'd been too upset by all that had happened to think clearly.

Becoming aware that the whole congregation had turned and smiled, greeting them again, Elizabeth felt shy. She tucked her chin and nodded.

Their acceptance warmed her to her soul. She just knew she'd made the right decision. She and Becca were going to be happy here.

As if to put the lie to the thought, a shadow fell across her lap. Looking at it, she felt a premonition of disaster.

"Do you think I could squeeze in?" said a deep voice beside her.

A voice she knew all too well.

It was dark silk, sliding through her mind, covering her thoughts with an awareness of the man's presence at her side.

Sit. He wanted to sit. Seated in the corner of the pew with no room to move over, Elizabeth looked helplessly at Mabel, willing the older woman to tell the intruder that there wasn't any room—since she didn't trust her voice at the moment.

"Why of course, Sheriff." Mabel beamed. As everyone on the pew shifted down, even Becca, Elizabeth had no choice but to slide down as well.

"Thank you, ma'am."

All too aware of his shoulder brushing hers as he sat down, Elizabeth scrunched her cheeks up in what she hoped would pass for a smile, at least to the casual observer. "You are welcome. Sheriff."

Rand was aware of the subtle sarcasm in her voice. He found himself wanting to explain that he took the job seriously. But now wasn't the time or place.

He should have done more talking last night, he thought ruefully. That was what he'd gone to the Sedricks' to do. If he'd stuck with his plan, he might not have spent most of the night sitting on the ferry dock, staring at the stars and calling himself seven kinds of fool.

What had happened between them was like a prairie fire, engulfing them in white-hot flames. But even though he was her first, he'd never imagined a woman like Elizabeth would waste her time pining for the likes of him.

He was surprised that she'd seemed to hold such bitterness because he hadn't returned for her.

It was even more strange when he considered how quickly she seemed to have married and started her family. She couldn't have grieved for him for long. Her little girl was a tiny thing; still, the child had to be at least three. Maybe even older.

The pastor launched into his sermon, taking his theme from the story of Jacob's ladder. Her hands clasped in her lap, her gaze straight ahead, Elizabeth gave the pulpit her rapt attention. Rand's gaze strayed to her wedding ring, and he wondered what type of man she'd wed.

And just how long she had waited after he'd gone.

"Are you the sheriff?" Her little girl leaned around her mother and asked, blinking up at Rand with great dark eyes.

"Yes I am, tadpole," he whispered.

She giggled. "Why did you call me tadpole?"

Casting a reproving glance in his direction, Elizabeth put her finger to her lips and signaled Becca to be quiet. "Because you jumped into the water like a frog,'' her mother said. ''This is the man who pulled you out. Now, you mustn't talk while the pastor is speaking.''

Nodding, Becca kicked her foot.

As the pastor talked of the angels going up and down the ladder in Jacob's dream, Elizabeth felt herself relaxing. She and Rand were supposed to be strangers. If she mostly ignored him, it wouldn't look strange. That was what strangers did.

And sitting by him was certainly easier when she ignored him.

Feeling an insistent tugging on her sleeve, Elizabeth looked down and met her daughter's ebony gaze.

''Mama—''

''Becca, you have to be quiet.''

''But he's talking about angels. Grandma's an angel,'' Becca said excitedly. ''I saw her when I was in heaven!''

''Yes, dear.'' Elizabeth gave her a look that said she should mind, then slipped her arm around her daughter and held her close. It was so hard to be stern when just the day before, she'd almost lost her.

Becca squirmed free. ''But I remember why Grandma said I had to come back.''

Her heart squeezing, Elizabeth put her finger to her lips again and signaled her daughter to be silent.

''But, Mama . . . !''

''Can you tell me after the service?'' Elizabeth whispered. She didn't want to hear what her daughter thought her grandmother had said, even if it had only been a dream. Becca had nearly been taken from her. The thought of losing her was too much to bear. Elizabeth didn't want to be reminded of it.

Suddenly, Elizabeth became aware of Rand watching their daughter, and the tension that had taken hold when he sat down tightened a notch.

How could he fail to see the resemblance that was so obvious?

Tucking the child back against her side, Elizabeth half turned her back to Rand, shielding Becca from his view. As the pastor droned on, she counted the minutes until she could escape.

Later, as she shook the pastor's hand, Elizabeth hoped her smile looked genuine. "Lovely service, Reverend Lyle."

It wasn't the good pastor's fault she'd spent most of the last half hour in dread, waiting for someone to notice how alike Rand and Becca were—for her sin to find her out.

"So nice to see new people," the aging pastor said, then smiled, then turned his attention to Rand, who was right behind her. "And we don't see you often enough, Sheriff! So glad you joined us today."

As Elizabeth made her way down the steps, small knots of people stood about the churchyard, talking and socializing. She had a sharp memory of the last time she'd attended church in Kansas. As she'd stood on the church steps after services, Becca just a baby in her arms, everyone had stared or turned their backs. This was the first time she'd been to services since.

Elizabeth was aware of Rand following her down the steps—in the same way she had been completely aware of him since he'd stood beside her pew, of the faint scent of his shaving soap, the slight nick on his chin, the way his bronzed skin contrasted with his starched white collar on the Sunday shirt.

She had a strong urge to break and run for the Sedricks', to escape before she did or said something to give herself away. However, Mabel Sedrick spotted her, and the feathers on her hat danced energetically as she motioned for Elizabeth to join her and the people she was talking with.

Though she wanted only to escape, Elizabeth plastered a smile on her lips and, leading Becca by the hand, headed toward the small group.

"There you are, dear." Mabel caught her elbow and pulled her into the center of the crowd.

Picking Becca up and setting her astride her hip, Elizabeth smiled and nodded to the people she'd met before services started.

"I wanted to introduce you to Hiram's sister, Maggie Jean Hoffpaur." Mabel beamed, directing her toward a plump young woman who held a babe in her arms. Several children crowded about her skirts.

"Mrs. Hoffpaur." Elizabeth extended her hand and swallowed past a knot of apprehension. ''I'm so happy to meet you. Hiram wrote so often about you and your family, I feel I know you.''

''Me, too.'' The woman beamed, then blushed, her ruddy cheeks going even redder. ''I mean, I'm happy to meet you, too! But please call me Maggie Jean.'' She gestured to a large man behind her. ''This is my husband, George, and this is our brood, except for the three redheads. They're Hiram's.''

''I'm Elizabeth,'' she told the boys.

The boys, with hair in shades varying from rust to newly polished copper, eyed Elizabeth curiously, but responded to her smile with shy grins of their own.

The baby began to fuss, and Maggie Jean bounced the child on her shoulder. Her gaze went to Becca. ''This must be your daughter.''

Becca, who had been eyeing the baby curiously, looked up and smiled. ''I must be.''

Everyone laughed. Becca blushed, taken aback, and hid her face against Elizabeth's neck.

Elizabeth had dreaded meeting her fiancé's family almost as much as meeting Hiram. But in the face of such warmth, the knot of tension in her stomach disappeared.

Only to coil again as Rand stopped at the other side of the circle, nodding to some of the men. He was tall, a head taller than most. His dark gaze met hers briefly, and Elizabeth felt a sizzle all the way to her toes.

How could he make her feel that way, she wondered, now that she knew the truth?

''Hiram is going to be so put out that he wasn't here when you arrived,'' Maggie Jean said, reclaiming her attention. ''But he took some logs down the river to be sawed into lumber to build his new barn. It might be two or three weeks before he's back.''

''It's my fault.'' As Elizabeth explained that she'd arrived sooner than planned, she was completely aware of Rand watching her silently. What did he want from her? Why was he staying around her? He had no right to expect anything, she reminded herself. "Although I wrote, Hiram must not have received my letter," she finished.

"I'm sure it's waiting for him with his other mail in my kitchen cupboard." Maggie Jean shook her head. "If I had just known, why me and the kids would a been there to meet you!"

As her future sister-in-law went on, Elizabeth saw Mabel catch Rand's sleeve and say something to him in a low voice. He nodded to Mabel and left. Relief washing through her, Elizabeth gave her full attention to what Maggie Jean was saying.

It was going to be okay, Elizabeth told herself later as she took plates down from a high shelf in Mabel's homey kitchen.

Mabel had allowed her to help, and now dinner was almost ready. The smell of fried chicken and apple pie filled the kitchen. She hoped Doc Sedrick would get back in time to join them.

Becca was sitting on the work counter, where Mabel had placed her, watching as their hostess vigorously mashed potatoes, adding milk and butter in turn. Mabel seemed to delight in answering the thousand and one questions the child asked about the process. It was a shame the Sedricks had never had children of their own.

Elizabeth knew she and Becca had passed their first hurdle. People in the town accepted them. No one questioned her story of being a widow.

No one noticed Becca's resemblance to Rand.

Now, if Rand Matthews would just go away—as he'd been only too happy to do before—she and Becca would be able to settle in and build new lives.

After she selected forks and knives from those standing in a small crockery jar, she picked up the plates, heading for the dining room.

"Oh, I forgot," Mabel said. "We'll need another place setting." She glanced up from the bowl of potatoes.

"Is Doc back?" Elizabeth set the plates on the kitchen table and went to the shelf for another.

After tapping the potato masher against the side of the bowl, Mabel gave it to Becca. "Do you want to lick this?"

"Yes!" The child's eyes grew round, and she swiped it with her tongue.

Wiping her hands on her apron, Mabel told Elizabeth, "No, he's not back. Though Jonas shouldn't be too much longer, without he ran into something unexpected. But Rand Matthews will be joining us for dinner."

The plate Elizabeth was taking down slipped from her fingers. Gasping, she caught it in midair.

Mabel never noticed the near-disaster.

"I feel for him," the older woman mused, beating the potatoes briskly. "He's such a good man. And being a bachelor, he doesn't have anyone to cook for him. So we often have him over to Sunday dinner. I like to think it makes him feel less alone."

Mabel lifted the bowl. "The potatoes are ready, dear."

Chapter Six

''Here you go, Rand.'' Mabel slid a large slice of apple pie onto a saucer and passed it to him. ''Would you like some clotted cream with that?''

''No. Thank you.'' He took a bite. ''Hmmm, this is delicious.''

Her cheeks pinking with her pleasure, Mabel smiled. ''I just threw it together.''

Rand winked at Becca. ''How about a slice for the pretty girl with the pink bow in her hair?''

Warily, Elizabeth glanced from the tall man at the end of the table to her daughter, whose dark brown hair and eyes were so nearly the same color.

Giggling, Becca touched the large bow nestled in her soft curls. She pulled it free and studied it. ''That's me! My bow is pink!''

''So it is.'' Mabel smiled at the child. ''Do you want pie?''

''Yes, ma'am.'' Dark curls bobbed as she nodded with enthusiasm

''I thought you might. You do have a nice healthy appetite, despite your dunking in the river.'' Mabel placed a child-sized piece on a saucer in front of Becca, who dug in as though she hadn't eaten a thing in days, when in fact she'd just emptied her plate of two servings of mashed potatoes and gravy and both chicken drumsticks.

Feeling tension knotting her stomach, Elizabeth looked back at the glazed carrots on her own plate and moved them about. Though she'd been careful not to stare at Rand during the meal, she'd heard every tiny "clink" his fork made against the plate. Felt his gaze every time it touched her. As it did now.

"Elizabeth?" There was a question in Mabel's voice.

"Yes?" Looking up, Elizabeth saw she held the knife poised over the pie, a questioning look on her face.

"Pie? Oh, no, thank you." After touching her napkin to her lips, Elizabeth placed it beside her plate. "I'm much too full of your delicious fried chicken." She hoped her smile didn't look as strained as it felt.

The older woman beamed. "Thank you, dear. I'm afraid it was just common fare. Well, there is plenty left, if you change your mind later."

"The meal was delicious," Elizabeth said truthfully. She would have truly enjoyed it if sitting across from Rand didn't have her stomach in knots.

"Thank you. But you did as much as I did." Mabel resumed her seat at the opposite end of the dining table from Rand. "I just wish Jonas had made it back before now."

"I'm sure he won't be long," Rand said. "But if he's not back in a couple of hours, I'll be happy to ride out and see if he had trouble."

Mabel nodded. "Thank you. With his arthritis, if his horse goes lame or the buggy breaks, he could never walk back to town."

Conversation lapsed. Once again feeling Rand's gaze, Elizabeth tried hard to ignore him, watching Becca as the child finished her pie.

What did Rand think he was doing anyway? Elizabeth wondered. The way he looked at her and spoke to her—ever since he'd arrived at Mabel's, the interest he'd shown in Elizabeth had gone beyond that of a stranger. Mabel was bound to suspect that they knew each other.

If she didn't already see the resemblance between Becca and her father.

Elizabeth wished she had taken a slice of the pie, just so she would have something to occupy her.

Mabel broke the silence "Hiram gave me these apples last fall, and I dried them." Taking a piece of pie for herself, she went on. "He has a nice big orchard on his place. You'll like that, Elizabeth"

"I like to make apple butter." She sensed Rand tensing slightly at the mention of her fiancé.

Mabel said, "He has pear trees, too. His father brought them as seedlings over the Oregon Trail and planted them when he staked his homestead. Now that his father is gone, the place is Hiram's."

"Where did his father go?" Becca asked around a bite of pie.

"His father died, dear," Mabel explained.

"Oh." Silent for a moment, Becca looked thoughtful. Kicking her foot beneath the table, she tapped her fork on her saucer. "My grandma died," she said at length.

"Did she?" Mabel asked sympathetically.

Becca nodded. Mabel patted the little girl's hand "Well, I'm sure she's in heaven."

"She is." The dark curls bounced as Becca nodded again, her eyes glowing. "She's all sparkly and light. I visited her when I fell into the river."

Profound silence followed the child's statement.

"What do you mean, dear?" Mabel asked the child, but looked at Elizabeth, a frown drawing her graying brows together.

"She dreamed about her grandmother in heaven," Elizabeth said. Elizabeth's heart twisted painfully at how close she'd come to losing her daughter.

"It wasn't a dream!" Becca shot her mother an exasperated glance.

"Of course it wasn't. Tell us about it," Mabel said kindly.

"I *went* to heaven and *saw* Grandma. I wanted to stay with her, but she told me I had to come back. Then I wasn't in heaven. I was cold and wet and Mama was carrying me. Then we were inside the 'zamining room and Mama wrapped me in a big towel."

"Oh, dear," Mabel looked at the child in wonder.

"Can I tell you *now* what Grandma said?" Becca asked her mother. "Remember, I wanted to in church, but you told me in church I couldn't 'cause I had to be quiet?" Ebony eyes gleamed. "Can I?"

Nodding, Elizabeth stared at her child.

"I wanted to stay with Grandma, but she said I couldn't 'cause you would miss me too much."

"I would." Warm tears slid down Elizabeth's cheeks.

She caught her breath in surprise as Rand reached across the table and clasped her hand, his hand warm and his touch reassuring.

His hands had saved her child. Elizabeth wanted to kiss the callused palm and thank him again.

"She said you and Papa needed me with you," her daughter added, and forked in her last bite of pie.

Elizabeth's gaze flew to Rand's face. She caught her breath.

He was staring at Becca as if seeing her for the very first time.

Later, watching through the kitchen window while Rand and Becca were together on the porch, Elizabeth thought the truth must be obvious to anyone with eyes. So obvious her heart felt squeezed.

But had Rand guessed?

For an instant earlier at the table, she'd thought he must have. Then he'd acted so casual with the child, she'd doubted he had.

Mabel brushed through the door from the formal dining room. "How odd, dear, that Becca would say that about you and her father needing her." Frowning, she set a stack of plates and silverware down on the kitchen worktable beside the dishpan. "I mean, your husband is dead."

Her stomach knotting, Elizabeth nodded. "Yes, that is odd. But it must have been a dream anyway."

Rand sat on the swing on the side porch, and through the

open window, she could hear Becca chattering to him while she played on the floor. She was making a dozen old clothespins Mabel had given her to play with into a clothespin family.

A hundred or so yards beyond them down the broad street, Elizabeth could just see the ferry dock and the river. When Becca had wanted to go outside as Elizabeth and Mabel were clearing the table, the river and the memory of what happened the day before had been all too near. Elizabeth had refused to hear of it. Then Rand had volunteered to watch the child and keep her from wandering off.

Though Elizabeth's heart protested against it, she could have hardly said no without Mabel and Rand thinking it unusual.

"I'm almost done clearing the table," Mabel said, going back into the dining room.

"I'll start these," Elizabeth said. Pouring a kettle of hot water over the dishes already in the pan, she told herself she was being silly, that people saw what they expected to see. She picked up a bar of soap and began shaving slivers off into the water, trying to put the thoughts out of her mind.

Mabel returned with glasses. "I don't think it was. A dream, I mean. I've been a doctor's wife a lot of years, and Jonas has told me some strange things he's heard from his patients. One young man was kicked in the head by a horse and everyone thought he would die. After he came out of it, he told Jonas he was pulled down this tunnel filled with light to a beautiful place. Then his brother, who'd passed on years before, came to him and told him he had to go back because it wasn't his time—which is much what Becca said happened in her dream.

"And then there was a little girl who ate some poison berries and was delirious for days. She told us that while she was unconscious, she was floating above the bed, watching her mother take care of her." Mabel shook her head. "Maybe, by 'father' Becca means her new father, Hiram."

It was a simple answer. Elizabeth wanted to agree, but the lie stuck in her throat.

She was grateful when Mabel disappeared again into the dining room. After grabbing a dishcloth from a wire line stretched in the corner, she stuck her hands in the pan of water.

"Ouch!"

She immediately jerked them out again. Silly. She'd been acting silly since she'd realized Rand was here, in Willow. Letting the man's presence affect her. Letting the possibility that he would guess the truth worry her. And it had to stop. She had come here to marry Hiram Smith, and marry him she would, no matter. She had her daughter's future to think about.

And if she was honest with herself, her own future. Rand still had the power to affect her—he'd proved that last night. But she needed more from a man than pleasure in his arms, however wonderful and sense-stealing that pleasure might be. Tired of going on alone, she wanted to share her life, but with a man she could depend on.

A man she could trust to be there.

That wasn't Dalton McClure *or* Rand Matthews.

Shaking her red hands, waiting for the sting to go away, she felt the prickle of tears trying to force their way into her eyes. None of this would be a problem if only Hiram had been here when she'd arrived and they could have been married right away.

Sucking in a deep breath, she shook her head, irritated with herself for wishing things to be different.

If there was one thing she'd learned—slowly, but was beginning to sink in—it was that one had to make things different for oneself by making the right choices. She had given in to her infatuation and desire for Rand and become pregnant with his child. She had let her brother bully her into leaving Kansas sooner than she planned, and Hiram hadn't known to expect her.

Now, it was up to her to maintain control and not vary from her plans again.

After gingerly easing the plates into the pan of hot water, Elizabeth took the dishcloth and began to wipe down the large wood-burning stove, giving the dishwater time to cool down.

Becca's high-pitched voice came to her through the window, telling Rand how her clothespin family came to Oregon in a stagecoach, then a boat with a wheel that dipped into the water, and then another stagecoach—which was exactly how she and

Elizabeth had traveled. Then Becca told him the clothespin family's names, from the parents to the baby, and he joined in the game by asking their ages.

As Becca made up an age and a story about each one, her high childish voice drifting through the open window, Elizabeth felt the knot in her stomach begin to loosen.

Then she heard Rand ask, "What was your papa's name, Becca?"

And Elizabeth's heart froze.

Before she gave conscious thought to what she was doing, she was out the back door, the dishcloth still in her hand.

Looking up, Rand found Elizabeth rounding the corner of the Sedricks' porch. Her gaze was wary as it met his, then skittered to her daughter.

"Becca, pick up the pins and let's put them away. I think you should take a nap now."

The child looked up, frowning. "Why?"

"Never mind. Come on." Elizabeth twisted the dishcloth.

Thrusting out her bottom lip, Becca started gathering the clothespins.

Fear in every line of her body, Elizabeth bent and helped, never glancing at him. His heart beating slow and heavy with the realization, Rand asked, "Who is her father, Elizabeth?"

She glanced at her daughter, then him, then looked away toward the ferry landing, just visible past the house up the street. "Becca doesn't remember her father."

"You weren't going to tell me." It wasn't a question. He stood.

Glaring at him, Elizabeth said, "I'm going to marry Hiram and give my daughter a home."

Rand sucked in a deep breath, feeling as if he'd been punched in the gut. Halfway between them, the little girl—*his daughter*—looked back and forth from one to the other, a frown on her face caused by the adult tension she felt but didn't understand.

Elizabeth took a step and tucked Becca into the folds of her skirt, like a hen protecting a single chick.

He understood that she didn't want to discuss it in front of the child. A child who'd never been told the truth. Feeling his fists clenched, he uncurled his fingers. Elizabeth obviously had no intention of telling her the truth, now or ever.

"It's what's best for Becca," Elizabeth said. She raised her chin.

Rand looked at his daughter. Didn't Becca have a right to know the truth?

Damn it, hadn't he had a right to know? If he hadn't guessed, he'd never have known!

Hearing voices coming from the front of the house, he jammed his hat on his head. "You have company. Thank Mabel again for me for the dinner."

Looking at his daughter again, he half reached out, wanting to touch her soft curls. But he let his hand fall back to his side. Turning, he stepped off the porch and headed across the backyard.

With each step, he wondered how he could have missed the obvious. The truth had been right there all along, for him to see. Becca was his. His child. His little girl.

Part of him wanted to shout. Part of him wanted to throttle Elizabeth for daring to keep her from him—or trying to.

He was a father. That unexpected knowledge warmed him. Made him feel somehow anchored.

But now that he knew, what the hell was he going to do about it?

Elizabeth watched Rand go, wondering why she wanted to run after him and defend what she had or hadn't told her daughter.

Her fists clenched in the folds of her skirt. That was just it. Becca was *her* daughter! Rand had made his decision when he'd taken their best horse and ridden away years ago.

He could have contacted her after the furor over his escape had died down.

He could have written to her after he was reported dead, so she wouldn't have cried herself to sleep at night.

He could have come back for her . . . if he'd really cared.

Becca hugged Elizabeth's knees, looking up uncertainly.

Forcing a smile, Elizabeth stroked her daughter's curls. "Come on, pun' kin. We have company."

"Who?" Becca pulled away and blinked up at her mother.

"Well, I hear Lois, and it sounds like several other people. Maybe Lois's brother and his wife. Or Hiram's sister."

"Are there children?" The frown between the child's brows disappeared.

"Perhaps." Elizabeth glanced over her shoulder. Rand had vanished. "Let's go see."

Chapter Seven

The smooth hickory of the ax handle slipped across Rand's palms as he swung. It made an arc, and he guided the blade to the mark, letting the momentum it carried do the work. A large chip from the trunk of the alder flew through the air. Other chips already littered the ground. A second later, another chip flew as the blade bit into the other side of the tree.

When the tree was down, he'd limb it and split it into small pieces to use to smoke salmon, when the fish began their run upstream.

Cutting deeper into one side than the other, he guided the direction the tree would fall. Several ax swings later, it started to lean, slowly, the wood cracking. Putting his strength into it, Rand brought the blade down hard, making one last deep cut, then stepped out of the way.

The tree fell with slow grace, bouncing as the limbs bent against the ground, then springing back and settling in a swirl of young leaves, dust, and twigs.

His breath sounding loud to his own ears, Rand rolled his shoulders, stretching tired muscles. Physical exertion felt good. He'd been away from here too long.

Above the sheltered valley, a red-tailed hawk soared, hunting on the wing, almost obscured in the misty sky. A watery sun sat over the peaks in the distance. The valley stretched out, a hazy emerald bowl. Winding down the length of it, a creek roaring with spring runoff rushed around boulders and rocks. The newer spring-green leaves of aspen and birch along the watercourse added contrast to the dark evergreens.

Along the stream, several tiny gray birds with gold and red crowns patrolled the leaf litter, flitting, hopping, never still, while a Canadian jay moved from branch to branch in a nearby lodgepole pine, watching Rand curiously and occasionally daring to fly down and inspect his shirt and gun belt where they hung on a nearby limb.

Drawing in a deep breath of tangy, evergreen-scented air, Rand wondered why he'd stayed in town so much of his time. He could quit his job as sheriff and stay here. He was more at peace here than anyplace he'd ever been, even growing up in Illinois. The first time he saw this sheltered valley, which he'd bought sight unseen from an old man in the Montana gold fields, he fell in love with it. He could see a horse ranch spreading over the gentle slopes, with barns and corrals. The urge to invest his work and sweat had been strong.

Glancing at the shoulder of a nearby hill, where a charred, stone foundation was all that was left of the original house, Rand pictured how it would look when he rebuilt it.

And a hard, hurtful knot formed in his chest. He realized why he'd stayed away.

It felt like home.

Rand picked up his ax and swung hard, biting deep into a limb on the fallen tree. Being here tempted him to put down roots and start building dreams. And he hadn't allowed himself to dream since he'd left Kansas. A man on the run couldn't afford dreams. Or thinking of any place as home.

Or could he?

The thought had been teasing the back of his brain. It had been years since anyone had come looking for him, or recognized him. Could he take a chance and start again?

Or was he just fooling himself?

Rand swung again with force. The blow severed the limb

from the trunk. Then he moved to the next limb and hefted his blade.

"I'm glad you aren't as mad at me as you are that tree," said a raspy voice behind him.

Rand half turned as he swung. The ax blade hit wrong, glancing off the trunk and sending a vibration up the hickory handle that rattled his teeth.

"Damn!" Turning completely, Rand propped the ax head on the ground and glared at his friend. "Did you have to sneak up on me like an Indian?"

Charlie Fox grinned, his teeth flashing white in a face like old, wrinkled leather. Charlie and his grandson, Jake, had come with the property. *"Like an Indian* . . . That's a good one. But it wouldn't take an Indian to sneak up on you. Not with you attacking trees like a crazy woodpecker."

Rand fished a bandanna handkerchief out of his pocket and wiped sweat from his face and bare chest. "Work is good for the soul." He shouldered the ax again.

"Ah." Nodding, Charlie turned away. "Then I'll tell the young woman you are engaged in spiritual pursuits and can't be bothered to talk with her."

"Wom—" Rand missed his swing again and cursed fervently. When he looked back, the older man was some distance down the path. "Charlie, come back. What woman?"

Though he asked, his gut already knew.

Elizabeth.

"The pretty one waiting to see you." Without looking back, Charlie Fox continued down the gentle slope.

Rand swung the ax, driving it deep into the trunk, and left it sticking there for when he got back.

Of course it was Elizabeth. Who else would it be? But why was she here?

He hadn't spoken to her since Sunday, when he'd learned the truth. Not because he hadn't wanted to. No. He'd had a thousand conversations with her in his mind. Each one ending the same—with him losing his temper.

It still hurt that he'd had to guess the truth. She would never have told him. So he'd put off seeing her until he could think of the right thing to say. Without strangling her as he said it.

He closed his eyes briefly, then looked where Charlie had disappeared around a bend in the path. He should have asked if Elizabeth's—*if his daughter* was with her.

Thinking of the little girl, he felt warmth and anger mingle deep in his gut. His daughter. He'd be damned if he'd let her be raised by another man.

Plucking his shirt and gun belt from the branch, he strode after Charlie.

Elizabeth looked up as Rand rounded the curve in the rushing creek. Hatless, shirtless, his dark hair brushing his bare shoulders, he looked beautifully male and moved with the easy grace born of strength. Indigo denim stretched tight over his thighs, and her palms itched to smooth the fabric, to discover if the muscles beneath were as rock-hard as they looked to be. A warm tickle bloomed inside her when he drew near, and she could see the sheen of sweat slicking the muscles of his arms and broad chest. No doubt he was the person swinging the ax she'd heard earlier.

"I better tend to my stew." Charlie Fox looked from Rand to Elizabeth, then back to Rand, as if aware of the tension between them.

She had almost forgotten Charlie. She blinked, willing her brain to form coherent thoughts. "It does smell wonderful."

"Rabbit," Charlie said, then disappeared inside the cabin, shutting the door after him.

"Hello, Elizabeth." Rand nodded in greeting, then glanced at the wagon and around the open space in front of the barn.

"Becca isn't with me." Though the day was unseasonably warm, Elizabeth wrapped her shawl more tightly about her shoulders, as if the knitted wool would defend her against the emotions this man evoked in her.

Something like disappointment darkened his eyes—but was gone too fast for her to rightly interpret. "I see. Then to what do I owe this pleasure?"

"I . . ." Elizabeth watched, fascinated, as a drop of sweat made its way from between his dark brows down the length of his nose and fell off the tip. It would be easy to reach out and touch his chest, feel his perspiration-slicked muscles.

Impatiently, Rand wiped his face and neck on his shirt, then wrapped the shirt around his neck and laid the gun belt on the wagon seat.

She gave herself a mental shake, trying to focus. Why wasn't this easier? Why did the man's nearness have to muddle her senses? Swallowing, she looked down at the worn toes of her shoes, but only became aware of the scents of pine, clean sweat, and man emanating from him.

"Forget whatever speech you had rehearsed?" His tone was taunting.

"No." Raising her chin, she met his gaze levelly. "I didn't plan any speeches. I didn't *plan* to come here at all."

"Oh?" He hooked his thumbs in his pockets.

"No. Hiram's boys wanted to show me their farm. I . . . I didn't know you and he were neighbors. They wanted to stop by here on the way back to town to see the foal Hiram's buying from you for them. They're with Mr. Fox's grandson. He's showing them the foal." She glanced at the big barn. Sounds of boyish laughter and conversation trickled out the open doors.

Looking back at Rand, she added, "Anyway, I thought you'd stayed in town."

"I left my deputy, Willie Bates, to watch after things while I came out to help Charlie and Jake build a new smokehouse and get ready for the salmon run." Rand looked past her, toward the road she'd driven in on. "So why send Charlie for me if you didn't want to talk? You could have come and gone without me ever knowing you'd been here."

Elizabeth pulled her shawl tight again, then clasped her hands together and studied her interlocked fingers. "I thought, being I *was* here, we should discuss our situation and reach an understanding."

"She's my daughter." His tone was soft as silk, but there was steel in it.

"I'm marrying Hiram." She looked up, and almost quailed at what she saw. Inflexibility and anger tightened his jaw and made his ebony eyes glow like coals.

"You weren't even going to tell me."

The accusation hit home and she winced, but raised her chin. "And why should I have?"

"Why?" The word came out on an explosion of breath, his face darkening. His arms hung loosely at his sides, but his fists were clenched.

Elizabeth stood her ground and managed not to flinch. Finding her own sustaining anger, she hissed, "Yes, *why,* damn you! You planted your seed, then rode away on our best horse, leaving me to reap the harvest!"

"I never intended to hurt you." Rand clasped her upper arms. "And you know damn well I sent money for the horse a couple of months later. Just before I ran into that bounty hunter who tried to blow my head off."

Elizabeth gasped. "We never got any money." Frowning, she shook her head. "I don't believe. . . ." As she stared at Rand wide-eyed, a long unsolved puzzle suddenly fell into place.

"What is it?"

She shook her head. "My brother worked in town and he usually picked up the mail for us after—oh!" She put her hand on her mouth, realizing she'd been about to say after everyone knew about her pregnancy and she she'd started avoiding Salt Cedar Flats. But she caught the words back in time.

Her brother had bought a buggy about the time Rand spoke of, and she and her mother had wondered where the money had come from. Shamed that she'd thought the worst of Rand and that her own brother had most likely stolen from her mother, she felt angry tears threaten.

"Ethan must have. . . ." She straightened, wondering now if Ethan would really send her half of the money for the sale of the farm—her rightful due as half-owner. Ethan had promised to send it on to her, after the sale was completed. She'd always planned on having the money to repay Hiram Smith, if for some reason she didn't marry him.

Elizabeth said, "I'm sorry. I didn't know you'd sent payment for the horse. Mama never received it."

"I see." Rand looked up at the western hills, inhaling the

clean scent of the new evergreen logs the smokehouse was built from. He had felt so good that at least he'd been able to repay Elizabeth for the horse, if not for her great kindness to him, that it was a disappointment to learn she'd never received the money. "You never got my letter."

"No. No letter."

Laughter and shouts silenced whatever else he would have said. Glancing at the barn, he stepped away from her as Hiram's youngest son, George, scrambled through the open doors as if his life was endangered. A hail of dried horse dung and corncobs followed him.

The boy ducked and ran for cover behind the chicken pen, sending chickens in all directions, squawking and beating their wings against the fence pickets.

Jake Fox ran out after Little George. Another barrage of missiles followed him. Hiding behind the corner of the door, Jake aimed several corncobs of his own back into the dark interior.

A heavy thud and a yelp told Jake that at least one had found a mark. Grinning, he headed for George's safe cover. As he ran, he gathered more ammunition from the corncobs strewn over the ground.

Blinking away tears, Elizabeth was glad for the interruption. She'd almost lost control, and she couldn't afford to do that. Her brother's perfidy and his attitude toward Becca was a raw wound. But she needed to focus on the future. Becca's future.

Rand shot her a look that said they weren't finished, then turned his attention to the kids. "What are you boys doing?"

Though the tone was mild, the boys sobered immediately, looking guilty.

"Corncob war," Jake said. Dropping their potential missiles, the two came out from behind the chicken pen looking chastened. George gasped as a horse biscuit sailed past Jake's head.

"Donnie! Lance!" Jake called. "No fair. We gotta quit."

"Yeah, no fair!" George seconded, hiding behind his taller friend and looking askance in the direction of the two boys emerging from the barn.

The opposing army appeared, corncobs tucked into waistbands and suspenders and more held at the ready. Seeing Rand, they reluctantly disarmed, tossing their ammunition to the ground.

"If you make Lily or the foal nervous, they could hurt themselves in the stall," Rand told them.

Jake looked at his scuffed boots. "I'm sorry. I should have thought about that."

"No harm." Rand moved to Jake and put his hand on the fifteen-year-old's shoulder. "Tell you what. We were planning to move them out to the pasture anyway. Why don't you and the boys do it now, and you can show them Belle's new filly." He looked back at Elizabeth. "I'll keep Miss McKay company until you get back."

"Sure thing." Jake and the boys hurried into the barn, all but Hiram's oldest, who lingered at the door.

"Mr. Rand, it's *Mrs.* McKay." Donnie smiled shyly, dimples appearing in his round freckled cheeks. "She's gonna marry my pa. Then she'll be 'Mrs. Smith.' " He disappeared after the others.

Elizabeth shook her head. "*Miss* for *Mrs.* You see how easy it would be to destroy your daughter?" She had to make him understand what was best for Becca. He hadn't lived the shame, trying to protect their child.

Before Rand could answer, Jake came out leading the most unusual horse Elizabeth had ever seen. The mare had a long head with a distinctly Roman nose. She wasn't red or white, but an unhappy roaning of the two, as if nature had run out of one color and had to make do with a combination.

The animal had white speckles dotting her mouth and nose. White sclera surrounded her eyes, but instead of seeming nervous or frightened, as this usually indicated in a horse, the mare was relaxed. She turned her large head toward Elizabeth and snorted in greeting, then glanced behind her, where Donnie was leading out a dainty chocolate-brown foal with a snow-white rump.

A horsefly buzzed the foal's ear. Lance snatched it out of the air, and the little horse threw up her head and hopped in alarm.

''*Whoa! Whoa,* Lilybelle,'' Donnie crooned. The little filly gentled, turning an ear toward the sound of his voice. Donnie went on in the same soft tone. ''Lance, I know you ain't got spit for brains, but you ought to know enough not to spook her.'' He shot his brother a disgusted look.

''Sorry.'' Lance kicked a stray corncob. ''I was just catching a horsefly.''

Elizabeth said, ''The foal is beautiful. But there's something wrong with its hoofs.'' She looked from the foal's feet to the mare's. ''And the mare's hoofs, too. There are white stripes on them!''

The boys snickered.

Rand smiled. ''There's nothing wrong. These are Appaloosas, originally bred by the Nez Percé up on the plateau. The striped hoofs and mottled skin on the mouth and white around the eyes are characteristics of the breed.''

He nodded to the boys. ''While you take the mare and foal out to the pasture, I'll show Miss—*Mrs.* McKay the new smokehouse we just built.''

''Yeah, salmon will be running in a few weeks. Maybe sooner,'' Donnie said excitedly.

Lance nodded. ''I netted the most *and* the biggest one last year!''

As Hiram's boys followed Jake and the mare around the corner of the barn, Elizabeth drew a deep breath and tried to calm her nerves. She could see the corner of the pasture in the distance. It wouldn't take the boys long to get there and back.

Rand took her arm and she jumped. He frowned and dropped his hand. ''I didn't mean to startle you. Come on. The smokehouse is this way.'' He indicated a nearby structure of wood and stone. ''I assume you want to talk with me in private.''

Rubbing her arm where his fingers seemed to have burned through her sleeve, she followed him, deciding to clear the air once and for all. Since finding out he'd tried to pay for the horse he took the morning he left, the hurt she felt toward him had lessened a little. But anger still thrummed through her chest, anger that he'd let her believe him dead and hadn't cared enough to come back for her.

But most of all, she wanted to make him understand that he couldn't let anyone know he was Becca's father. She wouldn't let Rand destroy Becca's life.

The interior of the smokehouse was dimly lit, the only light coming in from the narrow vent along the peak of the roof and the open door. Positioned all around the walls were rows of slatted wooden racks, which she guessed awaited salmon steaks. Stones were arranged in the center of the earthen floor, as if ready for coals.

"You plan to smoke a lot of fish," she said. Looking around the room, she pulled her shawl tighter.

"It's a staple for the winter, when game gets scarce and the snow grows deep." Rand paused, then said softly. "Elizabeth, look at me."

She didn't want to. But how could she deny the simple request? Raising her gaze to his face, she found it harshly sculpted. His eyes were shadowed with pain.

"She's my daughter," he said. "I can't just pretend otherwise." Rand remembered Becca's dark eyes shining up at him as she introduced him to her clothespin family, the father of which was named "Sheriff Rand." Her delighted smile as he'd joined in her game of pretend had snagged his heart.

He'd never thought he'd know the joy of having a child. Now, he didn't want it to be snatched away.

"I'm marrying Hiram Smith."

"You liked his place, did you? It is a nice farm. Very prosperous." What possessed him to goad her, he didn't know. Maybe it rankled that Hiram could offer Elizabeth more than he could.

"I'm doing it for Becca's sake!"

"She's my daughter. I want to be a part of her life." His words were softly spoken, but a challenge nonetheless.

Clenching her fists, Elizabeth sucked in her breath, trying to control the fear the statement sent skittering through her. She had to make Rand understand the terrible consequences to Becca if he persisted. He didn't know. He hadn't seen people snub his daughter and jeer his innocent child.

Elizabeth swallowed her fear and anger and said as calmly as she could, "We were completely alone after Mother died.

Struggling to make ends meet. My brother leased out the homestead to be farmed, but he gave me only enough money from it to barely exist. Ethan said there wasn't any more, but . . ." But now and then she had doubted him. Her brother had always had a greedy streak, one she'd tried to ignore for the sake of maintaining family ties.

Elizabeth sighed and slid her fingers along the nearest rack, made of split alder. "No one in town wanted a fallen woman working for them. Now, I am going to marry Hiram Smith so I can be certain Becca will always have enough to eat, always be cared for. She'll have respectability."

"I can take care of her. Take care of you both. I want her to know she's my child—"

"*No!* Becca's got a chance for a future here and I won't let you ruin it and bring the shame of her illegitimacy out!" Elizabeth hissed. "I don't want to ever again hear my child called *a bastard.* Or have other mothers snatch their own children away when they get near her, like she has some terrible disease." Elizabeth impatiently dashed the tears from her wet cheeks.

Rand stood perfectly still. As if he'd sustained an unexpected blow "People did that?"

"Damn you! A lot you cared!"

All the anger and fear and loneliness she'd suffered through the years surged within her. Flying into him, she pounded his chest with her fists as hard as she could.

And he let her, taking the punishment as if it was his due.

Her anger left suddenly, taking her strength with it. Collapsing against his chest, she sobbed for all the pain she'd borne and all the loneliness.

"I'm sorry, Elizabeth. More than you can know." Rand caught her to him, stroking her shoulders and back, wishing to God he could go back and make everything different. "Not that it makes it better, but there hasn't been a day that I didn't think of you."

Her head came up He could see need and disbelief at war in her eyes. She wanted to believe him. That was something, at least.

In her place, he doubted he would.

He was aware the exact instant the energy between them changed. Her soft breasts felt warm where they flattened against his naked chest. Her sweet breath fanned against his throat.

Her lips were slightly parted, as if she was awaiting his kiss.

"I never stopped thinking of you." Rand lowered his mouth to hers.

Chapter Eight

He couldn't stop himself. Kissing Elizabeth. Tasting her. Inhaling her scent. Feeling her softness beneath his hands was more important than his next breath.

As Elizabeth opened her lips, pressing closer, Rand realized she wanted him, too. Perhaps even as much as he wanted her.

The thought sent heat surging through his groin and he groaned deep in his throat.

The sound set Elizabeth aflame. Twining her arms around his neck, she sought to be closer still, flattening her breasts against his hard chest. This was what she'd wanted, she admitted to herself. For so long she'd dreamed of this man. Even after she'd heard he was killed. The other night in the moonlight had seemed like an extension of those dreams.

But he was here now, real, flesh and bone, holding her as if he'd dreamed of her, too.

Need surged through her as he deepened the kiss, slanting his lips across hers as if he could never get enough of kissing her. Then his tongue began to probe the secret places of her mouth, and all her thoughts spun away.

There remained only sensations—his male scent, the texture

of his hair, too long, touching his shoulders, and slightly damp still from his recent exertion. And the taste of his mouth.

Her nipples tingled. She rocked against him, and they tingled more madly. Pleasure and need vibrated through her middle, and she gasped.

Taking advantage, he plunged his tongue into the sweet recesses of her mouth even more deeply. As he did, Rand stroked her back. He could never get close enough to this woman.

Cupping her backside, he spread his legs and fitted her between them. Pressing her close to his growing erection, he rocked her against his hardness, needing more. He needed to plunge inside her. To lose all the pain and uncertainty and longing for this woman that he'd felt over the years within her warmth.

He'd held onto the memory of their lovemaking so long, until it had become hazy and he had no longer known what was fantasy and what was real.

But Elizabeth was here, now. And the urge to lay her down on the floor was hard to deny.

When she reached between them and cupped his hardness through his breeches, it was almost impossible.

Unable to help himself, Rand covered her hand with his and encouraged her to stroke him. Trembling as sensations surged through him, he broke off his kisses and closed his eyes.

"I like this." Her words were the lightest of whispers. "I feel like . . ."

He looked down to find Elizabeth watching him, her eyes luminous. "What?" he asked. The single syllable was a croak more than a word.

She blushed slightly. "Before . . . when we made love before, you touched me and I felt helpless. Carried away by it all. I never realized I could do that to you, too."

"I realized it. Oh, sweetness, did I." Rand kissed her neck.

She tilted her head back, giving him access. Her pupils were dark, her lids drooping as she worked magic with her hand. "I feel . . . powerful."

He caught her waist, smoothing his palms up the flare of her rib cage to her breasts. His thumbs unerringly found the tight hard buds of her nipples, and Elizabeth gasped, her hand stilling.

"It's better when we are helpless together," he murmured against her temple.

As he rubbed her nipples, she trembled. He kissed her forehead and her temple, her cheek and the wispy honey-blond curls that had escaped from the bun at the back of her head.

Elizabeth caught his hands and held them, stopping what he was doing. She hid her face against his shoulder, barely able to breathe for the need she felt. "I want you so badly it hurts."

"I know. I hurt for you, too."

"How can I feel this way?" she asked harshly, angry with herself. "I *am* a bitch. A wanton, like the people back home said." Her shoulders shook. "Like Ethan said."

Rand realized she was crying. *"No!"* The word was an explosion of breath against her hair. "No, Elizabeth. You're human. It is natural to have these feelings."

"Hiram trusted me. Sight unseen. How could I do this to him?" she asked in self-disgust.

Rand stilled. He felt his heart stop beating at the reminder that she belonged to another man. She felt so right in his arms. How could he have forgotten?

"You don't want to marry Hiram, Elizabeth."

"I do want to. I am."

She tried to pull away, but Rand held her with one arm around her, smoothing her hair.

"I'm Becca's father. Let me *be* her father."

"No!" She pushed against him. This time he let her go. "You fathered her, but you've *never* been her father!"

The words hit like blows. He clenched his hands, wanting to deny the truth of them.

He couldn't.

"I want to, Elizabeth."

"For how long?" She glared up at him, her hazel eyes more green than brown. *"How long?* You might be masquerading as upstanding Sheriff Rand Matthews, but you are still Dalton McClure and there's still a rope waiting for you when the real law catches up with you."

"Look, I can't make promises about things I can't foresee, but—"

"Exactly!" she cut in. Dashing tears from her eyes, Elizabeth went on harshly. "If I let you be a part of Becca's life, if she grows to love you and they hang you . . ."

"They won't." He had to believe he could start living again, planning again. Being a father to his daughter. Shaking his head, he said, "They won't. It's been so long, it would have happened before now. Dalton McClure *is* dead and buried."

"You can't be certain of that. That's why I am marrying Hiram. It's the best thing for Becca. And besides, I gave him my word. My promises mean something to me." Turning on her heel, she rushed out of the door.

Looking after her, Rand realized his fists were clenched, and consciously relaxed his hands. But the tension in his gut refused to ease.

Of all the injustices he'd endured since being falsely accused of murder, this was the worst. Being denied the right to claim his daughter. Having Elizabeth refuse to give him a chance hurt more than hearing that jury pronounce him guilty. Or having the judge sentence him to hang.

What was worse, he couldn't blame her. He knew that when he'd let her think he was dead, though he was doing what was best for her, she'd seen it as abandonment.

She'd never received his letter, but that wouldn't have made a difference. Alone and pregnant, she would have felt even more betrayed if she'd learned he didn't intend to come back.

God help him, he'd never have left her at all if he'd known she would bear his child, though he would surely have ended up dangling from a rope. At least she would have had a wedding ring on her finger.

Now, she was only thinking of her daughter, trying to protect the child. Their child.

But the law thought he was dead. He had to convince Elizabeth she was wrong, that he could be a father to Becca. He wouldn't leave them.

Now that he'd thought about it, there was nothing he wanted more. He had a chance to have a life again and he was going to take it. Put down his roots here, invest his labor and sweat in building this into a horse ranch. Building a life.

Rand knew he had to show her she could trust him to be there with her this time, no matter what. He wouldn't leave again.

Hearing laughter as the boys returned, Rand pulled his shirt from around his neck and slipped it on. Buttoning it, he left the smokehouse. Elizabeth stood by the wagon, watching the boys approaching from the pasture, her shawl drawn tight across her breasts. She didn't turn and look at him as he walked up beside her. As Rand plucked his hat off the wagon seat and put it on, then strapped on his gun, she didn't acknowledge him at all.

He understood her attitude. That didn't mean he had to accept it.

Just how the hell he could convince Elizabeth to trust him when everything he'd ever done had convinced her she never should?

He didn't know. But he might as well start trying tonight, before she had time to forget what they'd just shared in the smokehouse.

He'd let her go on back to Willow for now, but as soon as he bathed and changed clothes he'd go to Doc Sedrick's and declare his intentions—to steal Hiram's bride.

The clouds thickened and rain started on the way home—not the hard downpours and lightning of a Kansas spring storm, but just light rain, falling straight down. It had rained five of the eight days she'd been here.

The boys seemed to think nothing of it, and merely pulled oilskin slickers from under the seat. Elizabeth was glad Mabel had suggested she take an umbrella in place of her parasol, and had loaned her one.

Angling the umbrella against the misting rain, Elizabeth carefully climbed down from the wagon. "Are you boys sure you don't want help putting the horse and wagon away?"

The three looked at her incredulously, peering out from under the hoods of their oilskins.

"No, ma'am. We don't need any. I been hitching and unhitching since I was big enough to pick up a trace pole," Donnie said.

Sensing that she'd made a misstep, Elizabeth smiled apologetically. "I'm sorry I doubted you. I'm not used to having capable young men around to take care of things."

Donnie sat a bit straighter at the compliment. "Yes, ma'am. I understand, it's just been you and Becca." He slapped the reins on the horse's rump and the animal started forward.

Elizabeth stepped back out of the way of the wheels and let it pass. She'd have to remember that the boys were capable of caring for themselves. They didn't need coddling.

She was lucky. All three were well-mannered and well-behaved boys and seemed ready to accept her, thank goodness.

Rand would never have a chance to know a father's pride in Becca, or only from a distance. Elizabeth hurt for him, knowing that. But she had to think of Becca first.

As Elizabeth headed for the front porch of the Hoffpaurs' small house, located directly behind the blacksmith and livery, the realization that she wasn't angry with Rand anymore caught her unaware.

Pausing on the porch to shake the water from her umbrella, she wondered when her feelings had changed. It must have been when she'd realized she wasn't the only one who had suffered because he'd left her. He had cared. And now he was suffering because he could never claim his child.

But Elizabeth knew it made no difference in what she must do. Marrying Hiram was still best for Becca.

"There you are!" Smiling, Maggie Jean opened the door, the baby in her arms. A toddler sucked her thumb and clung to her mother's skirt, looking up at Elizabeth with wide blue eyes. "Come in before you take a chill."

"Thank you." Elizabeth placed the umbrella in a stand by the door.

Maggie Jean stood back and allowed Elizabeth to precede her into the clean but well-lived-in parlor. "I just made coffee, and I believe there's some muffins left, if my girls didn't sneak back into them—I put some aside for you and Hiram's boys."

"That sounds wonderful. The boys are putting the horse and wagon away. Thank you for letting them take me out to Hiram's farm. He has a lovely place."

"It's nice, isn't it? That great big house and the orchard. He gives me all the fruit I need to make jellies and preserves and such, and he has plenty to sell besides. And when he gets the barn enlarged, he plans to get a half-dozen milk cows and go into the dairy business. There's lots of folks in town, like Doc and Mabel, who don't keep their own cows, and he's close enough he can sell milk in Eugene, after the railroad comes through."

Elizabeth smiled, admiring the other woman's loyalty to her brother. Maggie Jean didn't have to sell her on Hiram. She already knew he was a good man, and could provide for her and Becca.

She just hoped she could be the wife he deserved.

Guilt nibbled at her. Going willingly into Rand's arms, she had already failed.

She had to be certain it never happened again.

Chapter Nine

"Sit." Maggie Jean gestured at a worn armchair. "I'll fetch the coffee and muffins."

"Let me go into the kitchen with you," Elizabeth offered. "You probably have things to do, or to tend to on the stove, and I don't want to be treated like company."

"That's considerate of you. I can tell we're going to get along just fine." Beaming, Elizabeth's future sister-in-law led the way.

The kitchen proved to be a hub of activity. Two older girls were busy at the stove. One younger girl and boy, both looking a little younger than George's eight years, had several kerosene lamps disassembled on the table. They were cleaning soot from the globes and trimming the wicks. All smiled and said hello when Elizabeth entered.

"You just sit at the end of the table. I'll pour the coffee." Maggie Jean grabbed a potholder and lifted the blue enamelware pot from the stove as one of the girls set two cups on the table.

"Thank you. I'm afraid it will take me a while to keep all of your names straight." Elizabeth settled into a straight-backed chair.

The girl smiled. "That's okay, Mrs. McKay. Mama gets us crossed half the time."

"I do not, Ester." Maggie Jean poured the coffee.

"I'm *Hester,*" the girl whispered behind her hand to Elizabeth as the other children giggled.

"I know," Maggie Jean said with a smile. "Ester is the tall one burning the soup."

"I am not!" The tallest girl looked askance at her mother.

"You're not Ester?" Maggie Jean raised her brows in mock perplexity.

"I *am* Ester. I'm *not* burning the soup!"

The children laughed again, even Ester, and Elizabeth smiled, liking the warm family atmosphere.

"Hester, please fetch that tin of muffins from the cabinet. Lisa?"

"Yes, ma'am?" The girl who looked to be the oldest sister turned from the stove.

"I think the baby is asleep now. Please put him in his cradle." Maggie Jean gave the baby to the girl, then settled into a chair and picked up the toddler, sitting the little girl on her lap. She directed her attention to the children cleaning lamps. "Are you two finished?"

"Yes, ma'am."

"Good. The scent of kerosene doesn't go well with baked goods. Put the lamps away, then you can have some muffins, too. After you wash the soot off your hands."

"Yes, ma'am," the two chorused, and scrambled to clear the table.

"Muf-fins!" Removing the finger from her mouth, the toddler pointed as Hester placed the container on the red gingham tablecloth and opened the lid.

"Yes, sweetie, muffins."

As Elizabeth enjoyed a muffin with her coffee, she got to know the Hoffpaur children a little better. All were polite and well behaved, like Hiram's boys. All were a little curious about her, and she encouraged their questions about Kansas and her and Becca's trip.

As she described her former home, they found the concept

of almost flat land with hardly any trees a hard one to grasp. And they were definitely disappointed that there had been no skirmishes with Indians on the overland part of Elizabeth's and Becca's journey.

Becca had never had other children around to associate with, but now she would have lots of cousins, Elizabeth realized. Nice, well-mannered children with whom to play.

After the wedding.

Sipping her coffee, Elizabeth tried to gather enthusiasm for the prospect. But each time she tried to picture her fiancé, he had Rand Matthews's face.

Darn the man anyway! She had come here to start a new life, not be mired in old feelings.

The *ping, ping, ping* of a hammer hitting steel issued from outside. Elizabeth assumed Hiram's sons had joined Maggie Jean's older boys and their uncle in the blacksmith's shed.

"I do wish you'd stay here with us, until Hiram returns. I know he'd want that," Maggie Jean said later, as she saw Elizabeth to the door.

Touched by her sincerity, Elizabeth impulsively gave her a quick hug. "I thank you. But we'll stay where we are for now. Mabel has grown quite attached to Becca, and I've been helping Doc with some of his patients. His arthritis is making it difficult for him to tie bandages and such, and I've had some training as a nurse."

And though the offer was sincere, she knew the Hoffpaur family was overcrowded already with Hiram's sons staying there while he was away.

The rain had settled into a fine mist as Elizabeth made her way on the boardwalk toward the other end of Main Street. Willow was a pleasant little town. She liked it here immensely, except for the river being so close, a constant reminder of nearly losing her daughter. And Rand happening to be in town was an unfortunate coincidence.

Passing in front of the sheriff's office, she slowed, wondering if once she was married to Hiram, she'd be able to put Rand out of her mind.

She would have to, she told herself firmly. That was just the way things had to be.

Her attention was claimed by the boy running toward her on the boardwalk. When the lad got close, she recognized him as Johnny, the boy who did chores for Doc and Mabel. As she saw his expression, wide-eyed with fright, Elizabeth's heart took a painful thump.

Her hand to her throat, Elizabeth asked, "What is it, Johnny? Is Becca all right?"

Skidding to a stop, he looked up at Elizabeth from under the hood of his slicker. "Yes, ma'am. As far as I know. Mrs. Mabel sent me to find you for Doc. He's hurt his leg." The boy's face turned a sickly shade. "And it looks awful bad."

It was passing from twilight into dark as Rand went up the steps and crossed the porch to the Sedricks' front door. He raised his hand to knock. Then paused, lowering it again.

After Elizabeth and the Smith boys rolled out of sight, he'd bathed in the creek and put on clean clothes, deciding that since he'd made up his mind to marry Elizabeth, he might as well get on with the job of convincing her.

Maybe he should have put on his Sunday best. That was what he would have done if he'd gone courting back east. Maybe he should have brought a bouquet or candy.

Eyeing Mabel's pink seven sister's rose, which ran up the corner post of the porch, he decided a few blooms wouldn't be missed. Trying to break off a cluster of flowers, he found a thorn. "Damn!"

Bad idea, he decided as blood welled on the tip of his finger. Sticking the injured digit into his mouth, he went resolutely back to the door and knocked. Elizabeth would just have to take him like he was, without flowers to soften the blow.

Holding Becca on her hip, Mabel opened the door. "Rand! Oh, am I glad to see you. Come on in."

Her head on Mabel's shoulder, Becca smiled at him, and his heart did a warm flip-flop.

"Mabel. Is—"

"Come in, come in!" She caught his sleeve and pulled him inside. "I know Elizabeth said she's had experience in these things, but I feel better now that you're here. Willie is no help at all."

"Experience?"

"If something happens to Jonas . . ." Shaking her head, Mabel took Rand's hat and hung it on the hall tree while he peeled off his slicker.

"What's wrong with Jonas? Where is he?" He hung up the slicker beside his hat.

"You don't know? Oh, Rand, he's in the examining room. It's his leg."

Rand's gaze returned to his daughter. Her brows were puckered together in concern. Obviously, she was upset because the adults around her were upset. Rand touched her cheek. "What's wrong, little one?"

Dark eyes met his—eyes so much like the ones he saw in the mirror every morning when he shaved that he wondered how he'd failed to see their resemblance right away.

"Doc hurted his leg," she said, her mouth turning down at the corners.

"Your mother and I will help him. Don't worry."

Becca blinked up at him, her expression lightening, total belief in her gaze. "Okay. I won't worry."

Rand felt as if he'd just taken on an awesome responsibility. He'd made a promise to a child. His child.

"That's right." Mabel kissed the little girl's cheek. "There's nothing for you to worry about. Let's go find one of those cookies we made this afternoon."

Carrying the child, she headed toward the kitchen. "Tell Elizabeth I have more water heating if she needs it," she said over her shoulder.

Rand turned the porcelain knob and swung the door of the examining room wide. Elizabeth was fitting a thin pad of white cloth over a cone-shaped screen. Wild Willie Bates stood in one corner, stroking his thick ginger-colored mustache, looking ill at ease.

"Rand!" Willie greeted him as if he was a lifeboat in a storm-tossed sea.

"Oh, Rand, I'm glad you've come." Elizabeth's eyes shone. She meant it. That knowledge sent warmth curling around his heart. Frowning, she glanced at Doc, and Rand realized why.

The older man lay on the examining table, his face chalky-white and lined with pain. A white towel spotted with red was draped over one of his legs.

Scowling, Doc propped up on his elbow. "I don't need that damned stuff, Elizabeth."

"No chloroform? It's going to hurt like hell," she warned him.

"Well, that's good. It damn sure will have to ease up some to just hurt like hell." Sweat beaded Doc's forehead and he lay back. "I will take laudanum. You might give it time to take hold before you start. With laudanum, I can be awake if you need advice."

Sidling for the door, Willie said, "Rand, this bein' a awful small room, why don't I just ease out and let you in." His bushy red brows waggled up and down, signaling his distress.

"Go on home, Will."

"Really, Rand? Okay. If you say so." Willie made his escape.

Rand closed the door after the deputy. "What happened, Doc?"

"Slipped climbing down off the buggy. My foot went between the steps as I fell. Damn leg snapped like a dry twig." Doc shook his head. "Willie saw what happened and helped me inside—though I thought I was going to have to hold ammonia under his nose while he did it. The man's squeamish as Mabel."

Rand gently lifted the towel. It was a compound fracture. The flesh wound was not large, however. Doc might keep his leg, if he was lucky. During his short stint in the Army after college, Rand had seen this sort of wound go either way, healing up as though nothing happened, or with gangrene setting in inside of a week.

"What can I do to help?" Rand asked Elizabeth.

"Get Doc a glass of water from the kitchen and fetch me that brown bottle on the corner of the second shelf. Then wash your hands and take those scissors on the tray and cut off his pants leg."

She unwrapped a set of wooden splints and inspected them. "Doc, I'm glad you keep several sizes of these ready for use."

"I didn't expect to be using them on me." He looked as if the pain had exhausted his strength.

"You're in good hands, Doc," Rand assured him.

Elizabeth shot him a dark look. He wasn't supposed to know she had any medical skills, he realized as he left to get a glass of water from the kitchen. She had dug the slug out of his shoulder and cauterized the wound, no doubt saving his life. He hoped Doc would fare as well under her care.

After the laudanum had taken effect, Elizabeth washed the area around the wound carefully and applied a carbolic acid solution. Setting the leg required strength. Rather than hurt Doc more by possibly trying and failing, she directed Rand. After the leg was set and splinted, Rand and Elizabeth helped Doc into his bedroom, while the laudanum was still in full effect.

Mabel was there before them, and already had the bed turned down. Elizabeth and Rand helped him to sit on the edge of the mattress.

Mabel wrung her hands, looking frayed "Becca was tired so I put her to bed, Elizabeth."

"Thank you. I'd better go check on her." Elizabeth left.

"You can help Rand undress me," Jonas told his wife. "Get your scissors and we'll just cut off the rest of these blasted trousers."

Mabel nodded and hurried out, returning in a few minutes with her sewing basket. Leaving the couple together after he'd done what he could, Rand closed the door to their bedroom and looked around for Elizabeth. He found her coming out of a room at the end of the hall.

"Did you get Doc to bed?" she asked as she shut the door softly.

"Yes." Rand looked at the closed door.

"I should go in and check on him." She started to brush past Rand.

He put his hand on her arm and stopped her. "Mabel is helping him undress."

"Oh."

Glancing at the door to Elizabeth's bedroom, Rand said softly, "I want to see my daughter."

Elizabeth stiffened. "She's asleep."

Paying no heed to Elizabeth's whispered protest, Rand opened the door quietly. Light from the hall lamp on the wall directly behind them fell onto the bed and the dark head nestled against the white pillow. For a moment, he couldn't find words to speak.

"She is beautiful," he whispered at length. So small. Her hand was curled by her cheek; the fingers on it were so delicate. She was infinitely precious. And vulnerable. And she was his.

Watching the play of expressions cross Rand's face, the pride and wonder, Elizabeth felt her heart squeeze painfully. Pushing aside the feeling—she had to do what was best for Becca—she said quietly, "You know it will be better for her if I marry Hiram."

He was still for a moment. When he closed the door softly, his expression was etched with pain. Watching his face, Elizabeth realized she was holding her breath, hoping that she'd made him understand. That he wouldn't spoil her chances to give his daughter a good life. "Rand, you do know that. You wouldn't want to hurt her by telling people the truth, would you?"

"I'd never hurt her."

He stared at the closed door for a moment, and Elizabeth thought she'd won. Then he turned to her and cupped her face between his work-roughened palms. His dark eyes held hers. The intensity she saw there said he hadn't let go either, and he wouldn't let go easily.

"Rand, you have to know it's for the best!" She felt frantic.

"Hiram isn't her father." Still holding her face between his warm hands, he slowly lowered his mouth to hers.

No! She yelled the word in her mind. She'd promised herself just this afternoon that she wouldn't let this happen again.

But she could have no more turned from his kiss than she could have sprouted wings and flown away.

His lips caressed hers tenderly, in quick, gentle kisses. "I'm going to fight you on this, Elizabeth. Every way I can." He kissed her again. "I'm not going to just stand by and let you marry another man."

She pulled back, as far as his hold would let her. "You wouldn't tell that you're Becca's father. Rand—"

He silenced her with another quick kiss. "No. I won't cause you shame and Becca confusion." His lips found hers yet again, briefly. "But I'm not going to make it easy for you either. I want to marry you. I can take care of you and Becca."

He pulled her close, and this time his kiss was deep and soft. A kiss that was all tenderness and emotion. Warmth bloomed in her chest, though she fought to keep it out—warmth that touched a place deep inside her that had been cold and empty for a long time.

A warmth that stole her ability to think and react.

The sound of a doorknob turning down the hall barely registered, until she heard Mabel asking Doc if he would like an extra blanket.

Before Mabel came into the hall, Rand broke the kiss and stepped away. He moved and met Mabel at the bedroom door. "You're tired. Go to bed. I'll stay with Doc while you get some sleep, then you can relieve me."

Not knowing what else to do, Elizabeth ducked inside her bedroom and firmly closed the door.

Rand settled into an armchair in the corner of the bedroom and stretched his legs out before him. The laudanum Doc had administered to himself appeared to still be easing the pain. Though Rand guessed he wasn't asleep, Doc's eyes were closed, and he looked more relaxed than he had earlier when pain had him in its grip.

Shifting in the chair, Rand crossed his boots at the ankles, tipped his hat forward, and closed his eyes. Crossing his arms on his chest, he let his thoughts wander. He didn't expect to sleep. Even if he had gone back to his bunk in the sheriff's office, he doubted if he would have slept much.

Not after kissing Elizabeth in the hall.

Even if he hadn't, he had too much on his mind—the wonder of being the father of a beautiful, dark-eyed imp. And how Elizabeth seemed to make the sun shine on a cloudy day. She made him dare to dream again. Of rebuilding the old cabin on his place. Of building a life together.

But dreams were pointless if he couldn't earn her forgiveness and trust.

And how the hell could he do that, when he'd done so much to earn her distrust? He could only guess at the hell she'd gone through in Kansas, as an unwed mother. Her eyes held laughter and a joy of life when he'd known her before. Now, they were often shadowed. Though the old Elizabeth did peek through every now and then.

He knew now he never should have left her in Kansas. No matter what the cost.

Chapter Ten

Becca finished her porridge and dropped her spoon into the empty bowl. "I like Mr. Rand."

Reaching for a golden-brown biscuit from the pan she'd just taken out of the oven, Elizabeth stilled for a moment. She then took a biscuit, buttered it, and placed it on one of the plates of food she was preparing. "Why do you say that, pun'kin?"

Her daughter turned sideways on the bench and put her bare feet up on it. Catching her toes and bending them back, she looked thoughtful, then shrugged. "I don't know. I just like Mr. Rand. He calls me 'tadpole.' What are you doing?"

Elizabeth took another biscuit from the pan. "Fixing Doc and Mrs. Mabel some breakfast." Elizabeth laid pieces of ham beside the eggs on each plate, then set the blue enamelware coffeepot and two cups on the tray and lifted it.

"Mr. Doc hurted his leg." The child frowned.

"Yes. But Rand helped me treat it and put on a bandage. Doc feels bad, but I think he will be okay. Now, do you want to help me carry this food to him and Mrs. Mabel?"

"Yes!" Becca was off the bench in a flash. "Can I carry the tray?"

"It's a little too heavy for you to take. But you can go to

the bedroom where Doc and Mabel are and knock. After Mrs. Mabel answers, you can hold the door open for me."

"Okay!" Bare feet pattering over the wooden floor, Becca raced through the kitchen door ahead of her mother, then turned down the hall, her rapid steps muffled on the carpet runner.

As she lifted the lid and checked the pot of soup she had simmering for dinner, Elizabeth told herself it was okay if Becca liked Rand. Why wouldn't she? He was good with the child. And Rand had promised not to tell Becca the truth and confuse her. Elizabeth felt he would keep his word.

Still, life might have been simpler if Becca had taken a dislike to him.

As soon as the thought surfaced, Elizabeth was ashamed of it. It couldn't be easy for him. Falsely accused and convicted of murder, living on the run. He must never have felt safe anywhere. And though she didn't want to, she could understand why he'd left her in Kansas as he had. He said he'd wanted her to have a better life than he could give her. She was starting to believe him.

But he was still a wanted man. What was true then was true now. Though the fact that Rand cared he had a daughter warmed some corner of her heart, Elizabeth knew she must make him realize it didn't change anything. She couldn't let it. For Becca's sake.

Lifting the tray, she followed her daughter. Becca held Doc's bedroom door open wide.

"I'm not an invalid. I'm sure I could have hobbled to the table." A sheet drawn up across his chest, Doc winced as he shifted his leg beneath the covers. He looked almost as pale as his nightshirt.

"I never doubted it. I brought breakfast for Mabel," Elizabeth set the tray on a high chest. "Now, you might talk her into sharing it. . . ."

Mabel chuckled and moved to look over the contents of the tray. "This is very sweet of you, Elizabeth. I can use some coffee, I'll allow."

"You must be exhausted after sitting up all night. I'll stay with Doc after you eat, and you can get some rest."

Shaking her head, Mabel poured a cup of coffee from the pot on the tray. "I'm not so spent. Rand was here most all night."

"Rand stayed here?" Elizabeth smoothed her apron. It was just too silly—hearing his name made her heart thump harder. Of course, letting him take her into his arms and kiss her till her toes curled didn't help matters.

"I like Mr. Rand," Becca declared, to no one in particular. For the second time that morning.

Mabel said, "I woke up about four and took over from him. Of course, by that time the laudanum was wearing off and Jonas was getting fractious. I think his grouching was what woke me." She inhaled deeply of the coffee in her cup, then took a sip. "*Hmm,* this is wonderful."

"Hmph!" Doc snorted. "I don't grouch. Are you going to keep that coffee all to yourself?"

"I guess grouching means he's going to be okay." Smiling, Mabel poured another cup and carried it to the bed, setting it on the bedside table. Then she and Elizabeth helped Doc sit upright.

"I'll come back to check your leg after you've finished your breakfast," Elizabeth told Doc. Taking Becca's hand, she started to leave.

"Wait." Mabel moved to her and laid her hand on Elizabeth's arm. "If you see Rand at church, tell him I said 'thank you' again.

"And thank you, too, Elizabeth. I don't know what we would have done without your help. I don't think Doc could have set this leg himself, and I know I couldn't have handled this." Mabel hugged her.

"I'm glad I was here to help." Elizabeth patted Mabel's shoulder, feeling awkward. "I'm sure Rand feels the same way. But I'll tell him."

Herding Becca before her, Elizabeth left the bedroom and closed the door.

"I like Mr. Rand." Becca looked up.

"I know you do, pun'kin." Touching her daughter's soft curls, Elizabeth stifled a sigh. "Come on. We need to find your shoes, young lady, if we're going to meet the Hoffpaurs at church."

"I can sing?" Becca's dark eyes shown in anticipation.

"Yes. You can sing."

"Wait! Slow down!" Clutching her shawl around her shoulders, Elizabeth hurried down the boardwalk after her daughter, whose little shoes beat a tattoo as she ran on ahead.

Becca paused by the steps of the church and gave her mother a much-put-upon look. "They're *singing*. Hear it?" She cocked her head to one side, the red-gingham bow atop her dark curls slipping.

"Yes, sweet, but your bow is coming out." Catching the bow, Elizabeth removed it. "There's no time to fix it now. Go on inside—but let's not run, okay?" She placed the bow in her reticule.

"You weren't running." Becca took her mother's hand and tried to pull her up the steps.

"*You* were." Elizabeth caught her shawl more tightly together as they entered the dim interior. She guided Becca around the iron stove set in the center of the room. It had been fired to take the damp chill off the air.

As people turned and looked, Elizabeth felt a slight trepidation skitter along her spine, but recognized it for what it was—a learned reaction. Fear these people would somehow know the truth and reject them. She reminded herself that this town was different. These people were smiling and nodding in greeting, instead of frowning and whispering that she had no business there among "decent" folk.

Seated on the front pew with her brother and his wife, Lois Mayflower smiled and waved, easing Elizabeth's nervousness a little.

"Good morning." Nodding, George Hoffpaur stepped out of a pew into the aisle to let Elizabeth slide in beside Maggie Jean.

"Good morning." Elizabeth returned his smile.

Standing, baby cradled on her shoulder and toddler holding

onto her gingham skirt, Maggie Jean smiled warmly. ''I've been saving you a place—Lisa, take your little sister. Hester, Ester—*everyone*—scooch down, please. Let your new aunt and cousin sit. Go on around on the next pew if you have to.''

''Yes, ma'am.'' Lifting her baby sister, who reluctantly released her mother's skirt, Lisa did as she was asked. The rest of the occupants of the bench shifted, raising and lowering like the sections of a caterpillar.

''I'm not her aunt quite yet,'' Elizabeth protested.

Patting the baby's bottom as he fretted, Maggie Jean shrugged. ''So close as not to matter. So we may as well start treating you like kin.''

The comment made Elizabeth feel awkward and unworthy, especially when she remembered being in Rand's arms just the night before. How had she let Rand break through her defenses—*again?*

After she was settled in between the Hoffpaur children and their parents, Elizabeth patted the seat beside her. Selecting a hymnal from the repository on the back of the pew before them, Becca allowed her mother to lift her onto the seat. ''Is there going to be more singing?'' she asked hopefully, opening the book upside down.

''I'm certain there will be.'' Elizabeth smoothed the child's unruly dark curls. For so long they'd been isolated, only the two of them on the prairie. Now, being around people was helping her daughter to flourish. She was like a sunflower lifting its head to the sun.

''How's poor Doc?'' Maggie Jean whispered as the minister made announcements. ''Willie Bates said it was a bad break, with the bone sticking out and all.''

Elizabeth lowered her tone to match. ''I dressed the wound this morning. There's no reason to think it won't heal properly.'' She had been profoundly relieved when she'd changed the bandage and seen no signs of infection or inflammation.

''Thank goodness.'' Reaching out, Maggie Jean caught her hand and gave it a quick squeeze. ''And thank goodness you were here to help! Providence, that's what it is that brought you here to marry Hiram just when Doc had need of your help.''

''I'm sure glad to hear his leg is gonna be all right,'' George said, looking relieved.

''He's not out of the woods yet,'' Elizabeth cautioned. ''It will take. . . .''

Her voice trailing away, her gaze slipped by George and focused on a pair of dark trousers beside their pew, then traveled up to a black vest with a tin star pinned to it.

No! He couldn't! Not again!

''Mr. Rand!'' Becca clapped her hands in delight.

''Tadpole.'' His dark eyes rested warmly on his child, before shifting to her mother, his expression growing unreadable. ''George. Maggie.'' After nodding to the Hoffpaurs, Rand met Elizabeth's gaze again. ''Mrs. McKay, I need to talk with you.''

Conscious that everyone in the church was looking on, even the minister, who had finished the announcements, Elizabeth fought down a blush. ''I'm certain it could wait until after services.'' She forced the words out past stiff lips. Her face felt tight with the effort of keeping her expression bland.

Go away, Rand!

''Sheriff, is something amiss?'' Reverend Lyle asked from the pulpit.

Rand nodded to him. ''Sorry to interrupt, Reverend. Doc sent me to fetch Mrs. McKay. He needs her help.''

A buzz of concern went through the congregation. Maggie Jean asked, ''Is his leg going bad?''

''Can I help?'' George started to rise.

Rand stopped him with a hand on his shoulder. ''It's not Doc's leg.'' He addressed the whole congregation. ''I had stopped to see how Doc was doing when Texas Pete came barreling in. Seems it's Juanita's time, it's her first, and there's no women around. Pete didn't want to assist in the job himself, and from his attitude about the business, I'm certain Juanita doesn't want him helping either.''

Chuckles rippled through the congregation.

''Oh.'' Elizabeth rose. She hadn't had that much experience in helping with birthings herself, but she had assisted her mother enough to know what had to be done. "Come on, Becca. We need to leave now."

"I want to sing!" Her bottom lip thrusting out, Becca frowned up at her mother in a manner Elizabeth knew all too well.

"Becca, come on." Her tone stern, Elizabeth caught her child's hand. Becca's lip edged out further.

"Let her stay with me," Maggie Jean offered. "We'll take good care of her. Go on with Rand, and leave Becca with us. Mabel is busy with Doc and you can't very well take Becca with you. And besides, we'll enjoy looking after her."

Maggie was right, Elizabeth conceded. It would be impossible to keep an eye on her daughter and help out with the birthing.

Turning to her daughter, she hugged the child. "Okay, you can stay, but be very good for Mrs. Maggie Jean, like you were for Mrs. Mabel yesterday when I was gone. I might be away for a few hours. Maybe even overnight. Babies sometimes take a while to get here. But I will be back as soon as I can." After another quick hug, Elizabeth made her way out of the pew.

As Rand took her elbow and led her out of the church, she fought a reflexive need to pull away. She was all too aware of him. Of his warm fingers gripping her arm. Of the strength and the power of the man walking beside her, shortening his strides to match her own.

Outside the church, she pulled free and walked ahead of him on the narrow boardwalk, hurrying toward the Sedricks' white frame house down the street.

The memory of Rand's kisses the night before came unbidden. As warm thrills chased themselves through her stomach, she drew her shawl tightly about her shoulders and willed the sensations away.

It didn't matter what he made her feel. She was going to do what was logical, what was best for her daughter's future. She couldn't let him change that. But it would be easier to stay on the course she'd charted if she could just avoid his company.

That was proving damned hard to do.

Rand stepped ahead of her and opened the Sedricks' picket gate for her.

Angry with herself for allowing the man to stir her emotions, Elizabeth glared up at him. "I can find my own way to . . . wherever it is, Rand. I'm certain Doc will give me directions."

"You don't even know the people's last names." Letting the gate swing closed again, Rand pushed the wide brim of his hat back. "Why are you going to try to go out there by yourself?"

"I don't want to go with you," she said, low and furiously. "I don't want to be around you! I—"

"Don't trust yourself?" He gently touched her cheek, looking pleased.

Angrily, she pulled away, then shook her head. "Damn it, Rand, Hiram is taking me on faith. His trust deserves better than I've given him so far. And *you!* His boys said you are his friend."

He was quiet for a space, looking toward the ferryboat dock. When he turned back, his face was unreadable. "Okay. I'll draw you a map while you're getting the things you'll need together. It's about eight miles from town, mainly up a mountain. And there are four turnoffs in the road you have to take."

Rand opened the gate again, holding it open for her. "Of course, you know to avoid the bears—just stop or go around them. They won't attack you, unless you get between a mother and her cubs."

"Bears?" Hiram's boys hadn't said anything about bears yesterday when they'd driven her out to their homestead. She'd never seen a bear in Kansas. As Elizabeth passed through the gate, she glanced toward the deeply shadowed forest.

"They gather for the salmon run, just like people. Of course, right now, they'll be foraging in the woods while they wait for the fish to come upstream." Rand took her elbow again and guided her up the steps.

"How big are they?" She'd seen illustrations of large bears catching salmon out of a river in the *Overland Monthly and Out West Magazine*. Dr. Brown in Salt Cedar Flats had subscribed to the publication and often let her borrow issues when she was helping him in exchange for training.

"Don't worry. They aren't big, like grizzlies. They're just little black bears." He held the door open. "Three hundred pounds or so."

"Is that you, Elizabeth?" Mabel called from somewhere in the back of the house, an anxious edge to her voice.

"Yes. I'll be right there." Elizabeth paused, tugging the knot of her shawl tighter.

"Shall I hitch up Doc's buggy and wait around front for you?" Rand's expression was bland.

Grinding her teeth, Elizabeth glowered up at him. "So you'd frighten me into doing what you want. Does my reputation and Becca's future mean nothing to you?"

Tipping his hat back down, he frowned. "Look, men outnumber women out here three to two. I know this place seems safe and isolated, but there are lumber camps filled with rough men, and rougher men building the railroad between here and Eugene—in fact, the line is getting close to Pete and Juanita's. And cutthroats and blackguards pass through the area on their way from California to the Black Hills gold strikes."

Elizabeth asked drily, "You mean I might run into an outlaw?"

Rand's lips twitched wryly. Like the sun coming out from behind a cloud, the atmosphere between them changed. He leaned closer, so close she imagined for a second he would kiss her.

And heaven help her, she wanted him to.

Chapter Eleven

Rand straightened suddenly, putting distance between them as Mabel came down the hall.

Elizabeth coughed to hide the pink she felt warm her cheeks.

''I'm going with you to protect you,'' he told Elizabeth in a tone that said further discussion was useless. ''And you will get there faster if I drive you.''

''Of course you're going to drive her,'' Mabel said, looking from one to the other. ''Why wouldn't he?'' The last was directed at Elizabeth.

Tucking her chin, Elizabeth studied the knot of her shawl. ''I was just concerned with appearances.''

''Appearances? Oh, I see. I hadn't thought of that. Out here, we're more practical and don't put so much stock in things like that.'' The older woman pursed her lips as she weighed the matter, then shook her head. ''You can't go alone, Elizabeth. It's rough country. You'd certainly get lost. I assure you no one will think anything about you riding out alone with the sheriff escorting you, if you're on your way to help poor Juanita.

''Now, I've packed a few things you might need in Jonas's bag. Do hurry and change out of your good dress. Pete will have driven poor Juanita crazy there all alone!'' She turned to

Rand. "Now, go on! Get the buggy hitched while Elizabeth changes clothes."

As Elizabeth hurried down the hallway to change into her old shirtwaist and skirt, she felt defeated. There was no help for it. She would have to go with Rand.

Alone.

And she admitted to herself, it wasn't so much that she didn't trust him as she didn't trust herself.

"Oh, Rand—*Oh!*" As the buggy wheel found a hole, one side of the vehicle dipped, throwing Elizabeth against Rand's side.

She righted herself quickly, clutching the arm of the seat with one hand and her best bonnet—which she'd forgotten to change—with the other. Thank goodness she'd prudently placed the carpetbag Mabel packed for her between herself and Rand's lean hip, or she'd be practically on his lap

Warmth rushed through her at the stray thought. A glance at his dark trousers stretched tautly over hard thighs increased the feeling of heat.

Firmly pushing all such thoughts away, Elizabeth concentrated on holding on, to prevent further contact between them.

"Watch it," he warned.

"Watch what? *Oh!*" She looked up just as a low-hanging limb took a swipe at her bonnet and she ducked. Before she could right herself, the buggy wheel rolled into another hole and she fell against Rand's shoulder a second time.

"You're doing that on—"

The sentence went unfinished as the wheel on her side found a hole and her teeth snapped together. Then the buggy tilted too far backward for her peace of mind as the road angled almost straight up.

"Stop that! You're driving into all those holes on purpose!"

"No, I'm not." Rand slapped the horse's rump with the reins. "I will admit to enjoying it, though."

"You—!" Her teeth snapped again as they went through another bump.

He grinned, a flash of white teeth against the lean suntanned planes of his face, reminding her of the man she'd first met and how he used to find humor in the darkest situations.

He was different now. She noticed he didn't smile as often. Looking out at the forest, feeling unwanted sympathy for Rand, she supposed he'd had to become hard to survive.

She knew she was different, too. More suspicious, less trusting. In Kansas, she'd learned to avoid people, to protect her daughter. Here, having to hide the truth about Becca's birth made her wary still.

Deciding it was best to concentrate on holding on—since conversation seemed likely to end in her biting her tongue off, quite literally—Elizabeth let go of her bonnet and curled both her hands around the buggy arm. No one had told her the Adcocks lived on the *top* of a mountain. What passed for the road to their homestead zigzagged back and forth up the side.

"Pete and Juanita are new to the area," Rand said. "Haven't lived a full year up here yet. Pete will probably get around to improving the road when he has time."

"You mean he'll get around to *building* a road! I haven't seen one yet. You could advise him on it, if he needs help." Elizabeth remembered that Rand had once made his living building roads and bridges. "I was wondering why you haven't helped the town by designing another bridge across the river."

As the horse balked, Rand slapped the reins again, not looking at Elizabeth. "Dalton McClure is dead. Rand Matthews doesn't have an engineering degree."

It always came back to his past, didn't it? Elizabeth gave him a sidelong glance, wondering that there was no bitterness in his tone.

Under Rand's urging, the horse made a second effort and pulled the buggy up the incline. Afterward, the trek seemed to smooth out a bit, lulling her into a false sense of safety. Then the wheel fell into a gully covered over by leaves and masquerading as flat road, and Elizabeth was almost thrown out of the seat.

When the wheel hit a deeper hole, she lost the struggle. Rand caught her as she pitched forward. She clasped his strong arm, huddling against him and holding on for dear life as the buggy's springs were tested.

The clean smell of his shaving soap teased her nostrils, taking her mind off the bad road. His strength felt solid. With his arm protectively across her, she felt safe from harm.

"*Whoa!*" After they made it through the rough spot, Rand pulled back on the reins. The winded horse was only too willing to stop.

As everything stilled, Elizabeth was suddenly aware that her breast pressed against Rand's upper arm as she clung to his bicep. Warmth surged through her flesh at the contact and her nipples tingled.

Damn! She straightened and he let her go.

"Are you okay?"

"Yes."

After picking the carpetbag up from where it had fallen in the foot box, she scooted back onto her side of the seat. He made her want him so easily. Elizabeth felt a blush heat her cheeks at just how easy. She was an engaged woman—had she no moral fiber?

"Why are we stopping?" She tried to make her voice cool. However, her words came out rather breathless.

After he wound the reins around the brake handle, he tipped back his hat. "The horse has to rest after pulling the buggy up that bluff."

"I see." That should have been obvious to her. She had been so aware of Rand Matthews, she'd been oblivious to the poor animal's labors.

Putting a gloved hand to her bonnet, Elizabeth pressed it back firmly in place and straightened her shawl, retying the knot. She didn't want Rand to know how much his nearness affected her. He'd caught her off guard last night in the hall. She hadn't been prepared for his onslaught of her senses. Or his declarations.

Last night, his sincerity had slipped under her defenses.

Today, she would remain in control, she promised herself. She couldn't stop the effect the man had on her. However, she didn't have to let him know it at every turn.

The problem was the warm look in Rand's dark eyes said he'd been perfectly aware of the contact with her breast and he'd guessed what she was feeling. That he was feeling it, too.

Determined to try harder, to keep focused on something besides Rand, Elizabeth deliberately gave her attention to the scenery around them. They had stopped on the shoulder of the mountain, on a spot overlooking the McKenzie River Valley, and it had to be one of the most lushly beautiful spots on earth. Mist shrouded the valley, making it look magical and mystical, something out of a fairy tale. In the distance a waterfall cascaded down the side of a bluff. Around them giant Douglas fir rose two hundred feet, their tops a thatch of green blocking out the sky.

The beauty of the scene was a balm to her troubled mind. "No wonder so many people have left everything behind to come to Oregon," she mused. "I love it here."

Raising his brows, Rand looked at her. "I'm surprised," he said. "This area is so different from the dry, west Kansas prairie."

"That's just it. Everything is so green and verdant here, I feel . . . I guess *nurtured* is the word I want. It's as though I can breathe deeper here. It surprised me when you warned me there could be danger. It never occurred to me there was anything here I should fear."

Rand admitted ruefully, "You really don't have to be afraid of bears. The horse would balk long before you came in sight of one."

"I guessed that." Elizabeth smoothed the fringe of her shawl. She might have told Rand the truth, that Kansas had stopped being home to her a long time ago. Looked down on as a slut, her child treated as a pariah, she'd leapt at the chance to leave. That was why she'd read the advertisements for wives her brother brought to her.

But to say how unhappy she'd been would only serve to remind Rand of the hurt he'd caused, and she didn't want to do that. He was paying the price for it already, in not being able to claim his daughter.

As Elizabeth looked up at him, Rand was drawn into her

soft hazel eyes. The ugly straw bonnet hid her wonderful hair, except for a few corkscrew curls that had escaped and framed her face. Her cheeks were flushed with the excitement of the rough ride. But her eyes glowed softly. She was happy here in Oregon. Perhaps not comfortable with him, but happy with her decision to come.

And then her gaze went to his lips.

He leaned toward her, the action as natural as it was for the water to rush over the falls.

Shaking her head, she pulled back. "No."

He straightened. "Why?"

Looking down at her clasped fingers, she sighed. "I am engaged. I know, I seem to keep forgetting that, but I really don't mean to."

He smiled inwardly, pleased that he could affect her as much as she did him. Catching one of the curls by her cheek, he let it wind around his driving glove. "Don't marry Hiram Smith. Marry me."

Her lips tingled at the memory of his soft kisses the night before, and she shook her head to dislodge the warm feelings. "I was wrong to let you kiss me last night. Just as I was wrong earlier, in the smokehouse at your ranch. Rand, I'm marrying Hiram Smith, not you. It's best for Becca."

That took him aback, but only for an instant. She still thought she was doing the right thing for her daughter by holding to her plan to marry Hiram. Even though Elizabeth was wrong, it was for the right reasons.

"It wasn't wrong of us to kiss," he said. "You came here to marry Hiram, but it's you and me who were meant to be together, Elizabeth." He smiled. "We have a daughter. I want to be her father. I want to take care of the two of you, and I can. You just have to trust me."

"It's for Becca's sake. I can't." Her voice had a desperate edge, showing the war going on inside her. "Rand, you are still a convicted murderer. If they find you one day—*when* they find you—"

"No one will." He was at last certain of that. "There was a man in Deadwood who recognized me, about four years ago, but he was shot down in a gunfight the same afternoon. Getting on a train to Independence a couple of years back, an old conductor, who I'd met when I was working for the railroad, thought I looked familiar, but he shrugged it off, more interested in punching my ticket.

"There's been no one else since that bounty hunter in the Nations. As far as the world is concerned, Dalton McClure is dead. He has been dead for a long time. All the while I've been looking over my shoulder, waiting for the worst. But it hasn't happened. I believe now it's not going to. I can start really living again. And I'm not leaving here. I won't run again."

"Rand, you can't promise that."

"I just did." As much to himself as to Elizabeth, he realized.

Elizabeth untied her shawl and drew it more tightly about her shoulders. It was colder up here on the mountain than she'd expected. She should have worn a warm coat.

Rand tempted her to take a chance. The thought of making the wrong decision chilled her even more than the mountain air.

"We'd better get on now, or the baby will be born before we get there," she said.

Sensing the time wasn't right to press the issue, he didn't argue. Slapping the horse's rump with the reins, Rand dislodged a horsefly and started the mare on her way at the same time. He would make Elizabeth see that there was nothing to worry about. She could depend on him to always be there.

It would just take time.

He only hoped Hiram would stay away until he could convince her.

Carrying the carpetbag, Rand waited on the stoop of the Adcock cabin to help Elizabeth up the crude-hewn log steps. She took his hand, but paused. Looking back at the fir woodland, she drew a deep breath as though collecting herself.

Rand asked, "Are you all right?" She looked a bit pale.

"I've seen you in action with worse things than a birthing. You'll do fine."

The statement was meant to reassure. The words earned him a sardonic look. "Have *you* ever helped with a birthing?" Elizabeth asked.

"No."

"Well, at least I've helped my mother on occasion." Which was why she knew how many things could go wrong. "I might need your help."

As Elizabeth passed him and knocked on the crude-plank door, he tasted her words and found a slight warning flavor to them.

A short time later, as he was helping a very pregnant Juanita Adcock rise from her chair, Rand was feeling he'd very definitely managed to be in the wrong place at the wrong time.

Halfway out of the chair, she paused, her eyes widening and face paling as she bent over her swollen middle, gripped by a contraction. She held onto his forearms, her small hands digging into his muscles with the force of steel traps. A stream of rapid Spanish hissed between her clenched teeth. Rand recognized several saints' names.

As the spasm seemed to go on and on, Rand looked over his shoulder. "Elizabeth!"

Elizabeth glanced up from what she was doing and nodded. "Good. They are getting closer together." She added a sheet folded into a pad to the middle of the bed.

Even as Juanita continued to grip his arms in a way that seemed likely to cripple him for life, she nodded as if she understood what Elizabeth meant.

"Try to breathe," Elizabeth said. "And when it passes, walk around some more. It may be a while yet. Your water hasn't broken."

"Water hasn't broken?" Rand frowned at Elizabeth, not liking the sound of that at all.

Juanita nodded again. Panting, she said, "I am the oldest of ten children, Señora. I helped as the last of my brothers and sisters were born. I know what to expect."

"That's good." Looking less tense, Elizabeth went back to

smoothing the clean sheets and tucking the corners. "You're doing fine, by the way."

One of the first things Elizabeth had done, other than instruct Rand to fetch water, was to explain to the expectant couple how important it was to make everything as clean as possible, to prevent childbed fever.

Elizabeth then put the water Rand had brought on the stove to heat, and washed her hands with strong carbolic soap. Afterward, she ran the men out of the one-room cabin as she examined Juanita.

When they were allowed to return, Pete seemed determined to describe in vivid detail how he'd lost his best mare last year when the foal breached. Elizabeth shooed the man outside again, and forbade him to return.

Rand had rather wanted to keep Pete company, but Elizabeth cut off his escape, saying she needed help and Pete was obviously useless. Sensing her nervousness, Rand did the things Elizabeth asked, lending her what assistance he could.

Suddenly, Juanita's face twisted in pain and a low moan started deep in her throat. It grew into a high keening wail, before subsiding as the spasm finally passed. Which seemed an eternity.

"Go ahead," Elizabeth told Rand. "Help her walk."

Drawing a deep breath to steady himself, Rand did as instructed and helped the pregnant woman walk in a circle in the middle of the small cabin.

Texas Pete called from outside, "Is ever'thang all right in thar? I thought I heard 'Nita yell." There was a quavery, nervous edge to his voice.

Rand said, "Juanita is doing fine, Pete." However, he felt like adding that he himself felt a little green around the gills.

"Tell him to fetch more water and put it to boil," Elizabeth told Rand.

"But you have two kettles on the stove already," he argued. It was a logical argument. He felt he didn't deserve the sour looks both women heaped on him.

"Pete, fetch the water! A lot of it!" Juanita called as she waddled across the floor, still gripping Rand's arm for support.

"You!" She glowered up at Rand. "Do not question the señora!"

"Why is she angry with me?" Rand asked Elizabeth, at a loss.

"You're a man." She said over her shoulder, as if that explained it. She dashed a little scalding water into a basin and swirled it around, then emptied it into the chamber pot.

He looked at Juanita for an explanation. She only gave him a disgruntled look.

"Sí, Señora," Juanita said. "You understand. You have borne a child, no?"

"Yes." Elizabeth smiled over her shoulder. "I have a daughter." Her gaze flickered to Rand for an instant. Then she slid the chamber pot back under the bed with the toe of her shoe, and poured more hot water from the kettle into the basin.

"How long did your labor last?" Juanita put a hand to her distended abdomen as Rand helped her to slowly turn around and start back across the room.

Elizabeth sighed "Two days."

"Madre de Dios!" Juanita eyed her with a mixture of horror and sympathy. "Sometimes, that is the way."

"You went through this for two days, Elizabeth?" Rand asked hoarsely.

He never got an answer. Beside him, Juanita gasped. Rand looked down at the discolored puddle forming on the rough plank floor and jumped back, suddenly understanding exactly what the women had meant by "water breaking."

"I feel like something has slipped." Juanita doubled again with a contraction.

"Get her into the bed." Elizabeth took Juanita's other arm and she and Rand helped the woman.

After they had her settled, Elizabeth ordered him to join Pete outside.

Rand was more than happy to oblige.

Chapter Twelve

As Rand sat down on the steps, trying to ignore the pain-filled groans and shrieks coming from within, Pete stood by the corner of the cabin, chewing on the reed stem of a corncob pipe and looking off into the distance. His skin tone seemed a little pasty.

"Best left to womenfolk, I reckon," Pete said philosophically.

Rand wanted to agree. But he was too aware of what he'd left Elizabeth to go through all alone. Now, he understood her anger better when she'd realized he was alive and he could have been there with her. He wouldn't blame her if she hated him for it.

But Elizabeth was kinder than that. She always had been. However, it was no wonder she hadn't been able to bring herself to believe in him again. He only hoped he could regain her trust.

Before she married the wrong man.

She might be called on to fill in for Doc a few more times, Rand thought, and he could escort her. That might give him the time he needed to convince her he wasn't going anywhere. Maybe—

The sound of a baby's cries interrupted his thoughts.

"Hot ziggedy!" Pete grinned hugely, displaying a missing tooth. "Sounds like it has a fine pair o' lungs!"

Elizabeth opened the plank door. "It's a healthy-looking girl, Mr. Adcock. You can see her when I get her and her mother cleaned up."

After meeting Rand's gaze briefly, a gentle look in her eyes, she disappeared inside again.

"Hot dang! I got me a baby girl!"

Rand thought Pete might do a jig right there in the front yard.

Rand knew how the man felt. He had a daughter, too. And if God was kind, one day he might get to tell the world she was his.

When Elizabeth did allow Pete inside and gave him his daughter, the look of wonder on Pete's face was something to behold as he peeled back the soft blanket and looked into the tiny pink face. Juanita was exhausted, but smiling.

Elizabeth moved to beside where Rand stood, just inside the door.

"Was Becca that tiny?" he asked.

"Yes, about that size." She smiled up at him, her eyes soft with memory. Then she looked down at the blood staining her apron, and pulled it off and stuffed it into the carpetbag.

Becoming brisk, she bustled around the room, bundling up the soiled linens tossed on the floor, straightening up anything out of place. After Pete placed the baby back beside her mother, Elizabeth called him over and thrust the bundle of linens and nightclothes into his hands. "Find a washtub outside and put these to soak before the stains set," she ordered. "They'll need to be washed first thing in the morning."

"Yes, ma'am," the tall Texan agreed submissively.

"Juanita is not to do anything more than take care of that baby for the next few weeks—or until Doc Sedrick says it is all right." Elizabeth glared up at the man, as though daring him to protest.

"Oh, yes, ma'am."

"I mean not *anything.* Juanita and I have already talked about this."

"I'll take good care of her. You bet." Pete nodded, holding the dirty linen gingerly.

Moving back to the bedside, Elizabeth smiled as she peeked at the baby once more. "She is a lovely baby. I'll be back to check on you both in a couple of days, Juanita," she assured the mother.

Rand dared a glance over Elizabeth's shoulder at the tiny, scrunched-up face.

And felt infinitely cheated.

"You were kind of hard on the new father back there, weren't you, Elizabeth? He was just worried." Rand propped his booted foot on the dashboard.

Elizabeth turned to him and smiled. "I know. But Juanita didn't need to deal with any demands from Pete for . . ." She felt a blush warm her cheeks, and looked at her gloved hands. "So, I wanted to make certain he understood that recovering from childbirth takes time. Besides"—she grinned—"Juanita deserves to be pampered a little by having him take care of her."

As the buggy gained speed, Rand pulled back on the reins. "Whoa. Slow, girl." The horse needed no urging to pull the buggy downhill. To Elizabeth, Rand said, "Juanita has a beautiful baby."

Smiling, Elizabeth agreed, "Yes, she does."

After a moment, he went on. "Did Becca have black hair like that?" The words were tentative, softly spoken as he gazed at the sky.

"More. And it stood straight up."

"Really?" Looking at her, he grinned. Then returned his attention to the road ahead. "I'm sorry I wasn't there when it was your time, Elizabeth," he said, surprising her. "Two days of labor . . . I can't imagine how you suffered. And you were all alone, but for your mother."

"I was angry, then," she admitted. "Because I thought you

were dead and I felt so cheated that you couldn't be there with me.''

Her words stabbed his heart. ''I wish I had known,'' he said. ''I would have been. No matter if the devil himself had stood between us.''

He sighed. ''But I wasn't.'' He shook his head. ''No man should miss the birth of his child. Or miss giving his child's mother his support.''

She reached out and clasped his hand. ''It's all right. After the baby comes, you forget the pain. There's just the joy. And you would have been caught if you'd returned to Kansas. Someone would have recognized you.''

''But when I think of you going through that, and I wasn't even aware . . .'' He tugged back on the reins again, slowing the buggy to a crawl as they rolled down the steep bluff where the horse had balked earlier that morning when going up it.

''Still, I wouldn't change the fact that we made love,'' he said softly. ''Becca wouldn't be here if we hadn't.''

''I know.'' Elizabeth understood what he was saying perfectly.

''She's so precious.''

''She is.''

''And bright. She already counts to ten. I was amazed as she counted her clothespins when she was playing on Mabel's porch.''

''She is bright.'' Her mother's heart swelled and, aching, Elizabeth blinked rapidly.

The buggy gained level ground again, and Rand halted the horse, looping the reins around the brake. Turning to Elizabeth, he said, ''Besides, I held the memory of that night close more times than I can tell you. Sometimes, it's all I had to sustain me.''

''I did, too,'' she admitted, her words the softest whisper as she smoothed the fringes of her shawl. ''I held it close to my heart.''

''I thought of you and how it was to be with you so often, I began to feel it was all a dream. Nothing that perfect could have really happened.''

"It was perfect, wasn't it?" She looked into his dark eyes. "I might have thought it had been a dream, too, but for Becca coming along."

"Elizabeth . . ."

Pain twisting his features, Rand pulled his driving glove off and cupped her face gently, the look in his dark eyes going straight through her heart. She leaned into the kiss as he touched his lips to hers, his kiss gentle like a butterfly's touch.

More powerful than a sledgehammer.

She *shouldn't!* She couldn't do this! What kind of woman was she? Every time Rand touched her, she melted into his arms. What kind of woman was she?

Even as the thought took shape, Elizabeth pressed closer, deepening the kiss.

Rand groaned in response, and pulled back long enough to toss the carpetbag between them back down into the foot box. He caught her beneath her arms, and before she knew what was happening, lifted her onto his lap. Across those hard thighs she'd been thinking about earlier.

The next thing to be tossed down into the box was her chipped straw bonnet. Though she managed a whimper in protest—it *was* her best—she didn't stop planting kisses along his jawline and cheek long enough to retrieve it. His hat, however, did join her bonnet.

After pulling off his other glove, Rand grinned, his dark eyes luminous. "If you're going to match me tit for tat, this could be interesting." He started unbuttoning her shirtwaist.

Looking down, she wondered when her shawl had been tossed aside. It was draped over the back of the seat. Watching his fingers work against the white of her blouse was exciting.

Then he pushed the material aside and the tops of her breasts were visible, hidden only by her thin camisole—she'd forgone wearing a corset since her fainting episode. The sight of his darkly tanned fingers as he stroked her fair skin was wholly evocative.

When he tugged at the bow of the ribbon drawstring, which was all that kept the undergarment in place, her pale breasts spilled out into his hands. Elizabeth sucked in her breath as a shaft of pure need pierced through her.

And her need redoubled as his thumb found a nipple and toyed with it.

"Oh, Rand!" Involuntarily, Elizabeth arched against his hand. He planted hot kisses along her throat as his fingers worked magic, increasing her pleasure.

She caught his hand, unwilling to only receive. "What's that you said about tit for tat?" she murmured, tugging his shirttail out of his trousers and attacking the buttons on his shirt. Her fingers were clumsy, but she soon worked the buttons free. Noticing one had been sewn on with black thread while the shirt and the thread attaching the others were light blue, she guessed that he had re-attached it himself. The sight was somehow endearing.

Elizabeth kissed the button before she pushed his shirt from his broad shoulders and kissed the center of his chest. His skin tasted slightly salty. She grazed his pectoral with her teeth. Higher, she found the pink, puckered scar where she had once dug a lead slug from his shoulder. She kissed the spot.

Then she pulled his mouth down to hers and kissed him as she'd wanted to do all day, a melding that went on and on. As her senses swam, she wondered if it was possible to expire from a kiss.

Shaking, Rand broke the contact. "Elizabeth, I'm not made of wood!"

She wriggled atop his erection. "It feels like it from where I sit." Her voice was low and sultry. She didn't recognize it as her own. Who was this woman who'd taken over her body?

"You're determined to torture me," he groaned. Catching her waist, he moved against her bottom, slowly grinding his hardness against her most feminine spot. Even through her skirt and petticoats, it was delicious torture. It was her turn to groan, low in her throat.

"You want me as much as I want you," Rand said triumphantly.

Nodding, Elizabeth cupped his face between her hands and tried to kiss him, intent on showing him how much.

Rand avoided her lips, instead nibbling her ear. Then he whispered, ''Marry me.''

Elizabeth stilled. Then sighed. ''I can't.''

''We were meant to be together. You feel it, too. And we have Becca.'' He nibbled along her throat.

Closing her eyes, Elizabeth savored the sensations. Feeling just like a thief for stealing memories she shouldn't own.

''Let me be her father, Elizabeth.''

''I can't.''

Rand stopped his loving assault. Pulling away, he shook his head. ''Then we can't make love. I won't take the chance of creating another baby, unless I know I can claim it as my own. As I want to claim Becca.''

Feeling a heavy thumping, Elizabeth looked down at where her naked breasts were pressed against his darkly tanned chest and realized it was his heartbeat. ''This is so unfair to you,'' she whispered.

He sighed. ''Careful. I'll start to think you've forgiven me.''

Elizabeth looked up at him, her hazel eyes luminous with caring. ''I have,'' she said simply.

Unable to stop himself, Rand pulled her tightly against him and kissed her. But this time, he felt no response in her lips.

When he released her, she pulled back and started to straighten her clothes, visibly drawing away emotionally at the same time.

''This is unfair. Not being able to be a father to your daughter . . .'' Tears moistened her eyes, but she blinked them away, looking down at the buttons she was fastening. ''Rand, I don't want to add to the hurt. But I'm still marrying Hiram Smith.''

''I won't stop trying to change your mind,'' he promised. Now that he'd decided he wanted to build a future with her, he wasn't going to give up easily.

''Please. Don't make this harder on both of us than it has to be!'' There was a desperate edge to her voice that made him want to smile.

She was weakening.

Chapter Thirteen

Rand pressed his advantage. ''I want to be a husband to you. I want to be a father to my daughter. It's been a long time since Kansas. No one is looking for me anymore. No one is going to arrest me and take me away. I've hired Jake to cut some young trees down and skin the bark, getting them ready to build a cabin.

''I'm not a rich man. Not as prosperous as Hiram. But there's a demand for horses and I've picked up some good breeding stock here and there. If I really start working at it, we could build a fine—''

Placing her fingers over his lips, Elizabeth cut off his words. They were too painful to hear. ''I can't take a chance on loving you.''

Her eyes widened as she realized what she'd said. She looked down, giving her full attention to buttoning her blouse.

''Or rather, that Becca will come to love you . . . trust you. And then you'll be hauled away. Or, or shot. Or have to run again to save yourself. You can see it wouldn't be fair to her, Rand.''

''It's not about Becca. It's you who can't trust me to stay, isn't it.''

It wasn't a question.

Lifting her chin, Elizabeth said, "I'm protecting my daughter." Standing in the box, she tucked her blouse back in her waistband and wrapped her shawl around her shoulders, then sat on the seat. "Let's just go on back."

Rand picked her forgotten bonnet up from floor of the box and held it out to her. She stuck it onto her head, askew. He then retrieved his hat and began buttoning his shirt.

Glancing up, he saw the sun westering behind the big firs. Twilight was beginning to fall. After unwinding the reins and releasing the brake handle, he slapped the leather gently against the horse's rump.

The animal seemed to sense it was heading home, and started forward briskly.

"After seeing today what I left you to go through alone, not even knowing I was alive . . ." He shook his head. "Well, I can't change that. But living without you and Becca, without being part of your lives, really hasn't been living. I'll promise you this now, Elizabeth. I'll never run again. No matter what happens."

Digger Banks angled a look over his shoulder as well as he could. Since he was lying flat on his belly on a plank atop two barrels, it wasn't easy. "I washed 'er out with turpentine, after I yanked the stob out."

"You did the right thing." As Elizabeth examined the ugly, inch-wide hole in the calf muscle of the lumberjack's leg, Rand held the lantern up so the light was directed on the area. Squeezing the muscle together, she peered as deeply in the wound as she could. "There are still some pieces of bark in there that will have to come out. The limb that did this was rotten, you say?"

"Too durn rotten to pull out in one piece." Digger shifted and looked back over his other shoulder. "I'll never figger out how it chanced to stick in me like that. My lucky day, is all. Durn tree kicked back on me, 'cause the wind caught the top jest as it was about to go and kinda whipped it a little. I jumped aside and that danged rotten stick went up betwixed my breeches leg and my boot and stuck in my leg. Pulled out what I could. Cutter took the point of his jackknife and gouged some more out.''

Shaking her head, Elizabeth sighed.

''I don't suppose this 'Cutter' disinfected the knife before he gouged around in the wound.''

''Can't rightly say he did.'' The lumberjack looked thoughtful. ''What *is* 'dis-infected'?''

''Cleaned his knife by boiling it or even pouring whiskey or turpentine over . . . Never mind.'' Seeing the blank look that glazed over Digger's eyes, Elizabeth pushed up her sleeves.

''He cut 'im a big plug a tobaccy, a'fore he gouged around in it.''

Meeting Rand's gaze, Elizabeth saw his lips twitch. Looking back at the wound, she stifled an answering smile at the thought of disinfecting a knife by cutting tobacco. She didn't want to share amusement with Rand. Or anything else.

She'd been obliged to have Rand drive her around for the last several days as she checked on Doc's patients. There was no avoiding it. She would have certainly gotten lost a dozen times, and he knew the area. But she'd worked very hard at keeping her emotional distance.

''Shall I get the tweezers from the bag?'' Rand asked Elizabeth.

''Yes, for the bigger pieces. We'll have to try and wash the tiny ones out.'' She glanced up at the lumberjacks peering inside the tent. The way they ogled her made her feel like an attraction in a sideshow. This time, she was definitely glad Rand was around. He'd been glaring at the men to make them keep their distance since he and Elizabeth had arrived at the camp.

''You!'' She pointed at a ruddy-faced man peering through the tent flap. ''I'll need vinegar and powdered soda from the cook.''

''I'll fetch 'em!'' The man hurried off, returning a few moments later with the items requested.

''Thank you.'' She gave them to Digger to hold.

Rand glared at the ruddy-faced man until he left the tent.

Just as Elizabeth was about to use the tweezers on a sliver of wood in the wound, *boom-boom!* sounded in the distance and the ground shook slightly. "What on earth's that?" She looked at Rand.

"That's dynamite, sounds like," Digger supplied. "Nitro has a bit bigger boom to it. That's the crew layin' track for the railroad comin' through from Eugene. They use dynamite to clear stumps an' rocks. The boss here, he got himself a fat contract ta supply the ties. Means work for a while.

"You kin go ahead now. It'll be a spell afore they set any more charges. Usually, the way it happens."

"Then hold still." She frowned in concentration as she used the tweezers, ignoring Digger's gasps and grumbles as best she could. After the bigger pieces of wood were removed, Elizabeth took the tin of soda from Digger. "This is going to burn a bit, I'm afraid."

"Well, it ain't been no church social up till now," he informed her. "But do what'er ya got to, I reckon."

As Rand helped hold the leg, Elizabeth sprinkled the wound full of soda, then trickled vinegar into it. The resulting foam carried tiny pieces of wood and bark out of the hole. After the foaming stopped, she washed it out with boiled water and bandaged it.

"You need to keep it clean," she told the wiry little man. "Don't worry if it drains. It's better if it does. If it stops draining and looks red and puffy, come into town and see Doc. Don't wait if that happens, or you might lose your leg."

Sitting up, Digger nodded as he worked his pants leg down. "Much obliged, ma'am."

As Digger hobbled out, Elizabeth stretched aching muscles in her back. She'd come there to stitch up an ax cut on a man that bled badly every time they tried to put him in a wagon to get him down the mountain to Doc in town.

After she'd finished and dressed the wound, she'd found a queue of men outside the makeshift examining room, all with medical complaints for her to treat.

Other than taking care of Digger and a few others obviously

in need, she'd explained to most of the men that she wasn't a doctor and told them to make their way into town to see Doc Sedrick. At the mention of the crusty old doctor, most of the lumberjacks seemed to recover quickly.

Elizabeth did dress a few wounds in fresh bandages, inspecting them for signs of infection, and helped as Rand popped a dislocated shoulder back into place.

"Ready?" Rand had returned all the supplies back to the carpetbag.

"I want to check on the boy with the ax cut once more before we go."

Rand nodded. "I'll get the horse and buggy while you do that—unless you want me to walk with you." He looked at her questioningly.

"I think you've glowered sufficiently at every man here that they've gotten the message." Despite her best efforts not to, Elizabeth had to smile.

As Rand's dark gaze found her lips, her smile died. And her breath caught.

No. She couldn't let him affect her this way.

Hurrying out of the tent, she brushed past the men gathered around the opening and made her way across the lumber camp. All the while, she was reminding herself of all the reasons she couldn't let Rand get under her guard. And they were all named "Becca."

Entering another tent, she found the young man she'd stitched earlier sleeping, pale from loss of blood. Without waking him, she looked at the bandage to make certain the bleeding hadn't started again, then touched his foot, making certain it was warm and circulation was good. She then quietly left.

Outside the tent, the owner of the lumber company was waiting for her. A round, fatherly looking man with an easygoing manner, he'd introduced himself when she and Rand had arrived as Jacob Smith—Hiram's cousin. Elizabeth had liked him immediately.

"I know those hooligans have about worn you to a frazzle but I was wondering, before you and the sheriff leave, if you'd take a gander at my boy, Bobby." The words were said lightly, but there was an undertone of worry. The same worry shadowed the man's eyes.

"Certainly. What seems to be the trouble?" Elizabeth fell into step beside Jacob as he showed her into the bigger tent that served as his office. A cot had been placed in one corner, and a youth of sixteen or seventeen wearing only long underwear lay on his side, clutching his middle.

"I don't rightly know what's ailing him. He's been drooping like a little biddy with the dropsy for the last week or so. Then his guts started a-knottin' up. I wouldn't think much of it, but it's been going on kinda long. And now there's these rose-red spots all over his chest."

As the boy realized a woman was in the room, he yanked a blanket around him. "Pa, it's just something I ate," he protested. "No need to bother the lady."

"Well, I heard tell there's a couple sick with something like this here down at the railroad camp. So I wanted Mrs. McKay here to take a look," Jacob told the lad.

"Dang it, Pa," the boy said in exasperation. "A feller don't want to talk about some things." He pulled the blanket up to his neck.

"Well, as long as I'm here, let me take a look," Elizabeth said. Paying his affronted modesty no attention, she moved to the cot and touched his forehead. It was fever-warm, but not terribly hot.

"Now, is your lower right side tender? Where does the pain seem located."

"No one place is more tender, ma'am. It's tender all over. Hurts all over. Cramps, too. And I'm having the back-door trots something fierce." He blushed.

Smiling at him reassuringly, she persuaded him to tell her in more detail just how the illness had come on. As he talked, she deftly undid the buttons on his long underwear, suspecting measles.

The details of his illness seemed to strike a chord in her memory. Something was familiar about the rose-red spots on his chest, too. But she couldn't quite put her finger on what it was. And the spots were like no measles she'd ever seen.

Other than advising his father to use water to cool the fever if it got higher, and not to let the boy have anything more solid than clear, salty broth, or rice water, until his intestinal troubles were over, there was little she could do.

She did caution Jacob not to drink or eat after the lad, and to wash his hands after he cared for him.

As Rand drove Elizabeth back to town, they played the game they'd been playing for the last several days. She tried to ignore him, avoiding his touch by getting in and out of the buggy on her own, and studying the flora and fauna they passed at the side of the road. And Rand talked incessantly about how marrying him was the only logical course for her, and about his plans for his horse farm.

This afternoon he added a new element. He waxed long and eloquent as he envisioned a honeymoon going up the Columbia on a paddle wheeler, seeing the Columbia Gorge and the Dalles Rapids.

Sighing, Elizabeth rolled her eyes heavenward, eyeing the twined boughs overhead. "I have a headache."

He quieted immediately. She hadn't expected him to be subdued so easily, and cast a sidelong glance at the tall man beside her, wondering what he was feeling, wishing she could make all his pain go away. But she couldn't.

Discouraged, Rand studied a clump of wildflowers blooming at the side of the road, wondering how much time he had to convince her before Hiram came back and he and Elizabeth tied the knot.

He could always just have a talk with Hiram, and tell him the truth, Rand thought. He cared for Elizabeth deeply and Becca was their child. Hiram was a good man. He'd understand. After all, his and Elizabeth's arrangement was just a marriage of convenience. A business arrangement.

But Rand knew he wouldn't do that. He'd given Elizabeth his word he wouldn't tell anyone Becca was his daughter.

His illegitimate daughter.

As Rand wondered what hell they went through in Kansas

to make Elizabeth so afraid of anyone here finding out, guilt stabbed him anew. He should have stayed, found a preacher, and married Elizabeth. No matter the consequences, he should have stayed. Even if he'd been caught, Becca would have a name.

Hell, he couldn't blame Elizabeth for not trusting him now.

He propped his boot on the dashboard and said, "You look worried."

"Do I?" Elizabeth blinked, as though coming out of a daydream. "I'm not. I was just thinking about Becca. Mabel is good with her and doesn't mind keeping her. And I'm glad I can help Doc out, especially after all he and Mabel have done for me. But I just miss being with Becca every day. Seeing her smile, hearing her make-believe play. I—"

She looked at Rand, and his face lost all expression. He was hiding his pain, she realized.

The rest of her words stuck in her throat. While she was going on about being separated from her daughter for a few hours, he'd never known the joy of being with her every day.

But he knew what he was missing.

Twisting her gloved fingers together, Elizabeth looked straight ahead. She wished she'd let him continue his usual babbling. "How is the cabin coming?" she asked. "I guess you've been too busy driving me over the county to get anything done."

Almost at once, she realized she'd made another faux pas. She could have bitten her tongue. Asking about the cabin was the wrong thing to do. It would make Rand think she was considering his offer.

And hadn't she? a little voice said accusingly. In some corner of her heart, wasn't she dreading when Hiram would get back and she would have to make an irrevocable commitment?

Rand snapped the reins. "Actually, Jake already has two dozen suitable trees cut and peeled, and he's working on more. Since the stone foundation from the original cabin is still there, it won't take long to get the ends notched and the walls up."

Drawing in a deep breath of the evergreen-scented air, Elizabeth exhaled it slowly. Wrens were flitting in the underbrush. A chipmunk scurried across their path.

Knotting her gloved fingers again, she said quietly, "After Hiram gets back, and . . . and we get married, I'm certain he'll want to drive me around, until Doc's back on his feet. That should give you plenty of time to get the cabin built before winter."

But not a reason to build it. Rand thought the words, but didn't say them aloud.

Elizabeth looked up at him, her hazel eyes dark with unspoken emotions. "Rand, I—"

Boom, boom, boom! sounded in the distance—the railroad crew blasting again. The sound jarred the natural quiet of the woodland.

Elizabeth looked back at the wrens, obviously thinking better of whatever she'd been about to say.

They made it back into town as dusk was settling over the street. As Rand took the buggy around to the stable to unhitch the mare, Elizabeth hurried inside. Closing the Sedricks' front door, she realized Mabel had company in the parlor. She recognized Lois Mayflower's voice, but not the man speaking with Lois and Mabel.

Tired, not wanting to see anyone before she freshened up, Elizabeth went quietly to the room she shared with Becca. After stripping off her skirt and shirtwaist, Elizabeth thoughtfully bundled them in a tight ball, along with her apron.

There was something about Jacob's son's fever that sent an alarm bell clanging. Mentally going over his symptoms as she took down her sagging hair and brushed it, then pinned it in a neat coil, she tried again to put her finger on exactly what was niggling at her. Without success.

It was certainly common enough to get sick from bad food, the sickness sometimes lasting for days. A fever could explain the rash. With a shrug, she donned a fresh shirtwaist and skirt, then wrapped her warm shawl about her shoulders, again. She was finding the Oregon spring felt much cooler than she'd expected. Probably due to the high humidity.

Becca had spent the day at the Hoffpaurs, and Elizabeth was

anxious to go get her daughter. The family would be ready to go to bed soon, and Elizabeth didn't want to inconvenience them. And she missed her daughter.

Looking into the mirror, Elizabeth decided she appeared respectable enough. She took the clothes out to Mabel's wash shed, and on impulse, she washed her hands with the strong lye soap Mabel kept there. She then went in search of Mabel to tell her she was back

After a light knock, Elizabeth entered the parlor and closed the door behind her. "Sorry to interrupt."

"Elizabeth." Mabel stood at once, beaming. "Not at all, dear. Come in." She added with a twinkle, "We've a surprise for you."

"A surprise?" Elizabeth stepped farther into the room and smiled at Lois, who spared her an absent nod, keeping her main attention focused on the man, who'd risen as Elizabeth entered.

"Elizabeth . . . ? Dagnabbit, I m-mean, M-Mrs. McKay?" the man stammered.

Not above average height with thinning reddish-blond hair, he tugged at his stiff-looking collar. His suit was neat, but worn thin at the elbows, and had obviously been made when he was a few pounds lighter. The buttons on the midsection were strained.

"Yes?" Elizabeth put her hand to her throat, filled with an unexplainable reluctance to admit her name.

The man looked at the bun Elizabeth had just coiled atop her head, then at the hem of her skirt. Then his gaze fastened on a spot on the wallpaper just above her right shoulder—several times coming near but never meeting her gaze directly.

"I'm real sorry I never got your letter. Afore I left, I mean. I sure would have done things better." His gaze shifted to the toes of her shoes again.

The door opened again, and Rand entered the room. His dark gaze went immediately from Elizabeth to the man.

He nodded to the latter. "Hello, Hiram."

Chapter Fourteen

Hiram Smith looked at his hands, looked at a spot over her head, looked at his shoes, and blurted out, ''Since you're here earlier than I expected, we could get hitched right now. Well, if the reverend is in town.''

''Married?'' Elizabeth glanced longingly at the door Mabel had just ushered Rand and Lois through. As Rand had left, he'd cast a dark glance at Elizabeth that seemed to ask if she could really go through with her plans.

When he'd gone out the door, she'd had an insane urge to call him back.

It had been Lois who seemed determined to stay in the parlor, continuing to ask Hiram questions about his orchards and farm, and he'd answered enthusiastically. Until Mabel had practically pulled Lois out of the room.

Elizabeth decided Lois must have picked up on her nervousness at the prospect of being alone with Hiram, and so was reluctant to abandon them, bless her.

Looking again at a spot just over her head, Hiram nodded vigorously. Then he blushed and looked at her shoes. ''No reason to wait.'' He accidentally met her gaze, blushed redder, and swallowed visibly. "I got a license at the courthouse while I was in Eugene."

"Maybe I should see if I can help Mabel with something," Elizabeth said. "She said she was going for coffee and cookies. She could need help." Elizabeth looked at the door again, longing to dash through it.

"Unless, of course, you want to wait. That's fine, too," Hiram said, not to be distracted from his subject. "Real fine. It's just that finding you already here, seems like we could go ahead and, well . . ."

Swallowing visibly, rubbing his palms on the knees of his trousers, Hiram shook his head. Meeting her gaze straight on, he blushed furiously. "Dagnabbit, I ain't doing this so good. And I thought it would be just so much easier."

"Easier? To get married this afternoon?" Elizabeth folded her hands on her lap, forcing herself not to bolt for the door.

She'd come here for this; she wanted this. But now that Hiram was here and it was about to happen, she felt overwhelmed.

"Oh, no." He shook his head. "Marrying by arrangement. Like I wrote you, the boys have been after me about getting them a new ma. I ain't so good at talking to women. Oh, I tried walking out with a couple of widders, but I ain't very good at this courting stuff, and what with men outnumbering the women here 'bouts, it just seemed like it would be easier to find someone through the newspaper. . . ."

The sentence trailed into oblivion. He met her gaze again straight on, for a second longer this time before his skittered away. This time the results weren't quite so fiery.

Sighing, he picked at a loose string on his coat sleeve. A button fell off and he snatched it up, putting it into his pocket. Watching him, Elizabeth found his awkwardness endearing.

"Emmaline, my wife, was the only woman I didn't ever get all tongue-tied around. She said the first time she saw me she knew I was right for her, and she sure enough was right for me.

"But she's been gone three years now." He looked in the general direction of Elizabeth's face. "Was it that way with you and your husband? Love at first sight?"

As she made pleats with her fingers in her worn gabardine skirt, this time it was Elizabeth who couldn't meet Hiram's gaze. "No. I didn't know Becca's father very long. But I thought he was the most wonderful man I'd ever met."

"You never rightly said how long you were together. How long were you married?"

There was sympathy in his tone. Sympathy Elizabeth knew she didn't deserve. "He was gone before Becca was born." She forced the half-truth between stiff lips.

He nodded sympathetically. "That's why, when you answered my ad in the newspaper and told me how you was widowed and had a child to support, I thought this would be good for us both. Not expecting anything to do with love, you understand. Just like a business deal. I had the wife I loved; now she's gone." He sighed for the past, then shook his head, looked at her, and blushed. "And I wouldn't try to take the place of your husband, Elizabeth—what did you say his name was?"

"Jack." She blurted out the first name that popped into her mind. This time, it was her turn to blush. This was the first time she'd not been able to avoid telling Hiram a direct lie, and her conscience stung mightily. She'd never made a habit of lying. Fixing the image of her daughter firmly in her mind, she reminded herself this was for Becca. To provide a home for Becca.

The stable home Rand could never give them.

She pushed aside thoughts of how unfair it was to him, or how wonderful it felt to be in his arms. . . . Rand couldn't promise he'd never be caught and brought back to Kansas, no matter how much she wanted to believe him when he promised her he'd never leave again.

"It all seemed so simple when I thought about it," Hiram went on, wistfully focused on a spot somewhere above her head. Again, he rubbed his hands over his britches, as though his palms were sweating. "So, being you got here early and you been forced to bunk in with Mabel and Doc—I'm real sorry I wasn't here—I just thought you might be feeling a touch awkward about that and want to get on with things.

"I know it must a been real hard for you, leaving all you ever knowed and coming out here. Taking me on faith."

Elizabeth said softly, "You're taking me on faith, too. And Becca."

"So, do you want to go on to the reverend's and get hitched now?" Focused on her shoes, he gave her a self-deprecating smile. "If you ain't ready to take off back to Kansas after meeting me, that is."

"I'm not ready to go back to Kansas," she said truthfully, and found a smile for him. One thing was certain, Elizabeth decided. Hiram Smith would make the most considerate husband she could imagine.

She just wished he was the husband she wanted.

He nodded, looking relieved, and almost met her gaze. "Then, do you want to go find the preacher now?"

"No!" She half rose from her chair. Forcing herself to sit back down, she amended, "I mean, Doc needs my help. His leg hurts too bad for him to get around hardly at all right now."

Elizabeth looked down and smoothed out the pleats she'd made in her skirt. Finding the preacher was the last thing she wanted to do.

But why wait? She suspected it wouldn't be any easier if she waited a day, or a week. Maybe not even a month.

"Mabel said how you been a real help to them, being a nurse and all." Hiram smiled, his pride in her showing. "I think that's real fine."

She returned his smile.

In the kitchen, Rand sat with his arms folded on the table, his coffee untouched. Sitting across the table from him, Lois Mayflower seemed just as unenthusiastic about hers, stirring it absently.

Telling Rand to stay put, that Doc had said he wanted to talk to him and Elizabeth the moment they returned, Mabel excused herself to go help her husband get out of bed. She'd informed him that Doc's leg was still swollen and he spent a good part of each day flat on his back with his foot up on pillows.

Pain-filled grumbling drifted into the kitchen from the direction of the bedroom. Rand had sympathy, but he was more concerned with what he didn't hear—it was awful quiet in the parlor.

The more Rand thought about it, the more he wanted to go pull Elizabeth out of the parlor and tell Hiram he could find himself another mail-order bride.

"Reckon Mabel needs help with Doc? She's been gone awhile." Lois's spoon made a tiny clinking sound as she continued stirring.

"She would have asked." Rand lifted his own coffee, then set it back down without drinking.

"A body'd be crazy not to marry Mr. Smith." Lois sighed and put down her spoon, staring at the checkered tablecloth.

"Hiram's a good man. Better than most," Rand allowed.

"I could tell that right off." The woman sighed again.

Footsteps sounded in the hall, and Rand glanced up. Looking like a startled deer, Elizabeth paused in the doorway. She was wearing her bonnet. Hiram stood right behind her, looking so pleased Rand felt his hand curl into a fist of its own volition.

"Where's Mabel?" Elizabeth glanced at Rand, then at the floor.

"Gone to help Doc up," Lois supplied. Elizabeth nodded, and drew her shawl tightly across her shoulders. "Please tell her we're going to get Becca at Hiram's sister's, then going to find Reverend Lyle." She looked down at the knot she was tying with the fringed ends of the shawl. "We'll be back soon."

Rand watched as Hiram took Elizabeth's elbow and led her down the hall. The front door opened and closed

The heavy tick of Mabel's grandfather's clock in the parlor marked several minutes as Rand was lost in his own thoughts. All uncharitable and all aimed at Hiram.

Breaking into them, Lois said, "She'll be happy married to Mr. Smith. He'll take good care of her and her little girl."

Picking up her spoon again, she stirred her coffee and gazed toward the high kitchen window, a soft look in her small, round eyes.

The truth of the statement was undeniable. Though Rand acknowledged it privately, he wouldn't admit it aloud. Elizabeth would be crazy to cast Hiram Smith aside and marry him instead.

But he was going to try his very best to convince her to do just that.

And if he couldn't change her mind, his daughter could have no better stepfather than Hiram.

But how could he bear to lose Elizabeth again? And his child, now that he'd found her?

"I was kind of hoping she'd ask me to stand up with her," Lois said. "Guess they'll be back as soon as the minister says the words over them."

It took a few minutes, but her words eventually penetrated his troubled thoughts.

Rand's head snapped up and he stared at the woman sitting across Mabel Sedrick's kitchen table. "Miss Mayflower, what did you say?"

Lois looked at him. "I said—"

"Now? They're getting married *now?*" Rand answered for her. How had he missed that vitally important bit of information?

"They said they were going to find the minister. And Elizabeth—"

Not waiting to hear the rest of what Lois was saying, Rand bolted for the door.

Elizabeth turned as heavy footsteps sounded on the boardwalk behind her and her fiancé. A tall man loomed out of the dark. She recognized Rand in the faint lamplight spilling out of a window. His face was set in taut, harsh lines.

Her heart beating harder, Elizabeth asked, "What's wrong?

Does Mabel or Doc need me? His leg hasn't started bleeding again?''

Rand said nothing for an instant, his dark gaze going from her to Hiram.

''Rand?'' Hiram looked perplexed.

''You're not marrying her,'' Rand told him, his voice soft steel.

''I'm not?'' Hiram blinked.

''Rand?'' *What was he doing?* Looking up at him, Elizabeth willed him to be sensible, but more than anything wanted to kick him in the shin.

A look of determination on his face, Rand said, ''I mean you aren't—''

''Rand!'' Almost shouting, Elizabeth cut him off. What was he trying to do? He was about to ruin everything!

Dear Lord, didn't he know this was hard enough as it was? Didn't he know that every time she looked at him, she wanted to be in his arms?

Glaring up at Rand, ignoring the strange look her fiancé gave her, she said, ''I've already explained to Hiram that Doc needs my help and will for the foreseeable future, so we can't get married right now.''

Rand's dark gaze claimed hers again. The look of pain and hope in his eyes was almost her undoing. ''You aren't going to find the minister?'' he asked.

''No.'' At that look, something warm and wonderful blossomed inside her. Something she had no right to feel, she knew. ''Oh, we are, but we're just going to talk to him about a date.'' Next Sunday, they had decided. After church. If all was going well.

''Oh, I see,'' Hiram said, nodding.

Rand remembered his friend's presence. Relaxing a little, he asked, ''You see what, Hiram?''

Looking from one to the other, Hiram said, ''You're worried we were gonna get hitched and you weren't invited to the wedding, weren't you, Rand? Couldn't figure out what this was all about for a minute there. Well, we ain't getting married today. Doc needs Elizabeth's help.'' Hiram patted her hand and beamed. ''We'll give it a few days, then Elizabeth and me will tie the knot. She can still help Doc, if he still needs her, even after we're wed.''

Elizabeth tried hard to smile at Hiram, but suspected she failed miserably.

They weren't getting married now. Rand sighed inwardly, and decided to give in to Elizabeth's silent pleading look and not say what he really wanted to say.

He'd talk to her alone later.

Rand shifted uneasily, suddenly at a loss. ''Well, Doc wants to talk to you, Elizabeth. Mabel said it was something important. You might want to hurry.'' He turned on his heel and went back the way he'd come.

She didn't really want to marry Hiram, Rand thought, sticking his hands into his pockets. There was still time to convince her to marry him instead. If he could find a way to prove to Elizabeth once and for all Dalton McClure was dead and buried, as far as the world was concerned.

He'd heard a couple of familiar names associated with the railroad construction crew. Lucas Skinner, who was the straw boss when Rand had worked for the Union Pacific in Kansas, was running this project. Rand knew he hadn't changed a great deal. Skinner would recognize him. But then, Rand doubted he had anything to fear from the straw boss.

Skinner was the one who had placed the dynamite by the wall of the jail.

Just why, Rand had never quite figured out. Now, he might get Lucas Skinner to answer some questions Rand had been carrying around for a very long time.

And if they were the right answers, and he cleared his name . . .

Halfway back to Doc's, Rand started whistling.

When Rand returned to the Sedricks', Doc, Mabel, and Lois Mayflower were waiting in the parlor. Doc sat with his injured leg propped on an ottoman and a sour expression on his face.

"Did Elizabeth and Hiram really take off to find the preacher?" Mabel asked, hovering behind her husband like a hen with one chick.

"No. Not the way we thought. They are just going to talk to him." Rand pulled his hat off and turned it in his hands. "Doc, you want to tell us what's the problem?"

"They aren't getting married now?" Lois said. Her hand to her throat, she looked relieved. Then seemed flustered. "Well, I should go and leave you men to talk business, whatever it is," she said, rising.

Shaking his head, Doc frowned. "Miss Lois, you better hear this, too. The whole damned town might be involved before this is over." He shot Rand a worried look. "We have problems. Henry Cavanaugh came to see me today to get quinine for his wife and boy. Said they're awful sick. I gave him something for their stomachs, too. He said, by the rosy spots the boy's breaking out in, it looks like typhoid."

Rand stilled. Typhoid fever could spread faster than wildfire. "He's sure?"

"Pretty much. He had it as a child. And he lost two brothers to it."

"I *sang!*" Becca skipped into the parlor. Elizabeth paused just inside the open door, Hiram at her shoulder. Wrapped in a paisley dressing gown and looking decidedly irritable, Doc sat in a chair by the wall, Mabel hovering behind him. Lois Mayflower sat on the settee. Rand rose from his chair as they entered.

Elizabeth sensed something was wrong from their expressions. But before she could ask what the matter was, Becca skipped straight to Doc's chair. "I sang! Aunt Maggie Jean has an organ, like at church. Lisa played and Ester taught me a song about angels." She added, "Grandma is an angel."

Mabel smiled. "And I bet you sang beautifully."

Becca nodded. "I did."

Putting her hand over her mouth, Mabel seemed to indulge in a fit of coughing, her eyes filled with mirth. Lois chuckled aloud. Even Doc was drawn to smile.

"Becca!" Elizabeth eyed her daughter, trying not to smile.

"She did quite right, Elizabeth," Doc said with a chuckle. "False modesty will get you nowhere in this world, will it, young lady?" The last was directed to Becca.

"I guess not. What's 'falls *mod-esty?*' " Becca frowned.

"It's what you don't have," Doc said.

"Do I need it?" The child looked around at the laughing adults in the room as she waited for an answer. Becca seemed pleased to have entertained everyone.

Amazed at how much her daughter seemed to like being the center of attention, Elizabeth wouldn't have been surprised if the child had taken a bow.

"No, you don't need it at all," Doc assured Becca, chuckling.

Mabel sat down on a chair beside Doc and held her arms out. Becca went to her instantly, and Mabel lifted the child onto her lap. "I missed you today. Did you like playing with your new cousins?"

Becca nodded enthusiastically. "It was fun, but I missed you, too." She drew a small cloth doll from her pocket. "Look what Aunt Maggie Jean made me." The doll had button eyes, a wide smile drawn with red stitches, and yellow yarn braids. "She said since Miss Annie was in heaven with Grandma—she drowned, you know," she explained, her gaze serious, "I *must* have another doll."

"And this is a very nice doll. What's her name?"

Becca shrugged. "I don't know yet."

Doc asked, "How do you like your new father?"

Frowning, Becca turned to Doc. "Who?"

"Mr. Smith, of course," Doc said.

From the corner of her eye, Elizabeth saw Rand tense. And she ached for him.

Becca's attention snapped to Hiram, who smiled at the child. "He's not my father," she said decisively, and danced the cloth doll down Mabel's arm.

Sensing Hiram's discomfort, Elizabeth gave him an encouraging smile, then went and knelt beside her daughter. "Hiram will be your stepfather. We talked about this before. Remember?"

"Oh." Becca seemed to think this over. "That's okay then, I guess." Giving her daughter a hug, Elizabeth started to rise.

"But what about my real father?" the little girl asked innocently.

Elizabeth could only stare at her daughter, thinking she couldn't have heard right.

Or could Rand have talked to the child? Surely he wouldn't do that.

"Oh, honey. You don't have a real father," Mabel said, smoothing Becca's dark curls.

Frowning, Becca smoothed the doll's yarn hair. "When I was in heaven, Grandma said I did. She said that he and Mama needed me."

Blinking rapidly, Mabel hugged her again. "Honey, I think you were much too close to heaven to suit me."

Not knowing what to think, Elizabeth met Rand's gaze. Then she patted her daughter's hand. "You've had a long day. Let's put you into bed, so I can come back and talk with Doc about the people who are sick."

"Let me take her," Mabel offered, and set Becca off her lap. "I'm afraid we might have a crisis developing. Jonas can fill you in."

To Becca, Mabel added, "Ready to go? I bet I know some bedtime stories your mother hasn't told you."

Becca nodded. "Okay. I'm getting awfully tired of Cinderella."

Later, as she lay beside her daughter, Elizabeth watched a fingernail moon descending in the west and tried to picture her life after she and Hiram wed. She would have a house to keep and children to take care of. Hiram's boys were very sweet. Perhaps, she and Hiram would have children of their own.

She tried to imagine making love with Hiram Smith. And couldn't. Hiram had surprised her tonight when he kissed her as she was showing him out. A quick, wet peck on the lips. She hadn't felt anything when he did it.

Rand could make her blood sizzle with just a look or a touch.

Pushing Rand and his touches and his looks firmly out of her mind, Elizabeth turned on her side and fussed with her pillow, then pulled the blanket up to her chin. Because of the fever outbreak, she might not be marrying Hiram for quite a while.

Typhoid fever. The instant Elizabeth heard Doc say the words, she knew that was what Bobby Smith at the lumber camp suffered from, and told Doc about it.

Hiram was very concerned about his young cousin. She didn't blame him. Though she'd never seen typhoid, she'd heard about it striking down communities on the Kansas plains.

Many more people had died along the Oregon Trail from typhoid fever than from Indian attacks.

After Mabel put Becca to bed, all four of them discussed the situation long into the night, trying to decide how best to handle it to keep it from becoming an epidemic. Hiram volunteered to ride to Eugene the next day and bring back quinine and paregoric—Doc having given most of his small supply of each to Henry Cavanaugh.

Lois offered to help however she could. Elizabeth was pleased to learn Lois had experience caring for the sick. If there was an epidemic, they would need every pair of available hands.

What had upset Elizabeth most was when the group broke up, Rand had calmly announced that he was riding out to the railroad camp at first light to assess the situation and see how many of the workers were sick. Or if it even was typhoid fever.

Doc agreed there was no reason to assume. It was better to find out for certain.

Then Doc mentioned the construction boss's name was Skinner, and Rand nodded calmly.

Not Lucas Skinner, Elizabeth almost cried out. Skinner had testified against Rand in Kansas.

Tears pricked her eyes. What did Rand think he was doing anyway, riding out to the railroad camp alone? Flaunting himself in front of people who knew he was a wanted man? Just what did he think he was going to accomplish, except to get himself hanged?

After punching her pillow, Elizabeth squeezed her eyes shut and promised herself she'd not lose any sleep over his refusal to listen to reason.

Chapter Fifteen

"That coffee smells so good, it led me down the hall before my eyes even opened." Mabel tightened the sash of her dressing gown as she came through the kitchen door. "Not both of my eyes, mind you. But one anyway. And are those sausages I hear sizzling in that skillet?"

"Yes. Biscuits will be ready in a few minutes, too." Elizabeth rubbed the biscuit dough scraps off her hands into the scrap bucket Mabel kept to give the chickens, then wiped her hands on a dish towel and slid the pan of biscuits she'd prepared into the oven.

"Sit," Elizabeth told Mabel. "You look like you're still asleep. I'll pour you a cup, if you don't mind my having made myself at home in your kitchen."

"Mind? I could come to like it far too much! And dear, you've been nothing but a blessing since you've been here," Mabel said warmly. Hiding a yawn behind her hand, she slid onto the split-log bench beside the kitchen table, then propped her head on her hands.

Feeling warmed by the compliment, Elizabeth placed a cup of coffee in front of her, along with the cream pitcher and a honey jar.

"I take it black. Remember?" Mabel sipped, raised her brows, and reached for the cream. "Oh, my. I usually take it black. But this *is* real coffee."

"I did get it a bit strong this morning. I thought we might all need a little extra kick to get us awake."

Especially herself, Elizabeth thought. Despite every intention of putting her fear for Rand out of her mind, she'd lain awake worrying. Using a pot holder to open the cast-iron oven door, she checked her biscuits and found them rising nicely.

Mabel took another sip, then studied her cup. "I have to say, it is working. I think both eyes are open at once now."

Elizabeth smiled. She hadn't realized how much she'd missed other women's company until she came to Willow and found acceptance again. No one in Kansas had visited or been friendly to her after Becca was born. And after her mother died, she'd felt very alone.

"It is waking me up. I just realized you're already dressed." Mabel raised her brows.

"I've been out at the wash shed and washed my clothes from yesterday."

"Okay." Mabel took a large sip, then looked toward the window and blinked. "I'm not still dreaming. The sun really isn't up yet, and you already have wash on the line. You make me look like a slugabed!"

"I couldn't sleep," Elizabeth confessed. "And I didn't want you to handle those clothes. On impulse I changed them yesterday, when I came in. Now, I'm glad I did, so I didn't expose anyone to the fever. Rand should be safe—he never went near Jacob's son." He had, however, kissed her silly in the buggy, after she'd been near the boy. But perhaps that slight exposure wouldn't be enough to cause him to catch the fever.

"It must have been an angel whispering on your shoulder, telling you to do that and keep us all safe." Mabel smiled. "Perhaps it was Becca's angel—your mother."

Becca's angel was another thing that had made Elizabeth toss and turn. "She's so certain that she saw her grandmother in heaven. . . ."

"Perhaps she did," Mabel said simply.

"I want to believe that. My mother loved Becca so much; she'd always comfort her when—" Elizabeth put her fingers to her lips. She'd had been about to say, "When other people would point and make fun of the child." Certainly, Elizabeth would have been at a loss to explain such a statement.

Moving to the stove, Mabel put a motherly arm around Elizabeth's shoulders and gave her a squeeze. "You still miss your mother terribly, don't you?"

"Yes." Elizabeth sighed. "But about the angels, you know how cruel people can be. I don't want everyone to think Becca is strange."

Shaking her head, the older woman said, "It never occurred to me to think they might be mean to the child because of her angels. Well, I guess in other places, people are different. It's been a long time since we left back East, where everything was so rigid and proper. But it's not the same here, dear. People are nicer than any place I've ever known. That's why Jonas and I stayed, even though his medical practice would have been more lucrative in Portland, or even Salem."

Thinking it over, Elizabeth had to agree. Every time she'd expected a negative or mean-spirited reaction from someone here, she'd been surprised. Pleasantly. People were genuinely kind and helpful.

The odor of singed flour wafted up to her. "The biscuits!" Grabbing the pot holder, she rescued them just in time, then turned her attention to the sausages sizzling in the skillet.

After everything was ready to serve, Elizabeth pulled her apron off. "I have another favor to ask, I'm afraid. Would you watch Becca again? I can ask Lois, if you don't feel up to it," she added hurriedly.

"She's no trouble at all. Of course I'll watch her, dear. But where are you going?"

Elizabeth glanced at the window. Between the red checkered curtains, the pearl gray of daybreak was growing steadily lighter. Rand would be riding out to that camp soon—unless she could stop him.

Not wanting to explain, she said, "I have to see Rand before he leaves. I can't let him ride out to that railroad camp alone."

She reached for the woolen coat she'd worn outside earlier when she did the wash. The weather had turned cool, and even damper. As she put the coat on, and then her straw bonnet, she considered the arguments she could use to talk him out of going.

It was madness to tempt fate. And he had no authority out there. Any problem at the camp was the county sheriff's job to handle. If anything, Rand should ride to Eugene and talk to him.

"Why don't you want him to ride out there alone?" Mabel poured herself another cup of coffee and cradled the cup between her hands.

Not expecting the question, Elizabeth searched about for a plausible reason. As she tied her bonnet strings, she stammered, "He . . . he doesn't know anything about methods to avoid contagion. He might do something to cause himself to become infected. Or worse, bring the fever back into town in some way."

The half-truth almost stuck in her throat. "And I might be able to help those sick men. I can at least tell them what to do for fever and how to avoid as much stomach upset as possible, until Hiram gets back from Eugene with more medicines."

Mabel gazed into her cup. "That's a good idea, dear. I wouldn't want Rand to get sick. And you might check on the Cavanaughs while you're out that way. The railroad camp is just up the road from their homestead."

Setting her cup aside, Mabel took a basket down from atop a cupboard. "I'll just put some sausages in biscuits and pack them in here for your lunch, along with a canteen of water. Go catch Rand before he rides off without you. Then come back before you go and I'll have this ready for you, along with whatever medicines Jonas has to send."

A few minutes later, Elizabeth was walking down the boardwalk beside Main Street. Having forgotten her gloves, she thrust her hands into her pockets and hurried along. The street was nearly deserted in the half-light, but lantern light in windows showed people were up and starting the day. Some families lived above their shops. Stovepipes sticking out from the sides and roofs puffed wood smoke into the damp morning, scenting the air along with the smell of baking bread and frying eggs and ham.

A mongrel dog lurking in the alley by the sheriff's office was startled at her approach and barked. Cringing, it moved away.

After knocking on the weathered, unpainted door, Elizabeth went inside, without waiting for Rand to answer. "I have to talk—*oh!*"

Startled, Rand looked up. Then raised one dark brow and continued tucking his flannel shirt into his pants. His fly was open and his trousers rode low on his hips to accommodate the action.

"Can I help you?" His voice held a dark, teasing edge of invitation.

"I . . . uh . . ." Elizabeth wet her lips, watching as he efficiently smoothed one side of his shirttail into his trousers, then started on the other side.

"Or do you want to help me?" he asked when she made no coherent comment.

Forcing her gaze away from his pants, she turned her back. A rumpled cot in one of the cells captured her attention. He must have slept there.

Elizabeth realized that looking at the cot and imagining him sleeping there was not a good idea either She closed her eyes. "Tell me when it's safe to turn around."

After a moment, he said, "Okay, Elizabeth."

She turned and found him dressed and buckling his gun belt.

Raising both brows, Rand asked, "Why are you here? Decided you can't marry Hiram after all?" His tone was joking, but his eyes held a serious glint.

She clasped her fingers together, "Don't go out to that work camp."

"Why?"

"There are people there who know you. Your life here will come unraveled. You'll be hauled back to Kansas to hang."

"Careful." He finished buckling the belt and picked up his gun from the desk. "I'll think you care."

''I do,'' she said simply, raising her gaze to his, knowing her feelings for him were in her eyes, ''You don't know how much I wish I didn't.'' She'd thought him dead once, and the pain of it was more than she ever wanted to bear again. She wanted to know he was safe, even though she couldn't be with him.

He stilled, his gaze searching hers in a way that made her breath catch in her throat.

''But you don't care enough to change your plans. You're still set on marrying Hiram Smith?''

God help her, she did care enough. More than enough. Elizabeth wanted to feel his arms wrap around her and never let go.

Becca was the only thing more important to her than her feelings for Rand—important enough to keep them apart.

''Nothing has changed. We've been through that.''

Shaking his head, he said, ''I have to go. First, because I care about this town and the people in it. But also because there's no other way to prove to you I am in no danger of being arrested. At least, I believe I'm not.''

As Rand pinned his star to the woolen material of his shirt, she caught his arm. ''This Skinner knows you, doesn't he? I remember you told me once he testified against you, though you thought he was your friend. He'll tell the authorities who you are!''

''Skinner's no threat to me,'' Rand told her. ''At the trial, he only told what he knew of the truth—that I'd said I was going to talk to the farmer who was taking potshots at us every time we tried to go forward with the tracks. The man's son would spell him at night. Between the two, they had us at a standstill for a week. The sheriff wouldn't do anything. A lot of people sided with the man. His land had been taken by the government by right of eminent domain.

''I felt it was unfair, too, for that matter. As I was riding out to the farmer's place that night, I heard shots exchanged. The man was bleeding to death when I found him in his yard. I tried to stem the flow, but couldn't, and he died. So I rode hell-for-leather for the sheriff.

''Trouble was, the old man's neighbors heard the shots and

met me on the road as I rode out. They saw the blood on my clothes and hands. I told them what happened, but they didn't believe me."

"You told me all this in Kansas. I believed you then. I still do." Unable to stop herself, Elizabeth touched his arm, feeling his muscles tense beneath her fingers. "But I met this Skinner in Kansas. After you had gone. He's not your friend. He was talking about how he hoped you'd be caught because what you'd done was a bad reflection on the railroad. You can't trust him, Rand."

"He was always one to cover his own tail." Rand frowned at this new intelligence. "Where did you meet Skinner? The rail line wasn't anywhere near your mother's homestead."

"I saw him in Doctor Brown's office while I was still working there as a nurse. Skinner had a bullet wound—just a little flesh wound on his calf muscle. It wasn't a new injury, but it had become infected." Elizabeth shook her head. "That was before I even knew I was pregnant with Becca."

Rand remembered Skinner limping slightly at the trial, and for the first time wondered if Skinner might have known more about that night the farmer was murdered than he'd told on the witness stand.

What Rand had never told Elizabeth was that he trusted Skinner because he was the one who had blown the jailhouse wall and saved him from hanging.

But all that didn't change the present—the fever, the need to be certain he could start a new life and prove it to Elizabeth.

"I still have a duty to the town," he said.

"Damn it, Rand, I'm not worried about the town. I don't want you to go out there! I have a bad feeling about what will happen if someone recognizes you, or if this Skinner isn't the friend you think!"

"Someone has to go assess the situation, and there's no one else. But even if there was, I have to go. I want to prove to you that you can trust me to be here always. I'm not going to run again. And no one is going to carry me back to Kansas."

"And if you prove the opposite? If you find yourself a wanted man again?'' She blinked hard, daring the tears gathering in her eyes to fall. Why was he being so damned stubborn?

''Then you'll have been right not to let me into your and . . . my daughter's lives. You'll marry Hiram and live happily ever after.''

She could have hit him.

Studying her face, he caught her chin between thumb and forefinger and lifted it for a kiss, and she let him without resistance. His lips were soft and gentle, but the feelings they evoked inside her weren't. They were a storm tide of emotional need and physical desire.

After a small eternity, Rand broke off the kiss and asked hoarsely, ''When Hiram kissed you last night, did it make you feel like that?''

Elizabeth blinked up at him. ''How did you know Hiram kissed me?''

As he slipped into his Mackinaw coat, Rand gave her a sardonic look. He plucked his hat from its peg on the wall and started out. ''See you when I get back.''

''No, you won't leave me behind!'' Angrily, she stomped her foot. ''I'm going with you!''

Rand paused. ''I don't think that's a good idea.'' If he did encounter any problems, he didn't want her caught in the middle.

''Mabel will have a lunch packed for us, and some medical supplies,'' Elizabeth said, paying his protest not the least attention.

''Elizabeth—''

''Or, I can just wait for you to leave and follow you. I can ride a horse or drive a buggy as good as you, remember.''

Her gaze dared him to say he'd leave her behind. Rand sighed in defeat. ''You've grown more stubborn over the years, Elizabeth.''

''Thank you.''

She breezed past him and out the door.

Chapter Sixteen

Using the pocket watch Doc loaned her, Elizabeth counted as she checked Hazel Cavanaugh's pulse. Fearful of what would happen in the rail camp, Elizabeth had talked Rand into going to the Cavanaughs first. Though she knew she was only delaying the inevitable—since she couldn't talk him out of going to the camp altogether and confronting the people who knew his past. It was only a small reprieve.

And the Cavanaughs needed to be looked in on to make certain Henry understood and was following Doc's instructions. Many pioneers had succumbed to the fever through the years from treatments that did more harm than good.

Though the window was open, the log room was dark and damp. It smelled of carbolic soap from the brisk cleaning Elizabeth had given it. She also helped Hazel and her son bathe, and placed rubber sheets, which Hazel happened to have from when her son was a baby, beneath clean linen on their beds.

"There." Elizabeth finished counting Hazel's pulse and patted her hand.

The woman wet dry, cracked lips. "Not very good, is it?" A frown of pain twisted her face as she clutched her midsection.

"A bit fast," Elizabeth conceded. "The rice water I fixed

for you should be cooled in a bit. I want you to drink all you can. It's important to keep up your strength.''

''No solid food?'' Hazel asked when the spasm passed. ''Seems like something strengthening would be more the thing.''

''Not at all. It prolongs the stomach irritation. You can have clear broth. That's strengthening. And a bit of sugar water if you feel especially weak. Now, this is important to remember, because the medicine might make your stomach feel better before it's really well.'' Elizabeth had administered paregoric drops earlier.

Already, Hazel's son was responding to the medication and sleeping peacefully on a mattress drawn up on the floor beside his mother's bed.

Knowing she'd done what she could, Elizabeth still felt ineffectual against an enemy she couldn't see. She gathered the dirty sheets she'd stripped from the bed and pallet earlier. ''I'll send your husband in.''

Pausing on the porch, she drew a deep breath, wishing she could do more. Mist obscured the tops of the two-hundred-foot firs surrounding the clearing around the log house.

The woods were deeply shadowed, even though it was only around noon. A rushing creek, filled with snowmelt from the mountains, gurgled at the edge of the clearing. Above the sound of the rushing water, and the calls of trapper jays in the trees, she could hear the *tink, tink, tink* of sledgehammers hitting steel, and an occasional shout as the construction crew built the rail line.

A tarpaulin was stretched across a raised plank and the corners tied to four posts over the Cavanaughs' wash pot, beneath which a fire blazed despite the misting rain. Elizabeth was relieved to find Rand had done as she asked and found a way to get the fire going under the pot.

Holding her burden as far away from her as possible, she went down the hewn-log steps and trudged across the muddy yard, trying to ignore the cold kiss of the rain. Under the tarpaulin, she put the sheets into the hot water and poked them down with a long, heavy stick, which she found laying near the pot. Because it was worn smooth and round on the ends, Elizabeth knew it had been long used for such a purpose.

She hoped Hazel Cavanaugh would recover soon and be using it again on washday.

Gripping the stick in both hands, Elizabeth jabbed the contents of the wash pot, knowing she'd done what she could. But feeling it wasn't enough.

A strong scent of carbolic rose on the steam, nearly taking her breath away. Good, Rand had shaved plenty of the soap she'd given him into the water. While the fever ran its course, it was important to prevent the spread of the infection by employing the nursing methods Miss Nightingale had described in her writings from her experiences in the Crimean War. Cleanliness was the cornerstone of the lady's teachings.

Rand strode around the corner of the cabin, his head tilted down, a trickle of water running off the brim of his hat. An oilskin slicker was stretched across his broad shoulders, making them appear even wider than usual. He looked as solid as the tall Douglas firs behind him. And right now, she wanted nothing more than to lean against his strength. She felt so badly for Hazel and her son, and there seemed so little she could do.

Henry Cavanaugh was right behind Rand. She guessed Rand had been looking into the Cavanaughs' sanitary arrangements, as she'd asked him to do.

The two stopped under the tarpaulin. Pulling off his hat, Henry nodded to her. Worry lined his long face, and his gaze skittered away from hers, settling on the wash pot.

Rand said, "We set up rain barrels under the eaves by the kitchen, to catch clean water. The infection might have come from the creek. Henry says there were some sick workers up at the railroad camp as early as last week. I know these camps aren't very clean. They're likely tossing their waste into the water."

"I never thought about people being so nasty and neglectful of other people's health, but some folks is just got no sense when it comes to keeping water fresh and clean," Henry said, shaking his head.

"If there's a dry spell and your rainwater runs out, you must boil all the water you get out of the creek, even if you're only using it to wash dishes or clothes,'' Elizabeth told him.

Henry nodded, looking lost and alone. She thrust the wash stick into his hand. Putting his hat back onto his head, Henry started briskly poking the clothes, as if he was grateful for something to do.

''I left rice water cooling on the stove. Give it to your wife and son when they feel up to eating,'' she said.

He nodded again.

Elizabeth added, sympathizing with the heavy load the man was carrying, ''I've told your wife some of the things to do or not do, mainly no solid food until this is past. Both of them are strong and doing better than most people at this stage of the sickness.''

She wished she could assure him they would both recover, but she couldn't go that far in good conscience. Typhoid fever was often a killer.

''Well, that's good to hear. I sure am obliged.'' Henry's expression lightened perceptibly.

''Oh!'' As the wheel dipped into a gully washed across the rough track, Elizabeth struggled to hold onto the arm of the buggy and her umbrella at the same time. After she righted herself on the seat, she said, ''Rand, I really think we should try again tomorrow—if Hiram gets back from Eugene with the medications Doc ordered, we'll be coming back anyway.''

From beneath the dripping brim of his hat, Rand glanced at her, one dark brow raised.

Overcoming the urge to shout at him, she strove to remain reasonable. ''Really, there's not a great deal we can do without them. I'd—''

The wheels hit a deeper hole, cutting off the rest of her words as she was obliged to hang on. Muddy water splashed in all directions, and on the long slicker Doc had loaned her to help her stay dry. The rain came down harder with each passing minute.

The stream the rough track wound beside was rushing faster

and wider all the time. Despite the umbrella and the slicker, Elizabeth was cold and miserable. The hem of her skirt and her shoes were wet. The buggy had no protective bonnet they could put up. She felt a great sympathy for the poor mare laboring to pull them.

"Rand, admit it would be better to come back tomorrow!" Elizabeth tried to keep the exasperation from her voice. But knowing she'd failed miserably, she gave in to her irritation and snapped, "I mean, you can throw your life away tomorrow just as well as today!"

He glanced at her. "I told you this morning, I have to face the past. Besides, you know we need to see what's what. There might be problems we aren't anticipating, supplies we might not think to bring unless we see what is needed. You know that as well as I do."

She also knew there were others who could do it. But didn't say so. Rand was well aware of the fact, too.

Why was he bound and determined to do this—to get himself recognized and dragged back to Kansas? It was madness, sheer and utter madness, and there didn't seem to be anything she could do or say to stop him.

Eyeing the handle of her umbrella, she considered closing it and whacking him. But it was raining a bit too hard to do without the protection.

And it wouldn't turn him from the course he'd set. Even if she knocked him cold, he'd just wake up and start out again.

She should just let him! Forget about him. Go on with her life—he wasn't a part of her plans anyway.

Trouble was, she cared too much. When she considered what would certainly happen if people found out Dalton McClure was still alive, warm tears mixed with the cold dampness on her cheeks.

Coming to a natural ditch between two folds of land, the mare balked at going through the rushing water. It wasn't very wide and didn't look deep.

"Ho, there. Get on, girl!" Rand raised his arms, preparing to pop the reins.

"Marry me?" Elizabeth kept her eyes trained forward.

The horse swiveled an ear around as if it couldn't believe what it had heard.

Elizabeth couldn't believe she'd said it, but once the words were out, she knew it was the right thing.

Turning to Rand, she found longing and disbelief mingled on his face.

"Seems like I asked a question like that this morning," he said, "and you had all kinds of good reasons not to."

"Not one of those reasons is that I don't care. I care too much," she admitted shyly. Too much to let him throw his life away.

Elizabeth felt a momentary stab of guilt that she would be abandoning Doc when he needed her to help out. But perhaps there wouldn't be any more typhoid patients. Perhaps Lois could take over for her and help out. She'd said she'd had experience in caring for the sick, and Doc would instruct her on what to do for the fever patients.

"You better be sure, Elizabeth," Rand said. Cool and wet, his lips found hers. The kiss was brief and hard. Pulling back, he studied her sharply. "You are, aren't you?" He kissed her again before she could answer, as if afraid she might change her mind even as he questioned her about her resolve. "Don't say such things if you aren't."

Suddenly, the rain became a deluge, pouring down just as if some giant water bucket had been overturned. In her preoccupation with Rand's kisses, she let her umbrella tip too far forward, and cold water went down her back. She jumped, remembering where they were.

Water fell so hard and fast, it was difficult to even see the horse's head, just a few feet away. Water puddled on the slicker on her lap and sloshed over her shoes.

Knowing Rand's wide-brimmed hat was no protection, that the cold rain had to be finding its way down his collar, Elizabeth scooted as close as possible and shared what little protection the umbrella offered.

His dark gaze caressed her face. "I promise I'll do my best to make you happy," he said. The words were barely audible over the drum of water on the umbrella. "And . . . and to be a good father. I want to be a good father to Becca.'' Rand swallowed hard, as if struggling to keep control of his emotions. But happiness shone in his eyes.

''You will be. I know it.'' How could she even have considered going through life without him? Elizabeth wondered.

Rand started to kiss her again, but the horse's nervous whinny drew his attention. The stream of water in the ditch they'd been about to cross had doubled in size and force in just those few moments. The mare had been right to balk at going across it. They might have been swept away if they had tried.

''Looks like you're going to get your way about the railroad camp. This is starting to look too dangerous. We'll have to hole up somewhere until the storm passes.''

''Where?'' Elizabeth asked, realizing they were trapped on two sides by water, and on the third by an impossibly steep hill.

''There's a trapper's cabin back a ways. Hold the reins tightly. The mare is getting nervous.''

After thrusting the leather thongs into her hand, Rand jumped down from the buggy. He caught the mare's bridle, and Elizabeth could barely see him through the rain as he forced the horse to go backward, until they came to a wider place in the road where they could safely turn around.

Drawing in a deep breath, Elizabeth searched in her heart for regret that they wouldn't be staying in Willow. She did like the people, like Doc and Mabel. Lois and Maggie Jean, too. And Hiram. The town certainly would have been a good place to bring up Becca. Everyone seemed so accepting of her here, she was blossoming like a sunflower.

However, Rand seemed to already love the child, though he'd been around her very little. He would be a wonderful father, of that Elizabeth had no doubt. They would find another place where Becca could fit in and have friends. Perhaps in Canada. Or Mexico.

After Rand guided the horse and got the buggy turned around, he climbed back onto the board seat and took up the reins. ''I think we'd better find shelter, until this rain stops.''

* * *

Elizabeth turned slowly around in the one-room cabin. Someone had left everything neat. Cans lined the few rough wooden shelves on the wall. There was a fireplace with a hook for hanging a cook pot, pot hooks on the wall, and one rough-hewn chair. There was also a bed—the first thing she'd noticed upon entering—and a wooden chest.

"It's not much. But it is dry."

The words had scarcely left Rand's mouth when a large drip fell from a rafter across the open attic and splattered on the hard earthen floor.

"Well, mostly. There's a lean-to on the back side. I'll be back after I put the horse under it."

He started to turn away, then turned back and gave her a swift kiss. "I did hear you right, Elizabeth? It wasn't just the rain in my ears? You did say you'd marry me?"

"I did the asking."

The look in his eyes sent warmth surging in her chest. He glanced at the narrow bed, neatly covered by a blanket, and the warmth she felt moved around, pooling much lower.

"See if there's kindling in the box to start a fire," he said huskily. "We need to dry out our clothes." After another kiss, more lingering than the last, and promising more to come, he went back out into the storm.

Her hands shaking, as much from the raw emotions rioting in her chest as from cold, Elizabeth draped her slicker over one of the pots and let it drip, then pulled off her damp gloves. The warmth of Rand's kiss made her more aware of how cold she was, even though she still wore her coat. And no wonder. Looking down, she realized her skirt was practically wet to the waist, as well as her petticoat beneath it.

Rand was probably soaked through, too. He was right. They needed to dry out, before they caught pneumonia.

Inspecting the kindling box, Elizabeth found it well stocked with pitch-filled splinters, and after making a little hollow in the old ashes, she placed several curled shavings in the depression. There were no matches, just an old-fashioned tinderbox and flint. Luckily, growing up in a pioneer family, she knew how to use it.

By the time Rand returned, with something shielded beneath his poncho-like slicker, Elizabeth had a small but hearty flame flickering among the shavings.

"I found dry wood under the lean-to out back." Rand dumped his treasure of small logs at the side of the stone hearth. After Elizabeth placed several thin splinters of kindling into a loose cone over her tiny flame, it grew, becoming brighter and hotter.

Rand stacked the hardwood logs on stones placed inside either end of the fireplace as andirons. Heat from the kindling soon ignited the wood and they had a bright hot blaze.

"Now, if we just had coffee." Elizabeth moved back a little from the heat.

Slowly, his gaze moved from the steam rising from her wet skirt, to her face. Rand said, "I'll see if I can find some, while you get out of those wet clothes. You can wrap up in the blanket from the bed while they dry."

"You're wet, too." Her words were so husky, Elizabeth hardly recognized her own voice.

Grinning, Rand suggested, "Then we could share the blanket."

Rising, he pulled off his slicker and hung it beside hers, then put his wet hat atop it. Going over to the shelves, he began sorting through the tins.

Her fingers shaking, it seemed to take forever as Elizabeth undid the buttons of her coat. Remembering her damp gloves, she spread them out on the hearthstones to dry, then hung her coat on a peg by the mantle. She'd already hung her wet slicker on a peg by the door, and a small puddle had formed on the floor beneath it.

By the time she began unbuttoning her skirt, her every cell seemed aware of the tall man behind.

"What is this place? Except for the dust, it looks like the owner just stepped out for a minute," Elizabeth said, trying to divert her thoughts from the fact that she was alone with Rand and getting undressed.

"An old trapper named Jeremiah Hull lived here. He'd been in these mountains since the '40's. He died this winter. Heart seizure, Doc said. I've been trying to find a next of kin since then, but it looks like he didn't have any family."

Selecting a tin from the shelf, Rand opened the can and sniffed the contents. "Will tea do?"

The damp skirt pooled around her ankles. "Wonderful." The word vibrated as she shivered under his dark gaze.

Rand picked up the cast-iron kettle from beside the fireplace. "I'll get the water."

As he opened the door and held the kettle under the downpour falling off the roof, she quickly placed the cabin's only chair in front of the fireplace and hung her skirt over it. Untying the drawstring of her petticoat, which was just a little damp, she removed that, too. Then went to work on shoes and stockings. By the time Rand turned back around, Elizabeth sat gingerly on the edge of the bed, clutching the blanket around her.

She looked young and vulnerable sitting there. Not like a woman grown, one who'd given birth to his child.

"Thank you." Her hazel eyes shone as she looked up at him, her chin tucked shyly.

"For what?" He hung the kettle on the iron hook inside the fireplace made for that purpose, then swung it over the heat.

"You stood with your back to me long enough to fill that kettle four times over."

"I thought you might feel uncomfortable with me watching." Rand sat down beside her and started removing his boots.

"No. I mean, yes."

Picking his boots and socks up, he placed them near her shoes on the hearth. Then he started unbuttoning his plaid flannel shirt.

She watched him, fascinated, until she realized that he was watching her watch him and felt warmth surge through her cheeks. "Do you want some privacy?" she asked.

"No." He slipped the shirt off his wide shoulders and the long undershirt beneath. Then he unbuttoned his trousers and pushed them down. His drawers followed, and he stood in silhouette in front of the fire, limned in golden light.

''I feel as though it's immodest to look, but I want to see all of you,'' she confessed, blushing. ''I remembered that night we were together so often. I remembered you were beautiful. . . .''

''You were beautiful, too,'' Rand said, the mattress sinking with his weight as he sat beside her and took part of her blanket, so they were wrapped together in it, sitting side by side.

''I was?'' There was wonder in her thick-lashed eyes. ''I did feel beautiful, when you touched me.'' She smiled. ''For the first time—the only time, really—I felt special. Not just 'different' because I liked to read books and novels and learn of other lands.''

With infinite tenderness, Rand traced Elizabeth's high cheekbone. ''I was so certain that you'd forget me. Who was I, that you should bother to remember? An outlaw. Nobody.''

''You were everything to me,'' she confessed. Until she'd come to Willow and found he could have come back for her. That her trust had been misplaced.

But she pushed that thought aside. This was a new beginning. For both of them.

As a nurse, she knew that if one didn't pick at a wound, it would heal.

Eventually.

Chapter Seventeen

Rand tugged the pink satin ribbon holding her camisole together, untying it and exposing her breasts.

As the fire crackled, Elizabeth fought her shyness not to snatch the edges of the blanket together. Having Rand look at her body so intimately caused her to want to hide. But it excited her, too.

He cupped her breast, his sun-browned hand dark against her light skin, his callused fingers causing a delightful friction. He stroked the light stretch marks left when her breasts had enlarged as she nursed Becca.

''They aren't as high and firm as they used to be,'' she admitted. To her shock, her body had changed dramatically with the birth of her child.

''Your breasts are even more beautiful than before,'' he assured her.

She caught her breath as he bent to kiss first one, then the other, as though paying homage.

Rand raised his head, his dark eyes luminous. ''You are more beautiful.''

She caught the words to her heart, but wanted to protest that it wasn't true. But the look in his eyes said it was. To him, at least.

Reaching to remove the pins from her hair, he took it down, spreading it over her shoulders. The scent of lilacs wafted to him, and he brought a handful to his face and inhaled deeply of the remembered scent. And he was taken back to where they had begun.

Rand swore to himself that this time it would be different. This time he wouldn't be leaving in the morning.

He'd never leave her again. He would never run, no matter what.

Shivering with anticipation, Elizabeth touched his smooth chest, lightly, tentatively. She wanted to explore, but was unsure of herself. Or what he expected. Vaguely she remembered touching him before, holding onto his shoulders. But her memories had blurred.

His skin was warm and smooth, the muscle underneath hard.

She kissed the puckered scar where she'd removed the slug from his shoulder years before, then the hard ridge of his collarbone.

"I tried so hard to keep that night all fixed in my mind," she confessed. "Each touch. Each kiss. Then when we . . ." She hid her face against his warm shoulder. "It was so beautiful, like a fairy tale. But after a while, it all seemed unreal, like a dream. If not for Becca, I wouldn't have been sure you ever were there at all."

It had hurt so much when he left. She'd never wanted to bear such pain again. Never had she wanted to love anyone again. To take such a risk. Now she knew that her feelings for him hadn't left her heart, but had only been lying dormant, waiting to bloom again.

"I thought of you," Rand confessed hoarsely. "At first, I thought of little else. I don't think there was a single day in all the years we were apart that I didn't think of you, Elizabeth. You were the finest thing that ever happened to me. I held the memory of your sweet giving close to my heart, and I took it out when it seemed there would never be anything good in my life again."

He traced the line of her jaw. "I felt so cheated to have found you and been forced to leave you like that. I only found the strength to do it because I believed it was best for you."

"I know that now." Looking up, she saw the truth of what he said shining in his dark eyes. He started to touch her cheek, and she caught his fingers and kissed them. "I understand."

Rand whispered, "If I had known about our daughter, all Hell couldn't have kept me away."

"I know that, too."

"Elizabeth, is this real? Can we . . . are we really getting a second chance?" Some part of him was afraid it wasn't real. That there really weren't any second chances in life. He had lived without daring to dream for so long, it was difficult to believe.

"Ssssh!" She placed her finger across his lips. "Let's please start again. Pretend like the last five years never happened."

More than willing to comply, Rand kissed her fingers, then pulled her against him. His body remembered her scent, her warmth, her curves. And responded with a need to be one with her again.

This time, he'd not leave in the morning. This time, they could build a life.

Kissing her long and deep, he tried to convey what he felt, for which words seemed so inadequate. And she responded by pressing her firm breasts against his chest.

At her action, his need erupted into a consuming ache.

Groaning as he moved to kiss her throat, her shoulder, he felt her fingers wind tentatively into his hair. Her shy touch reminded him that Elizabeth was still almost a virgin, that he had been her only experience with a man. And that knowledge brought renewed tenderness for her.

Their one time together had been poignant and beautiful; however, because it was her first time, there was pain for her. Though he'd managed to give her pleasure, she had never achieved climax.

Silently now, Rand promised Elizabeth this time would be for her. For beginning a lifetime of enjoying each other. For teaching her what she still didn't know. All that he'd never had time to show her. He would bring her pleasure, to the fullest measure he could.

Brushing aside the silken fall of honey-gold hair, he kissed the soft skin on the point of her shoulder, then down her chest. Cupping her breast, he kissed it gently. Then he licked it, and hearing her sharp intake of breath, he did it again, laving the nipple with his tongue until it was hard and tight.

His reward was a moan from deep in her throat.

Passion rocked him as she pulled him closer, greedily demanding more from his mouth.

Fire, Elizabeth thought, clutching at his head. She was on fire, deep inside. The fire she'd remembered and hungered for so long. This consuming, insatiable blaze only Rand could ignite. His teeth and tongue on her breast was delightful torture.

She whimpered as Rand shifted, breaking off his assault. Without knowing just how he did it, she found herself lying on the narrow bed. He was atop her, chest to chest, his erection pressing against the apex of her thighs. Instinctively, she spread her legs.

Lifting her hips, she invited his entry. But he didn't fill her, as she craved. Instead, his mouth found her other nipple, and he began the delicious torture again.

"Rand!" Catching his shoulders, she tried to wriggle into position to join with him.

"Not yet, sweet. Not yet."

"But I need you!"

Though it was only by an effort of will that he could resist the need to plunge into her softness, he wanted to give her more. He wanted to give her everything.

"Rand!"

"Sssh!"

He moved lower, kissing her belly. Finding small lightning-shaped stretch marks, he kissed each one, filled with wonder that she had carried his child. Feeling infinitely cheated, he wished he could turn back the clock, touch her when she was rounded with his daughter. He had missed so much—Becca's birth, her first tooth, her first steps.

Holding her mother at night . . .

Elizabeth twisted restlessly, demanding more with her movements.

Rand moved further down, nipping the soft inside of her thighs, which spread wider at his touch.

"What are you—"

Her question ended on a sharp intake of breath as he found the hard bud of her desire and nibbled at it.

"Rand!" *This couldn't be decent. . . .*

The thought evaporated as soon as it formed. Need. Hunger. Heat. Coherent thought left her as she rose to a place where there was only sensation. Winding her fingers into his hair, she pressed his mouth against her center.

When he thrust his tongue into her moistness as he continued the assault on her nub with his fingers, Elizabeth unconsciously rocked in rhythm with his actions, needing more, ever more.

She was beyond anything but feeling these wonderful sensations Rand was creating. Some tiny part of her wanted to protest that he was taking nothing for himself. But the half thought was lost as sudden waves of pleasure and heat rocked her convulsively, whirling her away beyond the tiny cabin to where there were bright exploding stars.

When Elizabeth opened her eyes, she realized time had passed. Her head was cradled on Rand's arm as he lay beside her on the narrow cot, watching her.

"I must have slept." Memory of their intimacies flooded back and she felt shy.

"You must have." Rand smiled, a lazy, self-satisfied smile, and she couldn't help grinning in return.

Rain still drummed on the roof of the cabin, perhaps not as hard as it had. The cabin's single window showed the gray outside deepening.

Elizabeth became aware that his male member was still aroused, pressing against her thigh.

"You didn't. . . ." She blushed. "You know."

His dark gaze was warm, touching her heart. "This time was for you."

"Oh." She wondered then if there was to be more, but felt awkward and afraid to ask.

"You didn't experience those feelings the first time we made love," he said. Leaning over, he kissed her forehead.

"No."

"It was your first time. It was all too new." He sighed. "I thought about that and regretted it, because it felt like I cheated you. I'm sorry to say, it was my only regret, other than leaving you."

Elizabeth said, "It was beautiful. I treasured the memory. I just didn't know there's so much . . . more."

"Now, you do." Grinning, he traced her bruised lips with the tip of his finger.

She caught the tip of his finger in her mouth and sucked on it, and he stilled, his eyelids half closed. Realizing he found it erotic, she exaggerated the action.

Rand pulled it free of her mouth. "Minx," he said hoarsely.

"Why does that excite you?" she asked innocently.

"Because it's evocative of . . . other things. Now be still." He tried to gather her close and hold her still, but this was all too interesting and exciting.

She wriggled free, propping up on one elbow. "What other things? Like you did to me? Only my doing it to you?"

Memory of his mouth on her most secret places rekindled fires low in her belly. Squirming slightly, she realized to her surprise that she wanted him again.

Rand was not spent. The evidence was pressed sweetly against her thigh. There was no reason they couldn't make love again.

She wriggled against his erection. "Rand—"

"Elizabeth, go back to sleep," he ordered sternly, trying to bring her head back down to his shoulder.

"Why?" She grasped his hard male member and made a tentative stroke, finding it felt like velvet slipping over warm steel. "We need to make love again. This time for you."

"No." His hand covered hers. She thought he would remove her hand, but looking sweetly tortured, he showed her how to stroke him. Once. Then again. Then, shaking his head, he stopped her. "No."

"Why not?"

"I won't spill my seed inside you again until we are married. I won't take the chance of another child—"

Elizabeth stroked him despite his restraining hand. The moan deep in his throat made her feel she had power she'd never suspected.

"Elizabeth!"

It was a plea, but whether he was begging her to stop or to continue, she had no idea. And she was enjoying herself too much to stop.

After pushing him flat on his back, and half off the narrow cot, she sat astride his thighs, admiring how wide his shoulders were, and the way his torso tapered into a narrow waist and slim hips. From a shock of black hair at the apex of his thighs, his shaft curved back, almost to his navel.

She stroked the length of it with the tip of her finger, and it jumped.

Shocked, she jumped in response. Then grinned at him. "You're still ready. You haven't found release." She touched him again, and he leapt in her hand again. She gloried in her power over his desire.

"Careful. You'll get bitten." Rand's voice was a hoarse rasp. His hands trembled as they circled her waist.

"I already have," she replied huskily, and bent to take him into her mouth, instinctively bringing him to the same pleasure he'd shown her.

Chapter Eighteen

''We never did have our tea.'' Elizabeth sighed, huddling under her slicker. It might have braced them against this damp.

Glancing at her from beneath the dripping brim of his hat, Rand grinned. ''Must have gotten preoccupied.'' He snapped the reins and the mare pulled the buggy through the overgrown trail.

''Must have,'' Elizabeth agreed.

Feeling her cheeks warm as she remembered just how, she turned away from his knowing gaze and looked out at the forest. Ferns and undergrowth were heavy between the towering fir trees. Rand had explained that the west side of the mountain got more rain more often. Growth was verdant here.

The downpour had ceased, but the skies hadn't cleared completely. A wind swirling out of the valley blew rainy mist against her face, cooling her blush as she remembered the glorious afternoon they'd shared.

When they had made love when Becca was conceived, it had been wonderful. It had never occurred to her to think there could be more.

There was. So much more! Making love this time with Rand

had been magical—there was no other word to describe it. He took her to places inside herself she had no idea existed.

No wonder young girls were kept ignorant until marriage, she thought in wonder. If women knew the joys that awaited them, there'd be more children without names than legitimate children.

"Better hold on," Rand warned. The cabin sat on the shoulder of the mountain. The trek down looked even more treacherous than it had going up it.

Once again, Elizabeth clutched her umbrella with one hand, the buggy arm with the other, trying to remain upright on the hard wooden seat. Rand placed his arm across her, holding her, making her feel secure.

Seeming to sense she was headed home, the mare wanted to rush down the steep trail, and Rand had to keep holding back on the reins He had assured Elizabeth that they should make it back to town before dark, unless other areas along the road were washed out, or under severe flooding, and they had to make detours.

It would have been safer if they could have waited until morning, giving the rain that had fallen a chance to run off. They could have spent the night loving and cuddling as the rain drummed on the roof, and Elizabeth wouldn't have minded a bit.

But the need to get back to her daughter drove her to dress and insist they leave. She'd never been separated from Becca overnight.

Their daughter, she amended, a warmth growing inside her at the thought. At last they could be the family they always should have been.

Becca would easily accept Rand in the role of father—she seemed to have a natural affinity for him. As if her little heart had always recognized the truth.

Now, he'd have the chance to claim her as his own.

Thinking of the family they were forming, Elizabeth smiled, filled with happiness. Never could she remember being more content.

Oh, it was going to be a little awkward, breaking the news

to Hiram and Maggie Jean, especially after Maggie Jean had been so wonderfully accepting of them. But Elizabeth knew Hiram would understand. Hers and Hiram's arrangement had never involved the heart. And she'd be getting her part of the money from the sale of the farm. She'd always had it in the back of her mind to use it to repay Hiram if their arrangement didn't work out.

Everything was going to be all right.

As the buggy brought them back to within sight of the main road, just another turn or two through the trees, Rand looked at her. "Penny for your thoughts?"

Blushing slightly, Elizabeth realized he must have been watching her for some time.

"You aren't regretting your decision, are you?"

The tone was joking, but there was a serious light in his eyes.

"Actually, now that I've said I would marry you—"

"You asked *me,* remember?"

"Now that I've asked *you,*" she said with a smile, "I was wondering why it's been so hard to make the choice. It feels so right, the only choice really."

"You didn't trust me to be here for you." It was a statement, not a question.

She wanted to argue, but Elizabeth knew he was right. Mostly. "It could have been partly anger," she confessed. "When you—when I thought you were dead, I hurt so much. I grieved for you, for us, for the unfairness. Then to find out you were alive and I had suffered that hurt for no reason. And that you'd never even tried to come back to me. As if you hadn't really cared . . ."

"I'm sorry, Elizabeth. I cared. Too much to come back." He was amazed she had felt so deeply for him. "I can never make that up to you. But I promise you, I'll be here. I won't go away ever again." He grinned. "Not willingly anyway."

The truth of his promise was in his eyes. "I believe you," she said, surprised that it was the truth.

Suddenly, the buggy sank, stopping stock-still, mired. Rand hadn't been paying close attention to the trail. Now he cursed under his breath as he looked over the side and saw they had rolled into an old stump hole. The leaf litter floated on muddy water, making the spot look level. The horse had skirted it as she turned a sharp curve, but the buggy wheels were now sunk up to the hubs.

"Come on, girl. Get up, now!" Rand slapped the reins against the mare's rump. The horse strained and the buggy rocked, but couldn't roll free.

"I'll have to get out. Stay here."

The brim of his hat pulled low to protect his face from the fine mist, Rand thrust the reins toward Elizabeth. Juggling her umbrella, she took them as he stepped down onto the steps, then jumped to firm ground.

Going to the horse's head, Rand caught the mare's bridle and encouraged it to pull, but the normally well-behaved carriage mare refused. Tossing her head in agitation, the mare nickered.

And an answering nicker came from the forest.

Rand's attention snapped to the woodland road ahead, then the surrounding forest.

Looking around, Elizabeth felt someone watching, though all was quiet to her except for the steady drip of water off the surrounding foliage from the earlier rain.

The mare turned her head, ears swiveling forward. After a moment, she nickered again, and again the other horse answered. This time much closer.

There was a snap of deadfall and a subdued rustling in the wet bracken as whoever it was moved closer. Then all was quiet for a few moments more. Elizabeth felt every nerve in her body tense.

"Come out if you're friendly," Rand called, his slicker hiked up and the hollow of his palm resting on the bone handle of his Colt.

"*Eh?* Question is, I'm a thinkin', is you friendly?" a crackly voice called from the woods.

After a moment's pause, Rand said, "You'll have to come out and see if I am or not." He slowly raised the hem of his poncho-like slicker and draped it back over his shoulder, showing the sheriff's star on his chest.

And with the slicker out of the way, his gun could be drawn more easily, Elizabeth realized.

Slowly, two riders appeared from out of the underbrush, an old man on a startlingly white mule and a teenaged boy on a shovel-footed Appaloosa. Drawing his mule to a halt, the old man spat a stream of tobacco juice on the trunk of a giant fir, miraculously without getting any on the snowy beard that rolled over his chin like a cloud climbing over the shoulder of a mountain.

''Well, iff'n you ain't friendly, at least make it a clean shot with that thar big iron yo're totin'. Better to have one betwix the eyeballs than get shot in the gut.''

As he recognized the man, Rand tightened his grip on the gun.

The man's bright blue eyes lit suddenly. ''Well, I'll be damned! If it ain't Dalton McClure, ya can shit in my hat and I'll war it right on!''

Cold washed through her as Elizabeth looked from the man with the white beard to Rand, who stood perfectly still.

She'd known this would happen! She just wished she wouldn't have been so stubborn and mistrustful—she could have agreed to marry Rand sooner and they could have been safe in Canada by now.

The two men eyed each other. Time slowed. Each drip off the edge of her umbrella seemed to take minutes to hit the dashboard of the buggy. There seemed to be an hour between each painful beat of her heart. Even the forest around them had quieted. No birdcalls, no squirrels chattering, no animal sounds. Only the moisture dripping from the leaves to break the silence.

Then Rand visibly relaxed and gave a slight shake of his head. ''Sorry. You've got the wrong man.''

''Wrong man, eh?'' The blue eyes growing sharp, the man scratched his white whiskers and spat again. ''Well, I ain't see-nile yet. I know yo're s'pose to be dead, but yo're sure enough Dalton McClure, or his twin brother!''

The statement hung in the air, firm. He wasn't to be swayed into thinking he was mistaken.

"*Yes!*" The one word exploded from Elizabeth, surprising her that she'd said it.

The man looked at her as if remembering her presence, and snatched his hat from his head. "Afternoon, ma'am." Leaning in his saddle, he then used the headgear to swat the gangly youth on the Appaloosa, who was staring at her with mouth agape.

The boy shot the old man a startled look, then snatched off his own battered hat and nodded. "Ma'am."

His voice crackled, making three notes of the single syllable. Red color rushed across his freckled face, and an already prominent Adam's apple worked up and down.

Glancing at Rand, Elizabeth found him staring at her perplexed.

Drawing in a deep breath, she squared her shoulders. "The *sheriff* here is Dalton McClure's exact twin. Exact! As alike as two peas in a pod. Only, well, you know Dalton ended up on the other side of the law from Rand here. It's sad"—she shook her head—"but even out here, people are always mistaking poor Rand for that Kansas outlaw. Who *is* dead, by the way—has been in his grave for some time, I believe."

Realizing how hard she gripped the umbrella, Elizabeth loosened her hold and gave the pair of newcomers what she hoped was a smile.

"Exact . . . twin." Rand's brows rose as he looked at her in disbelief, sardonic amusement lighting his eyes. Elizabeth wanted to kick him.

"Well, sir, I'll be damned. Yo're shore that!" The old man jammed his hat back on his head, eyeing Rand critically. "His ex-*act* twin! I'd not believe it, but I had a pair of cousins like that. Couldn't tell one from t'other, 'cept one growed up mean. Always frownin'. That's how I knowed Joe from John.

"But yo're just like Dalton—and I knowed him good, too. He was a *con-struction* engineer, or some'ot like that. We was buildin' a railroad in Kansas, and I was cookin' for the camp.

We talked when he come into the cook tent to warm hisself and get a cup of coffee, and that was often.''

The old man shook his head. ''Damn coldest weather I ever passed in my seventy year—beggin' pardon, ma'am.'' He gave Elizabeth an apologetic nod for his language. ''Lost a toe to frostbite that winter. Which is how come I got my name—*Nine-Toed Bill* at yore service. This 'ere is my grandson, Buck.'' Pausing, he worried his plug around and shot the tree trunk again with amazing accuracy, splattering the same spot on the bark.

''I'm right please ta meet ya, ma'am. Sheriff.'' Buck bobbed his head up and down, matching the undulations of his voice.

The old man believed her?

Under the concealing slicker, Elizabeth put her gloved hand to her heart. It was still thumping hard, but beating with a little less uncertainty than it had before.

Becoming aware that the man and boy were watching her, she nodded to the pair and tried to smile. ''Pleased to meet you, Mr. Nine-Toed Bill. Buck.''

Rand touched the flat brim of his hat, not knowing whether to laugh at Elizabeth's ploy, or curse because he really hadn't expected to meet up with anyone he knew so well, other than Skinner.

''I'm Rand Matthews—sheriff in Willow. This is Mrs. McKay. She is a nurse. Been visiting some folks down with fever, just north of here.''

''The typhoid, I take it.'' The old man's action with the plug grew more agitated. ''That's why we're leavin' the railroad camp. Sent three near dead back to Eugene. But four more are down with it. A half dozen more sick enough to drop in their tracks, but that whoreson Skinner—beg pardon, ma'am—is workin' 'em anyway, threatenin' to withhold their wages rightfully earned iff'n they don't work. All he cares about is gettin' the track laid on schedule.'' He spat eloquently.

As if to emphasize his words, three dynamite blasts sounded in the distance, then the *tink! tink! tink!* of pickaxes hitting rock began again.

Skinner. Elizabeth looked sharply at Rand. He thought he

could trust Skinner. A man who would force sick men to work didn't sound trustworthy to her.

Nine-Toed Bill went on. "I cooked at 'is camps an' other Union Pee-cific camps, too, fer a long time. Even before Buck joined me, when my ole fingers got the rhuemeetism and I couldn't peel taters so good no more. I tol' Skinner to take our back pay and stick it in his narrowest crack—beg pardon, ma'am. Can't spend no money when yo're dead, and when the fever gets a grip like 'at, 'at's all those what stay are like to get."

He paused, and the old man's blue eyes narrowed. "Eh, did you say yo're named Matthews? I thought you said yo're Dalton McClure's twin brother?"

"Matthews was my mother's name." Rand turned away and smoothed out a kink in the mare's reins. "Changed it when my brother Dalton was on the run." He shot the older man a wry look. "If you looked just like a man with a bounty on his head, would *you* keep the same last name?"

"No, I don't think I would." White whiskers quivered as the old man chuckled. Then he shook his head as if suddenly sad. "Weren't fair, what happened to yore brother, ya know. Waren't fair a'tall. Him and me, we talked some, like I said. He was a right fine man. I never could see him doin' what those folks in Kansas said he done."

Rand nodded. "That's what I thought, but now that my brother is dead, it doesn't matter much."

The man spat again. "Dalton McClure waren't the type to shoot that farmer over makin' his stand ag'in the railroad takin' over his land. In the first place, Dalton didn't care overmuch iffin the track got laid on schedule. He would a just waited, patient-like, for the law to work things out. There waren't a doubt the railroad would win.

"But that Skinner was the one shittin' on one foot and stompin' it off with the other about losin' his bonus money because of that sodbuster—oh, beg pardon again, ma'am." The old man flushed. "I ain't been around decent folks enough to remember my manners anymore. But be 'at as it may, if ya wus ta ask me, I'd say Skinner shot the old farmer so he could get on with layin' his precious goddamn tracks."

"Bonus money?" Elizabeth prodded, more interested in what Nine-Toed Bill meant than in his language.

"As straw boss, Skinner allus gets so much a day fer ever' day he gets a rail line finished up under schedule. Sometimes, the bastard gets as much as twenty dollars a day. An' he's right fit to be tied over this fever right now, puttin' the work so far behind."

"We were on our way out to the camp to assess the situation and see what help was needed when rising water cut us off and we had to take shelter," Elizabeth said. "Medicine should be available tomorrow."

"I know those poor wretches w'ots sufferin' will bless you for it, ma'am, if you could give 'em some relief." Bill nodded. "Skinner could have sent for medicine or a doctor, but he's afeared of a quarantine stoppin' the work, I reckon."

"I'd like to get Mrs. McKay back to Willow before dark catches us in these hills," Rand said. Taking hold of the mare's bridle, he looked at the youth. "Mind lending a hand, Buck, and giving a push while I pull?"

"Sure, Sheriff."

The young man scrambled down from his mount. Glancing at Elizabeth, then down, then back at Elizabeth, he made his way to the rear of the buggy. Leaning over the wide mud hole, he pushed against the tailboard as Rand pulled and the mare strained.

"Thar it goes!" Buck windmilled his arms to keep from falling into the mud hole as the buggy moved, the wheels making a loud sucking noise as they pulled free.

"Ho!" Rand stopped the horse after the buggy was out, and patted her flank as he strode back to the seat.

Elizabeth smiled. "Thank you, Buck."

Red flooded between the boy's freckles again. "Yes, ma'am. You're welcome, I'm shore." Eyes focused on his boots, he hurried back to his horse. His grandfather handed back his reins.

"Much obliged for the help." Rand nodded, climbing back

on the buggy. "I don't have any authority anywhere but Willow, but I ask that you stay clear of any towns for a couple of weeks. Until you know for certain you don't have the fever."

Bill nodded. "I wouldn't want to bring the misery to decent folk, iff'n we do 'ave it."

Pointing at the trail they'd just come down, Rand said, "If you go up the shoulder of the mountain about a quarter mile, you'll find a cabin you can stay in for a while. No one will bother you and game is plentiful. Someone will check on you in a few days, to see if you're sick and need medicine."

"Much obliged, Sheriff," the old man said, nodding. "Very much obliged. Iff'n one of us do get sick, we'll need a snug place to hole up."

He touched his hat and put his heels to his mule's flanks, riding up the trail that Elizabeth and Rand had just come down.

"Ma'am." Nodding and blushing, Buck kicked the Appaloosa's flanks and followed at a trot.

Looking pensive, Rand slapped the reins and the buggy started forward again.

Barely waiting until Buck and his grandfather were out of sight, Elizabeth clutched Rand's wrist. "I was so frightened when I realized he knew you."

"I know. You handled it well." He touched her cheek lightly with his gloved hand. "Making me my own twin." Rand chuckled. He doubted Bill had truly believed her. The old man was no one's fool. But he'd been willing enough to go along with the farce. That seemed to say that he felt Rand's business didn't concern him.

Rand sobered. "Things must be bad at the railroad camp for Bill to leave. As soon as I get you safely back to town, I'll go out there. On my horse, I should be able to get through or go around high water, just as old Bill and his grandson did."

"You'll do *what?*" With a chill washing through her, Elizabeth stared at him in disbelief.

"I'll go out to the camp." Rand frowned, noticing how distraught she was. "What's wrong?"

"Don't go. Bill just said what kind of man Skinner is. If

you go, it will be a mistake. And it's not even your jurisdiction. You have no authority. There's no reason to risk yourself!"

"There are sick men who need help. I can't just abandon them—particularly if what Bill said is true." Having known Bill, Rand was inclined to doubt it. The old man had been fond of exaggeration. "If Hiram has made it back from Eugene with the medicines, I can bring them out there when I go."

Twisting her gloved fingers together, Elizabeth wondered what she could do to dissuade him. And realized there was nothing. Because he was the man he was, he would do what he saw as his duty to others. Even when it wasn't his responsibility. Even if someone else could do it.

But after he'd delivered the medicine and given the sick men some basic advice, there would be little else Rand could do. Nursing was better left to women, and Lois was supposed to try to recruit some women from town to help out.

"If you're set on going, go. I understand." She sighed.

"You'd do the same thing, Elizabeth."

"I suppose I would. If Hiram's back with the medicines, I'll get mine and Becca's things packed, while you take the medicines out to that camp. When you get back, we can head for the Canadian border and get married somewhere along the way."

"You want me to leave Willow?"

At his look of disbelief, Elizabeth was taken aback. "I thought it was settled."

As he continued to stare at her, she said, "That's why I asked you to marry me. To take Becca and me away. My heart tells me if you go out to that camp, and we delay in leaving Willow, then you'll end up being hanged."

Didn't he understand? She had mourned for him once. She couldn't bear to mourn for him again.

Shaking his head, Rand said softly, "I never told you I would leave town."

Chapter Nineteen

Elizabeth glared at him. ''What do you mean you're *not* leaving?''

He couldn't be serious. Not after what they'd shared. The loving. The closeness. He wouldn't toss it all away, would he?

''I'm not leaving.''

Elizabeth stared at him, feeling a stone form where her heart had beat so happily just moments before.

Not looking at her, Rand clicked his tongue and jiggled the reins. The horse picked up its pace, as if it knew it was headed for its warm dry barn and a feeding of oats and hay.

''You said you'd marry me.'' With an effort, she kept her voice low and even. ''That's why I *asked* you. So you would leave with me and Becca and we could be a family. We could be safe. Not so you could go around that railroad camp, around people that know you're a wanted man, then just wait for a federal marshal to come and haul you away.''

Rand sighed, but stared straight ahead. After what seemed an eternity, he said, ''I didn't promise you I'd run. But that I will marry you.'' He looked at her and asked, ''You care that much?''

In answer, Elizabeth balled up her fist and hit his arm. After the afternoon they'd just spent together, how could he ask that?

"No, damn you." She blinked back tears anyway. Angry tears.

"I never said I'll leave Willow." Looking at her, Rand went on softly. "I meant that I'd provide that stable home for Becca you came here to find. Right here."

"If you stay after you go around people who know your past, you can't build anything. Listen to me, Rand. We *can* build our lives together, but somewhere else. Canada. Mexico—anywhere you want. If you stay on the course you've set, you won't have a life."

Her voice broke on the last. She knew in her gut it was true. If he stayed in town, she'd lose him. Again.

And this time forever.

"I told you I wouldn't run away again. I gave you my solemn word. But I didn't only mean I would never leave you. I meant I wouldn't run at all. This has stayed unfinished for far too long. For five years, I haven't had a life. I've just been eating and sleeping and breathing. But not living.

"Now that I've found you again, I want to be free of it, so it can't come back to haunt us. Elizabeth, if we run, I know I'd never feel free again."

She glared at him. "And if they hang you? How much life will you have?"

Rand's face was set in determined lines. "I have a duty to the town to try and stop this fever from becoming epidemic. A duty to friends like Doc and Mabel. I'll stay and fight this thing."

Tears drowned her anger. She swiped them away, refusing to let them fall. "Then I can't marry you. I can't lose you again."

Silence stretched between them, broken only by the forest sounds and the squeak of the buggy springs and the clip-clop of the horse's hoofs. Rand wanted to ask what strange logic made her believe she couldn't lose him if she *didn't* marry him. But he wisely said nothing.

Later, when she had had time to think about it, she would

realize he was staying because he wanted them to have a real life, not the uncertainty he'd lived with for the last five years.

"Look," he said, "I may have been right in the first place—nothing may come of it because no one cares anymore. As you pointed out to Bill, the reward has been collected."

Skinner was still the man who had helped him escape. If the straw boss was the only one left at the railroad camp that knew him, Rand felt he could trust Skinner.

And Rand didn't think Old Bill would cause him any trouble either—even though he doubted the older man had really believed Elizabeth's story.

Regardless, Rand knew he couldn't run again. Not when the town faced a crisis. And not for his own peace of mind. When Elizabeth had time to consider why he was staying, she'd realize he was right.

Turning away, Elizabeth silently gazed at the ferns and brush at the side of the road, seeing little. Just a short while ago she'd been so happy, so certain that marrying Rand was the right thing, for her and Becca.

How could she have been so wrong?

"If I let Becca get attached to you, then . . . I won't let you break her heart. But she needs a home and I can't stay with Mabel and Doc forever. If you won't leave with us, I'm going to marry Hiram, like I came here to do."

"You aren't serious." The words were quietly spoken, but emotion vibrated through them.

Raising her chin, she declared, "I am. I have to put Becca first."

She felt Rand's gaze, but continued to stare at the forest. If she saw the pain her words caused, she could never keep her resolve.

Hearing his sigh, she thought she might have changed his mind. She hoped she had. She didn't want to lose him. Not again. How could she bear it?

Holding her breath, she prayed he'd say he would leave with her in the morning.

"If you can marry Hiram after what we shared this afternoon, you aren't the woman I thought you were, Elizabeth.'' His words fell between them like a blade.

Letting her breath out slowly, Elizabeth stared at the forest.

''Mama, Mama!'' Running across the porch, Becca threw her arms around Elizabeth's legs, nearly knocking her back down the steps.

Dropping her damp oilskin slicker, she scooped up her daughter and gave her a tight hug. At least she still had Becca. And no matter what Rand thought of her, Elizabeth told herself, she had to think of Becca first. The little girl's heart would not be broken.

Little arms twined around Elizabeth's neck as Becca hugged her back. The hug salved Elizabeth's bruised heart.

As long as she had her daughter's love, she could survive anything.

She had before.

Standing in the open door, Mabel said, ''Becca's been anxious about you all afternoon.''

''Mama, you were *gone* when I woke up!'' Her gaze was accusing. ''I missed you!''

''I missed you, too, pun'kin.''

Becca leaned back in her arms and studied her mother critically. ''You were helping sick people?''

''Yes, I was. A mother and her little boy—he's just a little older than you.''

''Why are your eyes and nose red? Were you crying because the little boy is sick?'' Becca asked, her mouth turning down at the corners.

''No. I think the little boy will get well. And his mother will, too. It's just the cold and damp making my nose run.'' Caught completely off guard, she gave the only explanation for her appearance Elizabeth could think of. She certainly couldn't tell her daughter the truth.

Rand might have let her know how she looked before he took Doc's horse and buggy around to the barn, she thought in irritation.

But Rand hadn't said anything to her after his last hurtful statement.

Balancing Becca's weight on her hip, Elizabeth busied herself picking up the slicker and blinking back tears. She had hoped just saying she would still marry Hiram if Rand didn't leave with her and Becca would make the stubborn fool reconsider what he planned to do.

What made her cry was knowing that she had little choice but to go through with the arranged wedding. Thank goodness, Hiram didn't expect more than a business arrangement.

"You must be chilled through," Mabel said, frowning in concern. "Come on inside and we'll get something warm into you, Elizabeth." She ushered her into the hall. "I guess Rand will be tending to the horse? We'll fix him some hot chocolate, too."

"Hot chocolate?" Becca's dark eyes rounded in anticipation. *"Mmmm!"*

"Yes, hot chocolate. I don't suppose you'd like any, would you, Becca?" Mabel asked the child, her lips pursed doubtfully.

"Yes, ma'am, please!" Becca nodded vigorously, her dark curls bouncing.

Hanging the slicker on the hall tree inside the door, Elizabeth said, "After Rand talks with Doc, he's going back out to the railroad camp. We couldn't go after we . . . finished at the Cavanaughs. I've never seen rain fall that hard. There was flooding. I was afraid we'd be swept away trying to cross a small creek. We had to wait for it to quit before we could get back to town." She added, as she followed Mabel into the warm kitchen, "It doesn't look like it rained that much here, though."

"It didn't. Your clothes you'd put on the line this morning had time to dry before it started. Then it was just a light mist, though it has stayed with us for the rest of the day. Weather up on the mountains is often quite different, I understand." Mabel frowned as she took a tin of chocolate down from the cupboard. "I hope Hiram and Lois haven't run into any storms on their way to the lumber camp."

"Hiram and Lois?" After letting her daughter slide down,

Elizabeth took off her bonnet and touched her hair, wondering what it looked like. There'd been no mirrors in the old trapper's cabin that she could check after she pinned it back up into a bun.

Becca climbed up on the bench by the table and rested her chin in her hands, assuming an attitude of patient expectation.

Mabel pried the lid of the tin with a spoon handle. ''Hiram got back from Eugene about two this afternoon—he said since it was a good wide road from the stage using it and all, and since there was some moonlight, he decided to leave last night after we all talked over the situation. He was worried about Jacob's son, and wanted to get the medicine to him as soon as possible.

''Lois was here when he got back. She had come to see you, I think, to talk with you about some ladies who have volunteered to help out if need be. Anyway, she went with Hiram to the lumber camp, in case the boy has worsened and needs someone to tend him.''

''I'm glad she was here to go with Hiram.'' As Elizabeth set the heavy pot Mabel used to heat milk onto the stove, there was a brief knock on the back door. Rand entered at Mabel's invitation.

He nodded to Mabel, then set the carpetbag Elizabeth used for supplies down beside the door. ''You left this in the buggy,'' he told her. He was no longer wearing his damp hat and slicker. Elizabeth decided he must have left them outside on the porch.

''Thank you for bringing it in for me. I saw Becca waiting on the porch and I guess I forgot to get it out.'' Lifting her chin, determined not to let him know she was hurting, Elizabeth added, ''Hiram got back with the quinine and paregoric. He's taking some out to the lumber camp now.''

''That's good.''

''Mr. Rand, don't you want to say hello to me?'' Turning completely around on the bench, Becca looked askance at his having ignored her, her lower lip thrust out.

''Hello, tadpole.'' Rand smiled.

The look on Rand's face—the pain behind his smile—tore at Elizabeth's heart.

Becca held her arms wide, expectantly. Taking one long stride, he scooped the little girl up, and she hugged him just as exuberantly as she had Elizabeth.

Then pushing back in his arms and studying him, just as she'd done her mother before him, Becca said, ''Your eyes are red.''

Elizabeth's gaze flew to his face. His eyes were red. She busied herself ladling milk from a large crockery pitcher into a smaller one that was easier to handle, willing her hands not to shake.

Raising his brows, Rand said, ''I guess that's because it's cold and wet out.''

''That's what Mama said, too, when I asked her why her eyes were red.''

In the sudden quiet in the kitchen, Rand sensed Mabel's curious glance from him to Elizabeth, but he didn't look at either woman. He hugged his daughter again before he set her on her feet. He held onto her small hand a few seconds longer. ''I'd better go talk to Doc, tadpole, then be on my way.''

''I *never* get to talk to you for long.'' Becca sighed, and took her doll from her pocket. ''Miss Annie wants to talk to you, too—I decided to name her Miss Annie, just like my first doll.''

''A very nice name.'' His heart twisting as he reached out and stroked the doll's yarn hair, Rand wondered if he was being a fool not to take Elizabeth and Becca and just leave. He'd have his daughter.

Straightening, he said, ''I have to go, tadpole.''

''Isn't it too dangerous to go to the railroad camp?'' Elizabeth suddenly said. ''I mean, those roads were hard to pass over in daylight.'' She hadn't meant to protest, but she could help making one last plea.

If he went, everything would fall apart. She just knew it.

''I'll be okay on my horse. I can ride around flooding, cutting through the forest, where we couldn't pass today with the buggy.''

''You're not going anywhere,'' said Mabel firmly. She had shaved slivers off the block of chocolate into the pot. Elizabeth slowly added milk as Mabel stirred. "Not until you've had something warm to drink and a hearty supper."

One gray brow cocked, she looked at him, daring him to disagree. "I have some biscuits, black-eyed peas, and ham hocks left over from dinner. Now go on and talk to Jonas. Some supper and hot chocolate will be waiting for you when you get back."

Rand smiled. "How could I pass up that invitation and settle for a hunk of cold jerky on the trail?"

"You're staying?" Becca looked up hopefully.

"Just for a bit. I have to talk to Doc right now." Rand tousled her curls.

"He's in his bedroom with his bad leg on a chair, reading a book without pictures." Becca made a face, indicating what she thought of such books.

Mabel said, "Wore himself out seeing patients all morning. The old coot, I told him not to overdo. He's fractious at not being in the thick of things, going out and about with you. I think his leg hurting—as is normal—is probably the only thing keeping him inside." She shook her head.

"Come on, I'll show you where," Becca said. "Sometimes I go and tell him stories, so he won't be bored." Becca caught Rand's index finger and pulled him out of the kitchen.

"Don't stay long, young lady. This hot chocolate is almost ready," Mabel called as the two disappeared into the hall.

Then holding up the wooden spoon to Elizabeth, Mabel said, "Taste it and see if we've added enough sugar."

Obeying, Elizabeth nodded. "It's fine."

As Elizabeth was turning to put the spoon into the dish pan, Mabel commented, "It's amazing how alike those two look. Becca and Rand, I mean."

Elizabeth felt the whole world still for a heartbeat. She swallowed and asked brightly, "What do you want to serve this in? The teapot you used before when we had hot chocolate?"

Keeping her gaze fixed on the shelves where Mabel stored her dishes, Elizabeth tried to breathe deeply and slowly, trying to calm her nerves.

"That'll be fine, dear," Mabel said.

Elizabeth got the teapot down from the high shelf, and the lid rattled as her hand shook. She caught it and held it with her other hand. "Becca looks like her father," Elizabeth said simply. Unwilling to lie to this woman who'd been a good friend. But not daring to tell the truth. "Do you want to serve this in here, or bring it into the parlor?"

"Fire in the hole!"

Holding his hat, the blaster slid down the side of the boulder, which sat square in the path of the track. He ran like the dogs of Hell were after him and dove behind the bole of a giant fir.

Men all around the area crouched behind whatever cover was handy, heads ducked down, fingers in their ears.

Watching from a distance, Rand unwrapped his arm from around his horse's neck and patted it on the nose. "Good boy. Easy now."

A second later an explosion shocked the night. Great prongs of fire rose and raked at the dark sky; then a rain of rock chips and dust pelted the area. After the blast, men moved on to the next obstacle in the projected path of the tracks, to lay more explosives.

Taking the reins, Rand walked his horse into the camp, such as it was. It was spread out in a haphazard manner. One long tent stood out in the pale moonlight. There were a couple of chuck wagons with tin plates and cups on the tailboards. A few smaller tents were scattered about the perimeter.

An iron pot on a low fire and coffeepots near enough to keep the coffee warm showed that someone had taken over the cooking chores after Buck and Nine-Toed Bill had left. The aroma of beans mixed unpleasantly with the faint scent of human refuse.

Rand guessed there was an open latrine nearby. No wonder typhoid was spreading through the workers.

Flames from a half-dozen other fires could be seen round the camp. A few men sat quietly hunched around them, or stretched out in bedrolls near the flames. From inside the long tent, there came an occasional moan or curse. A lantern or two inside it cast eerie shadows against the canvas walls.

Rand tied his horse to an alder limb and decided the small tent in the middle of the compound was the one he wanted. It was the only one with a stovepipe sticking out the side, and that meant it was Skinner's.

As he started to enter it, a voice said behind him, "Hold there, stranger."

The distinctive click of a cock being thumbed back sounded, reinforcing the order.

"I'm holding." Lifting his hands slowly, Rand said, "I'm sheriff in Willow, here on business."

His pistol was plucked from his holster. "Turn around," the man said. "Slow."

Keeping his hands up, Rand obeyed. He found a short man dressed in tall black boots and a plaid coat that would have been more appropriate for a gambling saloon in Portland.

"Well, I'll be damned." Skinner looked Rand up and down, disbelief on his long face.

"*Sooner* rather than later, if you don't lower that gun," Rand said easily.

Skinner grinned and did as Rand asked, giving back Rand's gun. "Can't be too careful out here. But you know how it is. Damn, but it's good to see you, Dalton. It's been a while. How you been? And what the hell you doing wearing a badge?"

"Name's Rand Matthews. Like I said, I'm sheriff in Willow." Rand shook hands, meeting the other man's gaze steadily. He was all too aware of the interest the men around the fires were showing in their conversation. "I'm here on business. Mind if we talk inside?"

A myriad of emotions crossed Skinner's face in the dim light of the fires and the slender moon, before it settled into congenial lines. "Eh? Well, you just look like someone I used to know then. Come to think of it, I had heard that fellow died down in the Nations a few years ago. Must have been true."

Skinner went inside the tent and struck a match, lighting a lantern. Rand followed, pausing just inside the door. "I know the fellow you're talking about. He did die." Studying Skinner, assessing whether it was surprise or fear on his features, Rand paused for a moment.

"Now that I've got a good look at your face, you do remind me of someone I used to know," Rand went on. "Last I saw of the fellow, he was lighting a dynamite fuse by a jailhouse wall. He used a cigar stub just like the one in your jaw."

Skinner grinned, took the unlit stub out, and thumped it out the open tent flap. "Funny how people can look alike, ain't it? Never blowed a jail. Name's Skinner, by the way. Lucas Skinner." Moving behind the desk, which took up most of the small space, Skinner gestured toward a chair. "Have a seat."

As Rand sat down, he guessed Skinner was speaking for the benefit of anyone listening in from outside the thin canvas walls. Rand nodded to show he understood. "I'm here because I heard you have fever in the camp."

"True. But just what business is that of Willow's sheriff?"

"I don't want it to spread into my town. I want to know how many are sick and how bad. And if the railroad is willing to cooperate, I just might be able to help you keep the workers you have left healthy."

Chapter Twenty

"Whoa!" Hiram pulled back on the reins, and the buckboard rolled to a stop in the center of the sprawling, muddy camp.

Seated between Hiram and Lois on the hard wooden seat, Elizabeth felt the smell of the place assailing her nostrils long before the wagon stopped. Potato peelings and other debris had been tossed on the ground near the cooking area, where it all was now rotting. Flies swarmed over the refuse.

Even more flies swarmed over a shallow ditch they'd passed about a hundred yards back. From the smell of the thing, it obviously served as an open latrine.

The ditch angled downhill toward the creek, and it was certain the rain the day before had washed raw refuse into the stream.

Looking around at the squalid conditions, Hiram shook his head. "Pigs is cleaner. No wonder there's sickness in camp."

"Yep," Lois agreed. She and Hiram had gotten back to town long after dark last night. They'd told Doc this morning they wouldn't have made it back at all because of flooding if they hadn't ridden horseback, instead of taking a wagon.

Rand halted his horse beside the buckboard. Shaking his head, he rested his forearms on the saddle horn. "Looks even worse in the daylight than it did last night. Smells just as bad, though."

The camp seemed almost deserted. A Chinese man with a long, thin gray beard tended a huge cooking pot suspended on a tripod. Obviously, Nine-Toed Bill's replacement. He looked up briefly, and went back to stirring the pot. The sound of steel hitting steel and men's voices rang out in the distance.

"Look." Lois pointed to a communal water bucket with a single dipper sitting on a stump near the center of compound. She shook her head. "It's a danged wonder they ain't all sick."

Daunted, Elizabeth nodded as she considered the work ahead. Rand had reported seven sick. More of the workers could come down with the fever at any time. Taking in the filth of the camp, she thought the wonder was any had escaped the fever. Or dysentery. Or cholera.

Hiram said, "Good thing we brought those sacks of lime to cover the latrine. That creek empties into the McKenzie. If we don't get it cleaned up, when the salmon starts, a lot of folks could get sick from eating bad fish."

"I hope it helps the stench, too." Lois wrinkled her nose.

"Oh, it will. We'll cover it up with dirt, too. That's why we brought the shovels."

Hiram was a good man, Elizabeth thought. He'd had no sleep at all the night before. Nevertheless, he'd appeared at Doc's at daybreak. Lois was there soon after, dressed in old clothes and obviously prepared to work.

Rand was an even better man than Hiram. He was risking everything to battle this outbreak. Even his life.

Elizabeth laced her gloved fingers together, wishing Rand would look at her, talk to her. Agree to leave with her. Or just leave. She couldn't bear it if he was arrested and hanged.

Elizabeth had no idea when Rand had made it back to town last night. And no one else knew what chances he was taking. Even though Elizabeth had begged him yesterday to take her and Becca and run, she admired his sense of duty and loved him all the more for it.

Unfortunately, that wouldn't keep him from being hanged. She loved him. How could she bear it if he was?

But even though she had admitted that she loved him, to herself if not to Rand, it made no difference at all in what course she had to take.

Elizabeth knew she would marry Hiram.

Pushing her disappointment in Rand aside, Elizabeth directed her attention to the problems at hand. How to disinfect this sprawling, filthy camp and keep the sick from infecting the healthy. After Rand had arrived at Doc Sedrick's this morning, they'd discussed the situation at the camp and decided they would use a buckboard to carry the lime and other supplies, though it was certain to be hard to drive it in.

Thankfully, even though there were a couple of deep ditches washed across the track, the buckboard had made it through.

Hiram hopped down from the buckboard, then caught Elizabeth around the waist and helped her down. As he set her on her feet, she noticed Rand watching, his expression showing his pain. Quickly, she stepped away from her fiancé, feeling she'd somehow been unfaithful to Rand.

When just the opposite was true, her conscience reminded her. How could she go on with the marriage and live with herself?

If Rand was determined to get himself hanged, how could she not do what she had to in order to provide for her daughter?

She had to think of Becca. She couldn't live on Doc and Mabel's charity forever.

If she only knew how Rand's meeting with Skinner had gone—was the man trustworthy as Rand thought? Did he count Rand an old friend?

She doubted it. The one time she'd met Skinner as she'd assisted Doctor Brown in cleaning an infected wound on Skinner's leg, the man's comments had either been bragging on himself, or bordering on rude.

The second Rand rode out of camp last night, Skinner had probably used the telegraph line that was strung along the tracks as the railroad was built to alert the authorities. The truth was, she'd half expected to see a federal marshal awaiting them when they arrived. Worrying over Rand, Elizabeth had gotten little sleep herself. For the second night in a row.

As Hiram helped Lois down, the hem of Lois's skirt became caught on the brake handle of the buckboard, showing a goodly portion of her long bloomers and stockings Casually, Hiram reached out and unhooked it, then smoothed the skirt down. Seeming to realize what he'd done, he and Lois looked at each other and both turned red.

"Sorry." Hiram gazed at the top of Lois's sunbonnet, then the toes of her shoes. "Emmaline's skirts were always getting caught like that, and it just seemed natural to unhang it, like I used to do for her. Only, I ort not to have done that for a female I'm not married to."

Lois blushed, gazing straight at his face. "I'm grateful, I'm sure. I didn't know it was hung and it could have got ripped."

"That's true, and you're welcome." He fervently focused on a fir tree behind her.

Dismounting, Rand said, "The sick men have been isolated in that biggest tent. At least, that's what I told Skinner should be done when I talked with him last night."

Elizabeth heard low groaning and other sounds of distress issuing from the tent he indicated. She guessed Skinner had listened to Rand's advice.

"Let's get the womenfolk's supplies unloaded." Hiram caught the mare's bridle and led the animal around so the buckboard was right beside the tent.

Following him, Elizabeth unbuttoned her coat and took it off, leaving it in the wagon bed. Then she pushed up her sleeves, ready to get to work.

Reaching in her carpetbag, she took out an extra apron. "Lois, I brought this for you. I made several large ones of heavy cotton to wear when I was working with the doctor in Kansas."

Lois took the white square from her and unfolded it. "Much obliged!" She smiled, rather resembling Hiram in that she didn't quite look Elizabeth in the eyes. Which Elizabeth found very unlike the usually straightforward Lois. "This will really be a help to protect my clothes."

After taking her own coat off, Lois slipped the strap for the bib over her head and tied the strings in back.

As Hiram and Rand unloaded their supply of scrub rags and carbolic soap, Rand said, "Doc is sending a bill to the Union Pacific for these things. There was no need for these men to suffer so badly. This man, Skinner, telegraphed for medicines and other supplies sent out on the supply train. One comes from Eugene and brings more rails almost every day. But the railroad refused to fill his request."

"Then he is a good man, like you said he was?" Elizabeth had to ask. If Skinner was trustworthy as Rand had thought, maybe talking with him wouldn't put a noose around Rand's neck.

"Don't worry about me." Rand shot Elizabeth a warning glance as he brushed by her.

"Eh? You know this Skinner?" Hiram asked.

Realizing her mistake, Elizabeth wanted to catch back the question about Skinner. But of course it was too late.

Rand said casually, "I'd met him before. I'll stake the horses out where they can graze, after I drop the lime sacks by the ditch where we're going to need them."

Hiram lifted the last of the women's nursing supplies from the buckboard, then a keg of fresh water. "This ain't going to go far. While you do that, Rand, I'll take some of the buckets we brought and look around for more clean water for the women."

Looking at Lois, Hiram added, "You ladies need help with anything first?"

"No. Clean water is the most important thing," Elizabeth assured him.

As Hiram trudged off carrying buckets, angling to intersect the creek upstream from the camp, Elizabeth checked the contents of her carpetbag. Paregoric and quinine, rice to boil for rice water. These seemed like pitiful weapons to fight such a horrendous disease.

Lois slipped her cloth sunbonnet off and let it dangle by the strings. Glancing up at the thinly overcast sky, she said, "Looks like the rain might hold off a spell. That's in our favor, at least."

"Yes." Drawing in a deep, steadying breath, Elizabeth lifted the tent flap a few inches. The stench of illness roiled out. Several men were inside on crude pallets. A couple lifted their heads and looked toward the light she let in. One moaned.

"Looks like we have our work cut out for us," she said softly, so only Lois could hear. Stepping inside, she clutched the carpetbag and pasted a bright smile on her face for the benefit of the sick men. "Hello. My name's Elizabeth, and this is my friend Lois. We've come to help those of you who are sick, if we can."

"Lord, this is hard," Lois said much later as she followed Elizabeth down the steeply inclining bank.

"It is rough country." Elizabeth dropped her buckets by a tree. Putting her hands on the small of her back, she bent backward to ease tired muscles.

They had administered quinine to the fevered, brought fresh water in pans so the men could bathe, or bathed those who were delirious with fever. They'd cleaned and washed and scrubbed where men had been sick, and they'd used all the water Hiram had brought earlier.

Rand and Hiram were busy digging a new latrine. Rather than interrupt them, Elizabeth and Lois decided to fetch what they needed themselves. They had needed the fresh air.

"I meant, tending those fellers." Lois stared at the rushing stream.

"I know." Elizabeth caught her hand and squeezed it. "There's so little we can do out here. No way we can make them comfortable. Even washing their clothes is difficult without a proper wash pot."

"I'm a-feared that beardy feller ain't going to make it. The young Chinese is in even worse shape." Sighing, Lois tossed a bucket into the stream and used a rope tied to the bail to haul it out. Then she filled the other bucket she'd brought, and started back up the path.

"You coming?" she called over her shoulder.

Elizabeth leaned against a young aspen. The stream tumbled over rocks worn smooth by the action, roaring as it rushed on.

"I'll be on in a bit. I just want to take a minute to gather my wits."

After Lois disappeared up the bank, Elizabeth drew in a deep breath of the clean mountain air, scented with decaying leaves and moss. It was a beautiful scene, with ferns growing lushly by the path. So beautiful, it was hard to go back and face the ugliness in the camp.

She'd done what she could for the young Chinese boy—who looked no older than Hiram's oldest. He was delirious and wouldn't drink. She knew in her heart there was nothing she could do to save him. Her efforts wouldn't make much difference. Catching the skirt of her apron, she wiped moisture from her cheeks.

Rand had been right. It would have been wrong to abandon these men, mostly Irish immigrants or Chinese. The poorest of the poor.

All the railroad bosses cared about was how much labor the men could provide. The sick had no one on their side, no one to care for them.

Elizabeth loved Rand more for his dedication to what he saw as his duty. That was why this risk he was taking hurt so badly.

Unable to help herself, she cried for the young boy, with no one to care if he lived or died, no family to comfort him. And for the other sick men, who were alone.

And for what Rand was risking to make a difference.

And because she couldn't marry Rand, when it would be her daughter at risk if she did.

After she felt she could cry no more, Elizabeth drew a deep breath and willed herself to have more control of her emotions. After hauling up a bucket of water from the stream, she washed her face, then used her apron to dry it.

Suddenly noticing how soiled her apron was, she shook her head at her carelessness, then washed her face again, wishing she had soap. But she'd brought none with her.

Fine curls had escaped her bun and tickled her cheeks. After taking the pins from her hair, she smoothed it with her hands, trying to put it up more neatly, but lost one pin when it fell into the leaf litter.

Inexplicably, the lost pin made her tears flow again. Sniffling, she knelt and brushed through the dead leaves, searching for it.

A breaking of twigs told her someone was coming down the path. "Elizabeth?" Rand called. "Lois said you were down here."

"I lost a hairpin " Elizabeth didn't look up. She didn't want Rand to see her crying.

He moved beside her and knelt down, raising her face with a finger under her chin.

She sniffed, trying to control her emotions. "The Chinese boy is going to die. There's nothing I can do to help him."

"I'm sorry. I came to tell you that he's gone. I know you did all you could," Rand said gently.

Fresh tears streamed down her cheeks. "You were right to stay and help. I feel so selfish now that we didn't come sooner." On her knees, she went into Rand's arms. "If we'd come yesterday, we might have helped him."

"We might have, but we had no medicines then. And we tried to get through, but couldn't," he reminded her, gently stroking her back, savoring the feel of her in his arms when he had no right to. "There would have been little we could have done."

"He was so alone, with no one to care that he's gone, no family. You were right to bring help to these men, b-but you c-could still be arrested." She dissolved into sobs.

"I hope not." Holding her close as she cried, Rand doubted that she heard him. He stroked her hair. "I have to believe I won't."

But he wasn't as certain as he had been. When the crew had come to the camp to eat dinner, he'd seen several more men he'd known—foremen working under Skinner. He should have guessed Skinner would have some of the same people around him.

True, no one had paid him much attention or acted like they

recognized him—it had been a long time since he'd last seen any of them, and then only casually.

A stick snapped behind them, and Elizabeth felt Rand's arms tighten.

Looking over her shoulder, she found Hiram standing on the bank above, for once looking her squarely in the face. She realized how close she and Rand were.

Rand released her and stood, holding out a helping hand to her. Getting to her feet, unable to say anything, she walked up the sloping bluff past Hiram and headed back to the camp.

"She's upset because the young Chinese died," Rand explained.

Hiram nodded. "She has a big heart." Glancing at the limbs overhead, he shifted awkwardly. "Came to tell you a man in a suit and one of them round bowler hats got off that supply train that just pulled into camp. From the way Skinner was bowing and scraping, I reckon he's somebody important."

Hiram paused and looked into the tumbling stream, then gazed in the direction Elizabeth had gone. "You care about her, do you?"

"Yes."

"I 'spected that when you chased us down on the boardwalk the other evening."

"I thought you might have."

"I think it was the way you looked like you wanted to give me a sock in the jaw that gave you away." Hiram shook his head. "Why didn't you say something?"

"I should have." Rand thrust his hands into his pockets. "There are . . . complications."

"Allus are, where the heart's concerned," Hiram mused. He looked Rand in the eye again. "Can you tell me what?"

"No. Not because I don't trust you. But it's best if I don't involve you." Seeing Hiram's quizzical expression, Rand grinned ruefully. "It would make you an 'accessory after the fact.' "

Hiram was obviously shocked, and his pale brows rode up on his forehead. "That sounds like a legal something."

Rand sighed. "Very legal. Elizabeth already knows. I've tried to convince her that it doesn't matter. . . ."

Hiram nodded. ''I guess this means Elizabeth has a choice to make.''

Rand picked up one of Elizabeth's forgotten buckets and tossed it into the creek, hauling up water. ''She already has.''

''She has?''

Rand nodded. ''She chose you.''

Hiram looked shocked. Then flushed red and stammered, ''S-she's a fine woman. I 'spect she feels bound to keep her word.'' Frowning, he met Rand's gaze straight on, for a third time. ''You gonna let her and me get hitched without trying to change her mind?''

Rand tossed the other bucket into the stream. ''Hell, no. But because of what she knows about my past, I'm having a hard time convincing her to take a chance. I guess I can understand. She's concerned about . . . her daughter's future.'' Looking up at the tall firs as if they held answers to his problems, he shrugged. ''And it has to be Elizabeth's choice.''

Handing one pail to Hiram, Rand picked up the other and carried it back up the steep path. When they reached the camp, Rand let Hiram take both buckets into the tent they'd converted into a makeshift infirmary.

Hooking his thumbs into his pockets, he watched the man in the bowler hat who Hiram had described earlier. The dandy disappeared into Skinner's office tent, Skinner right behind. Rand recognized him instantly—Gerald Carnegie, a Union Pacific boss. Now a vice president, or something like that. Rand had seen the man's picture in a Eugene newspaper when the new rail line was announced last year.

More to the point, Rand knew Carnegie would recognize him. He was the man who'd hired him years before, after the war was over and Rand had resigned his commission in the Corps of Engineers.

Seeing no point in putting off the inevitable confrontation, Rand started across the muddy compound, feeling his luck was about to change.

And not for the better.

Chapter Twenty-one

"Don't I know you?" Gerald Carnegie rose from the rickety chair behind Skinner's desk and shook Rand's hand. "I can't quite recall the name, but I never forget a face. I hired you right after the war—you'd worked a few months with the Corps of Engineers. What did you say the name was?"

Rand smiled blandly. "Randal Matthews."

"Of course. Matthews. I remember now!"

Rand's grin widened.

"I had no idea you were working on this project with Mr. Skinner." Carnegie smiled cordially. He was as dapperly dressed as though he'd just stepped out of a fashionable Boston men's club.

"I'm not on this project," Rand said. "I haven't worked for the Union Pacific for quite a few years."

"Oh," Carnegie said. His whole demeanor changed as his gaze went to the tin badge on Rand's chest.

He resumed his seat. The action indicated that Rand's change in status meant he was no longer of importance. "Well, it was nice of you to stop by and say hello, but you'll have to excuse my lack of hospitality," Carnegie said. "Mr. Skinner and I are discussing official railroad business. You understand, I'm certain.''

''I do understand. That's why I'm here.'' Without being invited to do so, Rand pulled up the only other chair in the small tent and sat down, crossing his long legs in front of him.

Eyeing Rand as if he'd lost his mind, Skinner stood nervously in front of his own desk, while Carnegie sat behind it.

''In what capacity are you here?'' Carnegie asked Rand, raising one black brow, its color in contrast to the gray of his bushy side-whiskers.

Rand ignored both the question and the imperious tone. ''You have a typhoid fever epidemic in camp. Why haven't medicines to fight that outbreak been supplied?''

His gaze narrowing, Carnegie shrugged. ''Skinner has reported a few sick men. Disease is not unusual in these backward places, and these men are hardly the railroad's responsibility. But do stay around awhile, Sheriff. We'll have need of you.''

Carnegie turned to Skinner. ''I want to know why these men that are too ill to work haven't been turned off. As I've said, their health is hardly the railroad's responsibility. And why are they still on railroad property, occupying beds that belong to the line and which are needed for able-bodied men?''

Skinner's jaw dropped. ''You can't mean for me just to pitch sick men out of camp?''

The imperious brow rode up again. ''You will do exactly that. If there are any problems''—Carnegie nodded toward Rand—''the sheriff here is no doubt used to handling evictions.''

''What evictions?'' Elizabeth asked as she came through the tent flap.

Both Rand and Gerald Carnegie stood.

''Madam, I do not believe we've been introduced,'' Carnegie said in chilly tones, looking over her dark, serviceable dress and apron.

''Mrs. McKay, Mr. Gerald Carnegie—of the Boston Carnegies,'' Rand said. As he did so, he could tell by the way she clenched her fists that Elizabeth was seething. "District manager of the railroad, I believe?"

Carnegie puffed up, as though grossly insulted. "Vice president of special projects."

Elizabeth stepped forward and glared at Carnegie. "I asked *what* evictions."

"A pleasure to make your acquaintance, too, I'm sure." The man dipped his head ever so slightly. "Now, Mrs. McKay, I have to ask what you are doing on railroad property."

Elizabeth's chin snapped up. "Helping give aid to typhoid victims."

"Ah, you are a doctor then, and have diagnosed this dread disease?" Carnegie asked in mild interest, glancing at his pocket watch.

"No, a nurse. Our local doctor is ill. I am acting as his representative. I—"

"A nurse is little more than a servant." He snapped his watch closed. "Hardly qualified to diagnose serious illness like typhoid. I say these men are suffering from nothing more than a mild stomach upset and bountiful sloth. They will be removed."

Elizabeth eyes gleamed fire. "I see. Then you may give me instructions on removing one of them right now. I came to ask where we should bury the young boy who just died of bountiful sloth."

Carnegie was momentarily taken aback, but collected himself quickly, plucking his bowler hat from the center of Skinner's paper-strewn desk. "That's hardly my concern, madam."

Turning to Skinner, he said, "When I return tomorrow, I expect these unproductive men turned out and replaced." He stalked out of the tent, ducking to go under the flap.

Skinner shook his head, eyeing Rand. "Now you've done it. When he comes back tomorrow, you can bet there'll be men with him who'll turn those poor bastards out."

"Is that what happened in Kansas?" Rand asked. "Did the railroad bring in some hired gun to get rid of the old farmer who was holding up progress?"

Skinner looked away. "It was different in Kansas. More civilized, less frontier. Out here, Carnegie can pretty well do what the hell he wants—beggin' your pardon, ma'am. It ain't necessarily what's Union Pacific policy, but he gets results." Skinner ducked out of the tent.

Peering through the flap, Elizabeth saw the man hurrying after Carnegie.

"Is that true, Rand?" Elizabeth turned toward him, her fingers laced together.

Rand took the chair behind Skinner's desk that Carnegie had just vacated, and pulled the telegraph transmitter and receiver toward him. "There might be a bit more law in Lane County to deal with than Carnegie thinks. Did I ever tell you I worked for a while in a telegraph office in Sacramento?"

"No." Elizabeth watched in growing hope as Rand began tapping out code she was unfamiliar with. "Who are you telegraphing?"

"Judge Blackwood in Eugene."

Elizabeth put her hand to her throat. "A judge? Rand, you can't get a judge involved. What will happen if . . ."

She couldn't finish the sentence or the thought.

"Don't worry. He's a fair man. And an old fishing friend of mine." Rand grinned. "He's the one who appointed me acting sheriff in Willow."

"Do we have enough soap, Lois?" Elizabeth pushed through the Sedricks' front door, arms laden with blankets, scrub brushes, rags, and linens the people in town had donated for the men at the camp.

"Yes, I think there's enough." Catching the door, Lois held it open until Elizabeth was through it. She then took part of Elizabeth's burden from her and started down the steps.

"We've used all the carbolic soap in Lane County, but Maggie Jean and some ladies from church gave us just about enough homemade lye to scrub the Three Sisters," she said, referring to high mountain peaks visible in the distance. "Ought to do as good, I'm thinking. The butcher's wife is making some more today, if the rain holds off."

Elizabeth followed Lois to one of the waiting wagons and

deposited her stack inside the bed. A watery sun was just peeping above the mountains, but already a small crowd of people was getting ready for the trip to the rail camp.

Since Judge Blackwood had issued a court order forbidding men to be evicted from the camp, or the tent they were using as an infirmary to be moved or anything inside the tent taken away, Carnegie had left the sick men alone and hadn't tried to prevent the townspeople from helping them.

Over the past several days as they'd been fighting the fever outbreak, the number of volunteers had steadily swelled. Many people in Willow had had the fever before and felt safe from reinfection. Others simply felt pity for the men who were suffering without even their families nearby, and offered to help out.

After Elizabeth's encounter with someone as heartless as Carnegie, it was touching to see that so many people cared. Some even stayed through the night with the sick. While some of the fever victims were on their way back to health, six more had been taken ill. Three had died, in addition to the young Chinese boy.

"At least Hazel Cavanaugh and her boy are on the mend," Elizabeth said. Doc had managed—over Mabel's loud protests—to get out to the Cavanaughs' place, and had pronounced Hazel and her son out of danger.

"Yep. That's shore good to hear. Hiram's cousin in the lumber camp is improvin', but slow." Lois tucked her stack of supplies into a corner of the wagon bed, between a cast-iron wash pot they were bringing and several wooden tubs.

Most of the railroad workers had little in the way of clothes and bedding. When typhoid fever moved into the second stage of the disease and attacked the intestines, soiled clothing had to be boiled and disinfected.

"Yes. But I'm wondering what happened to the old man and his grandson we met on the trail the first day we'd gone out to the Cavanaugh place," Elizabeth said.

Rand had checked the cabin a few days later, and said they had been there, but had cleared out. Skinner had told Elizabeth that Nine-Toed Bill and Buck hadn't left voluntarily, but had been fired for stealing. Bill had been ordering supplies that were never delivered, then splitting the money the railroad paid for those supplies with a store owner in Portland.

Rather liking the old man, except for his crude speech, Elizabeth had been disappointed to learn the pair were thieves.

She'd found out also that Nine-Toed Bill had lied. The sick men were being paid for the days they worked. Skinner said they were paid by the day, and he couldn't pay them for the days they didn't work, however.

Skinner had remembered Elizabeth from Dr. Brown's in Salt Cedar Flats, but other than remarking on the fact, he didn't bring up Kansas or what had happened there to Rand.

Perhaps Rand was right, and the man was trustworthy.

But, oh, what a terrible chance for Rand to take. Now that there were others taking up the fight against the illness, she wished Rand would just ride away so he'd be safe. Every time he'd tried to talk with her alone, she'd told him so.

He still refused to listen to reason.

"Mama, you forgot to hug me and say good-bye to Miss Annie." Still in her nightgown, Becca came onto the porch, knuckling sleep from her eyes with one hand, while Miss Annie dangled from the other.

Elizabeth went to the edge of the porch and scooped her daughter off, swinging her around in the air and eliciting giggles. "Yes, I did kiss you good-bye. But you were still sleeping."

Becca held up her doll.

"Good-bye, Miss Annie. Stay out of trouble and behave for Mrs. Mabel now."

"She will," Becca assured her mother.

"I'll miss you." Elizabeth kissed the top of her daughter's soft curls, promising herself that when this crisis was over, she would spend all day with Becca, just the two of them. Funny, but she really missed being alone with her daughter.

She just never wanted to be as alone as they'd been in Kansas ever again.

"Mr. Rand!" Seeing Rand beside his horse, which was tied to the Sedricks' picket fence, Becca leaned as far out in her mother's grasp as she could, holding out her arms and Miss Annie as if certain both would be welcomed by the sheriff.

Rand looked up. "Hello, tadpole."

When Elizabeth stood rooted to the spot, Becca looked askance at her mother. "I want to hug Mr. Rand, Mama."

Elizabeth had no choice but to honor the simple request, though as Rand lifted Becca over the fence and the child wrapped her arms about his neck, Elizabeth saw pain in his eyes.

He hid it behind a smile as he handed his daughter back to Elizabeth. "I have to go now," he said.

As he untied his horse, then mounted with easy grace, Elizabeth couldn't help watching him. It seemed it was impossible for her not to watch him whenever he was near.

He seemed to sense her attention, and his gaze met hers. And something warm and disturbing flared in her chest.

If he'd just say he'd go, Elizabeth realized to her shame, she'd go with him anywhere.

Why was he being so stubborn? Didn't he see he was leaving her no choice but to marry Hiram Smith?

"Hello, young 'un." Lois smiled at Becca, showing the wide space between her front teeth.

"Hello." Becca yawned and put her head on Elizabeth's shoulder.

"Seeing the Hoffpaur kids down there playing in the street reminded me there's no school today 'cause it's Saturday." Lois looked at Elizabeth as if that should mean something to her. Though what it could be, Elizabeth hadn't a clue.

Clarifying, Lois added, "You know, I know you have things to see to. You ought not to be going with us today. There's plenty of us women to handle things without you."

"Why? What things?" Elizabeth blinked

"Tomorrow's your wedding, ain't it? Or did you and Hiram push the date back again?"

"Oh." Blushing, Elizabeth was deeply chagrined. "I'd forgotten," she admitted sheepishly. Put it out of her mind, more like—not the fact that she was engaged to Hiram, but that the date of her wedding was so near.

"You've been busy, right enough, what with helping with this fever, and all Doc's other patients. Hiram has been bowed up, too." Lois shook her head and focused on something just past Elizabeth's shoulder. "But you have to think of yourselves now."

Elizabeth couldn't forgive herself for forgetting that easily. It should mean more to her. She should have been counting the hours.

Hiram was a good man. He'd been the soul of patience, helping them with the sick when he could get away from the farm. Treating her like she was the decent widow he thought her to be, instead of the fallen woman she was.

And tomorrow, she would marry him.

The stone she'd felt in her stomach over the last few days suddenly became a boulder.

"Now, you stay here today and take care of some of the things you probably ain't had time for," Lois said. Stepping on the hub of the wagon wheel, she hiked her skirt up and swung her leg over the wooden side.

"I don't know. What if more people are sick, or—"

"Now don't you fret." Settling on the stack of blankets in the wagon bed, Lois told her, "We'll take care of things at the camp."

She patted Elizabeth's hand, her round face losing its smile. "You need to be gettin' ready fer your wedding. It's what you come way out here from Kansas for."

"Yes. I suppose you're right." Hearing a noise behind them, Elizabeth turned and found Hiram a short distance away tying his horse to the Sedricks' fence. He nodded to three women volunteers, who were passing on their way to the back of the wagon.

When he saw Elizabeth and Lois, his face lit and he ambled forward. "Mornin', ladies. I see we're all ready to go." He looked at the supplies and the sky, and then nodded to Arkansas Neb Erickson as Neb climbed onto the wagon seat and took up the reins.

Neb asked, "You want to ride, Hiram? Mrs. McKay?"

"I'm not going today, Neb," Elizabeth said. Though she

didn't look at him, she was completely aware of Rand, who'd halted his horse on the other side of the wagon.

Squaring her shoulders, she said, "Lois just reminded me that I have a wedding tomorrow to get ready for." She forced a smile.

"So do you, Hiram Smith!" Climbing onto the tailboard, Sara Edwards giggled. Already seated there, her sister, Deborah Quantrain, smiled. Their friend, Millie Vale, the only unmarried one of the three, sighed, a dreamy expression on her thin face, and took her place between the sisters.

"Well, then, we best get going." Neb winked at Hiram and slapped the reins on the horse's rump. The animal started forward.

Elizabeth's gaze flew to Rand. Without a word, Rand touched his heels to his horse's flanks and rode down the street.

"You don't have to go today, either," Elizabeth said as she found herself alone with Hiram. "I know you have work on your farm. With Neb and Rand and the other men, there's enough to help with any heavy work the women have." The buckboard creaked and rumbled down the street. She fought a strong urge to run after it.

Farther along the roadway, Rand spurred his horse into a gallop.

"That's just what I was thinking," Hiram said. "About me not going, I mean." He took her hand and squeezed it lightly, then stared after the departing wagons. "I got something I been wanting to show you. Had it ordered from San Francisco. But with the fever raging, it just didn't seem like the right time for giving surprises."

"A surprise?"

Hiram blushed. "A wedding gift."

Chapter Twenty-two

"What's a matter, pun'kin? Aren't you feeling well?" Elizabeth placed a hand on the child's forehead. Finding no fever, she smoothed Becca's dark curls.

"No, I'm not not feeling well." Sitting uncharacteristicly still on the buckboard seat as they bounced down the rutted road toward Hiram's farm, Becca smoothed her doll's yarn hair.

"Then you *are* feeling bad," said Donnie. He and Lance sat on the tailboard, letting their feet dangle. Donnie added, "We learned in school when you say two 'no' words in a sentence, it makes it mean 'yes.' "

Turning, Becca gave him a scathing glance, but made no comment. She returned her attention to her doll, smoothing the yarn hair.

Worried over her daughter's attitude, Elizabeth met Hiram's gaze over the child's head.

His gaze skittered away and settled on the horse's rump.

"Don't worry, Elizabeth. Give it time." He propped a foot on the dashboard. "She's used to having you all to herself, and she's had to share you a lot lately, what with all the work you've been doing because of the fever. Now, with you and me getting married, and all—''

''You can't get married to my mama.'' Becca's lower lip thrust out.

Hiram's brows rode up and he and Elizabeth exchanged another glance.

''Why not?'' he asked kindly.

'' 'Cause you're *not* my daddy.''

''Oh.'' Hiram nodded in the attitude of one discovering a great truth. ''I know that. But when your mother and me get married, I will be your 'stepdaddy.' Like Mrs. Mabel told you the other night. Will that be all right with you and your doll?''

Becca shrugged. Except for the action, the child continued to give the doll her full attention.

Catching Hiram's hand, which rested on the back of the seat, Elizabeth squeezed it in gratitude. She would always be grateful for his concern for Becca's feelings.

''Did you tell Mrs. McKay about the surprise?'' Lance called from the tailboard, above the wagon's rattles and squeaks.

''No. If Papa did that, it wouldn't be a surprise, would it?'' Donnie glared at his brother. ''You had to yank that cat out of the bag, didn't you?''

''A surprise?' '' Becca turned and peered over the back of the seat at them. ''You mean like Christmas?''

''I don't know about no surprise.'' Little George rode farther up in the wooden bed, where he'd been busy driving his toy block-wheeled wagon over the sacks of coffee and flour stacked behind the seat. ''Papa, is it Christmas again?''

''No, son. That's a few months away. But I think Elizabeth will like this surprise. I ordered it from San Francisco, then had it brung out from Eugene on the freight wagon.'' Hiram glanced at the top of Elizabeth's bonnet, then at the bow under her chin. ''At least I hope she likes it.'' He blushed.

As they rounded a bend in the muddy road and the tall firs gave way to a sheltered valley, Elizabeth understood Hiram's love of his land. He was always talking about it, and his plans for it.

After she got out of the wagon and helped Becca down,

setting her on her feet, the two older boys eagerly took Elizabeth by the hands and pulled her into the kitchen of the sturdy log house. Becca made no protest when Hiram picked her up and followed.

In the corner of the long room sat the biggest, fanciest stove Elizabeth had ever seen. One look at the expectant faces around her and she knew that this was indeed the surprise.

"Here it is. The surprise." Donnie's face glowed with excitement.

"Do you like it?" Lance asked eagerly.

"Like what?" Little George echoed, bringing up the rear. "Hey, we got a new stove!"

"You've been staying at Maggie Jean's and didn't know we we were puttting it in," Hiram told his youngest son.

As he turned to Elizabeth, Hiram's look was expectant. "Well?"

"I've never seen such a wonderful cookstove." Elizabeth trailed her fingers over the shining black surface. It was a full five feet wide and had a deep hot-water well at one side. There were places for six pots on the top, a warming oven, and the baking oven was huge, too. Looking inside it, she exclaimed, "This is so big, I could bake three cakes and a turkey at once in there."

"Wow. A cake for each of us!" A bright lock of his red hair falling onto his forehead, George looked at her wide-eyed. Then he glanced at Becca, still on his father's hip. "But I'd share mine with Becca."

That earned George a shy smile from the little girl. "And Miss Annie, too?" Becca asked, struggling to get down. Hiram put her on the floor.

Holding the doll out to George, she asked, "Could Miss Annie ride in your wagon? She needs to go to town to buy flour."

After a considering frown, he nodded. "Okay. But I'm driving the team." George pulled the toy out of his overalls bib, and soon both children were on their knees on the kitchen floor, heading toward the hallway.

"You do like it, don't you?" Donnie asked, his bright blue eyes shining.

"I like it a lot. It's the nicest stove I've ever seen." Elizabeth smiled.

"I helped Papa run the new stovepipe outside," Lance said.

"A fine job you did, too." She tousled the boy's dark auburn hair, a more subdued shade than his brothers'.

Donnie said wistfully, "It's been a long time since we had a cake or a pie at home. Aunt Maggie Jean bakes nice cakes, but there's not a lot left for seconds."

Lance sighed. "No, that there isn't."

Her heart full, Elizabeth blinked back tears. They were all so eager to please her, so in need of being mothered again. And when she had come to Willow, she'd only been worried about herself, that her deception wouldn't work and she'd be found out.

Elizabeth moved to the wide window overlooking the orchard. Lifting the red gingham curtain, she said, "These curtains are nice and cheery."

"Emmaline made those, just before she died. After she got too sickly to do much else but sew." Hiram paused and stuck his hands into his pockets, staring through the window.

Elizabeth heard the pain in his voice as he continued. "She said they'd brighten the place up for us. After she was gone."

There was sudden quiet in the kitchen, except for the sound of George and Becca in the hall, driving Miss Annie over obviously treacherous mountain roads lined with hostile outlaws and bears.

Straightening her shoulders, Elizabeth pulled off her gloves. "Well, I can't wait to try this out," she said, dispelling the sudden somberness in the kitchen. "Hiram, you wouldn't have enough flour and sugar to make tea cakes, would you? And maybe just a little cinnamon or vanilla? That does make them tasty."

"Tea cakes?" Donnie and Lance said as one, awed anticipation in their voices.

Hiram grinned. "I'll see if we do."

"And it'll be dinnertime soon," Elizabeth went on in the

same bright tone. "I was thinking of frying up a little ham, if you have it, and making biscuits with red-eye gravy, since we don't have time to cook beans."

"We probably have eggs in the henhouse," Donnie said hopefully. "We got some ham in the larder. And I like eggs a lot. Jake has been feeding the chickens while we were away and gathering the eggs as payment, but I don't think he's got them today."

Elizabeth said, "You could go see. And we'll need some wood, too, for the stove. Chop a lot. It'll take it to get this big oven fired up. Now hurry."

Lance and Donnie scurried out the back door.

She could do this. The boys needed her. And this would be a wonderful family for Becca to grow up in.

Elizabeth tied on an apron she found hanging from a peg on the wall, and turned to find Hiram staring.

He quickly found interest in the toe of her shoe. "You're a good woman, Elizabeth."

Abashed, not feeling that she was a good woman at all, she found interest in the toes of his shoes. "You don't really know me, Hiram."

He took her red, work-roughened hand, holding it up between them. "I know you've worked your hands raw trying to tend sick people you don't even know. And for no gain, excepting it's the right thing to do. And I know you speak kindly to my boys and you'll be a good ma to 'em."

The weight she'd been carrying on her conscience was getting impossibly heavy. Looking down, Elizabeth shook her head. "Hiram, don't—"

"And you're such a fine woman," he said, cutting her off. "With nice manners and all . . . I know I must shore be a sore disappointment to you—"

"Hiram, you're a fine man. After we're married I'll be the best wife I can."

"But you're keeping your promise to marry me 'cause you're a woman of your word." He squeezed her hand, his expression knowing. "Not 'cause you want to get hitched to a backwards man like me."

"You're one of the nicest people I've ever known." Elizabeth blinked furiously.

Hiram's gaze shifted to the new stove. "My ma had a stove like this. We had to throw it out of our wagon on the trail on the way here from Missouri, to lighten the load going over the Green Mountains. I remember she cried for days." He sighed. "I thought if you had a fine stove like this, it would make up a little for my backward ways."

She couldn't prevent the tears that ran down her cheeks. "Hiram—"

"If you say again how I'm a good man, I just don't think I can take it, Elizabeth."

"You *are* a good man." Crying, she wrapped her arms around him and hugged him tightly, pressing her face into his shoulder. *"I'm just not the good woman you think I am."*

While the children were busy elsewhere, she told him the truth. Or most of it.

"Why on earth would you put off the wedding again? The salmon will be running soon—Elizabeth would be a big help to you then." Maggie Jean eyed her brother curiously. "And the boys, they're all excited about having a new ma."

Standing on her front porch, she shook her head, bouncing the baby on her shoulder in counterpoint. "Hiram, what ain't you telling me?"

"Seems to me when we get hitched is my and Elizabeth's business, Maggie. When Big George gets back from Eugene, thank him for me for the use of the buckboard. I wiped down all the tack and brushed the mare." Hiram nodded to his sister and turned away, taking Elizabeth's elbow to escort her back to Doc's.

Little George and Becca ran on ahead, pulling his toy wagon by a string with the new Miss Annie in it. Hiram's two older boys had elected to stay at the farm until their father returned from bringing Elizabeth back to town. Their decisions might have been inspired by the last of the tea cakes Elizabeth baked being in the larder.

"*Elizabeth!*" Maggie Jean's call was more of a wail, expressing her unsated curiosity.

Turning back, Elizabeth shrugged. "I'm sorry. Hiram and I talked about it and we decided it will be best if we delay getting married for a little while."

"Cold feet!" Maggie Jean called. "That's all it is! As if there's anything to fear in getting wed!" Showing her irritation with the two of them, she went inside the house and banged the door closed.

"I feel bad that she's so upset," Elizabeth said. Walking comfortably hand in hand with Hiram down the boardwalk, nodding to the people they passed, she felt better than she had in weeks, now that she'd told him the truth about Rand.

It had been far easier than she'd thought. Hiram had held her close, comforting her as she cried and told him how she met Rand in Kansas and fell in love with him. But he'd been on the run, unfairly convicted of murder.

Hiram had never flinched as she told him how Rand left before she knew that she carried Becca. Lest he think badly of Rand, Elizabeth had explained how Rand let her think he was dead, killed by a bounty hunter, because he wanted her to have a better life than he could give her on the run.

And then she'd come to Willow.

After her confession to him, Hiram had gotten down his family bible. Expecting him to preach her a sermon about her lack of morals and break their engagement then and there, Elizabeth had been slow to realize what he was about. He showed her the inside of the front page, with the date of his marriage on it, then the entry recording Donnie's birth seven months later.

Almost looking her in the eye, he told her how he and Emmaline had been too in love to be patient, and what a fine fat, healthy baby Donnie had been.

And Hiram didn't want to call the wedding off.

He understood her reasons for not wanting to marry Rand, even though she confessed she still cared about Rand deeply and had tried to get him to take her and Becca away with him before he ran into someone who knew him, like Skinner.

But Rand had refused to leave. So she had to do what was best for her daughter. Hiram understood because he'd asked her to marry him for the sake of his sons.

Hiram did suggest they delay getting married until the typhoid outbreak was over, and that would give her time to think about it and make certain it was what she wanted.

He was a special man, Elizabeth thought, wishing she could love him as he deserved.

But then, he hadn't asked for her love. After the bond he'd shared with his wife, he'd said in his letters, he wasn't looking for someone to replace Emmaline in his affections. Just someone to be his wife and a companion and mother to his sons.

"Maggie Jean has always been a curious sort. It will do her good to wonder." Hiram grinned. "Besides, it is our business, ain't it?"

Elizabeth returned his smile. "I count myself a lucky woman."

At that, he stammered something that might have been a denial, turned red, and looked up at the overcast sky, then down at the boardwalk.

Music from an out-of-tune piano wafted up the street from the saloon on the outskirts of town. A few people nodded in greeting as they passed her and Hiram. Shop owners were pulling down their shades, and a few lanterns could be seen in windows already, though it was only dusk.

Rand rode past them, stopping down the street at the hitching rail in front of the sheriff's office. Watching his easy grace as he dismounted his horse, she felt a warmth begin deep inside, and wished just the sight of him didn't affect her so.

Before she married Hiram—if they married—Elizabeth knew she would tell him about the afternoon she'd spent with Rand in the trapper's cabin.

She hadn't quite been able to bring herself to unburden her conscience of that. Perhaps because the time together with Rand had been so special, so filled with loving. And she had given herself freely, believing they would be together always.

It seemed she was always reading more into Rand's actions than were promised in fact.

Feeling Hiram's grip on her hand tighten slightly, Elizabeth wondered if they could really make it work out. Now that she'd told Hiram who Becca's father was, would he be able to accept her as his stepdaughter?

Or would it eat at him every time he saw Rand?

As her own heart twisted painfully, Elizabeth admitted to herself it was going to be hell living in the same town.

Spotting Rand, Becca ran to him, flinging her arms wide. "Mr. Rand! Mr. Rand!"

"How are you doing, tadpole?" His smile almost hid the look of pain that crossed his face as he scooped his daughter up and swung her playfully around.

"I've been playing with George and seeing our new house. What have you been doing?" she returned brightly.

"Fighting dragons." As he put Becca down, Rand's smile was sad around the corners.

"Real ones?" George asked, big-eyed, as he caught up to them, his toy wagon trailing after him at the end of a twine string.

"Not real ones," Rand admitted, solemnly shaking hands with the boy. "The kind in bowler hats."

Glancing at Hiram and Elizabeth, Rand nodded. Elizabeth managed to return the greeting.

"Howdy, Rand. Hiram." Two lumberjacks passed by them on the street, nodding respectfully to Elizabeth. "Ma'am."

Hiram and Rand nodded back.

After the pair passed, Rand said, "Hiram, tell Doc I'll be down to talk to him in a little while. I'll need him to write up something to take to the Board of Health in Salem, so we can get an Order of Quarantine for the camp."

"What's happened today, Rand?" Hiram asked.

"Carnegie was there again today."

"The dragon in a bowler hat," Elizabeth murmured.

"Exactly." Rand's gaze rested on her for an instant; then his gaze shifted to her and Hiram's intertwined fingers.

He thrust his own hands into his pockets. "Skinner went behind Carnegie's back and warned me he's bringing in a train car full of Chinese workers fresh off the ship in San Francisco.

Seems Judge Blackwood's order said that the sick men couldn't be turned out of camp, but it didn't say anything about bringing more in."

"I'll tell Doc to write up the request," Elizabeth said, looping her arm through her fiance's. "Come, Becca, George. We need to go talk with Doc."

As Elizabeth and Hiram hurried on toward the Sedricks', Rand watched. He understood why Elizabeth was going on with her engagement. But it tore at his heart nonetheless.

Maybe Elizabeth had been right after all. Maybe he should have ridden out with her when she asked him to go. When Rand had gotten Judge Blackwood to issue the court order, the judge had warned Rand that he knew Carnegie and to be careful not to underestimate the man. That Rand had better watch his back.

And if Carnegie remembered Rand's real identity, getting him out of the way would be simple.

Maybe Rand should just take Elizabeth and Becca and run like hell, until he was across the Canadian border.

If Elizabeth still wanted to go.

She and Hiram looked pretty cozy, walking hand in hand as they were.

She'd said she would marry Hiram if Rand insisted on staying and taking a chance on getting himself hanged.

Looked like she'd meant it.

Chapter Twenty-three

Elizabeth carried a basin of dirty water out of the infirmary tent, past a giant fir tree on the edge of the compound. After she emptied the pan, she set it down and put her hands on the small of her back, stretching.

She winced at the deep ache that had settled there. Too many hours bent over, she supposed. Or she'd strained her muscles carrying fresh water up from the stream. Or maybe in helping the red-haired Irishman named Mickey to get out of bed for the first time in three days. He'd been very unsteady.

But she sensed Mickey was on his way to recovery. Slowly, but on his way. That made her smile, despite the muscle aches.

A fine mist filled the air, settling on her face. The mountain air held a chill that seemed to seep into her bones this morning, and her body felt achy and tired. A dull headache throbbed in her temples.

It was probably more than strained muscles, Elizabeth decided. It was exhaustion. She had been working long hours, then not sleeping well at night.

It was a good thing there were more workers than sick here today. Two of the sick men had gotten well enough to leave their sickbeds, and as they convalesced, they were helping out with the others.

With several volunteers there from town, the sick were outnumbered for a change, and well cared for. She supposed she might leave early and just rest this afternoon, if anyone headed back to Willow.

Rand would take her if she asked. . . .

The thought slipped into her mind, tempting her. She knew Rand was the last person she should ask, or allow herself to be alone with. She knew it, but her heart still warmed and fluttered at the thought.

"Woolgathering?" Coming up beside her, Lois tossed a pan of water onto the thick mat of dead leaves and fir needles at the same spot Elizabeth had.

"I suppose so." Elizabeth smiled. "It's nice to have enough help, so we aren't hard-pressed."

"Yep," Lois agreed. "The first day we come out here, I was runnin' around like a chicken with its head cut off. There was so much to do, and the men were so sick."

She propped her pan on her hip and cocked a questioning brow at Elizabeth. "Now that there's plenty to help, I can't figure why you're not in town getting hitched after Sunday services this mornin'."

Elizabeth smiled and toyed with a loose string on her apron pocket. "It's complicated. Besides, I'd want you there, and both of us couldn't stay away from here. So there you are. Getting married had to wait."

Lois was not to be mollified so easily, and her other brow rode up. "Most things are complicated where the heart is concerned," she said softly.

"With Hiram and me, it's not our hearts that are concerned." Not with each other anyway, Elizabeth amended to herself. "It's a business arrangement. For reasons I can't really go into, both Hiram and I agreed that it will be better to delay getting married. When this fever outbreak is over, we'll set a date."

"Hmph!" Lois eyed her as though she was short of wits. "I wouldn't take a chance on a man like Hiram Smith changin' his mind, or bein' ensnared by some connivin' woman."

"I suppose it *is* silly to delay." Elizabeth sighed. It was. She knew marrying Hiram would be for the best. She said, "But once the vows are spoken, they'll be forever. You can understand we need to be certain neither of us regrets it. We talked it over and decided to delay. As much for Hiram's sake as for mine."

Elizabeth wanted Hiram to have time to think about what she'd confessed yesterday and to be sure he would never regret getting married to her. And she wanted to tell Hiram about being with Rand in the cabin before they set another date. It was the right thing to do.

"Does Hiram seem to be havin' second thoughts?" There was an odd look on Lois's face.

"No. I just want to make certain he doesn't later on. When it's too late."

Lois looked up at the overcast sky. "I s'pose that it makes sense when you say it that a way." Lifting their skirt hems out of the mud, they started back. "Where is Hiram today? Takin' his boys to church?"

"No." Elizabeth stopped outside the infirmary tent. After looking around to make certain they weren't overheard, she said quietly, "He's riding to Eugene and catching the train for Salem. He is taking a letter from Doc Sedrick asking to have the camp put under quarantine to the head of the Board of Health.

"Rand got word that the railroad was going to bring in a carload of Chinese workers straight off a ship in San Francisco."

Lois gasped. "Why on earth would the railroad expose more folks to this fever?"

Elizabeth shook her head. "It's not the railroad, per se. Rand says he has heard that Carnegie is aiming for a seat on the Union Pacific's Board of Directors. Carnegie only wants to show he can get results and get the rails laid down fast and cheaply. He doesn't care how he does it. He certainly doesn't care about these workers."

Elizabeth felt anger surge within her at the memory of her encounter with the man and his attitude of superiority.

When Rand had gotten a restraining order from Judge Blackwood keeping Carnegie from having the sick men removed from the camp, or the tent or bunks removed, Carnegie had been livid with rage, Skinner reported.

Elizabeth knew Rand had made an enemy, and she couldn't help worrying what Carnegie would do in retaliation. He wasn't the type to be thwarted without taking revenge. And if he found Rand's vulnerable point . . .

"A quarantine means nobody can go in nor out till it's lifted," Lois said thoughtfully. "Whoever's in camp when it's posted will be stuck here."

"I hope Hiram will be able to give us some warning before the county sheriff comes and posts it. I wouldn't want to be separated from Becca for what might be weeks," Elizabeth said, rolling her shoulders to ease the tired feeling between them.

The whistle of the daily supply train sounded in the distance, chugging heavily up the grade on the newly laid tracks.

"Train's a mite earlier than usual," Lois noted.

"Seems like," Elizabeth agreed as she followed her friend into the tent. "Maybe the railroad has finally decided to start supplying quinine and paregoric for these men. Or just send more blankets and sheets."

"'At would be a blessin', right enough. But it'll happen when pigs fly," Lois answered.

Across the compound, Rand noted the train's earlier-than-usual arrival, too, and wondered if Carnegie was aboard, accounting for the special schedule. Or the construction engineer, who, Skinner said, spent more time in Eugene than in the mountains, leaving Skinner to figure out most problems for himself.

The handcar was blocking the tracks, where Skinner and his crew had ridden it back for the noon meal. Every now and then, a blast in the distance shook the ground as the blaster took out obstacles on the route while the workmen were well out of the way.

Rand knew a great many men had left when the fever hit camp. Those that stayed had made slow progress through a difficult area, but the rails were laid a good five miles up the line. He might just offer Skinner something in return for the help the man had given to him.

Warning about the quarantine.

After all, it didn't make sense to keep healthy people enclosed with the sick. As long as they stayed out here in the wilderness, until the outbreak was past and they were certain they didn't carry the disease, it wouldn't matter.

As he ducked into Skinner's office tent, Skinner looked up from his plate of beans and frowned. "What is it now, Sheriff?"

"That's no way to greet an old friend." Rand settled into the rickety straight chair by the canvas wall.

After shoveling a spoonful of beans into his mouth, Skinner said around them, "I wouldn't exactly call you friend, Matthews. You been nothin' but trouble since I first knowed you in Kansas—greenhorn with your engineer's degree."

"I'd been in the army."

Skinner snorted. "I was an infantry sergeant for four years, knee-deep in blood and guts at Gettysburg and them places. You came out of college a know-nothing lieutenant in the Corp of Engineers and rebuilt railroad bridges for a while."

"I can see how you would resent me being put over you on the project," Rand allowed. "My being your superior must have rankled."

Snorting again, Skinner shook his head. "You ain't never been my superior." He shoveled in more beans, then pointed his spoon at Rand. "I saved your bacon twice in Kansas. The first time, I took a bullet to do it, too. Ort to have just let you ride into that hornet's nest!"

Uncrossing his legs, Rand sat up straighter. "What do you mean, 'saved me twice'? What happened that night in Kansas?"

Skinner's face closed, becoming unreadable. "Ne'er you mind. It's enough fer you to know you owe your hide being here to me."

"Someone hired a gunman to shoot the old farmer. Was it you?"

Casting Rand a disbelieving look, Skinner shook his head. "You ain't real good at listening, are you? I told you, I saved your bacon two times. I didn't try to fry it. Your young, ignorant, know-it-all self did that right well on your on. 'Goin' out to try to talk sense to the old sodbuster,' you said. I told you wait till mornin'—real meaningful like. Then I looked around and you were a-ridin' off.''

Rand tried to remember if Skinner had said something of the sort. But it was just too far back. And maybe he wasn't paying close attention at the time.

Rand decided to try a different tack to try and get the information. ''Nine-Toed Bill said you rode out right after me, hell-for-leather, only took a different route, so you could get there quicker. Then shot the old farmer and let me take the blame.''

''What?'' Skinner looked shocked, then shook his head. ''That old bastard! Would have let him go years ago if I hadn't felt sorry for the old fart!''

''That's not what happened then?''

''Bill was mad 'cause I fired him,'' Skinner snapped. ''When I took him on again, I had told him this was his last cookin' job for the Union Pacific. I had to hire his grandson and another man fer him on the last two jobs. Too old, he just couldn't keep up, and he wasn't that energetic even when he was young. And frankly, 'at grandson of his is as useless as tits on a boar hog.

''But seemed Bill took what I said to mean he better skim off all he could get, instead of the little bit he usually made do with. I knew he was skimmin' a little bit for years, like gettin' the grocer to throw in his tobaccy fer him. That didn't matter too much. But this time his skimmin' was cuttin' my men short of food.

''After I went behind him on one shipment and checked the supplies he signed for—half of which didn't ever get put on the train—I told him to clear off. He has a habit of holdin' a grudge. I'd think he'd say anything to get me back.''

Skinner finished his beans, slurped his coffee, and wiped his mouth on the back of his hand. ''Rand, I ain't gonna help you no more.''

Raising his voice to be heard over the heavy chugging of the approaching train, he went on. ''Can't help you no more.

I told you about the Chinee-men comin' in, 'cause I fought for the Union against slavery. They get those poor bastards, not even speakin' English so they don't hear about the sickness, bring 'em out here, and the fever goes through 'em like salts through a widder woman. A man ort to at least know what he's goin' into.

"But I can't help you no more. Carnegie ain't a man to cross, and he's suspicious of me as it is. I'm not a young man anymore. I'd have a hard time startin' over."

The train whistle sounded, than a hiss as the locomotive let off excess steam mixed with the squealing of iron wheels braking against iron rails as it stopped at the camp.

"That train's early, isn't it? Wonder if Carnegie's on it," Rand mused.

"I hope not," Skinner said with feeling.

"It might be poetic justice," Rand said enigmatically and stood. "I'm grateful for what you've done. So now I'll help you. The county sheriff will be here sometime today or tomorrow to post a quarantine on the whole camp."

"What the hell?" Skinner stood, too, disbelief written on his face. "Why the hell did you do that? Ain't I tried to help you ever way I could, even warnin' you about the Chinese comin' in?"

"I'm sorry, Skinner. An order of quarantine is the only way I could stop Carnegie from bringing in more men. Once it goes up, no one will be allowed in or out of camp until the fever outbreak is over."

Rand went on. "I notice the end of the line has moved on some distance from camp. Now, you're probably needing to move your healthy men and supplies on down the line anyway, to get them closer to the work.

"With the supply train here to carry everything, this afternoon would be a good time to set up another camp, I'm thinking. And if any do get sick, send them back here. Elizabeth has drilled it into everyone's heads to not drink after each other and to wash their hands. Maybe there won't be any more cases."

Grinning, Rand paused in the open tent flap. "But if Carnegie *is* on the train, I wouldn't mention the quarantine to him. I'd just ease out of camp before the sheriff gets the posters up."

Smiling, Skinner looked like he liked the idea. "It would serve that son of a bitch right, wouldn't it? Too bad he's safe from the typhoid, though. Being cold-blooded, snakes don't get fevers."

Sudden shouts and the sound of running feet snapped Rand's head around. A dozen or so men with clubs were charging toward the infirmary tent. Some were already going inside.

High-pitched and terrified, a woman's scream cut the air.

Elizabeth!

Running across the compound, Rand drew his gun.

Chapter Twenty-four

With a cup of broth halfway to Mickey O'Day's mouth, Elizabeth looked up as noise erupted outside the front of the infirmary tent—the sound of running feet, men shouting, cursing.

''Mother Mary preserve us!'' the young Irishman whispered as rough-looking men swinging clubs burst through the tent flap. They attacked everything in sight, kicking bedrolls, turning over the few cots that were there, breaking the stovepipe.

''Have at, me boyos! Leave no one here walkin' under their own pow'r.'' The big man who was first inside the tent strode to a man rolled up in a blanket, so sick he'd been delirious most of the morning. Drawing back his jackbooted foot, the ruffian kicked the man.

The sick man groaned.

''Yer been told ta leave here, all o' yer!'' The big man kicked him again. ''Now out with ya!''

''Stop that! Yer ruffian!'' Lois, who had been tending the ill man and was returning with a fresh pan of water, slung it on the big man with the cudgel, drenching him.

''Why, you bitch!'' The thug lunged at Lois and grabbed a fistful of her apron and dress front, shaking her like a rag doll.

Deborah screamed, dropping the chamber pot she'd been carrying. Other women ran, ducking through the back flap of the tent. A few tried vainly to protect the sick men from the men swinging clubs.

"Stop!" Not stopping to consider what she was doing, Elizabeth ran to where the man was abusing Lois, and kicked his shin as hard as she could.

Growling, he turned on her, raising a cudgel to strike.

She caught the big man's arm. *"Stop this instant! These people are sick!"*

He glared at her, eyes almost lost in the folds of skin around them, then shook her off as though she was no more than a fly. She went sailing backward, and was caught by another ruffian.

"A ripe 'un!" The second man leered at her.

His foul breath in Elizabeth's face almost made her retch. She struggled to free herself, but he held both her hands in one of his, then grabbed her apron bib and yanked as if he'd rip it off.

The heavy cotton held, but the string bit into the back of her neck.

"Stop!" Elizabeth demanded.

"The nob said we're are to turn out these squatters, then you harlots w'ot has taken up on railroad property, we can do what we wants with."

The big man, who Elizabeth guessed was their leader, raised his club again, intent on cracking the sick man's skull. Lois dove back between them and the vicious blow caught her shoulder.

"Are you daft!" she cried, going to her knees, her face twisting in pain. Nonetheless, she managed to bend protectively over the man on the bedroll, shielding him from the ruffian. "These men have the fever!"

"Fever, is it?" The ruffian raised the club again. "I'll show you fever."

Light slanted across Lois as someone came into the tent. A pistol shot rang out, and the cudgel exploded into splinters, flying from the man's hand.

The man howled in pain, grabbing his palm, obviously hurt by the vibration from the bullet shattering the wood.

Then the brigand turned, enraged, toward the newcomer.

"The next is through your gut," Rand promised.

Elizabeth broke free of her captor and ran to Rand. He pushed her behind him, and all went quiet and still.

The leader seemed to be assessing the situation. The others shot him glances through the thickening smoke from the broken stovepipe, as though awaiting his signal.

"He's just one man," the big man growled at length.

"He's wearin' a star," someone pointed out.

"I might even aim lower than your gut," Rand said meaningfully. "But then it would probably just be wasting a bullet. I doubt if a blackguard who'd attack typhoid-stricken men and the helpless women trying to nurse them would have much manhood down there to lose."

As the insult struck home, the big man took a half step toward Rand. Then he paused, obviously respecting Rand's gun. There was utter quiet for a space.

"We was hired by the railroad man to clear out a pack o' squatters and whores," the big ruffian said. "I'm thinkin' if you are the law, you've no call to side with these here squatters."

"Look around you!" Elizabeth gasped in disbelief. "I wouldn't have thought anyone could be so dense. Can't you see these men are sick with fever?" She held out her thick, all-encomposing apron. "Does this look like a harlot's dress?"

"The other woman said some'ot about fever before." The man who'd held Elizabeth took a step toward the tent flap. As he looked at the men lying on the bedrolls, horror dawned on his face. "By damn, if it ain't."

Then he glared accusingly at their leader. "You didn't say nothin' about no fever camp."

"Typhoid fever," Rand supplied. "It's not always fatal. But more often than not."

The leader's eyes narrowed. "I think yer bammin' us fair. If it's fever, why ain't you or these 'ere women afraid?"

Rand shrugged. "I've had it before. Can't get it twice. The women have methods for avoiding contagion. Now, someone straighten up that pipe.'' He motioned toward the smoking stove with his gun barrel.

No one moved. Rand fired a shot into the earthen floor between the feet of the man nearest the stove, then trained the gun back on the leader lightning fast. As the first man jumped long after the bullet had burrowed into the earthen floor, his face went pale.

''Do it now,'' Rand said. ''I still have four shots left. After I put one in your boss's gut, I'll have three.''

Skinner stepped through the tent flap and levered a shell into the Winchester he was holding. ''And I have plenty more bullets to back him up.''

Through the wide-open flap, Elizabeth saw railroad workers flanking Skinner holding iron spikes and clubs of their own. Breathing a sigh of relief, she realized Rand wouldn't have to deal with these ruffians alone.

''What exactly is going on here, Rand?'' Skinner asked. ''Which one do I need to shoot first?''

''All of them, if they don't get busy and straighten up the mess they've made, then get the hell out of this tent,'' Rand said. ''I still might shoot this stupid ass. Just because.'' He still held his gun trained on the leader.

''Might serve the bastard right,'' someone mumbled, ''leading us into a camp ripe with fever.''

Two men moved to put the pipe back together. After they'd wrestled it back into place, Skinner backed out of the opening, watching the ruffians as he did so.

Rand pushed Elizabeth gently through the flap and followed her, keeping his gun on the leader.

With the barrel, he motioned for everyone to follow. ''Everybody out. Nice and easy.''

As the men started filing out of the tent, he went on in a conversational tone. ''Now, it'll take a few days—as few as five or as long as fifty—but you'll know when you're coming down with typhoid. The first signs are feeling weak and sluggish, and achy, like you're getting a cold. You might not think much of it to start with. But the achiness just gets worse. Then you lose your appetite.''

As she listened, Elizabeth's knees felt suddenly weak.

Rand went on. "But it gets worse when you start running a fever. See, something like boils get inside your intestines—that's the guts for you who don't know. Boils that you can't lance or cut to get rid of. They just stay inside you, fester and grow. When they rupture, you start passing bloody pus, and you know you're like as not to see the morning.

"Of course, by that time, you're hurting so bad you just don't care too much one way or the other. I've seen men stick their guns in their mouths, just to end their suffering."

The ruffians, who had dropped their clubs, stood listening in growing horror.

Folding her arms over her middle, Elizabeth looked at the tent. She wanted to go to Lois, who had been rubbing her shoulder and muttering the last time Elizabeth had seen her. She needed to check the extent of her friend's injuries.

But she didn't dare, not now.

A sick feeling rose in her throat. *Dear God, how could she have let this happen?*

To her relief, Lois and the other women appeared, but stayed near the tent's opening, looking ready to take flight for safety if trouble broke out.

" 'At dirty bastard," the leader muttered, Irish brogue flavoring the harsh words. "That goddamn dirty bastard nob, in his bowler hat, wit a hanky to his nose, like he couldn't bear the smell o' us! He didn't say a word about there bein' no fever in the camp."

Rand frowned. "Carnegie?" The description could fit no other south of Portland. Rand had already guessed the dandy was behind this outrage.

"Aye, Carnegie." The ruffian turned and spat after he said the name. "Not a damned word said he. He didn't care if he sent us in to catch our death o' the dribblin' shits. Just some stupid Micks ta him."

He glared at the men surrounding him. "He bammed us all right. But be damned if I don't get back me own outta his toilet-water-smellin' hide."

There were murmurs of agreement and "ayes" from the rough-looking lot.

Skinner stepped forward. "He didn't offer you a job working building this line, did he? The fever has us short-handed and we could use some men. He might have offered you honest work."

"No, that he didn't. But if there's fever in the camp, a feller would have to be daft—"

"He didn't offer you a job because he wanted you to clear out the camp of sick men so he could bring Chinese in here, right off the boat, for a third of the wage he would have to pay someone who speaks English.

"As far as being daft to work here, we're moving the camp down the line, five miles further on. If anyone would want to make an honest dollar, you can come talk to me about it—after you've washed up with good strong soap and clean water to lessen the chance you'll take the fever"

He motioned to the woods. "That path leads to the creek. That is, if the women you were roughin' up will give you a bar of soap. It's a damned sight more than I'd do fer you, after what you done."

As Skinner looked around at the men working for him, he said, "Come on, boys, we got a camp to move. Load everything on the supply train and we'll take it to the end of the line." He stalked off, the railroad men following.

The brigands' leader made profuse apologies to Lois, who stood with the other women just outside the door of the tent. His rough cap in his hands, he asked if they might please have soap to wash with.

Before answering, Lois picked up a club one of the gang had dropped and bashed the big man on the upper arm. As he yowled with pain, she dropped the cudgel and reached into the pocket of her apron. She came out with a bar of homemade lye soap, and tossed it to the next-nearest man, who caught it.

"I hope the Good Lord'll forgive yer fer this." She glared at them all. " 'Cause if I had my way of it, you'd all die of putrefied bowels and go straight into the fires of Hell!"

Whirling, she disappeared into the tent. The other women

who had been brave enough to venture out followed close on her heels.

As Rand watched the gang of ruffians file down toward the creek, looking for signs there'd be further trouble, Lois came back out of the tent.

"Where's Elizabeth?" she asked, a frown drawing lines over the bridge of her nose.

Looking around, he shook his head. "I thought she went back inside the tent."

"She's nowhere to be found in there. I wanted to ask her what to do about dinner for these men. Those hooligans dumped soot inta the broth pot when they broke the pipe." Lois surveyed the camp as she spoke. "You don't think someone took her off—"

"No." But unease skittered through him nonetheless. "Just do whatever you think best about food, Lois. I'll look for her."

"She might just be gone behind a tree to—" Lois flushed red as she realized what she'd been about to say, She ducked back inside the tent without another word.

Tracking through the mud, Rand made a round of the camp. Skinner and his men were rapidly disassembling everything but the big tent and loading it all atop the new rails and ties on the flatcars.

After searching everywhere else he could think of, he found Elizabeth beside his gelding, stroking the animal's shoulder while it grazed in the meadow where they'd staked the horses out.

"Horses don't get typhoid, do they?" she asked without looking at Rand as he approached.

"I don't think so." Rand frowned, a knot forming in his gut.

She held out her apron. The hem was stained with dirt and mud. Looking down at the stain sorrowfully, she said, "I was so careful. But just a moment's inattention, that's all, and there you are."

"Elizabeth—" He started toward her.

"Stay away." She backed up a step for every one he took.

Something was wrong. "Elizabeth, what is it?" Rand thought about rushing her and wrapping her in his arms. Fear clawed in his chest like a living thing as she looked into the forest, like a frightened deer about to bolt.

"Just stay back."

"Okay."

Her eyes were huge, dark with fear. He looked around for the source of it. The woodland was quiet and green. A watery sun peeped through the clouds and shone through the boughs of the Douglas firs edging the meadow. Clumps of pink and yellow wildflowers dotted the lush green grass.

Elizabeth's expression was at odds with the peaceful scene.

"What's wrong?" Very slowly, he took a step nearer. Then another.

Whimpering, she backed away. "Don't. Don't get too near. You just can't be careful enough. I tried. You know I tried."

"What's happened?" He took another small step.

She held out her hands as though to ward him off. "Don't! It's my own fault. I know just when I exposed myself."

His gut clenched. "Exposed yourself to what?" Though he guessed the answer, he hoped he was wrong.

"I have typhoid, Rand."

Chapter Twenty-five

"You're wrong." Needing to hold her, Rand took a step nearer.

Shaking her head, Elizabeth backed away. "No. I've been feeling worse and worse all week. It *is* typhoid."

"It could be anything. A cold from being in this damp when you aren't used to it. And you've been careful."

Not knowing if he was trying to convince himself or Elizabeth, Rand stepped toward her again. God, he needed to hold her. What she said couldn't be true.

But the look in her hazel eyes held a resignation that chilled him.

Squaring her shoulders, Elizabeth said, "No. I know just when I exposed myself—the day I was crying by the stream, because I knew the young Chinese boy was dying. After I stopped crying, I washed my face and dried it on my apron—before I realized my apron was dirty.

"Then you came and found me and told me he was dead, and you held me. . . ."

"That's no reason to think you have it."

Her expression bleak, Elizabeth seemed not to have heard.

She looked down at the mud-stained hem of the apron she was wearing now. "It's so easy, isn't it?" she said in wonder, shaking her head again. "I was careful today, see. But the mud is there. It only has to touch you, you see. And it stains it. And then it spreads."

Elizabeth pulled the apron off and wadded it up. "It was my mistake. I didn't go back and wash my face again with soap and dry it with a clean cloth. Now, I'll pay the price."

She looked up at him suddenly, her eyes rounding with concern. "Oh, Rand!" Elizabeth backed away. "Oh, I'm so sorry. I've exposed you, too."

"You couldn't." He eased nearer.

"I wish that was true. But I did." Her expression was horror-stricken. "I did. You held me that morning right after I washed my face, and I exposed you to it. And you'll get the fever, too."

"I won't get it." Rand made a sudden step and caught her, wrapping his arms tightly around her as she tried to pull away.

"Sssh," he told her, rocking her gently. "You're afraid you'll die, aren't you?"

"Yes. And now you'll have it, too." Though her face was turned away from him, he heard the tears in her voice.

"You can't give me the fever." Leaning back, he brushed tendrils of hair from her face. "I've had it. I don't think a person can have it twice. Didn't you hear what I told those men back in camp."

"I thought you were just bluffing them." She turned and pressed her face into his shoulder.

He stroked her back, feeling her tremble. The fine mist, which had let up during the morning, started falling again, dotting her honey-blond hair with tiny specks of moisture.

Rand pulled the cloth sunbonnet, which had been dangling by its strings, up over her hair.

"You aren't going to die. I won't let you."

"You can't stop it. I've pushed myself too hard. I . . . haven't been sleeping or eating well." She didn't like to admit that. If he guessed he was the cause, he would feel guilty. She didn't want that. ''I'm not strong enough to fight it.'' She murmured what she knew was true.

Cradled in his arms, pressing against his warmth and strength, she felt safe and sheltered. It was an illusion, she knew. But right now she didn't care.

Rand couldn't protect her from what was coming.

''I had a mild case. I had it when it hit a mining camp I was in near Bozeman, Montana. A few spots on my chest and stomach, and cramps. It isn't always severe. You know that. And some people don't ever develop the fever, no matter how many times they are exposed.''

''I feel feverish and achy. I've felt like I was coming down with a cold for the last couple of days. These feelings are usually the first stages—I should have realized it sooner. I just pray that I've not given it to Becca, or Doc, or Mabel.''

Looking into her upturned face, Rand noted her flushed cheeks. As he pressed a kiss to her forehead, his gut clenched. Her skin was far too warm. As much as he'd like to deny it, Elizabeth was more than likely right.

He stroked her back as she rested her cheek against his shoulder once more. ''You're young and healthy,'' he said. ''There's no reason to think you won't get through it. These might be the worst symptoms you have.''

Rand didn't know if he was trying to reassure her or himself. Both, he suspected.

Now that he'd found her again, he couldn't lose her again.

Elizabeth sighed and closed her eyes. ''I hope you're right.''

But her nurse's instincts told her she wouldn't be so lucky.

And if she died, what would happen to her daughter?

Rand let her go, but kept one arm around her shoulders, as if reassuring her of his support. ''Where's the coat I saw you wearing earlier.''

''Under the buckboard seat.''

Leaving her momentarily, he strode through the tall grass and retrieved it. After she slipped it on and buttoned it, he guided Elizabeth to his horse, as though she were too fragile to walk.

As she waited for Rand to work the cinch tight, she looked around the meadow. The clumps of lovely wildflowers did nothing to ease the cold fear coiling inside her.

"Where are we going?"

"I'm going to take you to Doc Sedrick."

"Rand, no. Becca's there. If I haven't already given this to her . . . No. No. I can't go there. I can't expose her again."

Finishing his task, Rand lowered the stirrup. "What about Jeremiah's cabin?" He could take her there and take care of her.

"The cabin where we . . ." Heat flooded Elizabeth's cheeks as she remembered the wonderful afternoon they'd spent at the trapper's cabin.

She wanted to say no. The memories were too strong. But in reality it was the perfect solution. She couldn't go back to Willow and expose people to the fever. She couldn't stay here.

"What about Becca?" She bit her lip. "If I don't see her and talk to her, she'll be worried and afraid. Before we came to Willow, we'd never been separated."

"We'll think of something." Rand mounted and held out his hand.

She took it and placed her foot in the stirrup he'd freed for her to use. The well-trained horse stood perfectly still as Rand helped Elizabeth swing up behind him. She circled his waist with her arms, and he felt her shivering.

With a growing sense of urgency, Rand turned his horse toward the camp and urged it into a canter. The area had already changed dramatically. Skinner's tent was gone, and so were the telegraph wires that had connected it to the main telegraph line being set up beside the tracks.

Men stacked boxes of explosives and other supplies onto the flatcar. Rand recognized the leader of the ruffians shouldering a dozen pickaxes and striding toward the train cars. Other miscreants were working, too.

Evidently, Skinner had managed to talk the gang into honest work. Good. Skinner needed the help, and keeping them up here would prevent them from possibly carrying the fever down to Eugene, or even Salem.

Spotting Deborah ladling broth into a bowl from the small cook pot the women had set up, Rand rode over. Sensing its master's nervousness, his horse pranced as Rand drew back on the reins.

"Is there something wrong?" The young woman looked from Elizabeth to Rand.

"Tell Lois she'll have to take charge. Elizabeth is sick."

"Elizabeth?" Deborah frowned up at her.

"It's nothing," Elizabeth said. "I'm sure. I haven't eaten right or slept properly for days. It's catching up." She hated lying. But it would do no good to frighten everyone.

Without giving her time to say more, Rand wheeled the horse around. Elizabeth wrapped her arms around his waist and held on as he gave the animal its head. Damp evergreen boughs brushed her skirts. The air smelled clean, tinged with evergreens.

As she held onto Rand's strength, feeling his hard muscles bunch as he shifted in the saddle, leaning to avoid a low limb, or to the side as the horse made a sharp turn, it was hard to imagine anything was wrong.

Carrying double, the horse soon tired. Rand slid off when they reached the steepest part of the trail to the trapper's cabin, and Elizabeth clutched the saddle horn as he led the horse the last few hundred yards.

Without Rand's warmth to hold onto, a chill seemed to seep into her very bones. It seemed terribly hard just to hold on, and her head pounded in rhythm with every step the horse took.

By the time they reached the cabin, she was more than ready to dismount. Rand caught her as she slid off. Holding onto his wide shoulders, Elizabeth was glad he did. Her knees seemed to belong to someone else. They refused to cooperate.

Could she be farther into the cycle of the disease than she thought?

"Hold on." He scooped her up and carried her inside.

Supported by his strength, Elizabeth felt sheltered and safe again.

But as her eyes adjusted to the dim interior of the cabin, she put her hand to her mouth to stifle a gasp. Everything had been so neat the afternoon they'd made love there. Now, nothing was in its place.

The tins were gone from the rough shelves, the table overturned. The narrow bed had been dismantled, the rope frame pulled away from the wall, and one end of the corn-shuck mattress ripped open. Half the stuffing had been scattered over the hard-pack dirt floor. What was left of the mattress lay draped over the overturned table.

The small tin trunk that had been at the end of the bed was open and a few articles of clothing scattered over the floor.

Everything had been gone through.

"Bill and his grandson did this?" she asked as Rand put her down.

"Afraid so. I came to check on them a few days after we met them on the trail and this is what I found."

"Why would they?" Elizabeth placed an arm over her middle as a mild cramp caught her unaware.

Rand righted an overturned chair and guided her to it, making her sit.

Elizabeth wanted to protest that she wasn't an invalid yet. But his concern warmed her, reenforcing that feeling that all would be right as long as Rand was with her. However irrational, she clutched at it, using it to keep her fear at bay.

What would happen to her daughter if she didn't recover?

"The way it looked to me when I found it," Rand said, "is the two spent the night here after we met them on the trail, then took anything they thought was of value. I think they figured whoever lived here might have some money hidden away." He motioned at two stones pried out of the hearth. "That must have been what they were looking for when they pulled the stuffing out of the mattress, too."

Grabbing the mattress, he stuffed fistfuls of corn shucks back into it. "After I fix the bed, I'll make a quick ride into town and get blankets and whatever else you'll need. I'll tell Mabel to pack your nightgowns and wrapper—I guess she'll know what to include. I'll tell Becca. . . ."

On his knees on the floor, Rand stilled, a fistful of corn

shucks clutched in one hand, the mattress ticking in the other. Changing emotions chased over his features as he looked up at her. "What do you want me to tell her?"

"I have to think about that." Elizabeth didn't want to frighten the child. But she didn't want to minimize the seriousness of her illness.

After he finished restuffing the corn shucks into the mattress, Rand stood and placed it on the bed. Then he stood her up, as if she was as fragile as a spun-sugar confection, then guided her to sit on the bed. He unbuttoned her coat—just as she might have unbuttoned Becca's, Elizabeth thought, tenderness for the man growing. His big hands were gentle as he slipped it off her shoulders.

Rand clutched the coat. It smelled of lilacs and damp wool. And it held Elizabeth's warmth. Laying it aside reluctantly, he knelt and helped her pull off her muddy shoes, somehow managing the tiny buttons.

Elizabeth lay back on the bed, and he spread the coat over her.

After Rand had built a fire in the fireplace, he said, "I'll be back with supplies and make you more comfortable as soon as I can. Will you—" His tone changed, becoming firmer. "You will be all right until I get back."

"If that's an order." She smiled, trying to hide her shivering. She felt cold to the bone. "Go on. I'll be fine. Just be careful not to come into contact with people, or handle things before you—"

"Wash my hands. I'll just stay outside of Doc's house and have Mabel gather supplies and medicines. And I won't let Becca get near me."

He paused in the doorway, his dark eyes uncertain. "What *do* you want me to tell Becca?"

"Tell her the truth." Elizabeth closed her eyes. "I'm sick, but I hope it won't be long before I can be with her again."

A hollow feeling settled inside as he closed the door and used the latchkey that he'd found lying on the mantle to drop the wooden bolt in place from the outside. Elizabeth would be able to get out if she needed to, but others couldn't get in easily.

Only the fact that Elizabeth needed medicine and supplies and he was the only one that could bring them gave Rand the strength to leave her at all.

Chapter Twenty-six

As she listened to Rand riding away, Elizabeth lay staring at rafters in the open ceiling. How could she have been so careless? She, who should have known better than anyone, except Doc, how easily contagions could spread. Dr. Brown had been adamant when training her, and though Elizabeth had often thought him lacking in compassion, he was a very good doctor.

She had only herself to blame for her carelessness. Now, she wondered what price she would pay.

Rolling over on her side, she studied the mess strewn over the floor of the once-neat cabin. Reaching out from the low bunk, she touched a piece of a broken bowl, half a painted pansy visible on the shard. It must have been a pretty piece—so out of place in the sparsely furnished cabin. Perhaps a keepsake from Jeremiah Hull's mother, or a wife.

The old trapper who'd lived here had owned so little, it [illegible] tragedy that even that little had been destroyed.

[illegible] the same thing had happened to her. She'd planned [illegible]ughter's future, choosing security over the urgings [illegible] So determined not to lose control of her emotions and let Rand ruin their lives. Well, Rand had had nothing to do with it.

She'd managed just fine all by herself.

"Look who came back with me." Rand held the door wide for the doctor.

Grumbling under his breath, his gray brows drawn together in a deep frown, Doc Sedrick made his way inside, maneuvering carefully on his crutches over the debris-strewn floor.

"Oh, Doc." Lying on the narrow bed, Elizabeth shook her head. "You shouldn't have come out here. The road is terrible."

"Terrible? Not at all. There *is* no road. How on earth could it be terrible?"

Rand placed a chair by the bed and Doc sat, propping his crutches against the wall. He winced as he stretched his splinted leg out in front of him.

"I know I didn't have to come, but you couldn't have expected me to stay away." Doc bent a sharp look at her over the top of his glasses. "I have to say you are looking puny, Elizabeth. For the last few days, I've wondered if you were taking ill."

"Flatterer." Elizabeth dredged up a smile. Now that the shock of realizing she was sick was wearing off, she'd begun to think more clearly. Make decisions. "I was careless, Doc. I know how this happened and I have no one to blame but myself."

"I'm not a priest. I don't need to hear a confession." But the harsh words were spoken in a caring tone.

Rand was hovering nearby, looking at a loss. Doc told him, "Bring me my bag, please. Then, if you'll wait outside, I want to examine my patient."

After Rand fetched the medical bag, he lit a lantern he'd brought back with other supplies and went out.

Waiting in the buggy, Mabel held Becca on her lap. Both watched Rand as he approached.

"Did Jonas confirm that it is typhoid?" Mabel asked.

"Not yet. He ran me out before he examined Elizabeth."

Rand glanced back at the rough cabin, wanting to go back inside, to stay by Elizabeth's side. "I'm no doctor, but I'm almost certain. Doc could have saved himself the trip."

"Nonsense. You don't know Jonas if you think he would have stayed away. We've grown very fond of Elizabeth."

Becca looked from one adult to the other as they spoke. Then with a sympathetic frown, she leaned over and patted Rand's hand, where it rested on the dashboard. "It's going to be all right, Mr. Rand."

Looking into his daughter's big, dark eyes, Rand felt a smile curve the corners of his mouth. Then blinking rapidly, he asked, "Do you know how many people care about you, tadpole?"

Becca nodded, her curls bouncing. "Lots and lots. That's why Mama brought me here. We were all alone at our old house. Nobody liked us."

Rand winced inwardly.

"Why do you say that?" Mabel asked the child.

"No one came to see us." Becca shrugged and looked up at Mabel.

The child's ebony eyes and winged brows were a reflection of the tall man's standing beside the buggy. As Mabel looked from the little girl to the man, understanding dawned.

"You never mentioned being in Kansas, Rand," Mabel said quietly.

Becca gaped at him. "We lived in Kansas, too."

He looked at his child and then back at the cabin. "I was there a few years ago, tadpole. Before you were born."

"About five, I'd say." Mabel smiled.

"Something like that." Rand stuck his hands into his pockets. "I never knew. . . . When I found out, I wanted to tell the world. But I owed Elizabeth. I couldn't *not* do as she asked. And she came here to marry Hiram."

"I expect you have something to do with Elizabeth putting that off," Mabel mused.

"I've tried my best, I admit."

Looking from Mabel to Rand, Becca frowned, obviously not understanding the conversation.

"I think Lois Mayflower is very glad of that." Retying the

strings her bonnet, Mabel looked at Rand with raised brows. "I don't think Lois would mind at all if Elizabeth and Hiram never got married."

It was Rand's brows that rode upward at this intelligence. But looking back, he saw he should have guessed how Lois felt. And he wasn't sure Hiram didn't have the same feelings for Lois. The two seemed so comfortable together.

But Hiram would never call off the wedding, not as long as Elizabeth was set on marrying him. It would be the honorable thing to do, to Hiram's way of thinking.

"You can come back and help me now," Doc called from inside.

After Doc had washed his hands in a basin of water Rand fetched him, Rand helped the older man back into the buggy, then unloaded the supplies of blankets, food, coffee, and a few other things he'd thought might be needed.

"Here's Elizabeth's things, Rand." Mabel placed a carpet-bag atop the crate he'd plucked from the tailboard of the buggy. "There are medicines inside."

"None until in the morning," Doc said. "I've given her paregoric, and it should have her resting soon. Make her drink all she can, at every opportunity. She knows all this, but like doctors, I suspect nurses make bad patients."

"Can I see Mama now?" Becca asked. "I've been patient," she added earnestly.

"Tadpole, you can't go too near, or you might get sick, too."

The lost expression on the little girl's face at Rand's words made his heart ache. "Tell you what. I'll help Elizabeth to the door and you can wave to her. Will that be okay?" Rand asked.

"I s'pose." Becca swung her foot in agitation.

Rand carried the crate and bag inside.

"I heard Becca." Elizabeth was already standing, carefully making her way across the debris-strewn floor in her stocking feet. Rand set the crate down, then caught her around the waist.

"What are you trying to do? Do you want to fall, or cut your feet open?" he asked in exasperation as he carried her to the door.

"I'm not completely an invalid," Elizabeth told him as he set her on her feet in the doorway.

Becca stood in the foot box of the buggy, waving madly.

Waving back, Elizabeth called, "I'll try to get well really fast, pun'kin."

"Mrs. Mabel says not to worry," the child said. "I can stay with them as long as it takes for you to get well." After a pause, she added, "But I don't want you to take too long, okay?"

"Okay, pun'kin. I'll do my best not to take too long."

Doc said, "I'll send Lois or one of the other women out to help you, Elizabeth, as soon as I can contact one." His splinted leg held carefully out toward the side, Doc unwrapped the reins from the brake handle.

"I'll take care of Elizabeth," Rand said, holding her shoulders protectively.

The older man frowned. "Rand, I'm not sure I heard you or you might have misunderstood—"

"I said I'll take care of her," Rand said again.

"Jonas, it's all right," Mabel told her husband. "I'll explain later."

Rand added, "I need to talk with Hiram. If you'd tell him when you see him, I'd be grateful."

"I can believe that you do need to talk to Hiram." Doc slapped the horse's rump with the reins.

As the buggy rolled away, Becca turned around on the seat, waving good-bye. *"If you have to go to heaven, tell Grandma hello for me!"*

"Okay!" Waving, Elizabeth felt tears prick her eyes.

"But try not to go, okay? I'd miss you too much!" Becca waved and blew kisses until the buggy was out of sight.

Rand scooped Elizabeth up and carried her to the bed.

Sitting her down, he took her hand and started undoing the buttons on the cuff of her dress.

"What do you think you're doing?"

"Undressing you."

"I can undress myself."

"I know." He took her other wrist and started on those buttons.

Elizabeth sighed. "I'm sorry. I do appreciate all you've done." A headache throbbed in her temples. She knew the opiate in the paregoric should go to work soon, soothing her stomach as well as her head and putting her to sleep as well.

"I don't have any designs on your body, if that's what you are worried about," Rand said.

"Actually, that's the last thing I'm worrying about right now."

After undoing the other cuff and the front buttons, Rand slipped the garment off her shoulders. Then he untied the string of her camisole. He couldn't resist pressing a kiss to the creamy skin of her shoulder. But he found it far too warm. Goose pimples sprang up along her arms as he pulled her sleeves down.

"Just a moment. I'll have you warm." Working quickly, he finished undressing her and pulled a flannel nightgown over her head. "There. All done."

"That's good. Because I think I have to lie down now." Elizabeth closed her eyes to stop the room from spinning.

Chapter Twenty-seven

When Elizabeth opened her eyes again, the lantern hung from the bare rafters, casting a golden light all around. She couldn't tell what time it was. But obviously it was very late.

She wondered how long she'd been asleep. Rand had been busy. The cabin was cleaned and straightened, all debris gone from the earthen floor. A cheery fire burned low in the stone fireplace. Despite the fire and the blanket pulled to her chin, she felt a chill. And her mouth was dry and her throat felt parched.

Fever. She would need quinine, though she hated the thought of taking the bitter medicine.

A murmur of low voices sounded outside. As she listened she wasn't certain how many people there were. One woman—oh, it was Lois. Then a man said something about Carnegie. Rand answered, but though Elizabeth tried, she couldn't understand what he said.

As her thirst and curiosity got the better of her, Elizabeth wet her lips and called, "Rand?"

Her voice came out a rasp. She wasn't at all certain he could hear her outside the cabin.

Hatless, his ebony hair splashed with gold lamplight, Rand

appeared at once. Moving to the bedside, he took her hand from beneath the blanket and held it, looking concerned. ''Elizabeth, what do you need?''

''Water, please.''

An oaken bucket with a dipper sat on the table. Rand dipped some water into an enamelware cup and brought it to her.

It was deliciously cool.

''More, if you don't mind.'' She gave him back the cup, pleased that her voice seemed to work better.

''Not at all.'' He refilled it and handed it back. ''We have company.''

Even as Rand said the words, Lois stuck her head inside the door ''Elizabeth? My word. I couldn't believe it when Deborah told me you'd took sick.''

She came on inside and brushed between Rand and the bed. Frowning, she placed her hand on Elizabeth's forehead. ''My, you are on the sickly side, ain't you?''

''The camp, the men—how are they doing? Are any more sick?''

''Don't worry about the camp. I got out afore the Board of Health posted the quarantine late this afternoon. A couple of the older women stayed to nurse the sick. The men what's got better are still helpin' out with those what's still poorly.'' Lois sat on the chair drawn up by the bed. ''Oh, and Deborah stayed to—I 'spect she's sweet on that young Irish feller, Mickey.''

''I could tell.'' Elizabeth smiled.

''Ever'thing is taken care of. The women will post a list of things they need on the big stump by the bend in the road—that's where the quarantine sign is posted—and Hiram or one of the others will go every day and fetch the stuff back. No new cases, and some improvin' right smart. Oh, and since Hiram's cousin is gettin' back on his feet, there ain't been any more cases at the lumber camp.''

''Well, there is one new case here,'' Elizabeth said. ''I was careless. Lois, promise me you won't be. I taught you what I knew, but I should have practiced what I preached.'' She closed her eyes.

''I will remember. But I ain't goin' ta be goin' back, now

that the quarantine's posted. Not unless they get real bad off for help. Doc Sedrick says my sister-in-law could have her young'un at any time. And the salmon are startin' to run. My brother and his wife need me more than I'm needed at the camp.

"With Sara and Millie, and the Widow Tompkins and Neb, I think the camp will do just fine without me and you. You taught ever'body real good—even if you messed up. Now, here's someone else to see you." Lois rose.

"Who?" Elizabeth opened her eyes and found Hiram standing at the foot of the bed. He looked at a spot on the wall somewhere over her head, then at the wool blanket covering her feet.

"Hello, Elizabeth."

"I'm glad you came," she said, and she was aware of Rand stiffening.

Hiram said, "Seemed the right thing."

"I hoped you would." She wet her lips and went on. "I need to set some things right. First, I want to tell you that I'm releasing you from our betrothal."

Everyone was silent for a few seconds. "Really, Elizabeth?" It was Lois who spoke first, her gaze flying to Hiram.

He looked into Lois's eyes, straight on and unblinking.

Looking from one to the other, Elizabeth smiled. How had she failed to see before how they felt about each other? She sighed, glad that Hiram's boys would get a mother. "I hope you can bake tea cakes, Lois. Donnie is especially fond of them."

"As a matter of fact, I can." Lois grinned, showing the wide space between her front teeth. "Won a blue ribbon for mine at the county fair in Salem last year."

Hiram gazed at Lois as though she was Helen of Troy. Then he glanced at Elizabeth and blushed, blinked, and finally focused on the earthen floor. "You sure, Elizabeth? I sent for you and you came on good faith. I want to do right by you now."

"You have. And I have money due me from the sale of my mother's farm. I want to use it to repay you, Hiram, the money you sent me for my and Becca's trip.'' She looked at Rand. ''And I want you to promise to see to it, Rand. If I can't for any reason. My brother hasn't been all that honest with me in the past. And if I die—''

''You will not die,'' he said as if that was an order.

''I certainly don't plan to. But I may not have a choice in the matter. And if I die, I'm afraid you might have to pry it out of Ethan.''

She went on. ''I'm almost certain my brother stole the money for that horse five years ago, and I was thinking a bank draft for sale of the homestead should have come before now. The mail isn't that slow.''

Rand nodded. ''I'll see to it.''

Hiram said, ''I ain't worried about the money, Elizabeth.''

''But I am.'' Elizabeth wet her lips. Her mouth was going dry again. ''I've always tried to be an honorable woman.''

''As far as I can tell, you're a right fine woman, Elizabeth McKay.'' Hiram looked at Rand. ''Any man would shore be proud to make you his bride.''

Lois moved beside Hiram, taking his arm. ''But I'm shore proud you changed yore mind, Elizabeth,'' she said.

After the two had left, Rand closed the door, then dipped a cup into a cook pot sitting on the hearth. ''Lois brought this chicken broth in a jar and I put it to warm. I think it should be about ready.''

Elizabeth sat up on the side of the bed, surprised at how light-headed she felt. ''Another thing, Rand. If I die, I want you to take Becca. I guess we need to make certain that no one objects.''

''You won't die.'' He handed her the cup.

''Chicken?'' Feeling no appetite, she took the cup from him and sipped. To her surprise, the salty broth tasted good and it warmed her. She drained the cup and gave it back.

''I'll get you more.'' Rand started toward the hearth.

''No.'' Elizabeth reached out and caught his arm, stopping him. ''Not right now. Thank you. Rand, what was Hiram saying about Carnegie?''

"Nothing." His expression bland, Rand looked her straight in the eye as he spoke.

"You are a good liar. I'll have to remember that. Now, do you mind telling me the truth?"

"I'm not going to discuss it with you, Elizabeth. It's not important." He touched her cheek, his callused fingers slightly rough against her skin. "The only thing you should think about is getting well."

"I have something more urgent to think about right now." She felt herself blush. "The privy."

"This is nice of you, Mrs. Lyle . . . I'll give her this broth later."

"Rand, we brought you some firewood. How's Elizabeth? Any change?"

"Don't worry about the linens. I'll send and get them every day."

"Increase the quinine and bathe her in tepid water. . . . If the fever gets too high . . ."

The voices worried her. She could never quite tell when they were real, or when she was imagining them. Although most of the time, she hurt too badly to care.

"What are you going to do about the county sheriff?"

"He knows where I am when he wants me."

At that statement, Elizabeth fought to open her eyes. Rand must have been giving her too much paregoric. The opiate had her in a stupor. . . .

But why then would she hurt so badly?

Elizabeth wet her lips. "Rand, who's here?"

Sitting in a straight chair drawn up beside the bed, arms crossed on his chest as he half dozed, Rand came alert instantly. "Did you say something?"

"I think I did." She touched his cheek. It was rough with several days' worth of beard. When had he grown that?

She let her hand fall back onto the bed, exhausted by the simple act of touching his face.

He caught her fingers and pressed a kiss into the palm, hope flooding through him as he realized Elizabeth was really awake this time. Not like other times when she'd talked out of her head with fever.

"You have a beard. . . ."

"You've been away for a while." He smiled and touched her cheek.

She wet her dry lips again. "Who is here? Who was talking?" The effort of speech was difficult. Almost beyond her.

"No one. Not for a while anyway." He dipped her a cup of water and held her up as she drank, hope surging in him as she accomplished the simple task. He'd been having to force water into her mouth as she was half-conscious and make her swallow.

"I think everyone in Willow has been by. Bringing broth and rice water. Firewood and food for me. You have made a lot of friends here, Elizabeth."

He didn't add that he'd been able to get her to take in far too little of the offerings. The only thing he had kept in her was water. Every hour, he'd held her head and forced a little down her. Even if she choked. Doc had warned him dehydration was her enemy.

He held another cup of water for her. He helped her lift her head. She took a few sips, then turned away from it.

"Becca?"

"Becca is fine. She sent you a picture." Rand took the drawing from a shelf and held it where Elizabeth could see it. Three stick figures held hands—a little girl, a woman, and a man with a star on his chest.

Exhausted, Elizabeth closed her eyes.

He put the picture back on the shelf and sat down again, taking her hand once more.

She murmured, "I was right to release Hiram from his promise. Now, Lois will bake for his boys. . . ."

"Yes. You were right."

"Who bathed me? Do I remember being bathed?"

"I did."

She stared at him wide-eyed for an instant, then shook her

head slightly. ''Tsk, tsk. Now you'll have to make an honest woman of me.''

''As soon as I can,'' Rand said. *If I ever get another chance,* he added silently, his cheeks wet.

''Becca . . . Rand, you will have to take care of Becca.''

She was suddenly unconcious again.

''I will try my best,'' he said, though he knew Elizabeth didn't hear. Raising her hand to his lips, he kissed her fingers.

He should have listened to her. Rand stroked her damp forehead and wondered how he could tell her, if she did wake up again, that she'd been right all along.

The sick had needed care, but the thing could have been done differently. He could have gotten a quarantine declared when he'd first heard of the illness in the camp and had Judge Blackwood see that Carnegie let the railroad provide essential care.

Rand wished he had taken Elizabeth and Becca and ridden like hell. Maybe the sick men wouldn't have fared as well, but then Elizabeth probably would not have contracted the disease.

They could have ridden for Canada. Or Mexico. Or sailed to the Sandwich Islands and looked down into the volcano, and to the Galapagos to observe the different forms of life, as he and Elizabeth had talked about a lifetime ago.

Becca's lifetime.

And they would have had their daughter with them.

But he had refused to listen.

This morning, Doc Sedrick had come out to the cabin again and examined Elizabeth again. Rand hadn't needed Doc to tell him the prognosis looked bad.

Now, touching her cheek, checking how warm it felt, Rand decided the quinine was doing its job. But keeping her fever down didn't seem to be making any real difference.

After Doc had gone, Rand had carefully brushed and plaited her hair, bathed her, and put her in a clean nightgown, wanting her to look her best. Willing her to get well.

Now, as he brushed wispy curls from her forehead, he tried to ignore how pronounced her cheekbones had become. She had lost a great deal of weight. Her ribs stuck out against her skin.

But it was the yellow cast to her skin that bothered him most. When he pinched a small place on the back of her hand, as he'd seen Doc Sedrick do, testing for dehydration, it stayed raised.

Elizabeth was barely hanging on—Doc had said as much. And if Elizabeth died because he'd been stubbornly insistent on staying here, believing he could build something more for them than castles in the air . . .

No!

Rand stood and went to the fireplace, raking the coals together, then putting more logs over them. He then swung out the hook, hung a pot of rice water on it, and swung it back over the heat so it would warm.

She wouldn't die.

Not if he could help it, he thought, watching the flames grow.

Becca wouldn't lose her mother because of her father's stubbornness.

Chapter Twenty-eight

"Drink, Elizabeth."

Without opening her eyes, she turned her head to avoid the cup.

"Drink!"

Rand had found a firm tone worked better than cajoling and trying to reason with her. Most of the time, even when she wasn't lucid, she responded to the tone more than his words.

Rand held her head in the curl of his arm and mercilessly forced a little broth mixed with rice water into her mouth, making certain she swallowed. After repeating the action, he set the cup aside, settled her back on the pillow, and pulled the blanket up beneath her chin.

Was it his imagination? Or were her struggles to avoid it getting stronger?

Maybe just wishful thinking. All through the long days and nights since that last time she'd spoken lucidly, he'd followed the same pattern—every thirty minutes or so, he'd forced Elizabeth to swallow fluids, either broth or rice water or water. After she'd taken at least three swallows, he would let her rest.

Rubbing tired eyes, Rand stood and stretched stiff muscles,

then hunkered down by the fireplace and poured himself a cup of coffee from the pot sitting beside the flames.

"Rand?"

It was just a whisper. He was by Elizabeth's side in an instant. "Elizabeth?" His heart thumped. Was she really awake?

Or was she talking in delirium again?

"Oh, I forgot to tell you. . . ."

He decided it was the latter, and swallowed hard. "Sssh. Whatever it is, it can wait." He took her hand and frowned.

Did her skin really have a better color, or was he wishing again? Rand pinched the back of her hand. Not believing the results, he did it again. The small ridge of skin created when he pinched smoothed out. Her skin's natural elasticity had returned, somewhat.

"No, I forgot to say . . . I love you." Elizabeth smiled up at him. He could no longer doubt she was truly awake.

"Oh, Elizabeth." Rand knelt and gathered her to him. "What a terrible thing to forget to say." He closed his eyes, hot tears on his cheeks. Hot pain ran through his chest—joy so great it hurt to feel it. "Even more terrible, I forgot to say it, too. I love you, Elizabeth. Oh, I love you."

"That's nice. But if you ever try to give me rice water again . . ."

"Never again." He laughed.

"Rand!" Suddenly distressed, she pushed against him. "Rand, I need. . . . Oh! *Oh, no!*"

"What is it? Are you in pain? Where does it hurt?" He pulled back and studied her face.

Tears darkened her hazel eyes. "I had an accident."

Jerking back the blankets, Rand saw the source of her distress and laughed aloud.

"It's not funny!"

"No, it's wonderful." He kissed her forehead. It was the first water she'd produced in he couldn't remember how long. "Really, it is wonderful. Doc Sedrick said if you started wetting again, you would be all right." He hugged her exuberantly.

"But the bed."

''Don't worry about the damned bed. Hazel Cavanaugh sent me her rubber sheets, and they're underneath the linen. I've plenty of clean sheets from Mabel.

''Elizabeth,'' he said seriously, stroking her cheekbone with his thumb. ''You're going to be fine.''

Rand's dark eyes glowed as they looked into hers. His tone told her that there had been some doubt, surprising her. She touched his damp cheek. ''How long have I been sick?''

''Almost two weeks.' ''

''Two . . . weeks? No wonder I feel weak as a newborn kitten. Becca?''

''Becca is fine and showing no signs of getting the fever.''

''That's . . . wonderful.'' Elizabeth's eyes closed. She tried to open them again, but they wouldn't stay open. The effort quickly became too much.

Kneeling beside the bed, Rand kissed her forehead, rested his cheek against her shoulder, and said a small prayer of thanks.

Elizabeth was going to recover. That was all he'd ever asked for during his long vigil. Now, he would take whatever came.

Looking down at the stew served over corn bread, Elizabeth felt as though she might explode if she ate another bite. She pushed the tin plate away.

''What's the matter?'' Rand asked, concern edging his voice. ''You are feeling well, aren't you?''

''I'm fine. The stew is wonderful. I find I just haven't much room to put food these days.'' She smiled. ''I can't eat anymore.''

''You mean after all that whining to Doc this morning about needing food more solid than gruel and farina, you aren't going to eat it?'' Rand grinned as he stropped the razor Doc had brought him—saying, as he gave it to Rand, that Rand looked worse than old Jeremiah and it was time he cleaned up.

Elizabeth had the feeling there was something more afoot than the men were letting on. She sensed a conspiracy, and decided to ferret out exactly what it was.

This morning, at last, Doc had pronounced Elizabeth no longer contagious and said it would be all right for her to see other people. She couldn't wait to hug her daughter. But Rand seemed reluctant to take her away from the cabin, making first one excuse and then another.

Now he had water heating over the fire to take a bath.

"Rand, I've been up for a week now. I haven't run any fever for a week and a half. I want to go back down to town and see Becca." Though Mabel had brought the child twice since Elizabeth began to recover and she had talked to Becca from a distance, Elizabeth couldn't wait to wrap her arms around her daughter and squeeze her tight.

"I miss her so much," she added.

"Soon. Very soon," Rand promised enigmatically.

A pair of strong arms encircled Elizabeth and squeezed gently, as though she was made of delicate porcelain. Heat rushed through her as she realized that he'd pulled off his shirt and his chest was bare.

Elizabeth swallowed, willing herself not to be distracted. . . . As she caught Rand's biceps, enjoying the hard feel of his muscles and the heat of his skin beneath her hands, it was hard not to be. For the last several days, as she had slept in the bed while he lay on a bedroll in front of the fire, Elizabeth had grown more and more aware of him, lying there at night, just a few steps away.

She took her renewed lack of self-control where her desire for Rand was concerned as a sign she was getting better.

Remembering that she wanted answers, she let go of his arms and folded her hands on the table. "What's going on?" she asked point-blank.

"Surprises." He kissed the top of her head, and slid his hands over her arms, warming her flesh wherever he touched.

Elizabeth swallowed. "I don't care for surprises. I've had too many in my life that were bad."

"Hmmm, I think you will like these." His voice was soft as silk as he rubbed his chest against her back.

So, she wasn't the only one feeling the heat over the last

several days. Elizabeth smiled, and leaned back into his embrace.

Then she realized what he'd said.

"More than one?" Intrigued, Elizabeth pushed out of Rand's embrace and faced him. Even with the beard, he was as handsome as the first time she saw him on the prairie. "Tell me?" She traced the line of his shoulder, then down to his pectoral muscles, well formed from hard labor.

"Then they wouldn't be surprises." He smiled. His smile faded, and there were the shadows in his eyes she'd noticed before.

He cupped her face, as if savoring the feel. "Believe me when I say you'll like them."

"Tell me one at least?" she cajoled.

Rand smiled again. Reaching into a box of things Mabel had sent that morning by Doc, he brought out a small, brown paper-wrapped square. It smelled of lilacs.

"Is this . . ." Opening it, Elizabeth found it was soap. "Real fancy milled soap." She inhaled deeply, savoring the smell.

"The sun is warm outside and the rain barrel is just about big enough you can sink down in it. And those cans of water I'm heating are for you."

"For me? Oh, Rand. A bath. A real down-in-a-tub-of-hot-water bath."

Rummaging in the box again, he brought out a towel and washcloth. "There's no one for miles. While I shave, you can soak and soap." A wicked glint in his eye, he added, "I'll even come rinse your hair for you when you're ready."

Tears sprang into her eyes entirely too easily these days. "Thank you. Looking my best—though I've lost so much weight—I'll feel better when I see Becca. She will believe I'm better."

"That, too."

"What do you mean."

Grinning, he went back to stropping the razor. "I just thought you needed a bath."

"Oh, you!" Elizabeth hit him with the towel.

The rain barrel was a tight fit. Her knees pressed against the oaken staves as she sank down until the water was lapping her chin. The two cans of hot water Rand added to the rainwater had made it wonderfully warm. Elizabeth luxuriated, used the fragrant soap to bathe and then wash her hair, then luxuriated some more.

Freshly shaven, Rand appeared in crisply pressed dark trousers and polished boots, and shirtless. He looked so handsome it made her heart catch.

Trying not to stare, Elizabeth asked, "Why do you have on such nice trousers?"

"I didn't want to put on my shirt until I helped rinse your hair." He lifted the can he'd brought outside.

"That didn't answer my question."

"It didn't?" As he poured the warm water over her hair, he said, "You'd better hurry if you don't want to get caught in that rain barrel when our company arrives."

"Company?" Shaking her head, slinging her hair back, Elizabeth fought the water out of her eyes. "What company? Who is coming?"

Rand looked down at the wet streak her action left on his pants and shook his head. "I told you there was more than one surprise. Now, try not to splash." With that, he lifted her from the barrel.

"Rand?" Glaring at him, she shivered. "Tell me, please?"

His dark gaze moved appreciatively over her wet body, warming her.

"No."

He handed her the towel and went back inside, leaving Elizabeth to fume silently.

Realizing she was standing there completely naked, she cast a wary look down the road as she hurriedly dried off and wrapped the towel around her.

When she got inside, she found the dress she'd brought with her to wear when she married Hiram laid out on the narrow cot—her mother's wedding dress. Plain white satin with a lace inset on the bodice and lace edging the cuffs. The blue-satin sash, which she'd planned to wear with it, since she was supposed to be a widow, was lying across the dress.

''It's a little wrinkled from being folded.'' Rand was buttoning a crisp white shirt. His uncombed hair touched his shoulders and fell forward in his face. A charcoal-gray coat was hung on the back of a chair, with a string tie across it.

His ebony gaze moved over her appreciatively as he finger-combed his dark hair back from his face. His gaze settled on her bare legs as he continued with the buttons.

''But if you continue to stand there like that, it's likely to get more wrinkled when I lay you down on top of it. Wet, too. You are tempting me to have the honeymoon before the wedding.''

Chapter Twenty-nine

Elizabeth wet her lips, not believing she'd heard right. "Wedding?"

Still buttoning his shirt, Rand smiled.

"Oh, Rand!" Dropping the towel, she flew into his arms. "Really? Today?" After all they'd been through, could it really be that they'd get to start their lives together?

Inexplicably, Rand's smile faded. "Today." He kissed her damp forehead. "This afternoon." He added, pulling back a little, "In my now-wet shirt."

His dark gaze settled on his chest, where her wet breasts had pressed against him and left a "heart" of dampness. Pulling her tightly against him, he slid his hands upward, cupping her breasts.

Elizabeth sucked in a harsh breath as his thumbs found her nipples.

"Hell, there's a lot more to be said for honeymoons than weddings," he murmured. Leaning over, he flung the door closed and slid the door latch into place. Then cupping her face, he kissed her deeply. As though savoring every detail of her lips, her mouth.

White heat swept through her, weakening her knees so that she clung to him for support. She never wanted to let go again.

And soon they would be married, together always.

Breaking off the kiss, Rand said hoarsely, "You have about a heartbeat to get your wedding dress off the bed, if you don't want it to look really interesting as you walk down the aisle." He began undoing the buttons on the shirt he'd just so meticulously done up.

Despite her shaky knees, Elizabeth had the dress draped over the chair atop his coat and was lying on the bed as Rand sat and pulled off his boots. Then he stood and stripped off his trousers.

"Are you certain?" Rand asked as he joined her on the bed. "And I'm not certain you're recovered enough. Elizabeth, I wouldn't want to do anything ever again that is going to hurt you."

There was a flavor to his words she didn't understand. He stroked her body tenderly, as though she might crumble to dust and disappear. But his slight touch was enough to stoke the fire building inside her.

Pressing boldly against him, Elizabeth closed her eyes, loving the feel of his naked body along the length of hers. "I feel ready now."

She reached between them and stroked his hardness. Grinning, she said, "You seem to be, too."

With a groan, he rolled atop her and kissed her neck, then the side of her jaw. He stroked her body as though unwilling to leave any part unexplored, and Elizabeth's desire for him soared until she begged him to take her.

When Rand joined with her, Elizabeth felt as though their souls merged. She could only hold on as the cabin swirled away and they rode a whirlwind to a place where stars exploded, bringing incredible pleasure.

When Elizabeth opened her eyes again, Rand was propped on an elbow, looking at her, tenderness in his dark eyes.

"I love you so much," she said. She pressed her cheek against his chest.

"I love you, too. Never doubt it."

"How could I? You took care of me in the worst kind of sickness. Doc told me I'm alive because you wouldn't give up. You willed me to live."

"But you got sick because of me. Because I refused to listen and just take you and Becca away. You went into that camp—"

"Ssssh." She placed her fingers over his lips. "You were right and I was wrong. But those men had no one. If we had left, more people would have died. We made a difference."

He kissed her fingers. "You made a difference. I love you, Elizabeth." After another kiss, he swung his legs off the bed and sat up. "But now, unless you want Hiram to find us like this, we'd better hurry and get dressed."

"*Whoa!*" Hiram pulled back on the reins, and the buggy rolled to a stop in front of the church. Dressed in his best suit, the one he'd worn in Mabel's parlor the first day he and Elizabeth had met, Hiram had come to get Elizabeth and Rand in Doc's buggy and deliver them to their wedding.

On the long drive into town, Hiram informed Elizabeth that Rand had asked him to stand as best man, and that Lois was prepared to act as maid of honor. If Elizabeth wanted her to. Elizabeth assured him that she did. She would tell Lois herself as soon as she saw her.

The churchyard was full of carts and buggies and horses at the hitching rails. People in their Sunday best waved and called greetings, though everyone acted rather subdued.

Rand jumped down and turned and caught Elizabeth around the waist, setting her on her feet. Looking about, Elizabeth felt a stirring of unease.

Something was wrong. She felt it.

"*Mama!*" Dressed in a frilly light-blue dress and with a big blue bow in her hair, Becca flew down the steps of the church and into Elizabeth's arms. "Mama, I missed you!"

"I missed you, too." Elizabeth blinked rapidly as Becca hugged her tightly. Then rising, she picked her daughter up. "My, you sure are pretty."

"Do you like my dress? It was Hester's. Aunt Maggie Jean made the bow for my hair. She said I can call her 'Aunt Maggie Jean,' even though you aren't going to marry Mr. Hiram. Did you get my picture?" the child asked, hardly pausing for breath between sentences, as if wanting to get everything out at once. It was as though she was afraid Elizabeth would disappear again.

"Yes, I got your picture. And a very nice picture it was, too." Elizabeth kissed her daughter's curls.

"Mrs. Mabel said you were very sick. But Mr. Rand was taking very, very good care of you."

"I tried, tadpole," Rand said, coming up behind them. He tweaked the child's cheek, and she beamed at him.

"How would you like to call Rand 'papa'?" Elizabeth asked Becca.

Big dark eyes rounded as the little girl looked from Rand to Elizabeth. "You're going to be my new daddy?"

Smiling, Elizabeth looked at Rand. Instead of the happiness she expected, the look in his eyes was infinitely sad.

"I'm going to marry your mother and take care of you both, the very best way I can," Rand told the child, but he was looking at Elizabeth.

"Something is wrong, isn't it?" Elizabeth asked.

"I'll explain later," Rand said.

Coming up behind them, Hiram cleared his throat. "Best get going. Lois"—he put his hand on his new fiancée's back and guided her near—"Elizabeth says she'd like you to stand with her."

"Of course I would!" Elizabeth assured her friend.

"I'd be proud," Lois said. But far from looking proud, Lois looked as if she would cry as she gazed at Rand, then at Becca.

Rand took Becca from her mother and helped Elizabeth up the church steps. Lois and Hiram fell in on their other side.

As they waited on the porch for everyone else to enter and get seated first, people nodded somberly, murmuring how glad they were to see Elizabeth up and about, giving her sad smiles.

"Tell me what's wrong," Elizabeth said. "Why are people

acting like this? Is it because Rand and me were all alone in the cabin?"

Lois shook her head. "It's just so good to see you well, Elizabeth. That's all. Kinda like seeing a ghost. You were so sick and all. That's a lovely dress." Lois touched the fall of lace at the cuffs.

Rand said, "It'll be all right. You're just nervous." Holding their child on his hip, he smiled at Elizabeth, his gaze full of tenderness and love. His caring did make her feel better. Until Wild Willie Bates came up to them, the last to enter the church before they did.

"I'm shore enough sorry, Rand," Willie said, hat in hand. He turned and shuffled inside, every line of his being sad.

"What is he sorry about?" Elizabeth asked. When Rand didn't answer, she turned to Hiram and Lois. "What's wrong with everyone? It seems more like people are gathering for a funeral than a wedding."

Lois looked at Rand. Hiram studied a passing cloud overhead.

Touching her cheek, Rand promised Elizabeth, "I'll tell you after the ceremony."

The wedding march started to play at that instant. The doors to the church opened, and the congregation turned.

Hiram and Lois looked relieved as they started down the aisle in front of Rand and Elizabeth.

"We're getting married," Becca said, then giggled, still perched on Rand's hip.

Elizabeth thought about balking until she got an answer. But seeing Doc standing propped on his crutches at the end of the aisle, obviously waiting to give her away, touched her heart. Mabel was seated on the front pew, hankie in hand.

Rand took Elizabeth's elbow and led her down the aisle, stopping beside Doc.

Reverend Lyle smiled and nodded in greeting, then opened his book. "Dearly beloved . . ."

For Elizabeth, the ceremony went by in a blur. Afterward, she only remembered Doc kissing her cheek as he gave her away, and that she said, "I do," at the appropriate moment.

And that a chuckle rippled through the congregation as Becca said, ''I do, too.''

Reverend Lyle intoned: ''I now pronounce you man and wife.''

Rand kissed her cheek, then kissed Becca's. ''Elizabeth, I'm sorry for not being completely honest with you. But I had to make sure you were taken care of. You and Becca.''

Everyone had risen, but there was utter quiet in the church.

''I don't understand.'' Elizabeth looked up at him and saw tears in his dark eyes.

Becca patted his cheek. ''Why are you sad, Mr. Rand—I mean, *Papa?''*

Chapter Thirty

"Rand?" Elizabeth's heart squeezed painfully as a man standing beside the first pew stepped forward. She saw a star pinned to his shirt under his coat.

Rand pressed a kiss to Becca's forehead, then gave the little girl to her mother. "I'm not sad for me, tadpole. But I'm sad because I have to leave now, and I won't get to be a real father to you. And I won't be around to take care of you and your mother."

Clutching Becca to her, Elizabeth shook her head. "No."

"I'm sorry I wasn't honest with you. I thought you might not go through with it. This way, you'll have my place. You can sell it or keep it for Becca. If I were you, I'd keep it." He grinned ruefully. "Widows with land are a special prize."

Rand's smile fading, he touched Elizabeth's cheek.

Elizabeth stepped away. *"No!"*

"Rand, I have to take you in now." The man patted Rand's shoulder, as though offering comfort instead of making an arrest.

"I know, Daniel." Utter quiet held the church as Rand kissed his daughter's cheek one last time. "Always remember that I love you, tadpole."

Frowning her lack of understanding, Becca gazed up at him solemnly. ''And I love you, too.''

Unable to bear the look of betrayal shadowing Elizabeth's eyes, Rand turned to the county sheriff. ''Let's go, Dan.''

I should have told him I love him, Elizabeth thought, looking out of the buggy on the busy Eugene street. It had been cruel not to. When he'd done so much. Rand had arranged everything. Going through Doc and Hiram to work out the details. Bargaining with the county sheriff to give himself up as soon as Elizabeth was well enough that he could marry her.

Sitting on Elizabeth's lap, Becca was unusually quiet. Poor heart, she'd just gotten her mother back and she had lost her new father. It must be impossible for a child to understand, Elizabeth thought.

She herself was having a problem with it.

''Here we are.'' Hiram pulled back on the reins. The buggy rolled to a stop in front of a freshly painted facaded building. *H.C. BLACKWOOD, ATTORNEY AT LAW* was painted in plain block letters on the shingle hanging outside the door.

Sitting beside her, Lois asked, ''What'cha thinking?''

''I was wishing I had those last few minutes back. In the church yesterday. I'd have spoken my heart instead of pulling away. Feeling betrayed. I know Rand did it all for me and Becca. So we'd be taken care of.''

Elizabeth touched the corner of her eye with her gloved finger.

''Mama, you got something in your eye?'' Becca asked, swinging her foot against Elizabeth's shirt.

Elizabeth kissed the top of her daughter's head. ''My eye is okay now, pun'kin.''

Going around to the boardwalk side of the buggy, Hiram helped Elizabeth down, then Becca and Lois.

''It's such a nice day,'' Lois said. ''While you're inside, Elizabeth, I think I'll stay out here with Hiram and do some looking around.'' Lois smiled at Becca. ''Do you want to take a walk up the street with us and look in store windows, or stay with your ma?''

While Elizabeth smiled her a ''thank you,'' Becca looked uncertain.

''It's okay if you want to go with Lois,'' Elizabeth said. ''I don't expect I'll be long.''

Becca caught Lois's hand. It was really no contest. She'd always loved store windows, but had had little chance to gaze into them.

''Look, I see hats!'' she said, pointing across the street at a milliner's shop.

''Well, let's go have a gander at 'em!'' Lois smiled and started across the street.

''You go on with them, Hiram. I'll be fine.''

Not waiting for an answer, she turned the doorknob and let herself inside the law office. She told the clerk her business, and he announced Elizabeth to Judge Blackwood as though she was an exalted personage.

''Mrs. Matthews, nice to make your acquaintance.'' H.C. Blackwood rose from behind a massive desk and extended his hand. A balding man with shrewd gray eyes, he was far shorter than Elizabeth, but seemed to stand taller than his size somehow. In his finely tailored suit and embroidered waistcoat, he looked the epitome of success. Except for the handlebar mustache—so large it looked as though it would overbalance him. It would have seemed more appropriate on a cowboy in Texas.

''Nice to meet you, too, sir. I only wish it was under better circumstances.''

''As do I. A shame about Rand,'' he added, making her brows ride up in surprise.

But of course, he would have handled some of the legal papers regarding Rand's arrest, she realized.

He indicated a chair, and waited until she sat down to resume his chair. The wall at his back was lined with leather-bound volumes Elizabeth took to be law books. He shook his head. ''Your wedding must have been a sore disappointment.''

So, he was more abreast of what was happening than she had thought.

"It was that," she admitted, twisting the strings of her reticule about her fingers. "Now, I need to hire a lawyer to represent my husband, to keep him from being extradited to Kansas. I came to you for you to recommend the best man for the job."

Leaning back in his leather chair, Judge Blackwood smiled, his mustache spreading to even grander proportions. "As a matter of fact, I can recommend someone. I recommend me."

"You? But how can you—won't you be on the bench presiding over the extradition hearing?" she asked in surprise.

"Now that would hardly be fair, would it, madam? As you know, Rand's an old friend and fishing buddy of mine. No, I've had to recuse myself because of conflict of interest, and Judge Owens is coming up from Salem to preside over the hearing.

"But I'm still a practicing attorney and I've no conflict in taking the case. Oh, while I'm thinking about it . . ."

He opened his desk drawer and pulled out an envelope. "This came for you today. I had it sent in care of my office, as I didn't know your address."

"For . . . me?" Perplexed, Elizabeth took the envelope, addressed to Elizabeth McKay in care of Judge Blackwood. Inside, was a bank draft from her brother Ethan in the amount of $330.

She swallowed. It was even more money than she was expecting. "How?"

Smiling benignly, the judge steepled his fingers over his waistcoat. "George Hoffpaur, whom I believe comes to Eugene every week to get his raw iron for his blacksmith's shop, brought a letter from Rand asking me to pursue a collection on your behalf of monies due you from one Ethan McKay, a clerk at the Salt Cedar Flats Bank."

The judge shrugged. "I merely sent Mr. McKay a telegraph—through his employers—detailing monies due. You see, Mrs. Matthews, the practice of law has more to do with how people act and react than it has these law books behind me. And a clerk in a bank can always be counted on to display scrupulous integrity to his employer."

"Scrupulous." For the first time since Rand was arrested,

Elizabeth felt herself smile. This man's help was far more than she could have hoped for. "Thank you for taking the case. And collecting my money. I'll pay whatever your rates are. Just set Rand free."

"I'll try my best. Rand is a good friend. Oh, and I believe there was a matter of payment for a horse a few years ago. I added that to the bill, too."

"You know about the horse?" She put her hand to her throat. Just how much did this man know about Rand?

The mustache spread again as he smiled. "Don't worry, Mrs. Matthews. A good lawyer never tells what he knows. Nor asks the right question when it will get him the wrong answer. Now let's talk about strategy. You won't mind if I'm a bit unorthodox?" His gray eyes twinkled in a way that a fox's might while contemplating how best to trap its prey.

When Elizabeth stepped back out on the street an hour later, the whole day seemed brighter, despite the overcast sky.

"Why are you sad, Mama?" Becca slipped off Lois's knee and went to Elizabeth, placing her hands on her mother's knees.

Forcing a smile, Elizabeth said, "I'm not sad. I'm thinking."

"Sad thoughts," Becca said wisely.

"Yes," Elizabeth admitted. She'd tried to see Rand that afternoon, after leaving Judge Blackwood's office. Rand had refused her visit, sending her word to go back to Willow. He didn't want her here. He wanted her just to let things take their course.

"Shore is a nice hotel the judge reserved us a room at," Lois commented, obviously changing the subject. They were sitting in the lobby beneath real crystal chandeliers as they waited for Hiram to rejoin them. Judge Blackwood had sent for him, no doubt still plotting strategy.

Plush carpets covered the floor. High-backed settees and mahogany tables abounded. Elizabeth figured it would take most of the money the judge had pried out of Ethan to pay their bills.

But she didn't care. The hotel was near the courthouse, and Rand's hearing was first thing in the morning.

When Hiram returned, he said, "Look who I found." He led Lucas Skinner into the sitting area. Lucas nodded to the ladies.

"Lucas is why Judge Blackwood sent for me," Hiram explained. "He thought we could bunk in together." Hiram's gaze held a hint of regret as it touched Lois's ever so briefly.

Watching the exchange, Elizabeth's brows rode up. So it was already like that, was it? She smiled inwardly, wishing them both every happiness. They had been good friends to her.

"Mrs. McKay—Matthews now, I guess—it sure is good to see you up and about." Hat in hand, Skinner nodded to Elizabeth. They'd grown to be sort of friends as she'd worked with the sick at the railroad camp. Lois and Hiram had gotten to know the straw boss well, too. To his credit, he'd done what he could to help them out, standing between them and Carnegie.

"Thank you, Lucas," Elizabeth said. "But why are you here? Don't you have miles of track to make up for, now that you've a full complement of workers again?"

"With both the Chinese and the Irish Carnegie was nice enough to provide, it's comin' along right swift. Be in Willow by next week, working on the new bridge." He grinned. "I bypassed Carnegie and requisitioned the main office of the line, and they sent me another couple of big tents for the men. 'Tweren't no big deal. The railroad has money. Carnegie just likes to act like the money is his. That, and he likes being the boss."

"Why did he hire those men to turn the sick workers out? I've never understood that," Elizabeth said. "And all over that old patched tent."

"Meanness. Just plain and simple. Rand went against him, getting those court orders, so Carnegie had to get Rand back. But Rand outmaneuvered him again with that quarantine, and Carnegie was so steamed up, he was like to explode over that. The quarantine should be lifted soon, by the way."

Lucas went on, shaking his head. "When old Bill looked Carnegie up here in Eugene, thinking there'd be a reward for

Rand—the railroad put up the original bounty, you know—it was just what Carnegie needed to get back at Rand.''

Elizabeth picked up her daughter and hugged her. So it had been Bill after all. And it had been exactly what Carnegie needed. ''How do you know all this?''

''Gossip in the railroad travels straight up the tracks, ma'am.'' Lucas chuckled. ''But don't count Rand out. I come here to Eugene 'cause Blackwood telegraphed me. Wanted me to provide an inventory and total of exactly what old Bill skimmed the railroad for on that last order of supplies. Judge Blackwood''—Skinner shook his head in admiration—''that man is a shrewd 'un, not a doubt about it. And he knows ever'body and ever'thang that creeps or crawls in this town.''

''What did the judge want the totals for?'' Elizabeth wondered aloud.

''I can't rightly say, ma'am. The judge, he told me not to discuss that with nobody. But he did ask me to give you this here note. Now, iff'n you'll excuse me, I'll be back later. The judge, he asked me to do him a little favor across town. I shouldn't be long. Eugene ain't that big a town.''

Becca yawned, and Elizabeth excused herself, too, to take the child upstairs to bed, leaving Hiram and Lois sitting side by side under the chandeliers.

After Becca was all settled in, Elizabeth opened Blackwood's note. In it, he simply told her the hearing was set for nine o'clock, and asked her to meet him on the steps of the courthouse at least fifteen minutes before time for court.

As Elizabeth slipped into bed beside Becca, she wondered just what Blackwood was up to.

Sadly, she decided, he'd have to be a magician to get Rand set free. Especially since Rand seemed determined not to help in the fight.

''Rand,'' Elizabeth called as he entered the alley, a deputy on either side. She'd been waiting at the side door for him to be brought to court, needing to see him, to speak with him.

Still dressed in the suit he was married in, now sadly rumpled, he looked down at the chains on his feet. ''I don't want to talk to you, Elizabeth. Time to put the past behind you and look to the future. For both your and Becca's sakes.''

''How can you say that? You talked with your attorney!''

''Blackwood is not a miracle worker. He can't undo what's done.''

''Don't be too sure. Just listen to his advice and for goodness sake, do what he tells you,'' Elizabeth called to his retreating back as the deputies led him through the side door. She fumed and ranted silently at him to listen to reason. If she had been close enough, she would have kicked his shin.

It would have made her feel better!

As one of the deputies closed the door and locked it from the inside, he asked Rand, ''Was that your wife?''

''Yes, it was.'' The word ''was'' said it all, Rand thought.

''Right purty woman.'' The deputies took his elbows and led him down a narrow hall.

''Yes, I know.'' She would have no problem finding another husband, Rand knew.

Listen to Blackwood, Elizabeth had said. *Do what he tells you.*

Well, Rand supposed that would be easy enough. All Blackwood had told him was to keep his damned mouth shut.

Elizabeth had looked pretty in her traveling suit, with a hat he hadn't seen before—he suspected she'd borrowed it from Mabel—sitting at a jaunty angle on her honey-blond curls. He supposed she was wearing the best garment she owned.

He regretted he hadn't had time to buy her and Becca the dresses and nice things they deserved.

Maybe her next husband would be generous.

Lifting her skirts, Elizabeth hurried back through the alley to the front of the courthouse, thinking vile thoughts about her husband as she did so. Lois and Hiram were already seated inside, and Becca was with them. But Elizabeth had an appointment to keep.

Elizabeth got to the steps of the courthouse just in time.

H.C. Blackwood was strolling down the boardwalk toward her, looking dapper in his charcoal-gray suit, his gold watch chain draped across his fancy waistcoat.

"Good morning, my dear. My, it is a lovely day." He smiled.

"If you say so," Elizabeth answered doubtfully.

"Oh, I do."

She twined her fingers together, wishing it was true. "Rand told me to put the past behind me and look to the future. For my and Becca's sake."

"Rand Matthews is that rarest of creatures. An honorable man. And that is precisely why we must save him from making some noble and unnecessary sacrifice."

Blackwood glanced at his watch, then snapped the lid closed and returned it to his vest pocket. "Now, if you'll excuse me, I am expecting someone else to meet me." He pointed with his umbrella at the open doors of the courthouse. "You might want to just wait for me inside, around the corner of the door, my dear." His gray eyes twinkled. "I think you can hear clearly from there."

Elizabeth did as he asked, glancing back from the top step just in time to see Gerald Carnegie shaking Blackwood's hand. Frowning, she ducked around the corner, and listened in shamelessly to their conversation.

Carnegie said, "I was a bit surprised when I received your message to meet with you, Judge Blackwood. Though we have attended a couple of the same social events, I'm honored that you remember me."

"Nonsense, the honor is mine. After all, it's not every day that I meet a fellow Bostonian. You *are* a member of the Boston Carnegies, are you not? And making a name for yourself as a man who gets things done—that's the word I heard about you in the main office of the Union Pacific."

Carnegie's voice was suddenly less authoritative. "Main office?"

"Yes. I get down there from time to time. By the way, how is the line into Willow progressing? As a large stockholder in the railroad, I have a keen interest, you understand?"

"Large stockholder?"

"Well, perhaps that is bragging a bit," the judge amended modestly. "I only hold a ten-percent interest."

"Ten . . . percent?"

"With voting proxy on another fifteen. I didn't want to have to issue those restraining orders stopping your plans, but image is important for the company. The West is growing more civilized every day. No longer is it possible to disregard the masses. You understand. Simply business. Better to delay the railroad a little than alienate the populace."

"The crew is making good progress on the Willow line, and I've brought in extra people to make up the delay," Carnegie said, his tone sounding as though he was recovering somewhat.

The judge said, "Ah, I see it's past time I meet with my client before the identity hearing." There was a snap as the judge closed his watch.

"Client?" Confusion colored Carnegie's voice. It grew more pronounced as he asked, "What identity hearing?"

"Yes. I've recused myself from this case so I can represent Rand Matthews. He is a very good friend of mine, you know."

"But—but I thought the man had been convicted and it was just a matter of extradition."

"Dalton McClure was convicted of murder in Kansas." The judge's tone grew infinitesimally harder. "He was also declared dead years ago."

At these words, Elizabeth dared a peek around the corner. Blackwood clapped Carnegie on the shoulder jovially and added, "Word has it that you are an ambitious man, and smart. I'll have my eye on you, Carnegie." With that, the dapper judge started up the steps, leaving Carnegie staring after him.

Hiding back behind the corner, Elizabeth giggled and clapped her hands, paying no heed to the people who passed by as they entered the courthouse and looked at her curiously.

Seated at the defendant's table, Rand was aware of exactly where Elizabeth was seated at the back of the courtroom, Becca on her lap. Of how she was tangling her fingers in the strings of her reticule.

Rand had wanted to make a statement, admitting his identity and waving extradition—he'd wanted to save Elizabeth the pain of being dragged through this.

Blackwood had squashed that idea in its infancy, telling Rand that if he admitted to being McClure, it wouldn't take people long to realize McClure and Elizabeth had been in Kansas around the same time and to see the resemblance between Becca and Rand. He went on conversationally, saying that it was funny Elizabeth's brother's last name was McKay and Elizabeth was going by the name McKay still, when she'd supposedly been wed.

Rand looked down at his manacled hands. It had been his intent to save her from all this. Now, he just prayed it wouldn't haunt his wife and daughter the rest of their lives.

"Don't worry," Blackwood said. "This won't take long." Then he winked as all were called to rise as Judge Owens entered the courtroom.

After the formalities were taken care of and the purpose of the hearing stated, the bailiff called the county prosecutor's first witness: Mr. William Erasmus Jones.

There was a stirring in the courtroom and murmurs as the witness failed to step forward.

After a moment, the county sheriff stood. "Your honor, if it please the court, may I speak?"

"Yes, Sheriff Williamson."

"I got an unsigned note this morning that said I might want to check on Nine-Toed-Bill—Mr. Jones. Seems he got word that the railroad was filing charges against him for theft by embezzlement, and he was planning to clear out. Well, the note was right. He and his grandson cleared out in the night—without paying their boardinghouse bill, I might add."

"Thank you, Sheriff." Judge Owens turned to the bailiff. "Call the next witness, please."

"Mr. Gerald Carnegie, Vice-President of Special Projects, Union Pacific Railroad."

As Carnegie took the witness stand, he gave Rand a look of pure malice. Then he glanced at Judge Blackwood and seemed to compose himself.

To the prosecutor's questions, Carnegie answered that several years before he had indeed hired one Dalton McClure, a well-educated, well-dressed young man with a bright future.

When the prosecutor pointed to Rand and asked if the man now calling himself Randal Matthews was in fact Dalton McClure, Carnegie raised a haughty brow. He declared that he could without hesitation say that the man in the rumpled coat bore little resemblance to the bright, well-dressed young man he'd once hired.

Blackwood moved for a dismissal, and as Judge Owens granted it, Elizabeth, Hiram, and Lois jumped up and cheered.

Chapter Thirty-one

"Here's to you, Mrs. Matthews." In the sitting room of the hotel suite, Judge Blackwood touched his champagne glass to Elizabeth's. "You are an exceptional woman." He glanced at Becca, who'd fallen asleep on the settee. "And your daughter is adorable."

"Why do you say that I'm exceptional?" Elizabeth asked, then giggled as bubbles tickled her nose "Oh, that sounds as though I'm fishing for more compliments."

"And doing it quite well, I might add." Blackwood's gray eyes twinkled as he sipped his champagne.

"She's exceptional because she had the good sense to marry me," Rand said. "Though it took a while to get her to the altar." Smiling, he took her hand. Heat seemed to travel upward from the point where his fingers clasped hers, and warmed her all over.

Blackwood cocked a derisive brow. "I was going to say, because she had the good sense to come to me for help. I was just about to visit you in jail, where you seemed quite content to rot despite this winsome creature awaiting you on your release."

The judge finished his champagne and set his glass down,

then kissed Elizabeth's hand. ''If I can ever be of service again, my dear . . .''

''We'll be stopping by on our way out in the morning to pay your bill,'' she assured him.

Blackwood's luxuriant mustache spread. ''No fee. But I will see you soon. Rand has some of the best fishing this side of Portland in that creek of his.'' He winked. ''Now, do you see why I couldn't stand idly by and let him be carted off to Kansas?''

After the judge was gone, Elizabeth set her half-empty glass down. This was the second time she'd ever had alcohol in any form. It seemed to be going straight to her mouth. She couldn't stop smiling. ''Where did Lois disappear to?''

''Hiram said something about getting Lois to help him pack before he leaves.'' He cocked a dark brow meaningfully.

''Oh, my.'' Elizabeth shook her head. ''I'm happy we were never so brazen.'' She giggled again.

Rand smiled. ''I think you have had enough. Okay, be serious for a moment. Help me understand. Blackwood made out a warrant for Bill's arrest because Skinner signed a complaint about the money Bill embezzled. That information got to Bill some way—''

''Not just some way. Last night, the judge sent Lucas to the boardinghouse where Bill was staying to tell him.''

Rand grinned. ''And in so doing, made certain Bill would take off, not showing up for court, although he'd been subpoenaed. With Bill missing, the prosecutor's case was cut in half.''

Elizabeth tsk-tsked. ''Now, that was not the judge's intention. He explained while you were signing the release papers that as an officer of the court, it would be unethical for him to influence anyone not to honor a subpoena.'' Elizabeth giggled as Rand caught her around the middle. ''But Lucas Skinner sat beside us in the courtroom. He spilled the beans after Bill didn't appear.''

''I see. But I'd like to know just what spell Blackwood cast on Carnegie. The man had me where he wanted me, then looked me straight in the face and said that I wasn't Dalton McClure.'' Rand shook his head as though still not quite believing it.

"That's not really what he said. It's just what everyone heard. What he said was, 'The man in the rumpled coat bears little resemblance to the bright young man I once hired.' "

Elizabeth added conspiratorially, "Did you know the judge owns stock in the Union Pacific—and as I understand it, holds a great deal of sway with the board. At least, that's what he told Carnegie when he met him on the courthouse steps this morning."

"The old fox," Rand said softly.

Elizabeth giggled again, remembering. As a soft snore sounded from the direction of the settee, she placed her hand over her mouth. Going over to where Becca had fallen asleep, Miss Annie clutched in her hand, Elizabeth placed her old shawl over the child.

Catching Elizabeth by the shoulders, Rand guided his wife to the bedroom and closed the door softly.

"I think I need a nap, too." He undid his tie and slipped his coat off, his dark gaze filled with purpose.

"Rand!" Elizabeth was suddenly warm all over. "Becca's just in the next room."

"We are married. And she is asleep." He gave up on his shirt buttons, and started undoing the coat to Elizabeth's dress. "And children get used to the fact that their parents sleep in the same bed." He kissed her neck as if he was starving and she was spun sugar.

Elizabeth arched against him. "I like the way you explain things."

"Besides, Mabel says Becca has been napping at least an hour every afternoon. That means we have about forty-five minutes before she wakes up." He kissed the other side of Elizabeth's neck as he slipped her coat off. After dropping it on the floor, he slid his hands up and cupped her breasts through the fabric of her blouse and camisole.

She moaned softly, deep in her throat.

"And we can order a trundle bed placed in the sitting room for Becca tonight, and have this bedroom all to ourselves." His voice was dark silk.

"Rand Matthews, I like the way you think." Elizabeth

wrapped her arms around his neck and kissed him deeply. "And I love you."

"I love you, too. Never doubt it."

How could she, when he'd been willing to give up all for her and their daughter's sake?

"But you do talk a great deal, when you should be doing other . . . things," she murmured, pressing against him in a way that ended all conversation.

Dear Reader:

I tried. I really tried.

All my friends who live in the Northwest assured me that readers living there would know I did my research for *Loving Elizabeth* if I would only include a slimy, five-inch-long, and much hated invertebrate called the banana slug.

It should have been easy. After all, I had an unplanned slug slide into my last book, *Marrying Mattie*—though it was a small brown slug and hardly of the grand proportions of its Northwestern cousins. However, all my plots to include them were foiled. The slugs refused to cooperate—which I understand is usually the case with these creatures.

I hope you enjoyed *Loving Elizabeth,* slugless though it is. You may write to me c/o Zebra Books, 850 Third Avenue, NY, NY 10022, or drop me an E-mail: victoriadark@yahoo.com.

Victoria Dark

(Web page: http://www.eclectics.com/victoriadark)

BOOK YOUR PLACE ON OUR WEBSITE
AND MAKE THE
READING CONNECTION!

We've created a customized website just for our very special readers, where you can get the inside scoop on everything that's going on with Zebra, Pinnacle and Kensington books.

When you come online, you'll have the exciting opportunity to:

- View covers of upcoming books
- Read sample chapters
- Learn about our future publishing schedule (listed by publication month *and author*)
- Find out when your favorite authors will be visiting a city near you
- Search for and order backlist books from our online catalog
- Check out author bios and background information
- Send e-mail to your favorite authors
- Meet the Kensington staff online
- Join us in weekly chats with authors, readers and other guests
- Get writing guidelines
- AND MUCH MORE!

Visit our website at
http://www.zebrabooks.com

Put a Little Romance in Your Life With

Fern Michaels

__**Dear Emily**	**0-8217-5676-1**	**$6.99**US/**$8.50**CAN
__**Sara's Song**	**0-8217-5856-X**	**$6.99**US/**$8.50**CAN
__**Wish List**	**0-8217-5228-6**	**$6.99**US/**$7.99**CAN
__**Vegas Rich**	**0-8217-5594-3**	**$6.99**US/**$8.50**CAN
__**Vegas Heat**	**0-8217-5758-X**	**$6.99**US/**$8.50**CAN
__**Vegas Sunrise**	**1-55817-5983-3**	**$6.99**US/**$8.50**CAN
__**Whitefire**	**0-8217-5638-9**	**$6.99**US/**$8.50**CAN

Call toll free **1-888-345-BOOK** to order by phone or use this coupon to order by mail.

Name____

Address______________________________________

City _______________ State ________Zip______________

Please send me the books I have checked above.

I am enclosing $__________

Plus postage and handling* $__________

Sales tax (in New York and Tennessee) $__________

Total amount enclosed $__________

*Add $2.50 for the first book and $.50 for each additional book.

Send check or money order (no cash or CODs) to:

Kensington Publishing Corp., 850 Third Avenue, New York, NY 10022

Prices and Numbers subject to change without notice.

All orders subject to availability.

Check out our website at **www.kensingtonbooks.com**

Put a Little Romance in Your Life With
Janelle Taylor

__Anything for Love	0-8217-4992-7	$5.99US/$6.99CAN
__Forever Ecstasy	0-8217-5241-3	$5.99US/$6.99CAN
__Fortune's Flames	0-8217-5450-5	$5.99US/$6.99CAN
__Destiny's Temptress	0-8217-5448-3	$5.99US/$6.99CAN
__Love Me With Fury	0-8217-5452-1	$5.99US/$6.99CAN
__First Love, Wild Love	0-8217-5277-4	$5.99US/$6.99CAN
__Kiss of the Night Wind	0-8217-5279-0	$5.99US/$6.99CAN
__Love With a Stranger	0-8217-5416-5	$6.99US/$8.50CAN
__Forbidden Ecstasy	0-8217-5278-2	$5.99US/$6.99CAN
__Defiant Ecstasy	0-8217-5447-5	$5.99US/$6.99CAN
__Follow the Wind	0-8217-5449-1	$5.99US/$6.99CAN
__Wild Winds	0-8217-6026-2	$6.99US/$8.50CAN
__Defiant Hearts	0-8217-5563-3	$6.50US/$8.00CAN
__Golden Torment	0-8217-5451-3	$5.99US/$6.99CAN
__Bittersweet Ecstasy	0-8217-5445-9	$5.99US/$6.99CAN
__Taking Chances	0-8217-4259-0	$4.50US/$5.50CAN
__By Candlelight	0-8217-5703-2	$6.99US/$8.50CAN
__Chase the Wind	0-8217-4740-1	$5.99US/$6.99CAN
__Destiny Mine	0-8217-5185-9	$5.99US/$6.99CAN
__Midnight Secrets	0-8217-5280-4	$5.99US/$6.99CAN
__Sweet Savage Heart	0-8217-5276-6	$5.99US/$6.99CAN
__Moonbeams and Magic	0-7860-0184-4	$5.99US/$6.99CAN
__Brazen Ecstasy	0-8217-5446-7	$5.99US/$6.99CAN

Call toll free **1-888-345-BOOK** to order by phone or use this coupon to order by mail.

Name ______________________________

Address ______________________________

City ________________ State ________ Zip ________________

Please send me the books I have checked above.

I am enclosing $__________

Plus postage and handling* $__________

Sales tax (in New York and Tennessee) $__________

Total amount enclosed $__________

*Add $2.50 for the first book and $.50 for each additional book.

Send check or money order (no cash or CODs) to:

Kensington Publishing Corp., 850 Third Avenue, New York, NY 10022

Prices and Numbers subject to change without notice.

All orders subject to availability.

Check out our website at **www.kensingtonbooks.com**